# The Wild One

## DENISE EAGAN

ZEBRA BOOKS
Kensington Publishing Corp.
http://www.kensingtonbooks.com

ZEBRA BOOKS are published by

Kensington Publishing Corp.
850 Third Avenue
New York, NY 10022

All Kensington titles, imprints, and distributed lines are available at special quantity discounts for bulk purchases for sales promotion, premiums, fund-raising, educational, or institutional use.

Special book excerpts or customized printings can also be created to fit specific needs. For details, write or phone the office of the Kensington Special Sales Manager: Attn. Special Sales Department. Kensington Publishing Corp., 850 Third Avenue, New York, NY 10022. Phone: 1-800-221-2647.

Zebra and the Z logo Reg. U.S. Pat. & TM Off.

ISBN-13: 978-1-4201-0122-5
ISBN-10: 1-4201-0122-6

First Zebra Printing: January 2009

10 9 8 7 6 5 4 3 2 1

Printed in the United States of America

*To my high school buddies,*
*Lou Ann, Karen, Jocelyne, and Sue,*
*for many, many years of love and*
*super-awesome promotion—*
*you're the best!*

*With big thanks to my "first readers,"*
*Rhonda, Betsy, Sharon R., and Sharon B.*
*for loving my work*
*even when it needed much editing.*

*And to my Scandalous Victorians at*
*slipintosomethingvictorian.com,*
*for guidance, assurance, and*
*general, all-around hand-holding.*

*As always, love to my heroes,*
*Tom, Sean, and Nat.*

# Chapter One

Jessica Sullivan lay dead on the polished wood floor, an overturned goblet of bloodred wine dripping near her hand. Her gold satin gown pooled around her body, except for a section of skirt pulled up to display a tantalizing portion of well-formed calf. Having fallen from her blond head, her crown still rolled slightly, its jewels gleaming in the gaslight.

But nobody noticed Jess. Everybody's eyes were glued to the scene two feet from her, of a man dying in his best friend's arms. Except for a few sniffles, the room held a tense silence, ears straining to hear the last words of a brokenhearted man. "Now cracks a noble heart. Good night, sweet Prince, and flights of angels sing thee to thy rest."

With that the curtain descended and a thunderous burst of applause ripped away the silence. Alive once more, Jess jumped up, swept her crown back on her head, and then smoothed out the wrinkles of her gown as she sped across the stage. Hidden among the side curtains, Michelle Dubois, gold curls bouncing excitedly, greeted her. "Oh, do you not hear them *ma amie?!* Are they not even louder than last night?"

Jess kissed her roommate's rouged cheek. "Of course they are, Michelle. They came for you."

"Oh *non!* Some are surely for you!"

Jess smiled indulgently as the curtain rose to expose the now-vacant stage. The narrator began calling out parts, and the actors glided out to center stage where they bowed and then formed a line. At "Ophelia" Michelle floated out. As if one person, the audience lunged to its feet, whistling and stomping, and warming Jess's heart, for her friend ate, drank, and breathed applause. When it started to wane, the narrator called out "Gertrude, Queen of Denmark," and Jess walked out to center stage. Curtsying, she passed an eye over the crowd, mostly male she noted with cheerful cynicism. As she took her place in line, out came troupe manager Robert Madison— Hamlet—and if noise could bring down a ceiling, it surely would have fallen then. Well, Jess thought merrily, there were a few women out there, too.

Several curtain calls later, the curtain fell for the last time. As the audience filed out of the theatre, stagehands scurried about moving scenery, and the actors grouped together to critique the performance, the crowd, the applause. Carefully avoiding eye contact, Jess removed the tin crown from her head and while pulling pins out of her hot, itchy wig, crossed the stage. Another performance, she calculated, another $1.25 toward her Jason-account—$1.25 nearer to redemption, $1.25 nearer to *home*.

"Jess! Jess, hold up a minute!" Behind her Jon, who played that most faithful companion Horatio, had broken from the throng of actors.

"NoJon," Jess answered, the two words spoken so often in the past, they'd become one. Moving down a hall toward her dressing room, she yanked off the wig, displaying jet black hair.

"Deny me not, fair Jessica! I beg but one minute of your time!"

"NoJon."

"You can't deny me forever!"

"NoJon," she said, opening the door to her dressing room.

"There, you admit it! Secretly you pine for my love!"

"NoJon." She shut the door in his face. Generally she was kinder, but after six straight nights of performances—and two matinees—tonight she was just too darned tired.

She turned a key to the gas lamps hanging on the wall. They sizzled slightly as they lit, revealing a large dressing room decorated with pink-and-gold-flocked paper, a thick pink carpet, a dressing table with two chairs, and a double-door wardrobe. Although no fan of pink, after six years in a traveling troupe Jess deeply appreciated the luxury.

Before she could seat herself, the rapping of knuckles on wood rang through the room. As Jess turned, Jon opened the door a crack and stuck his head in. "In all earnestness, Jess," he said, "a few of us are going out. We were wondering—"

She shook her head, flashing a smile to ease the rejection. "Thank you, but I have other plans."

He rubbed his chin and narrowed his eyes. "It's only supper and drinks, Jess," he said in a softly persuasive voice. "Nothing very expensive."

Nothing very expensive, her mind echoed, but between alcohol and flirtation, something remarkably sordid, for theatre people cared nothing about propriety or virtue. None except for Jess, who for six years had clung to both like a drowning man clings to a life preserver. "No, Jon, thank you anyway."

He sighed, and then shut the door with a disappointed click.

Alone again, she settled down at her dressing table and humming tunelessly—there were reasons she didn't act in musicals!—unpinned her hair, allowing her curls to swing free. With a jar of cleansing cream, she proceeded to wipe away her wrinkles, revealing the silky smooth skin of a young woman. To her chagrin a San Franciscan reporter had recently compared its texture to fine porcelain. So, she thought with a gurgle of humor, at twenty-four she resembled a chamber pot. Good gracious, what would they say at thirty-four?

Michelle swept in on a wave of expensive French perfume. "Jess! Always here before me, aren't you? I swear, I *cannot* understand why you never greet our admirers. That *is* the best part of the show, you know."

"The best part of the show is the cash."

"Well, yes, but all those *men*," she said with a deep sigh of satisfaction. She shook her head as she seated herself in front of the second dressing-table mirror. "And you are ever so pretty! You must know that if you ever showed your true face, men of every age would flock to you, and then you needn't worry so much about money."

Sighing, Jess sat back and shook her head in amused exasperation. "I'm not interested in men, Michelle. How often must I tell you so?"

"Oh, that William Acton again! Do not speak to me of him! He is nothing, not even a snap of my fingers," Michelle said, slipping effortlessly into a thick French accent as she snapped her fingers to emphasize her point.

Ever-ready humor bubbled up inside Jess. "You are entirely too combustible! And he *is* something. Acton's one of the most respected doctors of our time."

"He's a prude who knows nothing of women. He's probably terrifyingly ugly and unable to attract a woman were he as rich as Vanderbilt! Women are *not* naturally frigid."

"*You* are not, Michelle, granted, but Dr. Acton has studied the matter for years, and has discovered that most women are more like me, they do not *naturally* respond to the more intimate aspects of romance. It's no shame. It's how God made us."

"Bosh! That's pure bosh and you, *ma amie*," she said, her accent switching back and forth between Middle West American and French, "are merely suffering from a bad *affaire de couer* with that . . . that *Everett,* whose name I spit on!"

Chuckling through the stabbing in her heart, Jess replied, "It was a tad more than an affair. He's my husband."

"*Was* your husband. Surely after six years you cannot—"

A knock rang through the room interrupting them.

"Michelle?" Jon called through the door. "Are you in there?"

Jess frowned at her friend, who answered with a very French shrug. "*Oui,* Jean."

"There's a man here asking to see you."

Jess's frown deepened. The troupe never allowed admirers backstage, for in the past their admiration had manifested itself in uncomfortable, if not downright violent, ways. "She won't see him, Jon," Jess hollered back. "Send him away."

Outside the door Jon engaged in a short argument with a deep-voiced man. Just as Jon was saying, "He's pretty insistent," Michelle's eyes widened in sudden recognition, and she lunged from the chair, crying out *"Chéri! Chéri!"*

Jess's eyebrows shot up. Michelle loved her men, but during the five months that she'd been with the troupe, she'd not shown a preference for any certain one. Except, Jess recalled as Michelle flung the door open, when discussing one persistently absent—

"Lee, *mon chéri!* I have missed you so!"

Leland Montgomery.

Michelle threw herself into the arms of a tall, dark-haired man. Without speaking a word, he returned her greeting with a shamefully hungry kiss. Rolling her eyes, Jess waved Jon away. While waiting patiently for an introduction, she let her gaze drift over Michelle's Lee.

He was fashionably dressed in a black-caped coat hanging open over an evening suit of fine milled cloth. His shirt was made of crisp white linen, his black silk waistcoat decorated with a gold watch chain. His trousers were expertly creased and his boots so well shined they reflected the carpet. In his left hand he held pristine white gloves, a top hat, and a gold-topped cane. His black hair was slightly longer—rakishly so—than was stylish. A dandy, and one with expensive taste, as had all Michelle's men.

Mr. Montgomery lifted his head and his mouth curved into a deep smile as he raised his right hand to trace Michelle's jawline with his thumb. "Michelle, *chérie*," he said in a low voice "how I have missed you."

"And I you!" she replied.

"So it appears." He dropped his arm and turned to Jess. From this distance the color of his eyes was unrecognizable, but not the sparkle. He strode forward, extending his right hand, his smile falling into lightly etched creases as if he were perpetually amused. "Ma'am. I don't believe we've met. I'm Lee Montgomery."

"So I heard," she said, putting her hand in his. She expected a quick, light shake, but his long fingers wrapped around hers and held for a minute. A lightning bolt of heat sped down her arm and then radiated through her cold, passionless body. Mercy, what was that about? She was impervious to such reactions . . .

As he dropped his hand, he stepped back, chuckling—a deep-throated sound of unfettered humor. It was infectious, rippling over Jess's nerves and bringing an unaccountable urge to join him—an urge that Jess ruthlessly suppressed.

"Michelle was a trifle enthusiastic, wasn't she?" he said, turning his head to flash white teeth, while stretching his arm toward his lover. Michelle slipped into his embrace and stared up at him adoringly.

Up close, Jess's initial assumption of dandyism vanished. Powerfully built with wide shoulders, Mr. Montgomery seemed to fill the large room. His bone structure was harsh: strong cheekbones and a prominent nose. But that wide smile and the single dimple in his right cheek softened all. Handsome was how Michelle had described him. Jess would have called him breathtaking. If he didn't belong to Michelle. And if Jess didn't have a husband. And if she had any interest at all in single men or romance, which she did not. Honest to God, clean down to bedrock, did *not*.

*Could* not.

"And you must be Jessica Sullivan," he said. "I enjoyed

your Gertrude, although without your makeup you don't appear nearly old enough to be Hamlet's mother. Couldn't blame the uncle though."

It was time, Jess thought, and braced herself for the Leer given to every actress by every man who'd ever paid for a ticket and therefore believed he'd bought the right to eat the actresses with his eyes. Slightly repulsive, but part of the pay.

And Mr. Montgomery's eyes did run over her, but his gaze didn't repulse her. Not a leer, really, but warm appreciation, a compliment instead of an insult, which left her hot, shaky, and speechless. Foolish, foolish body—foolish, foolish nerves, for in the end that reaction was nothing but a fraud. A lie of her treacherous body, excited and tingly now, sure to shatter like thin ice if gentle touches or hot kisses turned to something more intimate. Shatter and then melt into stomach-churning revulsion.

*Not fair! Not fair!*

Mr. Montgomery turned once more to his ladylove. "And as always, *chérie,* your Ophelia was perfection. No wonder at all that you drove the fair Hamlet to insanity."

"Oh? But was he insane?" Michelle asked, raising her eyebrows mysteriously. "That is the question, *n'est ce pas?* Lee, do you like my hair? It is blond, now, like the British Blonds."

His smile deepened. "I do, but you've no need to imitate them, *chérie.* You grow more lovely with each passing day."

"And you more handsome! And you have shaved off that horrible beard and mustache, which tickled my face and hid your smile! Oh, Lee, *mon ami,* how long are you here?"

He shrugged. "A few days at least. There's a game being arranged at the Baldwin for Wednesday night. A few high rollers are expected."

"Oh, cards," Michelle said with a pout. "With you it is always cards! Do you think of nothing else?"

"It's how I earn my living, Michelle," he said mildly.

"But must you *talk* so much of them!"

He laughed. "I scarcely mentioned them! And those cards would like very much to take you to Armand's tonight. Are you available?"

Michelle's eyes widened. "Armand's? Oh, Lee, *vraiment?*"

"Really and truly," he said with another deep-throated chuckle.

"Oh, *oui, oui*—only." She looked at Jess, a plea in her brown eyes. "You do not mind, *ma amie,* do you?"

"Hey!" Lee protested humorously. "I thought I was your *ami!*"

"Silly man." Michelle giggled. "Jess? You will not be too lonely?"

Smiling, Jess shook her head. "Michelle, you haven't come home but once in five days. I'm used to an empty flat."

"If you are sure?"

"Absolutely. And now, Mr. Montgomery, if you don't mind? I'd like to change."

With a sudden look of speculation in his eyes—an interesting shade of hazel green Jess now noted—Mr. Montgomery nodded. "Of course. Michelle, I have a carriage waiting out front. With," he added, eyes twinkling, "champagne on ice. Hurry, *chérie,* or I shall drink it all!"

"Oh!" she said, and clapped her hands in childish delight.

A short time later, they were gone and Jess, seated at her dressing table, pulled a ceramic bowl toward her. It held only one article, a plain gold ring, scratched and worn from hard wear. Was she married tonight? Six years deserted, more than enough time for a judge to grant her a divorce.

But good girls didn't get divorced. Good girls remained in their small farming towns, and married small farmers and raised small farm children. Good girls did not pursue the limelight and live among people who thought fidelity archaic and the Good Book best used as a paperweight. So many rules broken already . . .

Jess slipped the ring onto her left index finger. Married.

* * *

Grimacing, Lee stared up at Hathaway's house, situated near the top of Nob Hill. A white wedding cake of a house, it awoke Lee's sweet tooth at the same time a lead weight settled in his chest, crushing the laughter generally residing there. For Hathaway, with his paunch and balding head, had done at twenty-three what Lee at thirty had yet to manage, found a woman with whom he wished to spend his life. It wasn't that Lee hadn't tried, but as soon as he played the "forever" card or even the "for a long time" card, an impossible-to-dislodge lump settled in his throat, and his heart started wandering. It was as if he'd been born with all the important cards missing from his deck, as if he'd been born a wild card.

With a deep sigh, Lee started down the walkway for the obligatory call, which came with the obligatory lecture. He ought to have visited upon arriving in San Francisco instead of spending a week playing poker and escorting Michelle from pillar to post. But he'd dreaded the visit from the moment he'd boarded the train to 'Frisco, and Michelle was so much more entertaining. As her friend would be if—

*She's Michelle's best friend, you cad!* his conscience squeaked.

And perfectly lovely, with midnight black curls framing a face that could launch more ships than Helen of Troy. She had the most beautiful eyes he'd ever seen, long lashed and luminous blue, which, he remembered, had appraised him with all the emotion of a Saratoga bettor inspecting a racehorse. Not your typical actress, Jess Sullivan, neither blowsy, breezy, and of easy morals like Michelle, nor spoilt and stuck-up as one might expect of such beauty and talent. But professional. Reserved. Poised.

Until some silly thing that Michelle said brought a sparkle of rueful humor to those eyes, melting the facade—and touching his shallow heart.

Oh, yes, Miss Jessica Sullivan was a true beauty. But she was also the only female friend he'd ever known Michelle to have, and blast his conscience, he wasn't cad enough to meddle in that. Not even for Helen of Troy.

Shaking the thought from his head, he fished through his vest pocket, searching for calling cards. Nothing. Damn. It'd been a dog's age since he made a social call; he was out of practice.

Five minutes later a gold-livery clad footman issued him into a huge green and white parlor with more gilding than the ocean had salt. Awful stuff. Michael's Yankee blood must run cold every time he entered the room.

Bernadette, a stylishly heavy woman dressed in primrose yellow, sat on a green damask chair, punching a needle through a standing embroidery hoop. Michael, sprawled on a sofa across from her, frowned over a book. When the butler announced Lee's entrance, Michael looked up, astonishment quickly melting into genuine pleasure as he rose to greet Lee.

"Montgomery! What brings you to San Francisco?"

"Quite a few matters, not the least of which is visiting an old friend," Lee answered.

At the sight of Michael, Lee's reluctance faded. He offered his hand for a hearty shake, but Michael, more brother than friend, shoved it aside to give Lee a quick embrace. "Poker and women, more likely."

Like women with skin the texture of alabaster and rose red lips perfectly shaped for kissing . . .

*Cad!*

Damned conscience!

"I confess those charms are not inconsiderable. And here is one of the city's loveliest ladies. Bernadette, it's been ages, ma'am," he said, bowing.

"Far too long." She had a cool voice in direct contrast to her fire red hair. It'd always bothered Lee. Weren't redheads supposed to be of a hotter temperament?

"Yes, ma'am," he said, flashing his dimple, "now that I see you, I must admit it has been."

She nodded as if compliments were her due, proving that Bernadette, like her gilt-infested house, was more show than substance, an upstart San Franciscan without an ounce of breeding. And *that,* he thought with a self-deprecating smirk, proved that he was a Boston Brahmin snob just like his father. He settled in an armchair.

They spent several minutes exchanging the kind of mindless pleasantries designed to make Lee yawn in his sleep. He much preferred that, however, to what came next.

"And how is your family, Lee? Mother and father well I hope?" Michael asked. Lee's stomach tightened.

"I expect so."

"And Star? And Port?"

"Last I heard Star had broken yet another engagement, this time to Sears. That makes her sixth, which is more than I can make out. They know she's pledged her life to women's rights, but still the men insist in pursuing marriage."

Bernadette scowled, but Michael flashed a grin. "She can't resist dangling the cheese in front of the mouse."

"And the mouse is caught in the trap every time," Lee replied, shaking his head.

"They appear to be fairly stupid mice."

"And your brother?" Bernadette interrupted. "Any children yet?"

"No," he answered shortly.

"He's been married, what, five years now?"

Five years and no sons to bear the Montgomery name. Port's heartache; Lee's problem. "Somethin' like that."

"And you, Lee? Might we expect wedding bells in your future?"

His throat clenched, but he managed to infuse lightness into his voice. "Why, Bernadette, you must know I surrendered all expectation of marriage when Hathaway stole you away."

As always, charm was lost on Bernadette. She pursed her lips. "You shan't find a wife among the actresses and dance hall girls with whom you regularly associate."

True. No Boston-bred gentleman would marry an actress, certainly not one who'd hike up her skirts on stage to draw male attention.

Or one that was Irish—the bane of Boston society.

"Why, not *all* actresses are unacceptable, surely. Only consider Jenny Lind. Didn't San Francisco open its arms to her when she came to town?"

Bernadette's lips tightened until just shy of disappearing altogether. "Jenny Lind is an entirely different matter, as you well know. She always behaved with the utmost respectability. The women *you* befriend are more likely to take after that Langtry woman. Who knows how many divorces she has accumulated now?" She shuddered in disgust. "If you've any hope of marrying well, you must amend your ways. You are thirty, Lee, and it is past time for you to consider your duty to your family and your future."

Damn the woman, he had no hope to marry well! He had no wish to marry at all, confound Port and his barren wife! A ring on Lee's finger, a noose around his throat. A knot formed there as he spat, "And what sort of woman, *precisely,* ought I to consider? A woman like you, so perfectly proper as to refrain from saying such nefarious words as 'chicken brea—'"

"Bernie, my love," Michael broke in hastily, "is there not some matter with the children you must attend? I swear you said earlier that Phillip's wardrobe needs review, as he's grown at least an inch in the last month."

Bernadette shifted her gaze to glower at Hathaway. For several seconds it seemed that she might turn her scolding upon him also, but she collected herself and rose. "If you'll excuse my absence, Lee, I must see to Phillip. As always, it's been a pleasure. I do hope to see you again while you're in San Francisco."

In fact, she hoped only to see him shackled to a woman

every bit as dull as she. Lee rose, as did Hathaway, and bowed graciously over her hand. "I shall endeavor to find the opportunity, ma'am. I should never wish to be deprived of your lovely company for long."

Her eyes spit back black anger, but she nodded and departed the room. Lee and Michael took seats once more. An awkward silence fell between them as Lee guiltily considered his behavior and his vicious thoughts about Port and Meredith, both suffering from a willing mind, but unwilling body. In the end, it wasn't Port's duty, but Lee's, as the eldest son, to marry well and pass on the name.

Michael coughed to fill the silence, and Lee took a deep breath. "I must beg your pardon, Hathaway. That was unforgivably rude of me. It seems the absence of polite society has dulled my sensibilities. You'll make my apologies to Bernadette, won't you?"

Shaking his head ruefully, Michael answered, "Never. She was every bit as rude as you were. You cannot help but butt heads, can you?"

Lee shrugged. "It's not her fault. I just can't abide all her silly conventions. It's why I left Boston, as you know."

"We had expected you to outgrow it."

Taking a deep breath, he forced his muscles to relax, and flashed Michael a grin. "Difficult to outgrow something that is part of one's nature."

Michael, his normally lazy face creased in concern, rubbed his temple. "Are we no more acceptable to you now than when you left home?"

"You, sir, have always been acceptable to me," he said, warmly. "It's society I can't bear, worse still the notion of marrying into it."

"Marriage is not so bad, Lee," he said gently.

Not for a man who had found love and fidelity with the "right" sort of woman. Lee hadn't even found it with the wrong sort of woman.

Michael leaned back, rubbing his chin. "Perhaps it is Boston you find so restraining," he continued. "San Francisco is light on company right now, but I daresay we might entertain you reasonably well if you would be so obliging as to accept our hospitality."

Lee shook his head ruefully. "Thank you, Michael, but I've sampled that company and am quite contented without it. Besides, the play is at the Baldwin, and I've come for business as well as pleasure. I should be much obliged, however, if you'd join me for a friendly game or two."

Michael barked a laugh. "No poker game with you is friendly, Lee. You're a damned sharp. I'll be glad for your company, however. Give me a few days and I'll see if I can't gather together some friends for a card party."

"Now *those* sort of friends," Lee said with a huge grin, "are the kind I should very much like to meet!"

"Then let us create a list," Hathaway said, leaning forward. As they discussed potential marks, Lee's relief at escaping society reignited his usual buoyancy. Five years, he assured himself, was not really so long. Port might yet father a son and leave Lee to live the bachelor life that suited his fickle heart so well.

# Chapter Two

Jess woke to the sound of a door opening, followed by a loud giggle. A bang followed the giggle, then a moan of pain and another giggle. "I am very sorry, *mon ami,* but there is a chair there," Michelle slurred.

"Now you tell me. Is there light also?" Jess heard a man ask, mirth and pain mingling in his voice. But who? Michelle rarely brought men back to their flat, preferring the more luxurious accommodations of her lovers.

"The building is too old for gaslights, *m'sieur,*" answered her dear, drunk friend, "but we do not need them. My boudoir is but on the other side of this sofa."

"What sofa—damn," he swore, as Jess heard another bump, "that sofa."

Lee Montgomery. Her sleeping nerves jerked to attention. Of course. Michelle had spent most of the week with him.

"Careful, there is a table before that."

"A table, too? Why the devil do you have so much furniture?"

"A table is useful enough, *oui?*"

"*Oui, mademoiselle,* but not very much in the dark. You must have a lamp. Ah, there, on the stove."

"But we do not need the lamp. I like it better in the dark, *oui?*"

"No. Michelle, no, Michelle, stop hanging on me! You need to find your bed."

"That is just what I have been saying!"

"*Alone.* Michelle, stop it, you're going to leave marks on my neck. By God, woman, but you're insatiable! Isn't once enough?"

"Never with you."

"It shall be tonight. You're quite drunk—Michelle, *chérie,* get your hand away from there, no—Oh chriiissst." Mr. Montgomery emitted a low, pleasure-filled hiss, which sent ripples down Jess's strong, straight spine.

Face burning with embarrassment, Jess curled deeper into her old straw mattress and tried to wash away the images in her head of exactly where Michelle's hand must be to create that sort of reaction. Not easy. Five months of living with Michelle had taught Jess a few things about men, lessons Jess had listened to with a combination of disgust and indecent fascination. Now, her mind filled with erotic visions, she regretted not covering her ears and humming every time Michelle opened her mouth.

Soft, inaudible whispers slipped through the cracks of Jess's door. Then Mr. Montgomery spoke in a voice husky with desire. "All right, *chérie,* you've convinced me." The sounds of movement, and then the closing of another door— Michelle's.

Jess rolled over and pulled her pillow over her head to drown out whatever noises they made. It was none of her business. None of her business that at this very moment Mr. Montgomery, with those long fingers, was slowly removing Michelle's clothes between long, deep kisses. Hot kisses, wet kisses, the giddy joining of lips and breath . . .

Another hot shudder ran down Jess's no-longer-so-straight spine.

"Damn, stupid woman!" Jess cursed herself in the dark. "It's none of your funeral!" Recollect, she told herself firmly, what followed kisses, recollect the pain of the marriage bed, the endless thrusting, the nausea-inducing rocking of the bed. No, she was *not* curious about what Mr. Montgomery did to Michelle, or Michelle did to him, and under no circumstances, *none at all,* did Jess wish to trade places with her. Everything Michelle had told her about the wonders of physical passion was just folderol. According to William Acton and George Napheys and a whole host of other writers, most women despised those acts, and, Jess reminded herself firmly, she was one of them. She didn't have Michelle's hot nature. Her blood ran cold at the thought of a man's touch.

Besides, men were good-for-nothing snakes. Everett had taught her that.

Everett had also taught her about kissing.

It was hours before Jess finally fell asleep.

Jess woke to the sun in her eyes. Grimacing, she rolled over, pulling her pillow over her eyes to block it out, but ever persistent, the sunlight slithered underneath. Finally, she tossed the pillow aside to glare at the faded brown curtains, which she'd forgotten to pull the night before, the dratted things. "It's San Francisco, for heaven's sake," she muttered as she padded across bare wood floor. "Where's the fog?"

As she passed her door, the smell of coffee filtered under the crack. She frowned. Was Michelle awake then? A quick glance at the clock on her night table told Jess it was barely ten A.M. Michelle rarely rose at such an hour, especially when she'd been out with a man—out with Lee Montgomery.

A rush of memories from the previous night assaulted Jess. Eyes widening, hand freezing on the curtain, she stared at the crack under her door. No, not possible. Michelle's men rarely stayed the night, and they all invariably fled in the early morning hours.

But Michelle never rose before noon. Never.

Jess dropped her hand. Useless now to shut the curtain. She would certainly not fall back asleep, not with *him* just beyond her door. Well at least he'd made coffee, she thought, as she stripped off her nightgown and turned to her small scratched wardrobe. She dressed in a plain blue cotton gown, splashed her face with water from the washstand, and then pulled her hair back simply with a velvet ribbon. Offstage, she paid only basic attention to her appearance and, she resolved, Mr. Montgomery's presence wouldn't alter that.

She opened her jewelry box and looked at her wedding ring. Married today or not? A wedding ring on her finger, but no husband in sight. Probably he wouldn't notice, but if he did—well, Jess preferred not to expose that miserable part of her life to Mr. Montgomery's mirth.

Not married. She slipped the ring on her right hand and then braced herself. She opened her door to stride into the parlor that separated her room from Michelle's.

*Oh Lord!*

If anything Mr. Montgomery was even more handsome than she remembered, sitting on the tired brown sofa in black trousers and a slightly rumpled white shirt, its sleeves rolled up to expose strong, male forearms lightly sprinkled with dark hair. He wore no tie or collar, and he'd unfastened the top buttons of his shirt. He'd crossed his feet, encased in gleaming black boots, on an ottoman. A light frown of concentration drew his black brows together as he held up a newspaper to read. His other long-fingered hand brought a mug to his lips as Jess closed her door behind her, doing her damnedest to catch her breath.

Mr. Montgomery lifted his head, then dropped his paper and rose in deference, Jess assumed, to her sex. His frown melted into a large smile—one no doubt calculated to turn a girl's resolution to mush. "Ah, Miss Sullivan. You're an early riser, are you?"

For all his aura of wealth, he appeared perfectly at ease in her shabby parlor, with its horsehair sofa, mismatched blue and red Persian armchairs, and worn rag rug. The parlor's only saving graces were the unfashionably painted lemon-yellow walls and two huge windows facing the street, through which the sun shone, creating oblong patterns on the floor. Between the windows, where it could catch the sunlight, sat a small parlor table. None of it would impress a rich gambler.

But gamblers were only rich until their luck ran out.

"Hardly early," she replied dryly. "It's past ten."

Mischief twinkled in his hazel-green eyes. "It's early for me."

"Apparently for Michelle also."

He laughed. "If you've lived with her for any length of time, you're accustomed to that. I've taken the liberty of making coffee and having muffins sent up from the bakery across the street. Help yourself," he said, nodding to a table near the stove. "There's cream and sugar also."

She nodded and moved to the table, her body growing stiff under his watchful eyes. Biting her lip, she chose a blueberry muffin. "Thank you," she said grudgingly, while pouring a cup of coffee. Black today. She needed it straight and strong to put the bone back in her backbone. What was it, she wondered, as she sat primly in the red Turkish chair, what was it in those eyes that melted bone?

Grinning, he reseated himself and casually folded his hands in his lap. "No cream? Like it barefoot then, do you?"

Barefoot—bare—naked—the words recalled the hot images that had haunted her last night. She took a deep gulp of coffee, scalded her throat, and answered, "You have an odd way of putting things, Mr. Montgomery."

"Not me," he said, shaking his head. "Those are ranching terms, ma'am."

"Ranching terms? I thought you were a gambler."

"I did a stint on a ranch first. And you may call me Lee."

Her back stiffened. "Thank you, but no."

"No? Why not?"

"You and I aren't on such familiar terms, I'm afraid."

Chuckling, he reached for his cup. "Afraid, are you? I assure you, Jess, there's not a single thing about me that you need fear. And if there were, using my first name certainly wouldn't negate it."

Flustered, she snapped, "I didn't say you frightened me. And I never gave you leave to use my first name."

Shrugging, he sipped his coffee. "No, ma'am, you didn't. But then you see, I'm not in the least afraid of being on familiar terms with you."

"You're very rude."

"And yet you're the one treating your guest to lectures."

"You're not *my* guest."

"Is this your home?"

"Yes, but—"

"Then I'm your guest. And considering the circumstances, your insistence on formality seems a little absurd."

"I did not invite you here. Michelle did. And frankly, considering the circumstances, I'd think you'd want to leave just as quickly as possible."

"Really? Why? Because you have enough frost in your voice to create another ice age? Tell me, are you always such a shrew when you rise?"

"I am *not* a shrew!"

Grinning, he said, "Oh, don't think I mind. I like a woman with a little acid in her soul. Makes her far more entertaining."

"I'm not here to entertain you, either!"

He chuckled again. "But you are, nonetheless."

"And I don't care what kind of women you like."

"Well, now, that *is* rude. Good manners dictate that you at least *feign* concern about your guest's comfort."

She glared at him, but held her tongue for it seemed everything that spilled from her lips only added to his amusement. And his amusement was definitely at her expense. She took a deep breath before saying carefully, "I am concerned about your comfort. Michelle will rise shortly, and I doubt you'll want to be here for that."

For the first time, the humor left his face. He grimaced. "Ah, so you heard us last night, did you?"

"I did."

Rubbing the back of his neck, he took a sudden tired breath. "Well, then, you know why I'm still here."

Disconcerted, she shook her head. "I'd think you'd want to, uh, escape."

"Believe me, I should love to. However, I possess this very annoying thing called a conscience and so . . . I'll stay."

Shifting in her chair, Jess frowned at him. "It won't be pretty."

"Ma'am," he said, rising. He crossed to the stove to pour himself another cup of coffee. "I've know Michelle for eight years, and the one thing I've learned is that on the morning after a spree she is *not* pretty. Still, fool that I am, I shall stay."

While Jess tried to reconcile this statement with the humorous, ne'er-do-well gambler she'd taken him for, a scrape of enamel on wood rang out from behind Michelle's door. A second later it was followed by a liquid wrenching and a splash. Jess wrinkled her face in disgust.

"Ah, hell," Lee said and put his mug down. "She's awake."

"I have a bucket in my room," Jess said. "I'll get it."

Heaving a sigh, Lee nodded. "And I'll see to her."

The next hour and a half passed swiftly for Jess as she and Lee attended the very sick, very green Michelle, who somehow managed to keep up a flow of French-accented chatter while emptying her stomach of its contents. Lee held his ladylove's head when she vomited, wiped her face with his fine linen handkerchief, and even offered to take the mess to the outhouse.

Touched by Lee's tender care, Jess shook her head. "I'll do it. If the Westgates see too much of you, they'll ask questions."

"And questions are bad?"

"The only way we could rent rooms in a decent part of town was by appearing modest and . . . conventional. And so Michelle's male friends are cousins."

"Cousins," he said slowly, his eyes studying her face. "They believe that?"

Jess grimaced. "They pretend to, at least. But if they encounter too many cousins or see too much of any one cousin, they may become suspicious."

"All right," Lee said, with a doubtful shake of his head. "I'll be a cousin, but damned if it doesn't sound incestuous to me."

And so she left Lee comforting Michelle while she visited the outhouse, rinsed out the bucket and filled it up with coal from the bin. When she returned, she added the coal to the stove, as Lee covered Michelle's shoulders with a shawl, then took a brush to her hair. Michelle's stomach had calmed and, sighing contentedly, she leaned against Lee. "You are always there for me, *chéri*."

"No, I'm not. I'm only there for you when I'm the one responsible for plying you with drink."

Finished with her errands, Jess perched on the edge of an armchair as Michelle giggled in reply. "I think you do very little 'plying,' Lee. I have a taste for wine."

"So it seems. I'd hazard to guess that most Frenchwomen do. Are you warm enough?"

She nodded. "I am fine now. Thank you. You did not need to stay."

Glancing at Jess, he said, "Yes, I did. Your roommate oughtn't to have to clean up after my messes."

"Ah, *ma amie*," Michelle exclaimed, leaning forward to give Jess's hand a squeeze. "You, too, are always there for me. I think I am fortunate to have such good friends, *oui?*"

With a wry grin, Jess answered, "Some days, Michelle, you're lucky to have friends at all."

"*Mais, non,* you are too hard with me! I am only fortunate to have a female friend. Of male friends, I have plenty."

With a small chuckle, Lee helped Michelle to a full sitting position. "And all these years, I'd believed that you loved only me, *chérie!* Now, if you're feeling well enough, I have business to attend."

Smiling brightly up at him, Michelle nodded. "I will see you again, soon, *oui?*"

Lee's eyes twinkled at her as he reached for his waistcoat and coat, slung over the back of Jess's chair. Jess leaned forward, assuring herself that she felt nothing at all when his hand accidentally brushed across her shoulder. "Of course. But," he started, as he donned his waistcoat. Jess tried not to notice the way the muscles of his chest moved under his shirt. "No more wine, understood?"

"Oh, but c*héri!*"

"I mean it! One morning of this is enough for any man." He pulled down his shirtsleeves and fastened them with shiny gold links.

With a petulant frown pulling down the corners of Michelle's lovely mouth, she crossed her arms over her chest and said, "All right, *m'sieur, mais ça ne me plaît pas!*"

Lee grinned and shrugged into his frockcoat. "Yes, well, you can do with a little less happiness." He turned to Jess, smiled down at her with those warm, laughing eyes and reached for her hand. Her eyes widened when he lifted it to his mouth to kiss the tips of her fingers, sending little thrills down her arm. "It's been an honor and a pleasure, Miss Sullivan. We must do this again sometime!"

Sudden amusement tickling her throat, she laughed. "And if Michelle has her way, we most certainly shall."

A glint of something other than merriment touched his eyes. "You almost make me wish for the occasion. Unfortunately,

Michelle's taste in wine is expensive. To see it in a bucket is more than a man should have to bear."

"Ah, but, Lee, you have the money for it," Michelle offered with a gleam of speculation in her eyes. "Perhaps, *chéri,* you have the money for us both to drink wine, *ma amie* and I?"

"I said almost, Michelle," he said, walking to the door. "Although," he continued, his hand on the knob. His gaze fell on Jess once more. "I don't see why we shouldn't include Miss Sullivan in our plans. I look forward to it, Jess." Then before she could form a polite refusal, he left.

Her face warm with a rising blush, Jess stared at the door and bit her lip. "Interesting," Michelle said, her French accent disappearing. "So the wind blows in that direction, does it?"

Resolutely, Jess rose and reached across the table to scoop up the empty coffee cups. "I don't know what you're talking about."

"No," Michelle said. Her eyes followed Jess. "But then, you don't know Lee."

"Nor do I have any intention of changing that situation," she said, placing the cups on a tray. She started to lift it when Michelle spoke in a voice that brooked no interference.

"No, now you leave those there, Jessica Sullivan, and sit back down. We're going to talk about this." Jess winced. When Michelle was in a certain mood, it didn't matter that she stood five feet nothing; she was a force to be reckoned with.

"There's nothing to talk about," Jess said, frowning.

Michelle's brown eyes ran speculatively over Jess and, with a little smile, Michelle nodded. "There is. I think you're stealing my love's attention and in that gown, too!"

"It's not such a bad gown," Jess grumbled.

"It's an abomination! Not so much as a tassel! It was out of date a hundred years ago, I swear it. For an actress to be seen in such as that . . . I am *very* sure that your brother can *never* appreciate the way you sacrifice for him!"

Jess flinched. "I don't have the theatre wardrobe you have

acquired, Michelle, and I can't afford appropriate costumes *and* elegant everyday clothes. Besides, you know full well it's not Jason's appreciation—"

"I know, I know, it's that ridiculous debt you believe you owe him." Michelle waved her hand as if to push the words out the window. "I won't hear of it. We will, instead, talk about Lee's interest in you."

"He has no interest in me. His eyes are only for you."

Michelle laughed and curled her feet under her legs as she reached over to pat a place next to her on the sofa. "Right now, he has *hands* only for me, honey, but his eyes were on you! Now sit."

"Oh, for the love of Pete," Jess said under her breath, but she granted Michelle's request, placing the tray back on the table. "There, now, are you happy? Honestly, Michelle, don't you think we ought to be cleaning up?"

"No, of all things, cleaning up is the least thing we ought to do. You must rid yourself of this neatness obsession, my friend. Now, tell me, do you like him?"

Jess sighed, trying to sound completely indifferent even though she couldn't imagine *liking* a man like Lee, ever. "I do not. He's rude."

"I think he's funny."

"He does, too."

Michelle laughed. "Yes, and I can see what he likes in you. Lee enjoys wit."

"I thought he liked French accents."

She shrugged. "He likes those, too."

Jess scowled. "Does he have any notion at all that you've never even been to France?"

"Oh, I'm sure he knows. But what of it? It amuses him and I like it, too. It suits us."

"Then I'm happy for you. And now—"

"I think you'll suit him better."

Jess shook her head as her stomach gave a little toss. "No,

no, no! Michelle, if you believe for one minute that I'm the kind of woman who would steal—"

"Oh, no, I don't think *that*. Good Lord, no, you're far too good a friend! I am *giving* him to you."

"Giving him? Good gracious, Michelle, you can't give men away!"

"Why not?"

"Why, for one thing, he might not want to go."

"Oh, but he does! As far as giving, I don't really own him, you know."

"You've known him forever. After, what—eight years?— he looks for you in every town."

"Of course he does. We're friends after all."

"Friends, no. That, Michelle, is the sign of a man in love."

Michelle burst into laughter, and while Jess glared, Michelle gurgled and burbled until tears trickled from her eyes. Jess crossed her arms over her chest waiting for her to finish. "In love with me," Michelle finally said, wiping her eyes. "I'm sure Lee *loves* me, at least a little, but *in* love, no, never. What we have is a . . . a casual friendship."

"It seemed a bit more than friendship last night."

"We know each other well, you see."

"And I'm very happy for you," Jess said, reaching for the tray. "Just as long as you keep me out of your plans."

Michelle watched her a moment. "Are you not at all attracted to him?"

The stacked cups slid on the tray and one crashed to the floor to break into three large pieces. Jess, her mind quickly calculating the cost of replacing it versus gluing it, sighed and started to pick up the mess. "I'd think every woman would be a little attracted to a man like that."

"I asked about you."

"I find him handsome. Is that what you wanted?" she asked, carefully placing the pieces on the tray. She'd glue it together later. "But I'm not of your passionate nature. 'Of your nature!' Will you listen to me? You're a bad influence, Michelle. I sound like a damned Jane Austen novel!"

"Oh, and how I love those books! Now, as to what I was saying—"

"As to that, I find Robert handsome, too. That doesn't mean I want to, uh, act upon it."

"I think you are deceiving yourself, *ma amie*."

"Will you, please, please refrain from using that phony French on me! I am not one of your men!"

"Still, I think you're lying. And I think that, as difficult as it will be, I will withhold my affections from Lee."

Jess's eyes widened in alarm. "Withhold your affections? Are you crazy? Michelle, you love him!"

"Oh, yes, I do. And," she said gently, "I love you, too, Jess. That is why I shall withhold my affection and he shall look elsewhere for his love," she said, rising and stretching. "Then I'll direct him toward you. It will work perfectly, I think."

"You shall *not!* Honestly, Michelle, when will you understand that I am married?"

"Never after that swine's actions. And what is more, once you have been with Lee, you will become less shrewish."

"Shrewish—you were *listening* to us?"

"Of course. Now, I believe I'll change and see if anyone is using the bathroom. Did I tell you? Mr. Westgate's agreed to allow us two baths a week instead of one, since we are actresses."

Ignoring the bath discussion, Jess snapped, "Michelle, this is madness. You love Lee and you'll lose him if you do this. Is that what you want?"

"My loss will be your gain."

"I refuse to be party to this scheme of yours! *And,* what is more, I'm not interested in men in that way. The notion repulses me."

"You are not involved in my scheming. And Lee does not repulse you. I can see things in your eyes, too, Jess. You do like him, you do find him attractive, and, I know this well, there is not a thing repulsive in him. But you will see. Now, I'm going to dress," Michelle said with finality and while Jess sputtered behind her, she went into her room and closed the door.

# Chapter Three

*"I should say the majority of women (happily for them) are not very much troubled with sexual feeling of any kind."* Jess read, sipping a hot cup of tea as she wormed herself deeper into the blue Persian chair, ugly in color but oh, so very comfortable! Dressed in her only nightgown, a threadbare but perfectly proper blue cotton, she pulled Acton's *Functions and Disorders of the Reproductive Organs* nearer to the kerosene lamp, which cast a halo of light around her in the otherwise dark room. *"What men are habitually, women are only exceptionally. It is too true, I admit, as the Divorce Court shows, that there are some few women who have sexual desires so strong that they surpass those of men, and shock public feeling by their consequences. I admit, of course, the existence of sexual excitement terminating even in nymphomania, a form of insanity which to those accustomed to visit lunatic asylums must be fully conversant with . . ."*

Which meant that Michelle, not Jess, was the mad one. Michelle, who had, almost upon meeting Jess, resolved that she was a soul badly in need of "saving," although not at all in the religious manner. For five nights Jess had avoided Michelle's latest ill-conceived scheme, but her occasional speculative gaze unnerved Jess. Tonight she had changed swiftly after their performance and headed home, avoiding her friend entirely.

Jess reached for a butter cookie, bought at the bakery across the street, one of her few luxuries. She continued reading where she left off, savoring each word like a piece of Swiss chocolate. *"But with these sad exceptions there can be no doubt that sexual feeling in the female is in the majority of cases in abeyance, and that it requires positive and considerable excitement to be roused at all; and even if roused (which in many instances it never can be) it is very moderate compared with that of the male."*

A knock sounded at the door and Jess lifted her head to frown at it. The only people who'd dare come knocking at this time of night wanted Michelle, and anybody even slightly acquainted with her would look for her at the theatre. Maybe if Jess ignored him, he'd go away. She focused on her book again.

Another knock, louder, more insistent. With a sigh of disgust, Jess rose, dropped her book on the table, and went to answer the door. Hand on knob, she glanced down at her gown and considered finding her coat. But whoever had come calling Michelle would surely not stay long enough for that to be necessary, nor would any of Michelle's friends have the least understanding of propriety. She opened the door a crack.

Lee Montgomery, top hat in his hand. He flashed her a smile. "Jess," he greeted, and her stomach flipped over, stupid, silly thing.

"Michelle's not here," she snapped. Of all the people she wished to see, he was at the bottom of her list, directly ahead of Genghis Khan.

"I know," Lee answered. "I left her in her dressing room. She requested that I wait here for her. May I come in?"

Damn, she ought to have grabbed that coat! "It would be best for you to wait downstairs."

With a flash of white teeth, he answered, "I should if it didn't look rather suspicious to the Westgates. After all, I am your cousin."

"I'm not dressed for company."

"I won't tell a soul."

Scowling, she allowed him entrance, then glanced around the hall. No one there, thank God. She closed the door and turned to see Lee removing his coat, not a good sign for a woman determined to spend her evening alone. He was dressed in casual eveningwear, a dark green suit that fit him like a glove—not good, either, for a woman determined to retain her peace of mind.

He laid his coat on a chair as Jess asked, "Just how long did Michelle say she'd be?"

Giving the cuffs of his shirt a quick, automatic tug, Lee crossed the room to their parlor table. "Five minutes, five hours, it's all the same to Michelle. Good God, Jess, it's black as pitch in here! Have you another lamp? Ah, here's one."

"Kerosene is expensive," she said, crossing her arms protectively over her chest.

"So is blindness." After fumbling with a match, he lit the lamp. The light sparkled on a newly acquired decanter of amber liquid and four crystal glasses. Lee pulled the stopper and ran it under his nose. "Brandy. Good girl, Michelle." With a mixture of exasperation and growing alarm, Jess watched him pour a drink. He held the decanter up to her. "Join me?"

"I don't drink hard liquor, but by all means make yourself at home!"

He chuckled. "Thank you, I believe I already have. She bought it for me, you know. Michelle doesn't like brandy."

"No, it's wine that's her problem."

Swirling the glass, he crossed the room, grinning. "I've known worse vices."

She frowned as she sat in her chair. "You oughtn't indulge her. It'll ruin her health."

Lee lifted his brows, while claiming the space nearest her on the sofa. "And her other indulgences won't?"

Jess sighed. "They'll most likely kill her."

"Probably." He sipped his drink, then closed his eyes with a deep sigh of contentment. "Ah, now that's fine brandy. Are you certain you won't try some?"

Something about the look of appreciation on his face reminded her of a man in the aftermath of passion, and a hot shudder flashed through Jess. "I'd rather see her amend her ways," Jess replied, then winced at the prudishness in her voice.

Opening his eyes once more, he shook his head ruefully. "Sweetheart, you don't have a prayer of that happening."

She stiffened. "You shouldn't call me that."

"Sweetheart? But don't you have a sweet heart? I beg your pardon, Jess, but from what I've seen thus far, you're exceedingly kindhearted."

Now, how on earth did he *do* that? Insult and compliment all at the same time? "I don't recollect giving you any cause to think so."

"No?" he asked, taking a sip and making another seductive sigh of appreciation. "You appear to take good care of Michelle, even though it must be a great burden."

She shrugged. "She's a friend."

"She's a friend with, I suspect, very different principles than yours."

"A little."

"A lot," he insisted, sipping more of his brandy. "Are you certain you won't join me? This is damned smooth stuff."

"No. I've refused it three times. When are you going to stop asking?"

He shrugged. "I probably won't. I don't care for drinking alone."

"Then maybe you ought to stop drinking."

"It'd be a deal more entertaining if you'd join me. Might take a little starch out of those stays of yours."

"I beg your pardon!"

The twinkling in his eyes turned to downright laughter. "Jessica, ma'am, you needn't beg me for anything! Your wish is my command."

She stared at him, her heart pounding in her chest as she struggled for an answer. None came.

Finally, he laughed and rose to fetch her a glass of brandy. "I was right. You do need a drink."

Her mind continued to sputter as Jess sought a reply that would shut him up. When he handed her a glass, she tried to push it away.

"Go on, Jess, take it." She shook her head and he said in a soothing tone, "All right, I apologize, *most* sincerely, for the remark. I never intended to insult you, but you left me an opportunity I couldn't resist."

"Oh, okay!" she said and took the drink. "I expect you don't resist too many things."

"Not many," he admitted, sinking into the sofa once more. "But a few. So tell me, sweetheart—we've established that, correct? You have a sweet heart—"

"It seems pointless to quarrel with you. You'll do exactly as you please."

"It is, really. How did a woman as straitlaced as you become an actress?"

"That doesn't seem to be any of your business."

"Most of what interests me isn't any of my business. That's why it interests me."

"So you're a busybody."

He considered for a minute, then nodded. "All right, I'm a busybody. Human nature fascinates me."

"It confuses me."

"Same thing. Are you going to answer the question?"

"No. What's taking Michelle so long?"

Smiling indulgently, Lee said, "Jess, she's not coming."

"But you said—"

"*She said* she'd be here. But she appeared a little distracted at the time. No doubt she's forgotten."

"Then I expect you want to leave," Jess said, starting to rise.

"Not really."

She stilled, frowning. "That doesn't make any sense."

"Why?"

"Because you came for her."

"I'm enjoying myself, nonetheless."

That was it. Her heart was going to take wing and fly. Death was but minutes away, for her heart could never survive at this pace. She sat back down, took a sip of the brandy and let its fire slide down her throat. Maybe it'd hit her heart and burn the damned, treacherous thing to ashes. Then, heartless, she would determine a way to dispose of Lee Montgomery. She'd never met a man more capable of disrupting her carefully ordered mind.

"You were expecting a certain kind of companionship tonight, weren't you?" she finally ventured. "I should think having been forsaken by Michelle, you'd look elsewhere." Her words were out before she'd thoroughly considered them. She bit her lip and decided she ought to damned well bite her tongue, too. *Oh, Michelle, I didn't mean to stab you in the back, truly I didn't!*

Lee's lips twitched. "I'm well past my teen years, sweetheart. I can do without a woman for a night."

"Oh." So he wasn't interested in her in that way. Why, that was a relief—wasn't it?

"I won't even attempt to seduce you, Jess. I promise. I only wish to talk," he said gently, confirming her thoughts in a damnable way. Probably men like Lee had a sixth sense about women. Probably they knew which ones were passionless.

Except for Everett. But he'd been blinded by money.

"Now," Lee said peering at her. "Are you at ease again?"

"I never was ill at ease."

He gave her another long hard look, as his eyes sparkled. "Of course not," he conceded. "My mistake. And so, Jess, kindly oblige my curiosity in human nature for a moment, will you? How did a woman like you end up on stage? Actresses aren't precisely known for their honor."

"I enjoy acting. Is that so strange?"

"No. You're quite good at it, too, but you don't crave the limelight as the other actors or actresses I've known. It appears to be merely a job to you."

"A well-paying job."

"When there's work."

"I haven't been out of work since I started."

He sipped his drink. "When was that?"

"Six years ago."

He nodded. "A nice long stretch. Why acting?"

She shrugged, fumbling for ways to ward off his questions. "I was broke and needed work."

"You couldn't have been very old. Where was your family?"

"I had no parents."

"Ah," he said, nodding as if he understood. He didn't, but she wasn't about to elaborate. "But the stage? Aren't there more respectable jobs?"

"Not . . . not where I was."

Another lifting of those eyebrows. "And where was that?"

"Deadwood."

He opened his mouth, lost his words, and said, "Oh." After a minute, he reached into his waistcoat pocket and withdrew a cigar and matches, glancing at her speculatively. "That *is* desperate."

"Yes."

He put the cigar in his mouth and prepared to strike a match. His eyes flickered over her. He paused. "You don't mind, do you?"

It was a simple process, nothing to make a girl's pulse race, but the movement of those finely carved lips created unwelcome pictures. Warm lips—long, lingering kisses.

He was staring at her, waiting for an answer.

"They're bad for your lungs," she answered.

He grinned and taking her comment as consent, puffed on the cigar to light it. After blowing a smoke ring, he said, "Most of what I enjoy is bad for me. That's why I enjoy it." He flashed her his dimple. "Please continue with your story. It seems rather fortunate that this troupe appeared at the right time."

Uh oh. "It was."

He raised his eyebrows, then let loose a laugh. "It didn't, did it?"

"Not exactly."

He tilted his head a little, a small frown appearing between his eyebrows despite his smile. "Did you seek other forms of employment first then?"

"I had no other choice."

"And they were?"

"Oh," she waved her hand airily. "A few things."

"A few things. I've been to Deadwood. There's not much work for a woman."

"I-I suppose not much."

"Not respectable positions, at any rate. What else did you consider?"

"You know, this really isn't—"

"Any of my business. Jess, I'm a gambler by profession, and my favorite woman is Michelle. I'm not likely to judge you harshly, am I?"

"No."

"And so?"

"Okay, okay! I tried selling love. Is that what you wanted to hear?"

His lips twitched in amusement. "Not exactly. I merely wondered if you'd considered it. What happened?"

She peered at him and shifted uncomfortably. "It didn't work."

"Ah, impotency!" he said, laughter deepening his voice.

"Oh, for the love of Pete, he wasn't impotent!"

"He?"

"Ye-yes," she said slowly.

"Only one man, then?"

"I-I wasn't very good at it, you see. After the one, it didn't seem worth another effort."

His face softened. "I'm sorry, Jess. Did he harm you?"

She grimaced. "No, not exactly."

"Not exactly?"

"I just—you see I, uh, met him on the street. He seemed . . . I don't know, clean enough. And young. And so . . . and so when he made overtures, I thought, why not? It seemed like— so many women do it, you know. And so I, uh, followed him back to his room. I really didn't want him in *my* room, you understand. And then, he undressed and he"—she took a deep breath—"kissed me. And then started to unbutton my bodice—" She stopped.

"And?" Lee asked, sitting forward in his chair, his hand hanging across his knees, with his cigar dangling between his thighs.

"And smiled . . ."

"And?"

"And I hit him over the head with a lamp."

Lee burst out laughing. "No doubt this enticed him."

She bit her lip. "I don't really know. I kind of ran."

"Ran?"

"It seemed like the logical thing to do."

"For him!"

She shrugged. "That was my one attempt at prostitution. Are you satisfied now?"

"More than your mark," Lee quipped, sitting back in his chair once more to take a puff on his cigar. "Did you ever see him again? Refund his money, perhaps?"

"Refund? How could I have collected any money?"

Grinning, Lee tapped his cigar against the ashtray. "Most prostitutes collect up front, Jess."

"Do they?"

"The successful ones do," Lee replied slowly. The more he talked to Jess, the more he realized that she was at heart a small-town girl, living in the very center of dissipation and debauchery. Yet she maintained a certain degree of naïveté— or a strong moral code. He'd never found either particularly interesting, but in Jess the contradiction fascinated him.

To hide his thoughts, he turned and stubbed out his cigar, flashing a quick glance at her. She was finally at ease, sitting back in her chair sipping brandy. If she knew what he thought every time his eyes strayed from her face to that body, she'd be a damned sight less easy. He had no intention of attempting a seduction; that didn't mean he didn't wish to.

"And you?" she interrupted his thoughts. "What brought you into your profession?"

"Ah, turnabout is fair play, right?"

She smiled. "Call it satisfying my interest in human nature."

A generous amount of wit also, but moral women and him were a hellish combination. Women of that sort wanted ties before bedding down with a man. And there was still Michelle . . .

He shrugged. "I left home when I was eighteen. Took a train West and discovered I have a knack for gambling. I've earned my living with it ever since."

"Oh," she said, her brows coming together in a frown of concentration. "Why did you leave home?"

"Boredom mostly." And the fact that alleviating it would disgrace his family beyond repair.

"Boredom?" she asked, disgust and shock tingeing her voice. "You left home out of boredom?"

"Boredom. Something wrong with that?"

She shook her head. "It sounds remarkably stupid to me."

He laughed. "No! Why?"

"I don't know. Don't you miss your home? Did you leave any family behind?"

"Mother, father, sister, brother. I've visited several times over the last eleven years."

"Were they angry that you left?"

"They expected it. My father made several attempts to interest me in the family business, but I didn't have the head for it. Since my brother and sister took to it like fish to water, he wasn't too disappointed in me. So I left to find my future elsewhere. Does that sound better? I wasn't bored, I was searching for my future," he said, flashing her his dimple-laced grin.

"Boredom," she answered, biting her lip. Watching the way those small white teeth worried her lower lip created such visions in his mind—of her lips and teeth working on the most sensitive parts of his anatomy—that he had to take a large gulp of brandy to hear her next words. "Not a broken heart or some past love haunting you?" she inquired.

"Why? Do I look brokenhearted?"

"No, but I always believed that rakes and libertines were merely victims of tragic heartbreak." With a disappointed twitch of her brows, she sighed. "I must say, I'm rather disillusioned."

Humor bubbled up inside him. "Am I a rake? I hadn't thought it!"

"I thought you might be, but apparently you're just an average, ordinary scoundrel."

"Really. And here I'd been thinkin' I'm just a nice, ord'nary sorta fella."

"Nice ord'nary fellas don't gamble for a living."

"Ah, of course. Only rakes, libertines, and scoundrels. Where did you get these notions?"

"Michelle."

"And her English romance novels, right? You believe that stuff?" he asked, and then noticed that her eyes were no longer just twinkling but actually laughing. "You don't. You're teasing me, you little shrew!"

She laughed, a light melodic sound that echoed sweetly in his brain. Lord, but a man could learn to love that sound. But *not* him, he thought, placing his glass on the table. Too many barriers for that to happen. So why in hell was he still here? Because he was a fool, that's why.

He rose. "And now I think I'd better go."

She nodded. "It is late."

He smiled down at her, shaking his head when she started to rise. If she stood up, the lamplight would shine right through that gown, exposing all her soft female parts. He was excited enough. Much more and not even a small-town girl would be able to deny the fact that he'd greatly prefer her company in the bedroom. He reached for his coat and pulled it on. "I'll let myself out. Thanks for the brandy, Jess." He had his hand on the knob when he remembered why he'd come in the first place. And, damn Michelle, if she'd been here his body would be far happier right now.

He turned to Jess. "Oh, and relay a message to *mon chéri* for me, will you? Tell her that abstinence neither makes the heart grow fonder nor the wine flow freer."

Lee steered the open-topped George IV phaeton toward Michelle's flat. Dressed in a gown of wine-red velvet and impatiently twirling a matching silk parasol, she decorated the building's dull walkway, catching the attention of every male in sight. Raising an eyebrow, Lee set the brake and smiled at her, his smile broadening appreciatively when he noted her deep V-shaped bodice, scandalously low for daywear. "Upset, *chérie?*"

"You are five minutes late, *mon ami.* Are you going to hand me up?"

"Of course," he said, jumping down. Gallantly, he took her pink-gloved hand and holding her gaze, pressed his lips to the back of her hand. "I apologize for being late. But permit me to say, Michelle, I had expected you to wait inside for me."

She tossed her head, blond curls bouncing. "I wanted a breath of air."

"Ah, so it wasn't the desire to show off your new gown?"

As expected, her eyes lit up and she smiled flirtatiously. "Do you like it?"

"I have always said that red velvet suits you, *chérie,*" he said, taking her parasol and handing her into the low-slung carriage. Daintily lifting her skirts, Michelle stepped into the carriage, then slid across the black velvet seat. After glancing up at the second-story window of the building, last room on the left, Lee followed her. Jess's room, he thought, taking up the reins. Was she up there?

*She's too straitlaced for you, Lee, old boy.*

He'd spent the better part of two weeks reminding himself of that. In fact, he'd spent the better part of two weeks avoiding Jess entirely, trying to destroy the memories of her eyes twinkling merrily as she shot retorts at him, matching him quip for quip. Not since he'd last seen Star had he enjoyed a woman's company so much. It didn't help that along with the platonic memories of Jess came the far more distracting recollections of the body that went with her mind. It'd have been a damned sight easier if Michelle hadn't been playing hide-and-seek.

Swallowing his frustration, Lee winked at Michelle, who was once more twirling her parasol. She'd perched it at such an angle as to expose most of her face to passersby while avoiding the browning rays of the sun. He gently slapped the reins on the pair of grays pulling the phaeton. "All colors suit you, *chérie*. And all fabrics. And all clothes. But do you know what suits you best, Michelle?"

Wiggling in delight, she stared up at him, eyes bright with anticipation. "*Non, mon ami,* but you will tell me."

"Scoot over here first." When she did, he draped his arm around her soft, familiar shoulders and leaned over to whisper in her ear. "What suits you best is wearing nothing at all."

Her soft giggle warmed Lee's hot blood. "I think that is what suits *you* best, *oui?*"

"Let us say that it suits us both best. Which begs the question, *chérie*, of your notable absence in my life these past two weeks."

"That does not seem to be a question, Lee."

"You shall answer it, nonetheless."

With a very French lifting of her shoulders, she replied, "I have been busy."

"No doubt. I believe, however, I made it clear that I'm staying in San Francisco particularly for the pleasure of your company."

With a pretty little pout of her mouth—amazing mouth, Lee thought with a sudden, vivid recollection of what she could do to a man with those lips—she said, "*Mais oui,* but I never said I would not be busy. Oh, Lee, do you see that woman there? In that *chapeau?* Is it not *très laid?* That big blue ostrich feather, it covers her eyes in the most amusing way."

Lee glanced in the direction of Michelle's outstretched hand. "I see it. It's rude to point, Michelle. She'll know you're talking about her."

"Hah! What do I care what she thinks?"

"Not much, I see. May I inquire as to where *your* hat is today, *mademoiselle?* It's unusual for you to go abroad bareheaded."

"Oh, but that is why I asked you to come! On Baker Street there is a shop, *comprenez-vous?* With *un chapeau très beau!*"

He barked a laugh and, muscles relaxing, steered the carriage down Baker Street. Michelle, with her easy morals and kindly avaricious ways, was just his sort of woman. Not Jess. Never straitlaced, moral Jess. "And here I hoped your summons was of a warmer nature."

"A *chapeau* is warm, *oui?*"

"Not, I daresay, the kind we're going to see."

She lifted her face to plead with her big, brown eyes. "And if you like it, maybe you will purchase it for a special woman in your life?"

He laughed. "*Oui, chérie.* I shall purchase it for a special woman in my life. Am I correct in assuming that it will complement red velvet perfectly?"

*"Naturellement!"*

Forty-five minutes later, as the sun was setting over the bay, Lee and Michelle exited the hat shop, a small red velvet hat with dyed-to-match plumes perched saucily on top of her gold curls. Carrying three large hatboxes, the clerk followed behind them and carefully secured their packages in the small back compartment of the carriage. Lee thanked him, slipped a bill into his hand, and then handed Michelle into the carriage. As they started off again, he smirked down at her. "Happy, *chérie?*"

*"Oui!"*

Her bright, childlike smile tickled Lee's throat. "And where to now? Am I expected to return you to your flat, or have you another errand for me?"

"Oh, not home! I must wear my *chapeau nouveau* first!"

"Ah, so I'm to drive aimlessly around the city so that *you* may drive every woman who might have been unwise enough to step outside this evening insanely jealous over your new chapeau. Is that correct?"

"Not *aimlessly*. You must drive through Golden Gate Park. That is where all the fashionable people go."

Chuckling, he threw his arm over her shoulders and gave

her a quick hug. "You don't need a hat to make them jealous, Michelle."

"*Oui.* I have Lee also!"

He shook his head ruefully. "I'm not as turned by a compliment as you, but thank you."

"You are very welcome." She sighed contentedly, then fell silent while Lee steered the carriage through the streets. A balmy breeze blew off the water, bringing with it the salty tang of the sea.

"Of course," Michelle said abruptly, "we must not stay out too late. I must show *mon chapeau nouveau* to Jessica."

Lee frowned. "I should have thought you above seeking the envy of your friends, *chérie.*"

"Oh, but she is waiting to see it! And it is not for envy that she will like it, but for her own use. I think perhaps she might like to borrow it some night. Do you think red velvet suits black hair as it does blond, Lee?"

Lee's jaw clenched as his mind created a picture of Jess, eyes flashing blue-black with desire, wearing that absurd hat—and nothing else. By God, he did *not* want to discuss Jess!

"I think the hat suits you, Michelle."

"That is not the question. It is whether it suits my Jessica." She heaved a stage sigh, chockful of feigned compassion. "Poor Jess. I think I might *give* her my new chapeau. I think it will lift her spirits, *ma petite pauvre.*"

"Your *petite pauvre*?" Lee asked, with a sudden touch of suspicion. "Does Jess have a problem?" It didn't matter—he didn't care to know . . .

"*Oui, chéri,* my Jess, she suffers from a broken heart."

"A broken heart? Forgive my stupidity, but I was under the impression that Jess habitually declines male companionship."

"Oh, but that is just it! She cannot bear another man because of her broken heart. It is so very sad."

He sighed. "All right. I'll bite. Why is Jess suffering from a broken heart?"

"It is," Michelle said, pausing for effect, "her husband!"

Stunned, Lee yanked on the reins, accidentally pulling the horses to a halt. Behind him someone swore. He slapped the horses' backs once more and turned off the main road. "Jess is married? She doesn't wear a ring. And her name is *Miss* Jessica Sullivan."

"Her stage name, merely, and she wears her band on her right hand sometimes. Oh, Lee, it is *trés* tragic! She was abandoned, by the, how you say, 'cad'?"

"You say cad. And this happened recently?"

"*Mais non!* It is five years, maybe six. I do not know, but it has put her off from men."

"Put her off from men? Because of one bad affair?"

"Because of a cad husband. It is enough, *n'est-il pas,* for a woman."

"Is it?" he asked, as his brain began to race. Married? Married. Miss—*Mrs.*—Small-Town America, it seemed, couldn't *ask* for ties, even if she wished to. It added a whole new dimension to the situation. If her heart ached for another man, he need never worry about it breaking over him.

"It is," Michelle answered. "And I have tried to help, but I do not know how to cure the ill. I begin to despair."

"I suspect," Lee said slowly, as he once more brought up that vision of Jess in the hat, "that the cure would require the attentions of another man."

"Oh!" Michelle exclaimed. "Do you think so, Lee?"

Caught by the sudden laughter in Michelle's voice, he glanced down. Her eyes gleamed with suppressed mirth. "Which is precisely what you were hoping I'd conclude, *oui?*"

"*Oui!*"

Perhaps Jess's veneer of morality was not so much prudishness as misplaced fidelity to a long-gone husband. If so, six years of abstaining from sexual pleasure was a very long time. "And I presume that you've already chosen a man for this cure?"

"*Naturellement,* but alas," she said with a deep sigh. Out of the corner of his eye, he saw that hers were dancing with mischief. "He is blind to my entreaties."

"Perhaps," Lee said wryly, "he hasn't understood your entreaties."

"You may be right, *m'sieur.* I have withheld my affections from this man and I have told *ma amie* of my plan, but it does not work, you see! I am cursed by those who refuse to cooperate with my best intentions."

Lee laughed. "So that's why you've been so, 'busy.' Good God woman, I've been running myself in circles wondering what I did to offend you! Next time you might consider honesty! I'm far more likely to cooperate if I know what's expected of me."

"*Mais non!* What would be the joy in that?" Michelle asked with a light toss of her head.

"Or the drama, eh? So tell me, *chérie,* what does '*ma amie*' say about all this?"

"She says I am, how you say, crazy. That you would stop loving me and seek out another woman."

"She said that? Huh." Interesting reaction. Had Jess played such a game with her husband and lost? Had he left her for another woman—other women?

"Huh? What means this huh?"

"It means huh."

"It means she is right, *oui?* You are no longer loving me!"

At the sound of false fear in Michelle's voice, Lee glanced down at her. Stage tears glittered in her eyes. Smiling, he gave her a quick hug. "First of all, *chérie,* I have already sought solace in another woman's arms—San Francisco is full of women willing to share a night's pleasure—yet here I am driving you all over creation so that you may show off the hat you just weaseled out of me. Second, after eight years I wouldn't stop loving you if you suddenly developed a deep and profound aversion to all men and joined a convent, although I confess I might visit you a little less often."

"Ah, so you do love me! I knew it! And why do I not wear your ring then?"

"Because, darlin', you'd make a hellish wife and I'd make a worse husband. I'm a sworn bachelor. However," he said, flashing a smile at her, "it seems your roommate doesn't understand that, does she? Perhaps I ought to prove my point. What do you say? Supper at Armand's?"

"Armand's! Oh, Lee, *oui, oui!* And wine, also?"

"The king of wines. Champagne. But I reserve the right to limit you to one bottle. First, however, let us stop at your flat, shall we, and invite '*ma amie*' to join us."

*"Mais oui, monsieur!"* Michelle said, clapping her hands in excitement. "So you are liking my scheme!"

"I'm not fond of any scheme that keeps you from my bed, *chéri.*"

*"Oui, mon ami,* it is sad, but you may not have us both and I have chosen for you. You shall be *très bon* for my Jess, and she will cease to be a shrew," Michelle said, sitting back with a deep satisfied sigh. "And I will have wine."

Lee groaned. "It seems abstinence makes the wine flow freer after all."

# Chapter Four

Armand's, Jess noted as Lee opened the door, housed a gambling parlor on the first floor. It was jammed full of men and women, all dressed in grand style, playing cards, dice, roulette, and a variety of games that Jess had never seen. Waiters carried trays of wine and hors d'oeuvres among the players, their feet silently skimming over the thickly carpeted floor.

"This way, sweetheart," Lee said in her ear, and took her elbow. Shivering at the whispering touch of his breath on her neck, she allowed herself to be led up a curving white and gold staircase to the main dining room. Michelle swept regally in front of them, a true San Franciscan picture of golden beauty dressed in shining amber satin. Having been here many times before, in the company of many different men, Michelle knew exactly where she was going. Not Jess, though, who had always been unwilling to pay the price, a price Michelle considered a reward in itself.

The headwaiter greeted Lee by name. It seemed that Lee had been here many times, too. Of course he had. He was one of Michelle's "rewards."

"In the back, Gaston, if possible," Lee asked. "I'd rather not hear the gaming room tonight."

With an obsequious nod, Gaston replied, "As you wish, sir. Right this way."

Lee motioned Michelle to proceed, then carefully guided Jess across the midnight-blue and gold carpet, between tables of laughing patrons drinking from crystal and eating off fine china. Jess tried not to stare, for the only time she'd ever eaten off fine china was at her grandmother's house. Guilt followed hard on that cheerful memory, as she recollected what had happened to grandma's money—and the criminal part she'd played in it.

Gaston halted in front of a table at the back of the large, gasolier-lit room, and pulled out a chair.

"Capital," Lee said, as Michelle slid into the chair. "Thank you, Gaston. And a bottle of your best champagne, if you will." He reached into his pocket to pull out a wad of money and slipped several sheaves into Gaston's hand. As Gaston slid away, Lee pulled out a chair for Jess. Painted white, it was so delicately crafted she feared it would break under her weight. It was covered in vanilla silk sprinkled with dark blue violets, in perfect contrast to the rug and blue-flecked cream wallpaper. "Michelle," Lee said, as he motioned to Jess to sit down, "I see you've taken a seat in the back. Are you quite certain you can see *every*one?"

"*Oui, ami.* I must look for my friends. You would not want me to be rude."

"We would never want you to be rude, *chérie,*" he said ironically.

Jess tested the chair. It not only held, but didn't even squeak. The soft cushion made her feel like she was sitting on a cloud. Luxury, she thought, smiling as she opened her menu. Pure luxury.

And pure French.

Damn it, wouldn't it just figure that she'd finally gotten to Armand's, only to discover that she needed French lessons in order to eat. Pressing her lips together, she tried to recollect

the little bits of French she'd learned from *Henry V*. Not a
single useful word came to mind, but she did suddenly recall
that the French ate snails. Mercy, but she did *not* want to eat
any slimy, gooey insect that dwelt on the underside of wet
leaves.

"Jess? Do you know what you want?" Lee asked.

She lifted her head to see his forehead creased in concern,
which belied the twinkle in his eyes, the rat. "Not yet."

He drew his chair nearer and scanned her menu. "You don't
speak French, do you? Allow me to offer my assistance. First,
beef, in French, is *beouf,* and lamb is *gigot,* and chicken is
*poulet*. This first section here is for soups. Do you like sea-
food? The *bouillabaisse* is a fish soup. It's wonderful, you'll
love it. And here . . ."

He spent ten minutes explaining it all patiently, while Jess
tried to make intelligent inquiries. She studiously tried to
ignore his hard thigh pressed lightly against hers and the fact
that he smelled deliciously of soap and wood smoke.

"There. Do you understand?" he finished.

He turned to her, and she felt his eyes on her face, which
decided to take that most inopportune moment to color up. "I
think so. Just one thing," she asked, turning to look at him. A
mistake. His eyes were warm with compassion—at her blush,
no-doubt—and admiration. Oh Lord, she thought swallowing,
oh Lord. . . . "What's the French word for snails?"

Lifting his eyebrows, he asked, mirth deepening his voice,
"*Escargot?* Do you wish to try snails, Jess?"

"No," she shook her head. "I sincerely do *not* want to try
snails."

His eyes laughed at her. "All right," he said with finality,
pulling the menu from her hands. "Do you prefer chicken or
beef?"

"Beef, I think."

"Splendid. I shall order for us both." When she opened her
mouth to protest, he raised his hand to stop her. "I know, I

know. You could do it yourself, and I'm certain you'd choose something edible. Everything at Armand's is exceedingly edible. But if you'll give me leave, Jess, I'm certain I'll find something that suits you much better than merely edible."

Scowling, she stiffened her backbone. "I think I'm perfectly capable of—"

"Fine." He looked down at the menu. "How about *Supremes de volaille farcies au fois gras?*"

"Why, since *volaille* is poultry, I suppose I'd consider it."

"Certainly, but *fois gras* is made from goose liver."

Oh, for the love of Pete, why hadn't she ever learned French?

"Okay, you order. You know, when you badgered me into joining you tonight I thought I'd at least have the option of ordering my own meal!"

"I didn't badger you. I merely requested that you accompany Michelle and me. Michelle was the one who badgered you," he said, shifting his chair back as the waiter arrived with the champagne.

"I did not badger," Michelle protested. "I would never badger. It is not my way. I only asked."

A slight pop and the champagne was opened.

"Over and over again," Jess replied, "while dragging me into your room, dressing my hair in this ridiculous style and forcing me into this dress." A fairly conservative violet faille gown with silver ribbons, purple silk flowers, and a white lace underskirt. Jess had secretly lusted after it for months. Actually, in spite of her protests, she liked the hairstyle, too, a quickly plaited chignon knot decorated with purple silk flowers.

With a French shrug of her shoulders, Michelle scanned the room for friends. "If you had agreed at first, I would not have asked again."

After taking a sip of champagne, Lee nodded to the waiter, who proceeded to fill their glasses. "As always, Michelle, your logic astounds me," he said. The waiter left and he lifted his glass. "A toast. To a night out with my two favorite ladies."

Jess frowned, for she did *not* want to be included in Lee Montgomery's list of favorite ladies. At best it was bound to be ignoble. At worst—did she truly want to know what it would be at worst?

"Ah," Michelle said, clinking glasses with him. "And to *mon ami*, who would not begrudge his *chérie* a glass of wine."

He grinned. "No, Michelle, it's the bottles of wine I begrudge you. Jess? Will you join our toast?"

Jess turned to look into Lee's hazel-green eyes. They were alight with merriment and some other emotion. A kind of lazy desire—for *her*. Lord, oh Lord, what on earth was she *doing* here?

Michelle's cry of surprise saved Jess from replying. "Lee! Over there! It is my good friend Arnold!"

Arnold. Oh no, he was another one of Michelle's men! As Jess turned to look a wave of unreality rushed over her, leaving behind abrupt, horrible clarity. She, Jessica Sullivan—really Mrs. Everett Dunne—from Charmaine, Illinois, daughter of a perfectly respectable cooper and a schoolteacher, was sitting at a world-renowned restaurant with a ne'er-do-well gambler and an actress. An actress who in all honesty was just a few dollars shy of prostitution.

"Oh, I must go visit with him!" Michelle exclaimed. "Arnold and his so-charming friend Suzanne. Oh and Carl and Robert! And there is Jean also! Lee, you do not mind? You cannot!"

There were times in life when a girl could suddenly see her past with utmost clarity. Jess's was a gray, bitterly cold road. And her future? Would she be Michelle in five years? In ten years? Twenty?

"Whatever pleases you, *chéri*. Jess?" Lee questioned, resting his hand on her forearm.

Jess looked down at his long, tanned fingers contrasting beautifully with her violet silk. The cuffs of his white shirt extended perfectly beyond the sleeves of his black jacket, his diamond-studded cuff links winking in the gaslight. His nails were neatly trimmed, but lacked the delicacy of a true dandy, like Robert. Lee had a man's hands, his touch was a man's touch. An unexpected shudder of delight coursed down her arm.

But she didn't like to be touched.

"Are you all right, sweetheart?"

She lifted her head to watch Michelle sashay across the room. Arnold rose to greet her. Taking her outstretched hands into his, he kissed her firmly—indecently—on the mouth. Jess shifted her focus to Lee.

The desire still sparkled in his eyes. Why hadn't she seen that earlier? Had it been there earlier? Maybe it wasn't desire, but only the warmth of friendship. Maybe the champagne had affected her powers of observation. Except that she hadn't had any yet.

Not friendship. It was passion. Lee meant to seduce her. Two weeks ago he'd denied it, but that was two weeks ago, and tonight was tonight. What if she succumbed? Oh God, *could* she succumb? Recollecting her months with Everett and how the wonder of his kisses had turned to disgust, she shivered. Of course not. As a typical, passionless, Victorian woman, she need never fear turning into Michelle.

But she was also an actress, expected to be promiscuous. If she wasn't going to be Michelle, then who was she going to be?

She had no notion. The road to her future vanished in a thick, white fog. Suddenly she longed desperately for home, longed to bury herself in Mother's arms, to plead with Father for forgiveness, to hold Jason's hand and never let go. But that was all lost to her now because of one reckless night— followed by another and another and another, leading her down a long road of misadventures to this place, this moment, sitting with a notorious philanderer bent upon seducing a passionless, abandoned wife.

"Jess?"

Her eyes ached with unshed tears. To hide the emotion, she lifted her glass and took a long sip of champagne. She'd never drunk champagne. It wasn't sweet as she'd have expected but bitter. Bitter and sparkly. "I'm fine."

"You don't appear fine. You're flushed. Are you ill?" He moved his hand from her arm to her forehead. "Well, you don't have a fever."

The waiter arrived and Lee ordered supper in what sounded like a flawless French accent. "And," he finished, "a bottle of Bordeaux, Chauteau Latour, *s'il vous plaît*, a '66 or earlier."

Jess stared at him, more unease plucking at her nerves, for the words rolled off Lee's tongue as a matter of course. Where would a simple gambler learn about wine and how to speak flawless French?

Jess took a longer sip of champagne. It sparkled down her throat as if it had a life of its own. After another sip, Jess decided she liked it after all. The fizzle dissolved the lump lodged in her throat.

Michelle returned and crouched down next to Lee's chair, lifting her face to plead prettily with him. "Oh, Lee, they have asked me to sit with them! It has been ever so long since I have talked with the *tellement très drôle* Suzanne. Say you do not mind me joining them!"

Lee's lips twisted into something between a smile and a grimace. "Is there something about my company you find distasteful, *chéri?*"

"Oh no, *mon ami! J'adore* your company. It is only . . . they will not scold me for wine, you see," she said biting her lip and looking for all the world like an expectant child.

Smiling affectionately, he tugged gently on one of Michelle's curls. "You're a little scamp. Go ahead then, but try,

try to go easy with that wine, will you? Jess doesn't need to clean up after you."

"*Naturellement,* I will try, but maybe she will not need to. Maybe I will not sleep at home tonight!"

"I wondered," he said with an exaggerated sigh of disapproval. "I've already ordered your supper. You'll need to ask the waiter to bring it to the other table."

"Oh, *oui!*" she said brightly, rising.

"And a promise, Michelle. Tomorrow night? Supper after the show?"

"But of course! First Robert is having this very boring cast meeting, so it will be late*, comprenez-vous?*"

"And I have a game Tuesday and Wednesday. Thursday? Promise?"

"*Oui*. Thursday. *Au revior,* Lee, Jess!" She swished away, waving to her friends as she crossed the room. She settled into a chair next to Arnold and leaned forward for another long, passionate kiss.

Jess focused once more on Lee, surprised and revolted by the ease with which he allowed his paramour to fall into the arms of another man. Having finished his glass of champagne, Lee leaned forward to pour another.

"That's it?" Jess asked. "You're going to just let her leave?"

He gave the bottle an expert twist and lifted his eyes to meet hers. "Why not? She seems happy enough."

"But . . . but Arnold is not merely a *friend* you know."

A wry smile tugged at the corner of Lee's mouth, as he leaned back in his chair. "I'm aware of that."

"Oh," Jess said. She looked to where Arnold laid his arm across the back of Michelle's chair and casually stroked her arm. "I thought that you cared for her."

"I do. Here." Lee leaned forward to grasp the bottle again. "Finish off that last swallow and I'll refill your glass."

"But—" she sputtered. When she peered into his eyes she saw not one ounce of regret. "I don't understand you!"

"There's not much to understand. Michelle has always had her men."

"And it doesn't bother you?"

He shrugged. "I knew she wasn't monogamous at our first meeting. She needs constant adoration and I don't have that in me. I doubt any one man does."

Jess frowned, finished her champagne, then held the glass out to him. He filled it to the rim. "And you aren't jealous?"

"Not in the least. I'm not particularly faithful, either, Jess. Besides," he said as the waiter arrived with their soup, "Michelle has broken off that particular aspect of our relationship."

Mercy no! Oh, Michelle could not possibly mean to continue this idiotic scheme of hers, could she? It was destined to fail, couldn't she see that?

"Go ahead, Jess. Try the soup," Lee said after the waiter had gone. "I've never had *bouillabaisse* with champagne before, but there's a first time for everything."

The soup was delicious, a light, tomato-spiced fish broth with chunks of various kinds of fish. After a few mouthfuls, she asked, "Then *bouillabaisse* doesn't go with champagne?"

Smiling, he shook his head. "It was originally a peasant soup."

"Then why are we drinking champagne with it tonight?"

"Michelle."

"Oh. Of course."

"Ah, here's the fish course."

The waiter took their bowls and left them with tiny fillets of some kind of saltwater fish, lightly flavored with a cream sauce. Salad followed. As they ate, Lee kept up a running conversation about the meal. Jess enjoyed it all, happily washing the food down with the champagne. Every time her glass got down to half full, Lee refilled it.

The main course arrived, accompanied by a deep red wine, which Jess admitted complemented the beef Wellington perfectly.

"How do you know all these things? I mean about food and wine—and French," she asked.

He opened his mouth to answer when a man appeared at Lee's elbow. Where had he come from? Jess hadn't seen his approach, but then the champagne had made her brain a little fuzzy.

"Montgomery," the man greeted Lee in a pleasant voice. He was stylishly dressed in a black suit, above average in height, with a slight build that couldn't hide a small paunch. He had thinning dark hair and a handlebar mustache, which moved as he talked.

"Hathaway," Lee said, turning his head to smile a greeting. "Something I might do for you?"

Mr. Hathaway laughed, shook his head, and reached into his pocket to pull out a wad of bills. "I think you've done plenty." He slapped the wad on the table. "Won it downstairs. When I saw you come in, I thought I ought to cash up before I lost it again."

A very large wad, Jess saw, her eyes widening in disbelief. Of fifty dollar bills. Lord almighty!

"Well timed," Lee said with a grin. "I daresay I'll drink the whole wad tonight."

Hathaway barked another good-natured laugh. "Drink that and you'll be pushing up daisies before the night's out. Listen, Lee, if you're free next Sunday night, Bernadette's throwing a party."

The amusement on Lee's face abruptly disappeared, replaced by cold wariness. Hathaway blinked and continued. "A soiree or sortee or something French, I don't quite remember. It'll end up a ball, regardless, you know how Bernadette is. I know it's late notice, but we should be honored to have you as our guest." Hathaway's eyes drifted over Jess a moment. Kind, respectful eyes—no doubt he'd never caught a perform-ance. A second later the light of speculation lit his face and he added slowly, "And of course we'd be delighted to have your lovely companion accompany you."

For an embarrassing space of time, Lee didn't answer, a muscle in his cheek jumping. Then he turned to Jess, and his expression softened to rueful irritation. "Forgive my rudeness, Jess. If you'll give me leave, I should like to present to you my good friend, Michael Hathaway. Sir, Miss Sullivan."

Surprised at his sudden formality, she stared a moment, then turned to Mr. Hathaway.

"Miss Sullivan," Mr. Hathaway said, and bowed. "It is a great pleasure to make your acquaintance."

When was the last time someone had treated her with such consideration?

Never. Certainly no one in the troupe cared for such formality. In fact, Charmaine had represented the high water mark of etiquette in her life, and formal introductions in a town of five hundred people would have been absurd.

A lump rising in her throat, Jess nodded at Hathaway, who addressed Lee once more. "Shall I send the invitations to the Baldwin, then?"

Flashing an amused scowl, Lee answered, "If you insist."

"I do. And now back to the Roulette table! My luck is in tonight." Hathaway bowed again, then walked away. Jess watched Lee stuff the money in his pocket.

He lifted one eyebrow. "Problem, Jess?"

Problem? Not one, but hundreds of problems! "That's a lot of money."

"A couple thousand," he said. "Last night's poker winnings."

Two thousand dollars—in one *night?* And he as casual as if it were an everyday occurrence, like formal introductions and expensive bottles of French wine.

Lee cut into his beef. "So, where were we? Ah, discussing where I received my knowledge of wines. I asked."

Slowly, she dragged her mind away from the impossibility

of winning two *thousand* dollars in one night and stuttered, "You-you asked? Who?"

He shrugged. "Anybody. Everybody. Family, friends. And I experimented, I suppose. Learning through experience, you might say."

Through experience. Or by example. She took several bites of her meal, her heart growing heavier. *She* had not learned through example, although the Lord had provided her two very good ones. After the mistakes she'd made, she had become the perfect example of what *not* to do.

After another forkful of beef, Jess noticed that Lee was leaning back in his chair, negligently balancing his glass on the table edge as he watched her.

"You're not eating," she remarked.

"I'm not hungry. You go ahead, though. Enjoy."

She frowned and took another bite, which she almost spit out at his next question. "And so, Jess, does it disturb you? My friendship with Michelle and our lack of, shall we call it faithfulness?"

She gulped her food down. "No," she lied, for the very word "faithfulness" ripped the scabs off the barely healed wounds of her heart. Everett hadn't been committed to faithfulness, either. But hadn't that been partially her fault? Oh hell, what did it matter? It was years past, she'd made her bed—badly—and she was very stuck lying in it. "Why would it?"

His eyes held hers in a hard, mind-reading stare, as he replied slowly, "Because it seems to me that you are. Faithful that is."

A quiver of discomfort wriggled through her belly. "What do you mean?"

"Michelle says you're married."

She jerked in sudden, stunned pain. *Lord almighty, Michelle, do you ever keep your mouth shut?* Appetite gone, Jess pushed her plate aside and reached a trembling hand for her champagne glass. "Did she? I asked her to keep that a secret."

"It's one hell of a secret. The question is, why is it a secret?"

"He left me. Did she tell you that, too?"

He fell silent as she focused her thoughts on the light sparkling on her glass. It turned the champagne a deep, bubbling yellow. It was beautiful the way the bubbles rose to the surface and broke with hundreds of tiny, sizzling pops.

"Many women are abandoned by their husbands," Lee finally said. "It's no shame."

No shame unless the woman forced him away with her cold, passionless nature. All well and fine for Dr. Acton to proclaim the majority of women naturally passionless; it was another thing entirely for a husband to bear it.

She shrugged and drank more champagne.

"Is your husband the reason you were in such dire straits in the Black Hills? Is that where he left you?"

She sucked in her breath. "Yes."

"And the reason you couldn't go home?"

Not even the mellowness contributed by the champagne could soften the arrows shooting through her heart. Lifting her glass, she replied, "I married Everett against my parents' wishes. They told me if I became his wife, I would cease to be their daughter." She finished the glass in two large gulps, not tasting it as it tripped down her throat.

"Which is what you meant when you said you had no parents," Lee said. "I thought they were dead." He leaned forward to refill her glass, a trickling river of gold filling a sparkling pond, she thought distractedly. She liked the distraction. She didn't want to think about Everett, wanted less to talk about him.

She took another long swallow of champagne. "My mother died shortly after I eloped, from heartbreak I suppose. My father followed two years later, leaving my brother, Jason, alone."

"How old was he?"

"Sixteen. My aunt took him in. I would have, but"—she drew a deep breath—"he wouldn't have wanted me."

"Angry you left?"

"Something like that."

He hesitated before saying in a voice thickly marbled with sympathy, "I'm sorry, Jess. It must have been very rough for you."

She blinked back tears and let her gaze rest upon his face. Such harsh lines, so marvelously softened by humor and compassion. "It was." She took a breath to bolster her waning courage. "And so you see, some of us do have ghosts in our past."

His eyes crinkled at the corners. "I suppose I should count myself a fortunate rake to be ghostless. Or was it scoundrel? An average, ordinary scoundrel, if I remember correctly." The warmth of gentle amusement flowed through his voice, crossed the distance between them, and settled like a soft cloud over her aching heart.

Or was that the champagne? The room seemed to be moving strangely, shifting and shivering like in an earthquake. But the ground didn't shake and no one else seemed to notice that the world wasn't acting normally. "And a completely immoral scoundrel at that," she added.

"I should think most scoundrels are immoral," he said with a twisted grin. "Tell me, do you still love him?"

Jess winced. Love Everett? After all he had done to her, after all he had *not* done? She couldn't possibly love him. And yet she kept his picture in a drawer next to her bed, and on a good day when she closed her eyes she could see him perfectly, his brown eyes flashing, voice aquiver with enthusiasm as he described his latest scheme for wealth. When she contemplated the tender emotion of love, she thought of her feelings for Ev.

But on bad days she recollected everything else, and she hated him. Hated him with the deepest, heart-burning version of the emotion, filling her brain with a curtain of black smoke, leaving the taste of ashes in her mouth. A gut-wrenching hatred.

They weren't the kind of feelings she wanted to expose to anyone, least of all a philandering gambler. "Maybe," she answered. "What interest is it of yours?"

His eyes flashed at her, but with her vision blurred by the shadows of gaslight and drink she couldn't make out the emotion in them. "I find human nature fascinating, remember?" She had emptied her glass again, and he refilled it, motioning to the waiter as he passed. "I should think, Jess, that after he deserted you, you'd hate him."

"I guess a part of me does," she admitted.

Lee whispered something to the waiter, then turned back to her. "Part of you? Have you seen him during the last six years? The troupe, I understand, has done some pretty substantial traveling."

"Robert's on a mission to bring Shakespeare to the illiterate in America. So we travel."

"And?"

She shrugged. Or she thought she did, anyhow. Her brain was awfully fuzzy. "In the beginning I looked for Everett. I heard about him in Denver, and Tombstone, and once here, in San Francisco. Later I got—angry—and decided to cut him out of my life like he'd done with me. That's when I took back my name."

"And what would you say to him if you did find him?"

"I don't know."

"Well, Jess," Lee said, crossing his arms on the table to lean on them. He held her gaze, and continued. "This is what I think. I think he's done you wrong, he's wandering this country believing it's of no consequence, and it's high time you get yourself a little revenge."

# Chapter Five

Lee watched Jess's eyes widen. As quickly conceived schemes went, he considered this one fairly inventive, but its success depended to a certain degree upon Jess's anger toward her husband.

"Revenge? How would I get revenge?"

By God, but she had the most beautiful eyes he'd ever seen, walnut shaped with huge blue irises. When she blinked, her long lashes kissed the velvet skin of her cheek, all but sucking the breath right out of him. Ah hell, the way she looked tonight just about anything she did could suck the breath right out of him.

"Why, here's the thing. Anyone who is at all acquainted with you knows that you spurn virtually all male companionship. To your husband—what's his name again?"

"Everett Dunne."

"Everett. If Everett hears of you—which I daresay he has since the troupe has traveled through most of the major western cities—it must appear that you're pining away for him. That you're completely faithful. He has no reason to regret having lost you since he hasn't lost you at all." He flashed her a dimple-laced smile. "In the meantime, he's been—forgive me, I don't mean to hurt you—with who knows who, believing he can take you back whenever he desires."

Jess winced and he held his breath, hoping the pain flashing across her face wouldn't ruin his plans. At some point over the years she must have questioned Dunne's fidelity.

She drained her glass of champagne again. Two bottles down, another on the way. Lee refilled her glass without shifting his gaze. "You must prove to him that you've forgotten him, even if in your heart you haven't. If you play the game well, you may even persuade him to return to you, if that's what you wish."

Her eyebrows drew together as she stared at her glass. "Lee, I'm a little drunk."

He chuckled. "A bottle of champagne will do that to you."

"I like it. The bubbles tickle my nose."

"Then by all means, have some more. I've ordered another bottle."

"Okay," she said, and took another sip.

"And so?" he asked.

"And so?"

"How do you like my revenge idea?"

"I don't understand. How do I prove that I no longer care for him?"

"By becoming involved with other men."

She frowned. "Other men?"

"Yes, by God, other men. In essence leaving *him*." Lee held his breath as he watched thoughts flowing through her eyes. *Come now, sweetheart. Say yes. You can do this, a simple yes, sweetheart. A simple yes.*

"It's . . . it's an idea."

An idea. Sweeter words Lee had never heard. The waiter arrived with the bottle of champagne. As the waiter opened the bottle, Lee ripped a few of the larger bills out of his clip and dropped them on the table. "The lady and I will be leaving. I'll take the bottle and the glasses. That ought to cover the expense. And," he added, ripping off another bill, "that's for finding us a cab as quickly as possible." The waiter stared at the twenty in his hand, then turned and sped across the room.

A short time later, while quickly giving the driver directions, Lee handed Jess into a hansom cab. After carefully stowing the glasses and champagne in the corner of the seat, he climbed up beside her. He took up a folded blanket on the seat between them and draped it across Jess's lap, tucking it around her legs. When he discreetly slid one hand down her thigh, she made no protest. Blood rushed to his groin in sweet, heady expectation. "So, Jess," he said, as the sound of the horses' hooves beat in time to the patter of his heart. "Let's discuss my revenge scheme in detail. Tell me your reservations."

"Your scheme," she said. "I don't know many men."

All right, what should he do now? The whole situation felt a little like wandering blindfolded through a battlefield. But when he reached the other side—he let his eyes glide over Jess's curvaceous body—why, the other side was a slow, pleasure-filled trip to heaven. Definitely worth the danger.

"You really only need one man to start. You'll want to flaunt him, of course. A quiet, brief affair won't be enough. We really want to enrage good ol' Everett, don't we?" Neither brief nor quiet, but torrid. Damnably torrid, with weeks—no, months—of long, hot nights. Endless kisses, naked skin sliding over naked skin, deep, guttural cries of satisfaction. *Just say yes, sweetheart.*

She giggled, a light, silly version of her laugh, which sent peculiar rays of light shooting through his heart. "You don't know Everett. I can't imagine him enraged."

Lee grinned as the cab bounced to a halt in front of her building. "Oh, we shall certainly enrage him." After which, he thought jumping down, he and Jess would go their separate ways, Jess's broken heart healed and he with memories sweeter than honey. He paid the driver, took up the glasses and wine, then reached up to help her alight. She swayed and Lee slid his arm through hers. "All right, sweetheart?"

She nodded. "Just don't let go."

"Not on your life," he replied, and carefully steered her through the front door. His heart pounded as they crossed the empty common room. Slowly, painstakingly, they made their way up the stairs. At her door, Jess fumbled with the key until Lee handed her the bottle and glasses, and took matters into his own hands. Once inside he slipped across the room to light the lamp by the stove. His hands shook with anticipation and the match scorched his fingers. A moment later he turned to see Jess leaning against the sofa. She was attempting to pour a glass of champagne, sloshing a deal of it over the side.

"Here, sweetheart, allow me," Lee said. In two strides he was at her side. He took the bottle and finished filling her glass and then filled one for himself. Handing her a glass, he said, "You know, you never toasted with Michelle and me."

"I didn't like the toast."

"No? How's this, then? To revenge!"

Smiling, she nodded. The movement caused her to sway and she giggled. "I'll drink to that." She hit her glass against his with such force it came within a hair's breath of shattering. Then she drained it in five gulps.

Lee grinned and tossed his off. "And now," he said, flashing her his best smile, "I'll take these." He took the two glasses and put them on a small table next to the sofa. "And I'll take this, too!"

His heart beating so hard it felt like it'd burst from his chest, Lee leaned forward and covered her mouth with his. Her lips were as soft as velvet and parted with little coaxing. Ah, but she tasted like sweetened champagne, and damned if kissing her didn't make his blood bubble, too. With a tightening down below, he wondered if all of her felt as soft, if her thighs would part as easily, if—

She wasn't responding.

In fact, she stood as still as stone, not so much as pursing her lips. What the hell?

He lifted his head and peered into her eyes. Even in the dimly lit room, he could see they were dark and glazed over. "Sweetheart, what's wrong?"

"Wrong? Nothing . . ." her voice trailed off.

"Don't you like my kisses?" He certainly wasn't Casanova, but generally he elicited *some* response from women.

"It's just," she said, lifting one hand to run a finger over her lips. His own twitched, longing to follow that finger. "I've never been kissed when I was drunk. My lips are numb. I can't feel anything."

"Nothing?"

"No. It's so peculiar."

Peculiar. His kisses were peculiar—and numbing.

She cocked her head. "You're upset," she said, and for the first time he noticed her normally crisp speech was slurred. "I'm not complaining, you know."

"All right, let's try it again." He reached up with both hands to hold her head steady. Again he lowered his mouth to hers. He put everything he had into the kiss, slowly, lingeringly sliding his tongue over hers, then gently drawing hers into his own mouth to suckle it. She tasted wonderful, and he stepped closer to press against her body, soft and yielding against the growing hardness—

No response.

He lifted his head. "Now?"

She shook her head as a small drunken smile settled on her face. "I'm sorry."

Very drunk. Numbingly drunk. *God damn it to hell!* Why the devil hadn't he considered the consequences of *too much* drink?

It didn't matter. He couldn't go through with it. With a deep sigh of frustration, he let go of her head and took one of her hands. "All right, then, it's bedtime for you."

"To bed? Already?" she asked, as he started to lead her to her bedroom. "I thought—what Michelle said—you'd want more touching."

"You misunderstand me," he said. "I'm not joining you. It's the sofa for me."

"Oh," she said, stumbling.

Lee dropped her hand and, wrapping his arm around her waist to brace her unsteady body against his—pure torture!—he picked up the lamp. Carefully, he guided her through the parlor to her bedroom where he gently deposited her on the bed. She leaned against the wall—no headboard on her barely serviceable bed—while he lit another lamp. He turned and squatted down to remove her slippers, displaying small, perfectly formed feet clothed in white silk. Bloody hell, who'd have thought feet could be seductive?

Taking a deep breath, he straightened.

"I thought," she said abruptly, "that you were going to help me get revenge."

Apparently the champagne had not slowed her thought processes as much as it had numbed her body.

"Not tonight," he answered. He sat next to her and leaned back to unbutton her gown, promising himself that the next time he did this, she wouldn't be falling-down drunk. Tipsy, perhaps. But not numb.

He pushed the gown off her shoulders, grinding his teeth as his gaze dove down to view the curve of her creamy white breasts displayed proudly by her corset. He closed his eyes and took several breaths. An eyeful, but not a handful, for she wouldn't feel a thing, so what was the point? He wanted more from a woman than just the use of her body. His enjoyment demanded hers as well, his desire increased by the smell of a woman's rising passion, the sound of her moans and the beauty of her skin, flushing deep red as she came to climax . . .

"Why not?" she asked, dragging him out of tormented reverie.

He swallowed and rose, pulling her to a stand. A quick tug and the gown fell to the floor. He reached down to untie her bustle. For all his inconveniently compulsive sense of honor, he couldn't resist running his hands over the curve of her hips. No response from her; his whole body tightened.

The bustle fell to the ground.

She was staring at him as if expecting an answer. It took a minute before his poor befuddled brain remembered her last words. "Why not what?" he asked, staring at the corset. That was next. Damn.

"Why not tonight?"

He took another breath. "Sweetheart, when I touch a woman I want her to feel it."

She couldn't sleep in the corset. It had to come off. At least, thank God, it was the sort that closed in the back. Grinding his teeth, he turned her around.

"I can't feel a thing," she slurred.

He started to unlace her corset. Useless thing. Her waist was plenty small without squeezing it into submission. "I know," he answered.

"It would be better that way you see," she slurred. "For me to feel nothing. I don't really like it."

The corset joined the growing pile of clothes on the floor. He turned her back around. Swaying, she placed her hand on his chest to steady herself. The heat of her touch burned through his vest and the linen of his shirt. He closed his eyes for a second, willing her to slide her hand downward.

Her words sunk in. He opened his eyes. "Don't like what?"

"I-It," she stuttered, blushing. "Men."

Oh, for the love of Christ, this could not be happening! He sent a wordless plea heavenward. "What about women? Do you like women?"

"Women? Why, yes, of course I like women."

That'd better be naïveté or he was going to wade neck deep into San Francisco bay and drown himself. "Some women like other women to kiss, Jess. And touch and go to bed with."

He held his breath. She stared a moment, then her eyes widened in shock. "Oh! Oh no! Mercy me! What kind of person do you think I am?"

Relief escaped him in a whoosh. "Right now, I think you're very drunk."

Holding one arm in a vice grip to prevent her from falling, he reached around to pull back her bed's coverings. She could damned well sleep in her chemise and drawers. If he had to touch her one more time, he'd drop stone dead from unsatisfied lust.

"I am drunk," Jess answered as he helped her settle into bed. "I am also passionless."

"Not entirely, I imagine." He tucked the blankets over her body—soft white breasts, small, tight waist, and gently sloping hips. "Everett must have stirred you a little or you wouldn't have eloped with him."

"I loved kissing him. But not the rest of it. That wasn't like kissing at all."

Oh damn, not frigid, too . . . "Not all men are good lovers."

"Ev tried," she said dreamily, as she closed her eyes. "But to me it was repulsive. Dr. Acton says that's normal for women," she said. A tiny flash of pain crossed her face. "But sometimes I wonder if he's wrong, if there's something wrong with me . . ."

Her voice trailed off as she fell asleep. With a frustrated sigh, Lee took the lamp and left to gather pillows and a blanket from Michelle's room. As much as his body beseeched him to seek out another woman to cure his lust, he refused to leave Jess alone. She was too drunk.

He dropped the pillows on the sofa, then slammed his backside into it, too. Damn, he thought, reaching down to remove his boots. This had to be some horrible joke. Some imp of an angel was no doubt laughing right now over having arranged that he, of all men, a confirmed bachelor and "rake," had fallen in love with a frigid woman.

The first boot came off. He threw it across the room. It hit the wall with a satisfying thud. His hands froze on the second boot.

In love?

In love.

Oh *hell!*

The second boot left a dent in Jess's sunshine-yellow wall.

Damn it, God damn it, he could not be in love with her! How in hell did that happen?

Lee's eyes lit on the champagne bottle on the table next to him. He grabbed it and took several swallows straight from the bottle, then wiped his lips with the back of his hand.

What did it matter how it happened? It had. He was in love with Jess. Why hadn't he recognized that before tonight? Although he hadn't so much as stolen a kiss, she slid into his every waking thought. Not merely visions of her in bed, but recollections of their conversations, her laughter, the way her eyes sparkled when she was amused, like two stars in the blue-black night of her eyes.

Blue-black night of her eyes? He groaned and ran his hand through his hair. He was a goner. Next thing he knew he'd be spewing bad poetry.

No, by God, this was impossible. It'd only been two weeks! He'd only talked to her three times! How could he fall in love so quickly? And with an actress, of all women. An Irish actress. Damnation, he could all but hear his father's rage ringing in his ears.

Which was a singularly senseless thought. His father would never hear of this, for even though he was in love, it surely wouldn't amount to much. He'd been in love a few times: Andrea in Boston—his one-time fiancée; Cheryl, in Chicago—beautiful widowed Cheryl, with her velvet touch; and redheaded Harriett in Portland with that gap in her teeth he loved to slide his tongue through. But the emotion had faded over time, leaving him with no desire for permanency. No doubt this would fade, too.

Except, he thought frowning, this felt different. For one thing, there'd been no lovin'. All the others, including Andrea whom he'd left a virgin in only one small way, had started out as affairs of passion. Love had followed on gossamer-thin wings of satisfaction, as light as it had been sweet.

With Jess, though, the telltale signs of love—the lightness in his chest when she was around, the desire for her company—had come first. And the signs were stronger. Not a desire for her company as much as a—well, hell, a *longing* for it, a sort of constant ache. An ache in his heart, and an ache in his body to stroke her breasts, caress the soft wet areas between her thighs. His thoughts were engrossed by the sort of sounds she'd make when lost to passion, what she would smell like, taste like . . .

Damn! Another long pull on the bottle.

Those questions had never arisen with all his other loves, because his curiosity had already been satisfied. Perhaps that was it. Perhaps once he took Jess to bed, thus satisfying his curiosity about her, his feelings for her would fade away, too. Quite possibly, he thought with a rush of relief, this would be the quickest of all loves. As long as he could satisfy it. As long as he managed to take her to bed, as long as she wasn't truly frigid.

She wasn't. She couldn't be.

If she was, he was going to lose his blasted mind.

# Chapter Six

Harsh morning sunshine slipped through the curtains and fell on Jess's eyes, waking her to a blinding headache. Groaning, she lifted her hand to rub her head. A mistake. The movement created a horrible spinning, which went straight to her stomach. Nausea took root and clawed its way up her throat. Hand over her mouth, Jess rolled out of bed and lurched across the room to her washstand, where she was horribly, miserably ill.

"Oh God," she whispered, sliding down to her knees. She closed her eyes and leaned her cheek against the cool plaster wall. Her head was going to explode for sure.

Behind her the door opened and a boot scraped the floor. Seconds later a large hand wrapped around her arm. She opened her eyes to see Lee squatting down next to her, his eyes, for once, bereft of merriment.

"All right, sweetheart, come with me into the parlor. We'll take it slowly."

Jess allowed him to lead her through the door to the parlor sofa. The room seemed to bend and sway as they moved. Dear Lord, she was *drunk. Still*. But how?

Champagne—a whole bottle of it. Or more. Much more, she recollected through a thick black fog.

She sat down as the nausea rose again. Lee sprinted to

her bedroom and returned with a bucket seconds before her stomach erupted in a gut-wrenching spewing. Awful! Awful! Closing her eyes, she whispered a thank you and leaned back. Mercy, but for the world to please, please stop moving!

The sofa sank next to her. A cold, damp cloth wiped her face, her mouth.

Lee, still here. What was he doing here at all? Hadn't he gone home last night?

A gentle splashing of water filled the silence of the room as he rinsed the cloth. A moment later he swiped it across her forehead, easing its throbbing. "That feels so good," she whispered in a rough voice that didn't sound even remotely like her own. No reply, just the continued motion. That was enough. Her dry tongue discouraged much speaking.

Time passed. Her stomach settled. Lee stopped wiping her face. "Better?"

She lifted her eyelids, wincing when they scratched her eyeballs. "Compared to what?"

He laughed and the twinkle appeared once more in his eyes. "Compared to when you arose."

Closing her eyes, she said thickly, "Let's just say I'm grateful to have an understudy."

"You may yet cheat her out of a performance."

"I shouldn't count those chickens if I were you."

"Well at least you've retained your sense of humor. If you're feeling well enough, I'll set the coffee to perking, then run to the bakery for some rolls."

"Coffee," she repeated and winced again. "I'm not certain if I ought to beg you for it or vomit. Damn, it's the vomiting."

She jerked forward as her stomach heaved. Nothing came up. After about a minute of pure, wretched suffering, Jess gave one final groan, closed her eyes and leaned back again, allowing her head to roll against the cool fabric of the sofa. The sound of dripping water tinkled through the room and then the wet cloth mopped her face. She moaned her thanks and forced herself to keep perfectly still until the nausea passed. Finally, she felt well enough to open her eyes. Lee sat peering at her. Smiling, he gave her thigh a quick pat and rose. "There, you seem a bit better. I'm off for those rolls. Back in a flash."

A moment later the door clicked shut behind him, and Jess sighed. What a kind, considerate man! A good man, a compassionate man.

The man who'd gotten her drunk.

Jess frowned, then winced, for even that small movement stabbed at her brain.

Presently, the pain passed and she recollected bits and pieces of the night, of Lee refilling her glass again and again. And Michelle's? No . . . Michelle hadn't stayed with them. She'd left them—abandoned Jess—before the evening was much advanced. And then . . . then what? She and Lee had eaten supper, drunk wine and champagne . . . and talked. Talked about . . . about . . . Everett.

It all rushed back to her in a nauseating flood.

Swearing, Jess grabbed for the bucket. But Lee had removed it and left a basin on the table. Moaning, she leaned over it and heaved unproductively for several minutes. Afterward, she slowly returned to her position and forced her mind to go blank. By and by her brain started functioning again.

Everett. She and Lee had talked about revenge and something about taking lovers. And then they'd come back here and then . . . and then . . . what? She glanced down at her clothes. She was in her chemise. She didn't recall undressing. But she did remember Lee in her bedroom, his hands running down her back, unbuttoning her gown.

Oh, dear God, what had she *done?*

Oh no, she couldn't have . . . she hadn't . . . never in a thousand years would she have . . .

Had she enjoyed it?

Oh no, how could she think such a thing? she asked herself,

pressing her hands against her burning face. What did it matter if she enjoyed it? It was wrong! She'd committed adultery, broken that most sacred of commandments, thereby securing herself a nice, hot place in Hell for all eternity. Damn Lee! And damn champagne, too! She was never going to drink another drop of the stuff. Or any other alcoholic beverage again, for that matter, never, never, never. The devil's brew, that's what it was. Just the thought sent her stomach tossing.

Jess was leaning over the basin once more when the door opened, followed by light footsteps crossing the room. She'd opened her mouth to tear a few strips of flesh from Lee's hide when Michelle exclaimed, "Oh Jess! Oh, my poor friend!"

Slowly straightening, Jess watched Michelle, a golden vision in her amber gown, sink into the chair across from her. Pulling off delicately embroidered kid gloves, she clucked sympathetically, "It was the wine, wasn't it? Oh honey," she said, scooting her chair forward to take Jess's hands, "after all the times I've drunk too much, I would've thought you knew better!"

Unaccountably comforted, Jess sighed. There was no one in the world like a female friend when a girl was sick. "I didn't know how much I was drinking. Lee kept refilling my glass."

"He did?" Michelle frowned. "Funny, he always puts his hand over mine."

Jess chuckled. It hurt less this time, thank God. "I can't imagine why."

Michelle's brown eyes smiled. She reached for a gray woolen blanket bunched up at the end of the sofa. Moving to sit next to Jess, she wrapped it around Jess's shoulders. "Has it been all night, then?" she asked, nodding to a pillow that had been hiding under the blanket. "Did you sleep on the sofa? My poor, poor *petite*."

Jess winced. "No, I went to bed. I think . . . I think Lee must have slept here." Which made no sense, if they'd . . .

"Lee? On the *sofa?*" Michelle exclaimed, eyes widening in astonishment as the door opened.

Lee's voice filled the room. "*Oui, chérie*. On the sofa. Jess was a trifle inebriated and I didn't want to leave her alone."

"*Oui*, but on the *sofa?*" Michelle repeated, confused.

"Yes," he replied firmly as he crossed the room to sit on the sofa next to Jess. "Listen, Michelle, the coffee's all ready to go. If you'll kindly put the pot on the stove, I'll feed Jess one of these rolls."

Michelle rose as Jess weakly waved away his offer. "I can't even think of food."

He opened a brown box. "It's the best thing for you, sweetheart. It'll soak up some of the poison."

"So you confess it at last, you've poisoned me."

Lee smiled, dimple and all, and in spite of her suffering, Jess's heart jerked. "Incorrectly employed," he said, "alcohol becomes a poison. Drinking too much can kill you."

Goodness, but he was still marvelously handsome, even after a night's carousing. He'd no right, none at all, to look so when she felt like warmed-over death, and he the cause of it. Closing her eyes against his charm, she answered, "Wonderful. How long before I die?"

He chuckled and, wrapping his arm around her, pulled her against his hard, lean body. "Lay your head on my shoulder and take a bite of this roll."

Jess complied. Closing her eyes, she willed the tiny morsel to go all the way down, but after a minute of stomach-whirling misery, she wished it would come up instead. Finally, with a tiny moan, she leaned forward and heaved once more into the basin, ridding herself of the tiny piece of bread along with some other awful tasting yellow stuff.

"Ah hell," Lee swore softly, while gently rubbing her back. "Michelle, you'd better send a message to Robert. Tell him that Jess's understudy is going on."

"*Oui*," Michelle answered. "It is for the best, *ma amie*," she said kindly. A moment later she left, gently shutting the door behind her.

Time passed slowly. The minutes turned to hours and passed on wings of lead. Over and over again Jess's stomach betrayed her, and over and over again, Lee, Cad and Creator of Suffering, rubbed her back and bathed her face. He didn't speak but for an occasional soothing comment. By and by, Michelle returned to report that Jess's understudy would indeed go on, and then left again to visit her dressmaker. It was an act of kindness. By that time Jess was heartily sick of being sick and wanted nothing more than to die. That relief eluding her, however, she was grateful for silence. Finally, she leaned her head on Lee's shoulder, closed her eyes against the whirling, and fell asleep. When she awoke, she was tucked comfortably in her own bed. Alone. Refusing to follow that thought to another place, she closed her eyes, wriggled deeper into her sagging straw mattress and fell back asleep. Hours later Michelle's irate voice yanked her out of a dream.

"Oh, it's impossible! Wake up, Jess, wake up! He's the most impossible man alive! How have you worked for him all these years?"

Jess sat up, squinting through the dim lamplight courtesy of Michelle. Her friend, still dressed in full Ophelia costume, slammed her bottom down on the edge of Jess's bed. "Who's impossible?" Jess asked, rubbing her eyes. She peered at her clock. One A.M. "Lee?"

"Lee? What does he have to do with it? Although he'll be furious, too! Oh! I cannot believe it. No, it's impossible," she said, vigorously shaking her blond curls. "We have to change his mind!"

"What's impossible, Michelle? Who has to change his mind?"

"Why, Robert, of course! He says our last performance will be Sunday's matinee and then we're closing down the show and taking it on the road! He's gone mad, stark raving mad!" she exclaimed and stomped out of the room.

"Closing down the show?" Jess asked. She swung her legs around the edge of the bed and wrapped her blanket around herself against the cold night air. Picking up the lamp, she followed Michelle into the parlor, where Michelle, contrary to all manner of economy, had lit every lamp in the room. "But . . . but why? It's been going so well!"

"Why?" Michelle asked, turning on her heel. Her face grew red, her fingers curled into fists. "Because Robert has lost his mind, that's why! I swear to you, we ought to commit him to an institution right now! This very minute." She stamped her foot to emphasize her point.

Although her stomach had calmed, Jess's head had not. Slightly dizzy, she sank into a chair and followed Michelle's pacing figure. "But he must have given some reason. Honestly, Michelle, you must compose yourself!"

"His reason? 'We are not accomplishing the mission for the troupe,'" she mimicked. "What mission is that? The mission is to perform, that's the mission!"

Jess shook her head. "That was never Robert's mission. He wants to bring Shakespeare—"

"Oh, to the illiterates of the world," Michelle finished, and threw her hands into the air. "But who is illiterate in Denver, I ask you?"

"Denver? Is that where we're going?"

"Yes, and in the middle of such a run! Such audiences! Every night a standing ovation! Oh, Jess," she said, her voice cracking, "I bet they don't even know how to clap in Denver!"

Rubbing her aching temples, Jess chuckled. "I expect they know that at least. It's just odd. Why Denver? Why now?"

"He says before the snows settle in," Michelle answered, starting to pace. "What snows I ask you? Where does he see these snows?"

Jess shrugged. "It can snow in the mountains as early as October. It's almost November. Maybe he's afraid the train'll get stuck."

"Oh, Jess!" Michelle wailed, tears springing in her eyes, "I don't want to go to Denver! It's so Western!"

Jess bit back a laugh. "San Francisco is much farther west, you know."

"Oh, but it's ever so cosmopolitan and Denver is full of all those . . . those *cowboys!*"

"It has a very nice opera house—"

"I won't go! I won't go!" Michelle flung herself at Jess's knees to wail miserably into her lap. "I won't!"

With a deep sigh, Jess wrapped her arms around her friend and made soft soothing noises, while her tired mind digested the information. Denver. Two mountain ranges away from Lee Montgomery. Was she happy about that? Or sad?

# Chapter Seven

"Denver?" Lee asked, leaning against the doorjamb as Michelle railed and Jess, hands crossed in her lap, watched. Ten hours had passed since Michelle had dropped Robert's pronouncement on Jess, and she seemed to grow angrier by the minute. "But why Denver?"

"Because he is mad!" Michelle cried, spinning on her heel. Her gaze raced around the room. "Oh, *je suis en rage! Où est un vase?* I must throw something!" She stepped toward the mantel.

Lee lunged and grabbed Michelle's wrist just as her fingers grazed the lamp. "No," he said firmly. "I fully comprehend your anger, *chérie,* but you shall not break anything while I'm here."

Michelle lifted her head, her eyes sparkling with tears. "I won't go, Lee! You must help us! Swear to me that you will stop Robert!"

He sighed, took both her hands in his and shook his head. "I can't. Unfortunately, that's not in my power. Now, stop stomping your foot," Lee demanded as Michelle, enraged once more, struggled to free herself from his grip. "Michelle, this tantrum stops now or I will leave!"

"*Non,* Lee," Michelle pleaded. She stopped struggling, and

lifted her eyes to his, tears running down her face. "You cannot leave me at such a time!"

Unmoved, he replied, "I'll walk out that door and you shall never see my face again."

Michelle crumbled in his arms. Burying her face in his chest, she broke into deep racking sobs. Drawing another huge sigh, Lee brought her to the sofa and spent several minutes rubbing her back and crooning softly in her ear. Jealousy twisting through her heart, Jess stared down at her hands. Why should she care that Lee loved Michelle, that at the merest crook of her finger he came running? A terse, tearstained note, and a half hour later he was holding her in his arms, generously dispensing comfort as if she weren't acting like a spoilt, spoilt child.

"Michelle," he finally said, "you must stop crying. You're making your eyes all red and puffy."

Nor should Jess care that barely thirty-six hours before receiving that note he'd tried—and who knew, succeeded?— to seduce Jess. Apparently he switched allegiances at the drop of a hat, and Jess was glad, mightily glad, that they were going to Denver and leaving the cad, the rake, the scoundrel, behind.

With one last wavering sob, Michelle stopped crying. She looked up at Lee, eyes wide. "Are they really red and puffy?"

He gave her a bemused smile. "A little, *chérie,* but on you it's lovely."

She breathed a little sigh. "*C'est très triste,* this Denver. I will miss you, Lee."

For the first time since arriving, Lee's gaze rested on Jess. So kind of him, she thought bitterly, to acknowledge her presence.

"Now that remains to be seen. When are you leaving?"

Michelle sighed dramatically. "The Sunday matinee will be our last performance. We bid San Francisco a last *adieu* on Monday."

"Well," Lee said, sitting back, his eyes riveted on Jess, his expression inscrutable. "Perhaps it's not so bad. I think I shall join you."

Michelle's eyes widened. Then clapping her hands, she exclaimed gleefully, "*Oui, oui*. That is an idea—how do you say?—*très bon!*"

"You say very good," he answered, smiling at Jess. Her jealous heart leapt. Goodness, but no man ought to be allowed to look at a woman like that, his eyes all dark and smoldering. She understood *that* emotion all too well, and it was not "*très bon*" by a long chalk!

Michelle's shoulders sank again. "Oh, but is not so *bon,* for what is there in Denver to do? We were there, Lee, *rappelez-vous?* Ten"—she stopped, her eyes calculating, then continued quickly—"*non,* five years ago! Nothing but cows and dirty men! Ha! It is no place for Michelle Dubois!"

Lee's attention shifted to Michelle again and chuckling, he twitched one bleached curl. "I remember and I assure you it's grown considerably since then. They have a beautiful opera house, along with a great deal of fine eating establishments, and yes, even *chapeau* shops."

"Shops? *Non! Vraiment?*"

"Absolutely. There's nothing in San Francisco that you may not also find in Denver."

"Oh!" Michelle exclaimed with another clap of her hands. She bounced around to face Jess. "*Avez-vous entendu, ma amie?* Lee says there are shops!"

Jealousy notwithstanding, Jess couldn't resist Michelle's childish delight. With a small gurgle of laughter, she said, "Yes, Michelle, I heard."

"So," Michelle said, sitting back with a beatific smile, "It is not *très mal* after all."

"No," Lee said, his eyes moving back to Jess. Her heart lurched again, joined by a small fluttering in her stomach. "And you, Jess? Do you think my idea is *très bon?*"

*Absolutely not.* Continued association with Lee promised

nothing less than the slow, torturous destruction of her carefully ordered world. "You'll do as you want, I'm sure."

He grinned. "Sweetheart, I always do what I want. What I would very much like to do right now is to take you for a drive. Michelle informs me that you don't get enough fresh air, don't you, Michelle?"

Michelle glanced from one to the other, her eyes gleaming— scheming! "*Mais oui!* I say it all the time."

And Michelle, damn the woman, conspired almost daily in the destruction of that world! Oh, Jess was going to strangle her! "I get plenty of fresh air. I take a two-mile walk every morning," she reminded her friend.

"That is walking, not driving," Michelle replied with fine disregard for logic.

Trying to control her irritation and the deceitful jumping of her pulses, Jess shook her head. "Thank you, Lee, but I'm afraid I have other plans."

He lifted an eyebrow over bright, laughing eyes. "Afraid again, Jess?"

"Oh, *ma amie,* you do not have other plans. I would know!"

And after Jess strangled Michelle once, she'd strangle her again. And again. "I don't tell you all my plans."

"Yes, you do," Michelle said. "That is because you have so few. Today you were going to do some washing."

"Washing?" Lee asked, his lips twitching.

"It's much needed washing," Jess defended.

"All right, I'll tell you what. If you agree to accompany me, then I shall pay to have your clothes sent to a Chinese wash-house."

She shook her head. "No, thank you. I don't send out certain items."

"I will do it," Michelle offered.

Oh Jess could not possibly strangle her enough! "That's not necessary."

"It is true, I do not like the washing. But I have washing,

too, and I will do yours with mine. This I do for *ma bon et très jolie amie,* who needs fresh air."

Jess sighed her defeat. With Michelle's indomitable will, the argument could last half the day. Besides, she told herself, the drive would give her a chance to discover, delicately, just what *had* happened last night. "Okay, okay, I'll get my wrap."

"*Non!* Not that horrible thing," Michelle said, rising. "You'll borrow one of mine. And a parasol! When you are with Lee, you must dress the part."

Lee had rented a Queen's-body phaeton and as fate would have it, the phaeton's gleaming cobalt-blue body perfectly matched Michelle's blue cashmere wrap shot with strands of silver. But it, like the blanket that Lee shoved behind them as he settled into the velvet upholstery, was unnecessary. With the canopy pushed back, the sun shone brightly upon them, and a warm ocean breeze heated the air to early summer temperatures. Risking the browning effects of the sun, Jess laid the parasol aside. But, she decided as Lee started the phaeton down the street, she'd wear the wrap anyway.

"You know," she said, in an attempt to create some distance between them. "Michelle is trying very hard to throw us together."

He flashed her a dimpled smile. "I know. Is that so bad?"

She sucked in her breath. Goodness, why hadn't she seen that coming? Of course he knew of Michelle's plans! They were as thick as thieves, these two, and doubtless scheming together. Well, she'd put an end to it right now! Blushing furiously, she snapped, "It's impossible."

"Is it? Why?"

Why? She recollected enough of their night of drunken revelry to know she'd mentioned her passionless nature. But she wasn't drunk now and really didn't care to discuss such an embarrassing secret in broad daylight. So she didn't answer, and

Lee let it pass as he steered the phaeton down the road to the end of town, and then turned left toward the hills. *There's gold in them there hills!* There was gold in the Dakota's Black Hills, too, but Everett had never found any. What he'd found was other female companionship. Jess flinched and shifted the focus of her mind to the passing scenery.

"Jess, may I ask you a question?"

She looked at him. A frown drew his eyebrows together as he carefully guided the horse up a small slope. "You've never hesitated before."

"I'm attempting politeness. Forgive me if I'm a little rusty."

She sighed. Lee polite. Would miracles never cease? "You may ask, if you'll allow me to ask you a few questions of my own."

He raised his eyebrows. "Interesting. What sort of questions?"

"They're of a—" She bit her lip. "Of a personal nature."

"All right. Fire away."

"You first."

"You first. You've piqued my curiosity."

"You first," she said resolutely.

"Stubborn, aren't you? Michelle is a poor influence on you. All right, here's the question. Michelle's right, you don't dress very well for a woman in your position. You yourself admitted that the stage pays well. So if you don't spend your money on clothing, what *do* you spend it on?"

"Why the answer's obvious enough. I save it."

"For what?"

She bit her lip. "For all the usual reasons. In case of illness or unemployment or for old age."

He concentrated on driving for a moment as the horses topped the rise. After steering expertly around a curve in the narrow road, he spoke. "Did you know that you bite your lip whenever you're uneasy?"

She started to bite her lip and then with a shake of her

head, stopped herself. "It's a bad habit. I bit my nails as a child, and that was the way I controlled it."

He turned his head and smiled down at her, a warm, affectionate smile that turned her stomach to jelly and her heart to mush. "I like it." He paused a moment, no doubt for effect, then added. "Nevertheless, it's a sure sign that you're lying."

"I am not!"

"You are. I earn my living reading faces and I know a bluff when I see one. So what's the real reason?"

"Why would I lie? It only makes sense to—"

"You're twenty-four," he interrupted her. "You can't possibly be concerned about your old age. You've been continuously employed for six years, and we both know Robert would be a fool to ever let you go. As for illness, your understudy was atrocious the other night—yes, I went to see her—because she's never been in front of an audience before. *That's* how often you've been ill. So, Jess, the truth if you please."

Oh, what the hell did it matter anyway, she thought crossly. Besides, maybe if Lee knew the worst about her, he'd leave her be. "I'm saving it for Jason."

"Your brother? What does he need with your money?"

"To set himself up in business, I guess, or go to school. Whatever he wants. The truth is, I owe it to him."

"For leaving home?" Lee asked, glancing at her in confusion.

"For leaving home and taking his inheritance with me."

Silence. No doubt, now knowing that she was in essence a criminal, he was considering turning the carriage around, willy-nilly, to drop her back at—

"And how, precisely, did you do that?"

She'd forgotten how indifferent Lee was to sin. "When my grandmother died she left Jason and me all her money. She said that my parents had provided for themselves just fine, so she decided to leave what she had to Jason for an education, and to me for a dowry, as silly as that might sound—"

"It doesn't sound—"

"—for an old maid. I didn't think much of it until I met Everett. He was a drummer at the time. Anyhow, we fell in love and he wanted to marry me, but claimed his sales weren't strong enough to support a wife. He insisted that it would take years to save enough and he didn't want to wait. So I told him about my inheritance."

"Ah, the infamous Everett again," Lee said, an edge to his generally amused voice. "I suspect Everett considered this something of a windfall."

Jess bit her lip and then nodded. "My portion was plenty enough for a good start, but he had other plans." She sighed, aching over her blind stupidity. "Everett always had schemes to earn vast amounts of wealth. This particular scheme meant investing in the stock market, only he thought he'd need more money than just *my* portion to make it work. I tried to convince him that he didn't, but he was adamant." She paused, guilt turning her conscience a dull, dirty gray. "So we took Jason's. Everett vowed that we'd pay him back and then some. The banker was a friend of the family and believed me when I told him that we were going to use the money to build a mill. The town needed a new mill."

She fell silent. Presently, Lee offered the rest. "And, at length, Everett lost it all, leaving you destitute and guilty in Deadwood. How did you come to be in Deadwood?"

Hot tears sprung up in her eyes and she glanced sideways, watching the trees go by as the carriage topped another rise. "That's an even longer story." With a quick flick of her hand, she wiped the tears away.

"All right," Lee said. "So now you're saving your money to pay Jason back. How much precisely?"

"Five thousand dollars."

She expected an intake of breath, a whistle, something, but none came. Probably, she told herself morosely, to Lee five thousand dollars was a few night's pay.

"How much have you saved so far?" he asked.

"About three thousand."

At that he did whistle. "Good for you. Have you told your brother?"

She swallowed. "I've tried to write him, oh, thousands of times, but I could never find the words. At length—" Another swallow. "At length, I decided to wait until I could pay him back in full."

They rounded a bend in the road, and Lee pulled the horses to a halt as Jess let out a gasp. The trees gave way to a sloping mountain meadow sprinkled with yellow and orange wildflowers. It ended in a cliff, which offered a breathtaking view of the bay. The ocean spread out for miles and miles, sparkling blue-green in the sunshine.

"Oh, Lee," she breathed. "I swear I can see all the way to China."

"Well," he said, grinning as he jumped down and reached for her hand. "Perhaps not that far. Pretty, isn't it?"

"Pretty? It's gorgeous! I didn't know there were such views up here!"

"Which was Michelle's and my point if you recall. Don't get too near to the edge there. I'd rather not try my hand at rock climbing today." He turned to reach into the carriage.

Jess crept carefully forward to stop within a few feet of the edge. Far below the ships in the harbor bobbed up and down with the waves like so many toy boats. If she looked really hard, she could see people walking along the piers, loading and unloading.

"Jess, come, join me. I've set a place for us to sit."

She turned. Halfway between the carriage and the edge of the cliff, Lee had spread out the blanket. He was kneeling in the center of it, removing wrapped packages from a small wicker hamper.

"What's that?"

"Crackers, cheese, lemonade." He glanced at her, his eyes twinkling. "I didn't think you'd want any more champagne."

She frowned. "I don't understand. How did you know I'd agree to come?"

He unstopped the bottle on the lemonade, poured some into a tall crystal glass and held it out to her. "Here. It won't bite. Not an ounce of alcohol, I swear." Slowly she made her way to the blanket. As she seated herself, he answered. "I didn't know you'd come. I took a gamble."

"Is that why you arrived so quickly after Michelle's summons then?"

He laughed and stretched his long, large body sideways on the blanket. "Yes, but don't tell Michelle. She'd much rather believe I was wearing a path in the carpet waiting for word from her."

Jess took a drink of the lemonade. Tart-sweet. Perfect. Of course. Lee probably never accepted anything that was less than perfect. "You seem to encourage that belief."

"It makes her easier to handle."

Jess tilted her head slightly. "I think you know Michelle very well."

He shrugged. "Eight years is a long time."

"I think you love her very much, too."

He jerked as if alarmed. He opened his mouth, then closed it again, and Jess congratulated herself for finally rendering him speechless. After another moment's thought, he said, "I suppose I do. Does that disturb you?"

And then, she thought disgustedly, he turned her statement into a question, which he had a remarkably annoying habit of doing. "Why do you always ask me those kind of questions?" There, a question with a question. He'd taught her a thing or two.

"I told you, human nature fascinates me."

"Did no one ever tell you about curiosity and the cat?"

He grinned. "My father. Often. It never deterred me in the least."

"Yes, I'm well aware of that," she spat.

He chuckled, his eyes warm with appreciation. "You know, Jess, you never bore me."

"Why, I'm sure you *must* know it's been my lifelong mission to entertain you."

He only smiled, sipped his lemonade and then nodded to the crackers and cheese. "Please, help yourself. And afterward, perhaps you'll oblige me by answering my question."

Confused, she frowned as she cut a piece of cheese. "Your question?"

"Does my loving Michelle bother you?"

She shrugged, inwardly warning her senseless heart to slow down. "Why should it? You make a nice couple."

The gleam in his eyes grew to a sparkle. "A nice couple? Oh, we're certainly that. Do you think we ought to tie the knot? Settle down with lots of little Michelles and Lees? I don't know about that, Jess. I'm not certain there's enough silk and satin in the world to clothe Michelle's daughters."

"Perhaps not now, but when you're older."

"I'll never be that old. Besides, as you may recall, we've ended that part of our relationship. We are now merely friends."

She shrugged and tried to tell her foolish heart that it had no right to suddenly lighten, for it could not matter one bit what Michelle and Lee did.

"And now," Lee said, after a minute of silence, "it's your turn. You had some questions to ask me? I believe you said they were 'of a personal' nature."

"Oh," she said, and grimaced. It had seemed like a remarkably intelligent notion at the time, a chance to discover what had happened last night. But now, alone with Lee stretched out oh-so-leisurely on the blanket, a vision of male virility, Jess wondered if she ought to leave well enough alone. "You know, I find I no longer care."

"Are you afraid you'll embarrass me? You won't. I told you, I have no ghosts. My life is the veritable open book. Fire away."

"No," she said, biting her lip. "I think not."

"You're biting you lip again," he said gently.

She sighed. "They weren't questions about you really. They were about me." Oh, was she really going to do this? Of course she was. She was no coward.

Lee frowned. "About you? Interesting. Go on."

"The other night, when I was so drunk . . ." Her voice trailed off as she searched for the correct wording. "Well, I don't recollect . . . I was just wondering . . . I don't recall changing out of my . . . of Michelle's dress."

He stared at her a minute. Her heart raced and her face grew very, very warm. What a ninnyhammer she was! Being a coward could be a good thing. A yellow-bellied, lily-livered coward. Who wouldn't want to be a coward?

"I thought that might be it," he said. "You were stumbling a bit, so I assisted you."

Appreciation heated his gaze. He ran his eyes down her face and over her person as if in recollection of seeing her un-clothed. A smile tugged at the corners of his mouth. A hot smile with no trace of mirth.

"And . . . and," she stuttered. Halfway there and since she was already uneasy, why not go for broke? "I recollect a . . . a plot for revenge and telling you—"

"Do you remember kissing me?" he interrupted.

For the barest moment she stopped breathing altogether. "Kissing?"

"Kissing. You claimed you couldn't feel a thing. You were devilishly proud of it, too. You were quite drunk, Jess." His voice was low, husky; his eyes had gone from warm to plain hot. Very bad. "Do you remember me telling you that there are a few things I resist?"

She nodded.

"Bedding down with blind-drunk women is one of them. Does that make you easy?"

At this point it offered but slight relief. What would *really* set her at ease, she thought wildly, was for him to stop looking at her like that.

He drained his glass of lemonade and sat up, his eyes never leaving hers. "I liked kissing you." He leaned forward, and her heart hammered in her chest. "Your lips were soft as velvet and sweet—"

"'There is more eloquence in a sugar touch of them than in the tongues of the French council,'" she quoted abruptly.

He stopped. "What?"

"It's Shakespeare. Henry the Fifth. I . . . I played Kate a few times."

"Hmm. Who'd have thought that Shakespeare was interested in kissing?"

"Romeo and Juliet, no doubt."

He laughed, his eyes crinkling at the edges. "And did you ever play the illustrious Juliet?"

"Once or twice."

"As I recall, there was a kiss or two in that play. I suspect," he said, leaning forward once more, "you remember how it goes."

His lips touched hers. For the briefest of moments, Jess drank in the feel of his mouth moving across hers. And for the briefest of moments she reveled in the tiny jolts of pleasure rushing over her skin. It had been ever so long since she'd been kissed. And even then, Everett's kisses had never felt quite this wonderful . . .

Then she recollected what accompanied kissing: grimy hotel rooms and the smell of stale perfume. Her stomach roiled. She jerked away, just as Lee was reaching to pull her nearer. "No!"

He halted, stunned. "What's wrong?"

"I think it's perfectly obvious! I don't want you to kiss me."

His eyebrows drew together in a scowl. "Last night you said you liked kissing."

Oh Lord, had she? She was never, ever going to drink champagne again!

He stared at her, long and hard. "I'd have bet the pot that you were attracted to me."

She tried desperately to catch her breath. "I don't know why. I never said anything to give you that impression."

He leaned back on the palm of one hand. "You didn't have to. You gave me signals."

"What signals?"

He hesitated. "Let's just say there are signals and leave it at that."

"No. If I'm unintentionally encouraging you, I'll stop it immediately."

He barked a joyless laugh. "You couldn't if you tried."

"I certainly can't if you don't tell me what they are."

Another long stare. "All right. First, there's the way you look at me. Your eyes follow me around a room. Even when Michelle's there, you don't see her. You're watching me."

"Of all the stuck-up, conceited—"

"It's not conceit, it's the truth. You know it as well as I do. Second, when we were reading your menu at Armand's you were breathing very heavily."

"I was nervous about the French."

"It was as if you'd found a fragrance that you liked."

She stilled, speechless as she recalled the soap and woodsmoke smell of his hair. She couldn't suppress a tiny, treacherous shiver of excitement.

"Third, and, sweetheart, you can't do a thing about this, a woman's eyes darken when she's interested in a man. When we're close, yours are almost black."

More deep breaths, for her heart was pounding again, stupid thing. "Okay. Okay," she said in a low, gasping voice. "I think you're remarkably handsome. Most women do, and I'm absolutely certain you know that!"

"Robert's handsome, also."

"Yes."

"You don't look at him that way."

She glanced around frantically, at the leaves of the trees casting shadows on the ground, at the horse happily grazing, at the grass moving with a gentle ocean breeze. A breeze? What breeze? She didn't feel a thing. She was as hot as hell.

"And so," Lee said, "I ask you again, Jess. Why won't you kiss me?"

*Why? Why?* She didn't know—why, she could scarcely think when he looked at her that way. She didn't want to kiss him for kissing led to—other things. And she hated other things. "I believe I explained that last night."

"Ah, so we're back to Everett and your less-than-stunning marriage."

She swallowed. "It wasn't him. It was me."

"You don't know that," he said gently.

"Yes, I do."

"He was just one man, Jess."

She took a deep breath. "I never responded to any other man's attentions. By the time I met Everett, I was eighteen, an old maid and resolved to spinsterhood. But when Ev kissed me . . . well, I liked his kisses. I assumed that it would be the same with the marriage bed, but—" Disgust tightened her throat. "But it was bad."

"Which merely proves that Everett was a poor lover," he said, leaning forward. His brow wrinkled in earnestness. "But just because Dunne couldn't make you feel—"

"No!" she cried, jerking back. Tears formed in her eyes. She dashed them away. "It wasn't that I didn't feel anything. I *hated* it!" Recollection flooded her senses in undulating waves of nausea: Ev slipping under the sheets, touching her, kissing her . . .

Lee's face went blank with shock. "Be that as it may," he said, swallowing, "you ought not to assume that you're frigid based upon your experiences with one man."

. . . and she sick as a dog, rolling away from him afterward to vomit in the chamber pot. Trembling, she wrapped her arms around her suddenly cold body. "You're wrong. I'm exactly like those women Dr. Acton writes about. Regardless, I'm married. What you want is impossible."

His eyes drifted from her face to her arms. After a moment, he took a deep breath and sat back. "All right, sweetheart. I won't touch you again. I promise."

# Chapter Eight

Lee was severely distressed. As he shook out the blanket, his eyes flickered over Jess. She sat in the carriage, her arms wrapped tightly around her body, her face as white as a ghost's. He dropped the basket in the back, then climbed into the carriage and leaned over Jess to wrap the blanket around her. She stiffened at his touch.

"I just want to warm you up."

She lifted her head to look at him. Her eyes black with suffering, she nodded. He tucked the blanket around her. Then he slapped the horse and started carefully steering the phaeton over the rough mountain road, pulling on the brake as they descended. Jess sat as still as stone next to him, unnaturally quiet. When the road allowed it he asked in as normal a voice as he could muster, "This money that you've saved for your brother . . . I assume you've invested it?"

She glanced at him. "Invested?"

"To make a greater return."

"Robert has it. I take three quarters of my pay and he holds the rest for me."

Lee didn't liked the sound of that. From what he knew of him, Robert had a penchant for gambling and a talent for losing. Michelle and Jess might not understand why they were leaving San Francisco; Lee had no such confusion.

"If you deposited it in a bank, you'd earn interest. At two or three percent, you could earn up to ninety dollars in a year. It won't do much to reduce your debt, but it's something. You could use it to purchase some new clothes, make Michelle happy."

She shook her head. "I don't trust banks. If you recall, I walked into one and stole five thousand dollars of my brother's money."

He hesitated. Considering the circumstances it was pure folly to create any sort of tie to Jess. She'd made it crystal clear that she'd allow nothing between them but friendship. A purely *platonic* friendship. He'd be more comfortable sleeping on a bed of nails.

But he loved her, however shallowly. After all the bad cards life had dealt her, she deserved to have someone on her side, if only for a day or so. "I have an associate in Denver who's a banker, Steven White. He clings so tightly to every dollar, I've almost had to hold him at gun point to make a withdrawal. I guarantee he won't let anyone steal your money. Chances are he won't even let *you* take it."

She shook her head. "Thank you, Lee, but we'll only be in Denver a month or two before moving on. It wouldn't be worth it. Our stay in San Francisco has been unusually long. Robert likes to keep the troupe traveling."

"You don't intend to use the money any time soon, and you'll probably pass through Denver a time or two before you do need it. You may withdraw it then. In the meantime, you could keep any additional savings with Robert."

After a moment's thought she said in a soft, wistful voice, "I would like a pretty gown someday. Okay, maybe it's worth a try. Would you mind dropping me at the theatre then? I'll let Robert know my health has improved enough to go on tonight, and ask him for my money."

He hesitated a moment, while logic struggled with his heart's emotions. "I believe I'll accompany you into the theatre," he said, forcing cheer into his voice. "And request that Robert purchase me a train ticket as well. That way I may introduce you to Steven." *Fool! Fool! You could send him a telegram, and stay here in 'Frisco, where hundreds of women would gladly help mend a broken heart!*

And yet he *had* promised Michelle that he'd join them. And he'd never slept on a bed of nails. Perhaps it wasn't as painful as one would imagine.

They'd reached the end of the mountain road, and he turned toward the theatre. He risked a glance at Jess. Some of her color had returned—rose-pink cheeks in an ivory face. Simply lovely. A lovely face with, he thought, remembering helping her out of her gown, the body to match.

And *frigid,* he admonished his quickening heart. Frigid as in a well-formed ice sculpture. Frigid as in stock-still and staring at the ceiling, trying to ignore him touching her.

Naturally frigid? He couldn't believe that. Nature just didn't create such beauty without the warm blood to go with it. Was it possible that Dunne had harmed her, sexually? Abused her? She didn't seem the sort to accept any manner of abuse, but his damned overactive mind insisted upon creating the sort of horrific scenes that could destroy a woman's passion. Finally, when a particularly infuriating scene flashed in front his eyes, he said, "Jess, there's one more thing I must know and then we need never discuss it again."

He glanced her way to see her face harden. "What?"

"About Everett. Did he ever harm you? Physically?"

She frowned. "No."

"Did he ever force his attentions upon you?"

She jerked her head around in shock. "No! Why ever would you think that?"

Relief melted the tension in Lee's muscles. "Your reaction seemed a trifle extreme."

She faced forward again. "You were pestering me. I

explained my difficulties, but you continued to pester me anyway," she snapped.

"I'm sorry."

"You ought to be. You've upset me. I let very few people upset me," she said with a tiny hiccup in her voice. It drove a spike through the middle of Lee's heart.

"I'm sorry, sweetheart, I didn't mean to do that."

She fell silent, and Lee damned himself for dredging up her pain again. If she were Michelle, he'd buy her some expensive trinket and all would be forgiven. Jess would merely throw it in his face.


The stage door was unlocked. Lee and Jess's footsteps echoed as they crossed the stage, then proceeded down a long corridor lined with dressing rooms. Robert's office was at the end, and as they approached Lee detected the sound of voices coming through the door. Not just voices, but moans. And groans. Damn, the man had a woman with him.

"Uh, Jess, perhaps we ought to return later."

"Oh, for the love of Pete," she breathed, her face tightening in irritation—Lee refused to believe it was revulsion. "He always has a woman in there. If we returned when Robert was alone, we'd both be wrinkled and gray." Without slowing her step, she walked up to the door and knocked, receiving only another moan in answer. Lee threw a sideways glance at Jess. Under normal circumstances he'd find this comical, but not after this day's conversations.

She knocked harder. "Robert, it's Jess. I must speak with you."

Behind the door someone swore, followed by scuffling. Face creased with disgust, Jess turned the knob and threw the door open. With an almost queenly air—she hadn't gotten Gertrude's part for nothing—she swept into a room richly papered in crimson and gold. Jess's eyes flashed over a woman sitting on a crimson velvet divan, who clutched a blanket to her partially nude body. The buttons on Robert's shirt hung open, but he had managed to hike up his pants. He started fastening them. "I've come for my money," Jess said.

"Your what?" Robert asked, glancing at the woman on the divan. The discomfort in his eyes made Lee glance that way, too. She was pretty enough, with large doe-brown eyes and long brown curls. Something about her struck Lee as familiar. He frowned, trying to place her face.

"My savings. Lee has suggested I deposit it in a bank where I can earn interest."

"I thought you were ill."

"I've recovered. I shall be able to perform tonight. My money, Robert?"

"I don't understand. We won't be returning to San Francisco for many months. It doesn't make any sense to put it in a bank now."

"The account will be in Denver. And I shan't need it for many months."

Robert glanced at the woman again. "Can't we talk about this later? As you can see I'm currently—engaged."

Jess rolled her eyes. "You're always 'engaged,' Robert."

"But you won't need the money until we're in Denver."

"I don't know what concern that is of yours," she said, wariness entering her voice. "Nor should it take much time. All you need do is open the safe."

Now Lee placed the girl. She was the daughter of a man whom he'd played with recently. Louis Temple, a large, blustering fellow who let money slip through his hand like sand, and bragged nonstop about his daughter's engagement to a Colorado congressman.

With a condescending sigh, Robert set to buttoning his shirt. His fingers shook. "It's not that simple. I don't have the money right now."

Jess's eyes went cold. "What do you *mean* you don't have my money? I can see the safe from here, there in the corner!"

Lee shifted uneasily. It was one thing to interrupt a man having some fun, another thing entirely when he was involved with a respectably engaged young woman. Her father would not be happy.

"Jess, please understand I use all our cash to pay for the theatre, the props, the scripts. It's currently tied up in the operation. Come the end of the week when the house owner hands over our profits I'll be able to pay you back."

"Oh no," she said, shaking her head. "You can not have done so! That was *my* money, Robert, not the troupe's!"

Robert grimaced, regarding Jess with something akin to fear, an appropriate emotion considering that the cold hostility in her voice could have frozen his nuts off. Which *did* amuse Lee immensely, but not enough to dispel his growing uneasiness. He reached for Jess's elbow. "Listen, Jess, Robert's right, We may discuss this at another time."

She looked up at him, her face flushed and her eyes sparkling with rage. Would she look that way under other extreme emotion? Desire . . .

Not a good time to think of that.

There was never a good time to think of that.

"Did you hear what he said? He doesn't have my money. I've scrimped and saved for six long years for that money!"

"Montgomery, for God's sake," Robert beseeched him. "You're a businessman. Explain it to her."

Lee attempted to rub away the prickles rising on his neck. "Actually, I agree with her—"

"I knew you would!" Jess said warmly, placing her hand on his arm.

"I also agree that it's not the time for this discussion. We'll not arrive in Denver for several days. We may deal with this matter then."

"But you don't know him! He'll have another excuse in Denver!" she said, her voice cracking as she turned to him. Tears sparkled in her eyes, lovely even in the throes of suffering. "Lee, it's all I have."

*Frigid, ol' boy.*

She sure as hell didn't look frigid.

"I know, sweetheart," he said gently. "He shall repay you, I promise." He raised his head to flash Robert his ugliest, most threatening scowl. The man flinched and stepped back. Good. His message had been received. He looked down at Jess and, smiling, took her hands to give them a reassuring squeeze. "But if he doesn't have it right now, you can yell from here to doomsday and the money won't appear."

"But—"

"You have every right to tear it out of his hide, Jess. But you know hide doesn't sell for what it used to." He watched as a glimmer of amusement trickled through her anger. "So we'll allow him to live for the present, all right? And," he said with a light laugh, "if he doesn't produce the money in a week's time, we'll sic Michelle on him."

"Oh, all right!" She turned to Robert. "You have until Monday, and then I *will* take it out of your hide!"

Jess pulled her hands free and made a wonderfully grand exit. Lee turned to Robert. "Another thing, Madison. I require a ticket on that train with your troupe." He reached into his pocket, ripped a few bills from his fold and grabbing Robert's hand, slapped them in his palm. "Keep the change. It appears you'll need it."


Jess fumed all the way home, swearing up and down that she'd tear Robert from limb to limb if he didn't pay her back, while Lee listened in silence. By the time they reached her flat, she was shaking. Not from anger, but from the horrible gnawing in her belly warning her that she'd most likely lost her money forever. A body, her father had been fond of saying, couldn't squeeze blood from a stone.

Lee jumped down, tied the horse to a post, and then reached up to help her down. "I'd like to say that I had a wonderful time," she started, stepping to the ground.

"But," he finished for her as he fetched her wrap and parasol, "hellish is a more apt description." The understanding in his eyes shot through her cold, weary heart like rays of sunshine breaking through a bank of rain clouds. "Come, I'll see you to your door."

She shook her head. "Thank you, but I don't need you to."

"Not every action in life is to satisfy a need, Jess," he said gently. "Sometimes we do things because we *want* to do them."

Not her, she thought dismally, allowing him to lead her upstairs. Tears prickled her eyes. For her, every action in life *was* about filling needs. Seven years ago she'd followed her wants, and it'd led to pure, unmitigated disaster. Not just for herself—oh no, she'd brought down her whole family with her.

They reached her door. When Lee didn't relinquish her elbow, she looked up, confused. His eyes gleamed darkly in the dim corridor, as he brushed her hair back from her face. A tiny spark of warning flashed through her, then his mouth was on hers and for the second time that day he was kissing her.

With a sigh, Jess closed her eyes and let his lips move oh-so-gently over hers. This time when Everett popped into her mind, she resolutely shoved him away. Maybe Lee was right; some actions in life ought to be about wants and she wanted this. Oh, how she wanted this—long lingering kisses. So much so that she allowed him to deepen the kiss, delving inside to stroke her tongue with his. Her skin tingled and her cold, desire-starved body melted in a rush of liquid heat.

Lee ended the kiss so abruptly that Jess swayed. His other hand grabbed her upper arm and steadied her. She swallowed hard and tried to catch her breath.

"Jess." His voice made a caress of her name. "No objection this time then?" he asked, soft laughter rippling along the bottom of his voice. She didn't answer him, for hadn't he said he knew when a woman was attracted to him? "Not even Shakespeare could describe your kiss, sweetheart," he said, then turned her around, opened the door, and pushed her into the room. After he shut the door behind him, she leaned against it for support. The sound of his boots echoed down the stairs, and she could have sworn she heard a whistle.

Michelle swept in from her room. "*Ma amie!* You are back!"

Jess touched her lips. They felt hot and her fingers trembled. Mercy, but her whole body shook. Swallowing again, she stumbled to the sofa where she dropped the parasol and wrap. Then she sank into her favorite blue armchair. It embraced her with soft, tattered familiarity.

"But where is Lee?" Michelle asked.

"He left."

She peered at Jess. "Honey, you look poorly. Are you ill? You're flushed." She frowned and then a huge smile curved her lips. "Oh!" she said, clapping her hands in excitement. "I see! Lee's ended your absurd dedication to celibacy, and it's about time, too!" She perched on the edge of the sofa, her eyes gleaming as she leaned forward. "Tell me everything! How was it? Where did you go? What did you do? Oh dear, I know *what* you did, but there are ever so many variations!"

With a quivering sigh, Jess shook her head. "We didn't do anything."

"No! I don't believe it. I know that flush! It's sexual satisfaction!"

"Good gracious, Michelle, must you always be so *explicit!*"

"Yes, for you are always so vague."

"Regardless, it's not what you think. It was just a kiss."

"A kiss?" Michelle sat back disgusted. "That's what this is all about?"

"It's about you becoming overly excited, as usual."

Michelle sighed and puffed her cheeks in thought. "Well,

a kiss is better than nothing at all, I suppose. It'll lead to more in time."

"It shan't lead anywhere. I made it perfectly plain to Lee that I'm not interested in him in that regard."

"Perfectly plain? Ha! It doesn't matter. *He* is interested and so, *voilà,* it will happen."

"It shan't. I told him everything, Michelle. *Every*thing, understand?"

"Everything!" Michelle exclaimed, jumping up. "Are you mad? Jess, there is no surer way to turn a man away than to tell him you're frigid!"

Jess winced at the word, but held firm. "It was best for both of us."

"It was not. Oh, poor Lee! Poor me!" she said, starting to pace. "When I think of all I've done for you, everything I've sacrificed, and you go throw it all way, it makes me want to scream! Oh!" she cried, stomping her foot. "I am outraged! It will take me ages and ages to bring him back to you if even I can!"

Tiny bubbles of humor rose in Jess, soothing her frazzled nerves. "It doesn't matter. I don't want you to bring him back."

"Ha!" she said, shaking a finger. "You are young and foolish. I *will* bring him back, but I warn you, this is not the best way to have your shrew tamed."

"I don't want my shrew tamed. I happen to like her just the way she is."

"No woman likes a shrew. Nor do men. They like shrews even less."

"It's much worse than that," Jess said. As the effects of Lee's kiss wore off, recollections of the rest of the day returned, squeezing her heart. "We went to see Robert, to get Lee a ticket to Denver and—"

"Ah, I'd forgotten. He's going with us to that awful Western place. Well, there is hope then."

"I asked Robert for my money. Michelle, it's gone!"

Michelle stopped a moment. "Your money? Gone? What do you mean it's gone?"

"I mean gone. I think Robert spent it." Jess rubbed her eyes as six years of frugality floated across her vision, six years of worn clothes and holey shoes, of soup for dinner and cold, dark nights, fearful of spending too much on coal and oil. For nothing, all for nothing.

"Spent it?" Michelle asked, puzzled. "Your Jason money?"

She sighed wearily. "My Jason money."

Michelle was quiet a moment. "And where was Lee when you found this out?"

"He was with me. What difference does that make?"

"Why, it makes all the difference in the world! You don't need that insane Robert! Lee will give you the money!"

Jess's head shot up. "He shall not!"

"Of course he will. What does he care for five thousand dollars—"

"It was three—"

"It's nothing to him. A snap of his fingers, that is all. You ask, he will give, and it is done. And now, we must think—"

"I will not take one penny, not one penny of his money, do you understand me, Michelle? And you shall not ask him for it, not under any circumstances, not if your life and the rest of San Francisco depends upon it!" She'd be damned if she corrected for her thievery by getting the money in an equally immoral way! From a gambler of all things!

Michelle waved Jess's protest aside with a flick of her wrist. "This is all bosh. Of course you will take it. That's what men are for, *amie*. Money! They work hard to earn it, for it pleases them to give it to women, especially pretty women."

"Not to me!" Jess ground out.

Michelle, eyes burning, turned on her. "Don't be idiotic! You're ruining everything!"

"Damn it, Michelle," Jess shouted, jumping up. "When will you understand that I'm not *like* you! I don't want men to give me things! I don't want to have to smile and simper and give them outrageous compliments just so they'll take me to Armand's!"

"And you'd prefer to sit at home night after night, drinking soup and reading Shakespeare—*a man,* Jess, who's been dead two hundred years!"

"Little you know," Jess spat, tears welling up in her eyes. "He's been dead almost three hundred years!"

"Two hundred, three hundred! He's *dead!* Dead, buried, and only so much dust now! And if you insist upon spending your life this way you will die old, wrinkled, and alone! Alone!"

"It is better than dying in an insane asylum like you! You are crazy, really and truly crazy, and I'm not going to stand here one more minute longer! As far as I'm concerned you and your precious Lee Montgomery may go straight to hell!" She brushed past Michelle and ran to her room, slamming the door so hard it sent a miniature earthquake through the building. With a gut-tearing sob, she threw herself on her bed and burst into tears.

# Chapter Nine

As the clock struck nine P.M., Jess let her book fall into her lap. Leaning back, she closed her eyes and sighed. Michelle had yet to return home. Over the last five days they'd barely spoken a word, and Jess was miserable over it. In twenty-four years, she'd never felt the need for a close female friend, but now, having lost Michelle, she realized how much she'd missed. Outrageous though she was, Michelle had always made Jess laugh, one of the few luxuries she could afford. Actually, now that Jess was dead broke, laughter was the only luxury she could afford.

Lee hadn't visited, either.

Jess rubbed her eyes.

No surprise there. As Michelle had so eloquently pointed out, telling a man that she was passionless was scarcely the best way to keep his attention. Nor had she any right to expect a man as sensual as Lee to be satisfied with kisses. Kisses from a married woman, no less. Lee was not the kind of man to accept that and, frankly, Jess didn't want the kind of man who would.

Which meant, as she'd been saying for six years, she didn't want a man at all.

Heavyhearted, she picked up *Hamlet* and shifted Acton's *The Functions and Disorders of the Reproductive Organs* to the cheap sewing table next to her armchair. It had offered her little comfort tonight. As much as she treasured Acton's reassurances—and despite her mother's warnings about the fiery end that greeted those who broke the seventh commandment—tonight Jess cared nothing about moral superiority. Tonight she felt lost and unloved and very willing to exchange a few days in Hell for a taste of true passion. Jump off the pedestal of female superiority for just an hour or two—just long enough to understand . . .

A knock on the door rang out.

Jess's head jerked up; her heart took a nasty flip. The Devil coming for her soul?

No, of course not.

Another knock, louder, and Lee's voice. "Jess? Michelle?"

Oh yes, Satan himself, in his most diabolical form.

Swallowing hard, she strode to the door, telling her absurdly leaping heart that he'd come for Michelle. Of course he'd come for Michelle.

She opened the door. And gulped.

He was dressed in an expensive black "tuxedo" suit, which fit him like a glove—black cutaway frock coat, white satin waistcoat and linen shirt. His rakishly long hair was neatly combed, his shoes spotless. The diamonds in his cuffs and tie pin glinted in the weak lamplight, speaking of understated wealth. In one hand he held a hat, a cane, and a pair of white kid gloves, in the other a posy of perfect blue violets and a snow-white orchid.

"Jess?" he said, smiling as he ran his eyes over her faded calico dress. "You're running late, I presume? Well, no matter, I'm quite contented to wait in the parlor if you've got some of that splendid brandy still. Here, sweetheart, these are for you." He dropped a kiss on her forehead as he handed her the flowers, then brushed past her into the room.

Dear heavens, Jess thought breathlessly as she closed the door, but he seemed to grow more handsome every day. She watched him hungrily as he dropped his gloves, hat, and cane in an armchair on the way to the parlor table. Shaking his head, he lit a lamp. "Dark as midnight in here again. I've half a mind to buy you a barrel of kerosene—no, *not* as charity so don't fire up at me, but to save my own eyesight." He poured himself a glass of brandy.

Her forehead was warm where his lips had touched. Had he somehow left a mark there? Marked for life by—*Late?* His words finally filtered through the fog in her brain. What was she late for? The train didn't leave until the following morning, not that Lee was dressed for travel.

He leaned against the table, sipping his drink. After a moment, a slight frown creased his brow. "Jess, sweetheart, forgive my rudeness, but as lovely as you are in that dress, it's not precisely a ball gown. We'll be late if you don't move along."

He'd gone mad. It was inevitable, of course. According to Acton, long association with loose women was bound to affect his brain sooner or later.

"I'm not going anywhere," she answered.

He flashed his dimple and quipped, "Why, I wish you'd informed me of that before I purchased the flowers." She merely shook her head in bewilderment. Abruptly, the amusement on his face turned into agitation. "You're not joking are you? Damn!" He straightened, glancing around the parlor. "Where's Michelle? She promised to arrange this for me."

"Jon and Miranda are throwing a small going-away party. I expect she's there."

"Jon and Miranda? Who in hell are they?"

"They're in our troupe," she said.

"Bloody hell," he swore under his breath. "I suppose I ought to have expected as much. Michelle's never been known for reliability." He heaved a disgusted sigh, then crossed the room to sink into the sofa. "It seems we're on our own, then, aren't we? But fear not, Jess, I am entirely at your service." He stretched his long legs out, crossing his ankles.

"And as discreet as a monk, to boot. Get started." He casually waved a hand toward her room. "Call me when it comes time to attend the gown's fastenings."

Jess shook her head. "Lee, I don't know what in blazes you're talking about! I had no plans for tonight other than to pack, which," she said, motioning to a pathetically shabby trunk in the corner, "I finished hours ago."

He looked at it, then back at her, a frown between his eyebrows. "Which says nothing to the purpose. I'm talking about the ball. Have you forgotten one Michael Hathaway? I assure you, he'd be quite disappointed to hear that, as I am quite certain he hasn't forgotten *you*. As you may recall, he invited you to his wife's party tonight, for which Michelle vowed to prepare you. Damnation, where is that woman?"

The door opened and "that woman" entered, her arms piled high with boxes. As realization sank in—but Lee must know that Mr. Hathaway hadn't really *meant* the invitation!—Jess noticed Michelle's boxes were falling over. She stepped forward to take three off the top, leaving one long, oblong box in Michelle's arms. Mercy, but how many gowns did one woman need?

"Michelle," Lee said, rising to take that box from her and laying it on the sofa. "Good God, never tell me you've been shopping at this time of night? You promised to assist me with Jess. I swear woman, I could wring your neck! It's quarter past nine already and we were supposed to arrive by ten sharp. Much past ten thirty and Bernadette will be serving my head on a platter for supper."

Michelle bit a fingertip, glanced at Lee, and then caught Jess's eye. At Jess's answering frown, Michelle's eyes grew bright. "I-I know. I'm sorry. It's just that . . . I thought it would all go away. I truly did . . . and then we . . . it just, oh Jess," she squeaked and abruptly threw herself into Jess's arms, crying pitifully, "I am so sorry, *ma amie*, ever so sorry."

Tears prickling her own eyes, Jess folded her friend into her arms and patted her ostentatiously bonneted head. "Oh,

Michelle, don't cry! I'm sorry, too. All those things I said! I never meant a word."

"Oh *non!* It is my fault, all my fault! I have hurt my sweet-hearted friend and I am a shrew—"

"No." Jess let loose a watery chuckle. "I'm the shrew, remember?"

"*Non, non,* but I am! The veriest shrew of shrews, a shrew enormous! Oh, the queen of shrews!"

Laughing again, Jess let her go and wiped her eyes. "Okay, if you want to be the shrewiest of shrews, that's fine with me. As long as you promise to be my friend."

"Oh, I am your friend, your very best friend! Always! Forever!"

Amusement rippling through his voice, Lee said, "Michelle, these superlatives are fatiguing. Would one of you be so obliging as to explain what the devil's going on here?"

With a little sigh of happiness, Jess turned to Lee, perched on the sofa's arm. Maybe her life wasn't pure tragedy, after all. The sun still shone some days, and even if she was broke and passionless, she had a friend, a good friend. And a person who could claim one good friend, could claim the world. Hadn't Shakespeare said that? If he hadn't, he ought to have. "We had an argument."

"All right," Lee said with an amused nod. "And?"

"And," Michelle said, happily swishing over to the long box, "*la couturier* has just this minute finished Jess's oh-so-beautiful ball gown!" She lifted the lid. "I had it measured on me, *ma amie,* but I made sure to tell her 'taller *s'il vous plaît!* And bigger in the bosoms!' *Oui,* I did! For *ma chérie amie,* I admit, my bosom is not so large!"

Michelle withdrew the gown. A *beautiful* gown, constructed of royal blue satin, with a square bodice and V-shaped back. It's beauty was mostly in the cut, for its only decoration was a set of silver tassels running down the shallowly trained back, and moderate trimming in blue velvet and silver lace. Jess swallowed, tears rising in her eyes, for Michelle had obviously put much thought into the gown; she'd never buy anything so exquisitely simple for herself.

Bending over Jess's shoulder, Lee nodded approval. "Bravo, Michelle," he said, "very well done indeed."

"And so," Michelle said, looking at Jess shyly. "Cinderella will go to the ball, *oui?*"

Jess let out a disbelieving laugh as she fingered the tiny puffed sleeves, cuffed in velvet and trimmed in lace. "Ball? Oh, Michelle, it's marvelous!"

"Ball or soiree or whatever the hell it's called. Who can remember all the names?" Lee asked as he seated himself in Jess's armchair and withdrew a slim silver box from his waistcoat pocket. He took out a cigar. "Doesn't matter," he said, striking a match. "The invitation says ball, thus the ball gown." He lit his cigar, squinting slightly as he puffed out smoke.

Bemused, Jess shook her head. "But Mr. Hathaway didn't *mean* it, Lee. He included me because I was with you. He only meant to invite you."

Lee shrugged. "He sent two invitations to the Baldwin. One is addressed to me, the other to Miss Jessica Sullivan. And now that you've got the gown, you've only to dress and we'll be on our way."

As understanding dawned, Jess said slowly, "Which you knew about. You didn't pay for it by any chance?" Firing up, she turned on Michelle. "Tell me the truth, Michelle! We talked about this! I will not accept—"

"Oh *non* and *non* and *non!*" Michelle said, her eyes wide. "It is my own money, *vraitmant!* Lee asked if you could borrow one of my gowns and me, I thought, '*Non!* I will buy one for *mon amie*, *mon petite pauvre,* who has had all her money stolen by that swine! I will buy her a gown and she will go to the ball and smile again!'"

Jess flinched at the reminder. "We're not entirely certain

it's gone. It's possible that I'll get it back in time. Robert isn't all swine."

"It does not matter tonight," Michelle said with a very French wave of her hand, dismissing all that was not of immediate concern to her. "Tonight, it is the ball!"

"Oh no! Now, Lee," Jess said, switching her attention again, "I appreciate the invitation, honestly I do, but this is absurd."

"How so? You have the gown, and it's perfect for you. And I'd bet the pot that in one of those other boxes are gloves, fan, slippers, the whole shebang. Michelle will lend you her wrap. I even brought you flowers for your hair, per Michelle's request."

"*Naturellement,* I would not forget the—how do you call it?—the shebang," Michelle said, and from another box she removed a fan of silver lace, ribboned with royal blue satin. Gorgeous, perfectly gorgeous.

But, Jess cautioned her fluttering pulses, she could not attend a *ball!* What would a small-town girl do at a party like that? She'd most certainly embarrass herself, for she knew nothing about fashionable etiquette, not even the codes of flirtation beyond the names—the Fan code, the Glove code.

But when she looked at the gown her heart lodged in her throat. It was so remarkably grand, and the color matched her eyes.

She'd keep it, at any rate.

Where would she ever wear such a thing?

"No," she said firmly, as much to herself as to Lee and Michelle. "It's impossible. I've never been to a ball. I wouldn't know how to act."

"You know how to dance, don't you?" Lee asked.

"Why, yes, of course, but—"

"That's all there is to it."

Dancing. Her heart ached with sudden longing. She hadn't danced in a dog's age! Oh maybe, maybe it wouldn't be so bad. After all Lee was a gambler. No doubt his friends were gamblers, too, not many more rungs up the social ladder than theatre people. Yes, Mr. Hathaway *had* dressed in high style, but that didn't mean much in San Francisco, where everyone dressed as if they'd walked out of Godey's magazine.

She bit her lip, narrowing her eyes. "I won't know anyone, Lee. Don't you want to talk with your friends?"

"Hell no. They're more acquaintances that friends, and I can barely stand Mrs. Hathaway. Prune-faced and sour, that's what she is. No, I thought we'd just dance."

"Just dance," she repeated. No long conversations about who knew who, and who was the best dressmaker in town. Instead, she would be whirling and twirling around the dance floor in Lee's strong arms, soft music floating all around them.

"Dance," he said, leaning forward, continuing in a devastatingly persuasive voice, "and eat and drink, although you might want to avoid the champagne."

Champagne. Almost a week had passed since she'd gotten so terribly ill, and now she could comfortably recollect the finer aspects of champagne, the fizzy bubbles tripping down her throat. Goodness, if they served champagne, what other delicacies would they serve? And if Mr. Hathaway could afford to lose two thousand dollars at poker in one night, no doubt he'd have no qualms about spending much more on a ball for his wife.

Lee leaned back and tapped his cigar in an ashtray. "Come, now, Jess," he cajoled, flashing his dimpled smile, "admit it, you know you want to go. I can see it in your eyes. It's your last night in San Francisco. What can be the harm?"

"Oh yes, *ma amie!* There is no harm! Go, go! You will dance and dance until these oh-so-beautiful slippers have worn off your feet," she said, and placed a pair of silver-embroidered blue satin slippers in Jess's hands.

Lee, his eyes still trained on Jess, laughed. "Perhaps not quite that much."

"Oh, all right!" she snapped, trying to sound irritated. But as soon as she said it she felt as if a rather large butterfly had spread its wings inside her belly. She was going to the ball.

With a sigh of pleasure, Jess sat back in the well-padded leather seat of the hansom cab. As expected, her new gown looked fairy-tale beautiful on her, even if it was skin tight in the front and the low bodice displayed far more of her breasts than Mother ever would have allowed; Lee had assured her that it was perfectly proper for a ball gown. In addition, Michelle had twisted her hair into a fancy French braid, using false hair to add thickness and depth and the violets for decoration. With the gown, the hair, the slippers, the long white gloves trimmed with silver lace—the whole shebang—Jess felt transformed from small-town Jessica Sullivan to an elegantly clad debutante.

Across from her, Lee's lingering gaze of male appreciation confirmed it.

The seconds passed into minutes, and she shifted uncomfortably. "So, Lee," she finally said to break the silence, "we haven't seen much of you the last few days."

He raised one dark eyebrow. "Miss me?"

For a space of seconds she considered lying, but what was the point? "Yes."

He grinned. "You are always so refreshingly honest. I've been busy earning a living. I wanted some extra traveling cash, and San Francisco is full of marks—pigeons—rich men—willing to part with their money."

"And Denver isn't?"

"They're not quite so rich."

She bit her lip and glanced out the window as she ventured, "Still, you weren't so busy you couldn't see Michelle."

"I believe you said 'we.' Are you now saying 'I'?"

"Does it matter?"

"You sound jealous."

She shrugged. "A little."

"Interesting," he replied and leaned forward, his folded gloved hands hanging between his legs. "I needed her services. Michelle, for all her faults, has a nice eye for clothing."

Jess chuckled. "I should hope so, considering how much of her mind it occupies."

His eyes gleamed. "Precisely. I wanted her help in dressing you for this shindig tonight."

"I still don't understand why. You could go just as well without me."

His dimple popped out. "And meet the prune-faced Mrs. Hathaway alone? Never!"

"I doubt she'd intimidate you for long."

"You're right. The truth is, I hate these things."

"Oh." She paused, sifting this new twist of Lee's character in with the other fragments of information she had about him. "So why go at all?"

He shrugged, leaned back again, and said, "I thought you might enjoy it."

"I could enjoy myself at home and thus not inconvenience you, which," she said, her acidic humor rising inside her, "as you know, is the very essence of my existence."

Chuckling, he answered, "Oh yes, I remember, shrew. It's been your 'lifelong mission' never to bore me. Nonetheless, you'll enjoy this more than sitting at home. And I suspect, in your company, I shall find it entertaining as well."

His words shot straight into her heart, then spread through her body in a warm glow.

Oh no, she would not fall for all his blarney! Men, she reminded herself firmly, were snakes, and Lee—gambler, womanizer—was one of the worst kind. Everett had been horrible in his way, but Lee, with his easy charm, could snap a woman's heart like a twig.

Clenching her jaw against her softening heart, she looked out the window, determined to avoid his gaze. The carriage was climbing a steep hill, and between the buildings they passed she caught faraway glimpses of the ocean shining silver and black in the moonlight. The ocean, and then as they turned left, a street sign lit by gaslight. Taylor Street.

*Taylor Street?* "Good gracious, Lee, this is Nob Hill!"

He glanced outside. "It is. Is that a problem?"

Her heart lurched into a fast, breath-stealing beat. "A problem? This is where the Floods live, and the Crockers!"

"It is. I suspect we'll see them tonight, although with any luck we'll avoid conversation."

"But . . . but these are your *friends?*"

He frowned "Where did you think I was taking you?"

"I thought your friends were gamblers. Professional gamblers."

"Professional gamblers don't throw balls."

"But . . . but . . ." she stuttered as the implications exploded in her mind in flashes of yellow light. "Lee, you can't bring me to a society party! I'm an actress, for the love of Pete!"

He shrugged. "So was Jenny Lind."

"I am *not* Jenny Lind. And I sincerely doubt Mrs. Hathaway wants an unknown actress at her ball!"

Even in the dark, she couldn't mistake the gleam of amusement in his eyes. "I'm sure she doesn't. That's part of what makes it so deliciously inviting."

"Oh, thank you so kindly, sir, for making me the object of your joke!"

He laughed and leaned forward to squeeze her hand. "Fear not, Cinderella, no one will recognize you without your makeup."

The cab slowed. Jess looked out the window as they stopped in front of a white mansion with thick Greek pillars and a tall wrought-iron fence. Light poured out of every window, and the sound of music drifted toward them.

"Just who," she asked breathlessly, as the coach came to a halt, "is Mr. Hathaway?"

"A childhood friend of mine. From Boston."

"Then what's he doing in San Francisco?"

"His father bought a bank and sent Michael to manage it."

"Bought-bought . . ." she stuttered, as the driver opened the door. He pulled down the steps and Lee, after giving her a quick pat on the thigh, descended. He turned, offering his hand, and she peeked her head out the door.

"Bought a *bank?*" she asked. The butterflies in her stomach curled into a hard, tight ball and died.

"A bank," he said, helping her down. When the ground greeted her feet, she raised her head to look into his eyes, glinting in the light pouring from the windows.

"How would you know a man who owns a bank?" she asked, although she really didn't want an answer.

Flashing his bone-melting smile, he took her other hand, too, effectively sandwiching them between his large, capable hands. "My father sold Hathaway the bank."

The doors of the house opened. A butler, joined by several crimson-liveried footmen, waited to greet them. Taking her elbow, Lee partially led, partially dragged, Jess up the steps.

"Your father sold it to him?"

"Yes. My father owns several of them."

Wealth, oh God, wealth beyond comprehension.

"Montgomery," she said. "From Montgomery Street?"

Lee chuckled and gave her elbow a reassuring squeeze as they entered the house. "No relation at all."

As the footmen attended their outer clothing, Jess surveyed her surroundings, reminding herself to breathe, for the hall alone was larger than all three rooms she and Michelle shared. Two stories high, it was paneled in gleaming oak with an enormous oak staircase carpeted in crimson sweeping upward and parting at the first landing, where it formed a double staircase. Above them a monstrous gold chandelier held back the night trying to enter through three enormous half-moon windows. And everywhere there was black-veined marble: marble stat-

ues, marble floor, marble pillars flanking the stairway. Jess's
heart raced as Lee took her arm and they followed a footman
along a two-story high corridor hung with life-size portraits.

"Don't worry, sweetheart," Lee whispered in her ear. "They
don't bite. At least, I don't *think* they do." The music grew
louder with each step. Then the footman bowed and swept his
arm toward a huge room with two sets of open double doors.
They entered, stopping just inside.

Gold. Lord almighty, everywhere *gold*—enormous, sparkling
chandeliers, paneling, wainscoting, everything covered in gold
leaf. The floor-to-ceiling windows, hung with delicate lace,
were trimmed in gold. The marble fireplace and the huge mirror
over it, trimmed in gold. Even the sky-and-cloud-painted ceiling was all but lost in gold-squared trimming.

And flowers, hundreds, thousands of flowers. The scent
almost knocked her over. "Good gracious, Lee," Jess gasped.
"I didn't know the world contained that much gold leaf! Do
they own a hothouse, too?"

Lee, scanning the crowd, grimaced. "Awful, isn't it? It's
Bernadette's doing. Hathaway's a Yank; you'd never see this
sort of ostentation in Boston. I see we're late enough to have
successfully avoided the reception line and the Grande Marche,
which, believe me, is for the better," he said smugly. "Let us see
about finding you a seat while I locate—ah, there's Michael.
Ah hell, he's with Greenway and Eleanor."

Blinded by grandeur, Jess only then noticed the people,
some dancing to the strains of an orchestra hidden behind a
row of palms, some sitting on cream silk settees and chairs,
while still others stood talking in groups.

Then the names sank in. "Greenway?" Jess repeated, in yet
another shock to her reeling mind. Over and over again she
tried to swallow the lump in her throat, barely controlling the
urge to flee. "Ned Greenway?" Dear God, and Eleanor
Martin, the queen of San Francisco society. Jess had only read
about her in the society pages. Oh no, she would *not* meet her,

she'd rather sink through the gold-parquet floor, turn into a bird and fly through the heaven-painted ceiling. To be anywhere but here, completely, entirely out of her realm.

Across the room Michael Hathaway spotted them. After reaching into a gold-edged white box, he withdrew a slim gold square and crossed the room. "Montgomery," he exclaimed, shaking Lee's hand. "Good to see you again! And Miss Sullivan," he said bowing. "It's an honor to renew our acquaintance. Your dance card, ma'am." He handed her a gold-leaf book with a tiny pencil attached by an ivory silk cord. She took it, using her best acting skills to appear perfectly at ease. Mr. Hathaway continued. "Lee, there are a number of people here who wish to talk to you."

Rubbing his neck, Lee grimaced. "Damn it, Michael, I came late hoping to avoid all that."

Hathaway laughed. "You'd have to arrive dead for that to happen. Come, we'll make it as painless as possible."

"Confound it, McAllister's here, too," Lee hissed, as he took Jess's arm to lead her across the floor. "Thought he was visiting his brother in New York. If he talks to Port there'll be the devil to pay. You'd better steer me clear of him, Hathaway, or it'll be pistols at dawn between you and me!"

Mr. Hathaway chuckled again. "Sorry, old boy, he's seen you."

A few breath-stealing moments later, Jess stood in frozen silence as Lee very prettily introduced her to *the* Eleanor Martin. Following that came introductions to Ned Greenway and the Crockers and the Floods. The next half hour passed in a blur as Jess attempted small talk with people of mind-numbing wealth, many of whom treated Lee to lectures about his negligence in attending social functions. Through it all he displayed a truly astonishing amount of charm. Even the oldest and hardest of women bloomed under his dimpled smile and silver tongue, their lectures skillfully averted with sincere apologies and well-targeted compliments.

Finally, Lee excused himself and led Jess to the dance floor. With his arm around her waist and enough distance between them for respectability, he whirled her around the room to a waltz. When her feet, from lack of practice, faltered, he merely smiled and told her that she was doing just fine. The music ended and Lee brought her to a chair, first steering her away from Mr. McAllister, who seemed intent upon conversation.

"So," he said in a conspiratorial tone, "did you get a good look at Eleanor Martin's brooch?" He shuddered in revulsion. "A beetle for the love of God!"

Jess bit back a laugh. "But *ever* so expensive."

"It doesn't matter. No amount of diamonds and rubies can make a beetle attractive. I shall never comprehend why some women insist upon wearing bugs on their clothes."

"It's the fashion."

"I've never seen you wear one."

Heat rushed to her face. "You've never seen me wear *any* precious gems."

Compassion flickered in his eyes, and he touched her hand briefly. "As it should be. You'd take the shine all out of them. Come," he continued in a rallying voice, "it's time to dance again."

Two quadrilles and another waltz later he led her to a seat where, exhausted and perspiring, she fanned herself. When he made a sly comment about another woman's huge dragon-fly broach flying away with her, Jess hid her laughter behind her fan. A devilish smile lit his face. "Better not do that. The fan across the lips means 'kiss me.' Not that I wouldn't love to oblige you, but this is hardly the place."

"Oh," she exclaimed, and let her fan drop to her side.

"Ah, the dance master is returning to the floor. If you'll lend me your arm?"

Breathless—from dancing, she told herself firmly, not from the idea of kissing Lee—she shook her head. "*Another* dance? No!"

"Should you consult your card, you'll see that you've already promised it to me."

"My card," she said, glancing down at the little book hanging from her left wrist. She'd completely forgotten about it. "But I never wrote anything in it." She lifted her hand and twirled the little book to untangle it.

"I did, while Del Huntington flirted with you, who, by the way, is married—at least occasionally—and a scandal in the making."

"Occasionally?" she questioned, as she finally pulled the card off her wrist and opened it. A list of dances and composers were printed down the left side of the book. On the right, written next to every dance in careful masculine script, was *Leland Montgomery*. "Lee," she said, shocked mirth shaking her voice, "you've claimed *every* dance."

"Have I?" he asked, laughter rumbling through his words as he leaned forward to read it upside down. "What a fortunate man I am."

"Fortunate! It's scandalous, even *I* know that! I am very sure that Mrs. Hathaway invited you expecting you to dance with many different girls."

"Bernadette didn't invite me. Michael did, and he knows full well that I'm only here because of you. Come, the orchestra is striking up," he said, taking her elbow.

"But—"

"Jess, if you keep complaining, I shall never invite you to another ball."

"At this rate *you'll* never be invited!"

"Then we had better enjoy this one, hadn't we?"

Shaking her head, she laughed and decided to stop trying to appeal to his better self. Probably, she thought as they whirled around the floor, Lee didn't have a better self. Two dances later Jess declared that she could not take another step. Tucking her arm in his, Lee led her to the "tea room" where he procured two glasses of champagne and settled her in a chair in a quiet corner. She sipped the champagne and surveyed the room and its occupants, somberly dressed men and gaily dressed women, chatting and flirting against a background of breathtaking opulence. Gold and ivory, crystal and marble; she could hardly believe someone *lived* here.

"Frightful, aren't they?"

She looked up. One shoulder propped against a wall, Lee was staring down at her, oblivious, apparently, to breathtaking opulence. His expression was serious for once.

"Are they all your father's friends?"

"Connections mostly, some family friends. A few, like Hathaway and Huntington, are mine."

"They seem to miss you."

"I don't miss them."

"That's a little selfish, isn't it?"

He shrugged. "A little. It would have been worse if I'd stayed. This," he said, waving his glass to encompass the whole house, filled to the brim with the cream of San Franciscan society, "made me a little mad."

"I thought you left home due to boredom."

His laugh was cold and mirthless. "Mad with boredom. It was"—he narrowed his eyes as if searching for the right words—"too confining. Too flat. I thought there had to be something more to life, something better. So I left."

She tilted her head slightly. "And have you found it? The something better?"

His lips twisted into a wry grin. "Every few months. It doesn't stick."

She sipped her drink and turned to watch the crowd a moment. "I suppose in some ways we aren't all that different."

"How so?"

"Life in small towns can be remarkably dull. I never minded until I met Everett. With his constant flow of new ideas, new thrills, he seemed the embodiment of excitement and romance. When he asked me to elope, I agreed, off in search of a better life. A more exciting life, I guess. He promised so many things." She sighed. "The thrill's worn off, though. And now," she said, her heart twisting at the thought of her parents' cold graves, "now I wish I could just go home."

His expression softened. "You've been dealt some bad hands, Jess, that's all."

"Lee, my whole life is a bad hand."

"Surely not your *whole* life," he said, spreading his hands in false supplication. "Think of all the hours you've spent in my sterling company."

"Oh, yes, and of course that makes up for everything!"

"It does, indeed! And now," he said taking her arm, "more dancing. I've brought you to enjoy yourself, Cinderella, and you shan't sit in the corner pondering the ashes of your life. And I promise you, the next time you ante-up, it'll be aces high."

"Aces high?" she asked, as he led her back to the ballroom. "That wouldn't be the ace of spades would it?"

He squeezed her elbow gently. "Nothing less than the ace of hearts for my Jess." With those words to warm her, Jess was once more whirling around the floor, laughing at Lee's steady stream of wit, while ignoring the scandalized frowns following them around the room. When the dance master announced that supper would follow the next dance, Lee took her elbow and led her off the dance floor.

"We'll get our supper, now, before the rush," he said. They went to yet *another* room, which was already beginning to fill with hungry dancers. At the head of the room and down one side were several long tables spread with tablecloths and laden with crystal, china, silver—and food. Jess's eyes widened in disbelief as Lee escorted her to the end of the line forming along the tables. "Anything?" she asked, as Lee passed her a supper plate.

"Everything," he said firmly, and proceeded to load their two plates with everything from lobster patties to cold duck, from asparagus to peas, stuffings and souffles—and dessert.

Oh sumptuous, light-as-air cakes and tarts, chocolate pastries, frosted fruit. When Jess lifted her eyes to glance at the other guests, they stared back, seemingly appalled at her and Lee's gluttony. With a gleeful twitching of her lips, she added a few more frosted grapes.

Lee motioned to a free table in a far corner. "Over there. Here, wait a minute," he said, motioning to a passing waiter loaded down with a tray of champagne. "We'll need a couple of these. Take one, sweetheart, I can't carry it all." A few moments later he laid down his burden and pulled out a chair for Jess. "Now, where shall we start? The duck? Or the lobster patties?"

Jess picked up a fork. "With dessert," she answered resolutely.

"Why, of course," he said, chuckling. "How could I be so dense?"

For the next half hour, they ate, drank, and laughed as they fought over the best of the food. Presently, Lee pushed his plate away and fell silent, sipping his champagne and watching her. As the silence lengthened, she became increasingly uneasy. Finally, she lifted her head to look him square in the eye. "What?

He lifted a brow. "I didn't say anything."

"You're staring at me."

"You're quite lovely."

Her heart flipped. Stupid heart. Why should it matter what Lee thought about her appearance? She'd long since become impervious to compliments on her beauty, hadn't she?

"It's not my doing," she blurted out.

He raised both his eyebrows. "Pardon me?"

An embarrassed flush warmed her face, but she continued anyway, determined to destroy his flattery and its unsettling reaction. "Men compliment women on their looks as if it's an accomplishment. I suppose it takes *some* work, but for the most part it's a twist of nature."

He tilted his head in interest, laughter sparkling in his eyes. "What an edifying thought. Please, do go on."

"Well, I didn't wake up one morning and decide I was going to be beautiful, then proceed to carve my face into agreeable lines. This is what God gave me. I had no hand in it. I didn't do anything extraordinary. What is there to compliment? Personally, I'd much rather hear praise for something I *have* worked at, like a particularly well-done performance."

"Ah. Of course," he said, leaning forward on crossed arms. Amusement marbled his voice. "Jess, sweetheart, allow me to compliment you on your capital portrayal of the twice-married mother of an insane son. You play matronly so well, I'm quite sure that you'll be marvelously realistic as, say, one of the hags from *Macbeth*, for which your—what did you call it? agreeable lines—will most certainly be useless. No doubt you'll find that immensely pleasing."

His amusement was infectious, and she laughed. "Certainly. I look forward to being scarred and one-eyed."

"You would. Did it ever occur to you that a man might compliment a woman's beauty for another reason?"

"Ha! You mean in order to extract a favor? Believe me, Lee, I have *intimate* knowledge of that manner of coercion."

The amusement on his face froze, and some dark emotion flashed through his eyes. "Everett again?"

With a little wince, she nodded. "I told you that he's never far from my thoughts."

"You did, Jess," he said, laying his hand over hers. Its heat flowed in soft waves down her arm. "Sometimes a man compliments a woman's beauty to let her know that he finds her extraordinarily attractive." His eyes held hers for several seconds, as the butterflies, alive once more, took flight in her belly again, their gossamer-thin wings tickling her heart. So much for destroying his flattery and its unsettling effect.

"And now," he said, giving her hand a quick squeeze before

he rose, "if you're done, it is time I bring you home, Cinderella. We have a train to catch this morning."

She rose and pulled on her gloves with trembling hands. "Why, I suppose that it *would* be best to leave before our carriage turns into a pumpkin."

"We certainly wouldn't want that to happen," he said, taking her arm to lead her from the room.

"And you," she said, on a hiccup of laughter, "turn back into a rat."

"A rat? I'm the footman then?"

"You are definitely the footman."

"Blast," he said with a rueful shake of his head. "And here I was hoping to play the prince."

# Chapter Ten

On the ride home, Jess sat next to Lee and easily accepted his arm draped around her shoulders. Would she, he thought with a slight clenching of his jaw, accept a more intimate embrace? Feeling like a blasted schoolboy dreaming of lost virginity, he tightened his arm and pulled her against him. She allowed that, too, with a little sigh that fluttered from his heart, to his stomach and down below. Damn, damn. She laid her head against his chest, and he took several quick shaky breaths. She had a light-sweet fragrance, which he couldn't place for the life of him. He spent the remaining minutes of the ride trying to remember where he'd smelled it before. Far better to concentrate on that than the wonderfully sensuous feeling of her soft body leaning against his, her breast pressed oh so sweetly in his side.

Still, for all the torment of holding her, when the carriage came to a stop he was reluctant to release her. It took him a few seconds to summon the strength to unwrap his arm, jump down, and lift his hand to help her out. She smiled up at him, an oddly, and damn it all, provocative, shyness in her eyes. "Now *this,* Lee, truly was a wonderful evening. Thank you so much."

His heart took a dangerous trip. She spoke as if he'd taken her for a ride to the moon instead of to an insipid high-society ball packed full of shallow-witted females and obnoxious men. And yet, he thought, staring into those soft blue eyes, he'd enjoyed himself. Jess's swift mind, that touchingly wistful quality and her strong sense of humor had all but shredded the monotony, adding a freshness to a generally stale affair. He'd seen it all with new eyes, and even if it didn't appear any better to him, it had been different.

"You're welcome. But I'm not leaving you here. Would Cinderella's prince abandon her on the street?"

A twitching of those perfect red lips. "As I recall, he abandoned her in his castle."

He laughed, took her hand and led her through the door and up the stairs, saying, "I'll walk you to your door at any rate. And, for the record, Cinderella abandoned the prince, leaving behind that idiotic glass slipper, which always annoyed me. Just exactly how do you make a glass slipper, why would you wear it, and what do you do if it breaks? I think it'd be damned uncomfortable."

"It sounds quite grand to me."

"Glass is inflexible. It'd give you blisters after one dance. And if the prince was a poor dancer, he'd step on your toes, crush the glass, and cut the hell out of your foot, thus rendering the stroke-of-midnight scene pointless. You can't run down steps with glass stuck in your foot," he finished, stopping outside her door.

"You're not very romantic, are you, Lee?" Jess asked as she reached for the knob.

Without thinking, he covered her hand with his. Her soft-sweet fragrance drifted off her hair and with an excited leap of his heart, he said, "Not yet."

She glanced up, a puzzle between her brows. Her eyes—damn—her eyes glowed in the light from the hall lamp.

He lowered his voice as his blood warmed. "I'm *very* romantic. In fact I'm quite attached to the part," he said, taking her arm and gently turning her to him, "where the prince kisses Cinderella."

"Kiss? But I don't recall . . ." she hesitated, her throat working, then continued in a light, thready tone, "I thought you were the footman."

"No, sweetheart. I am the prince. I am most decidedly the prince." Her eyes widened—and darkened. "And I *am* going to kiss you."

In response, her eyelids drooped slightly and, her heart battering his chest, he leaned over and touched her lips. Exercising all the restraint he could muster, he moved his mouth slowly over hers, letting her become used to the feel of him. He felt her muscles relax, and he brushed her lips with his tongue, requesting entrance. When she granted it, he slid inside to sweep her mouth, touching, exploring, savoring the taste of sugar-sweetened champagne. Finally, when his restraint started slipping, he lifted his head.

Her cheeks were flushed pink and her eyes were glowing with soft desire. Drawing a deep breath, he whispered, "And so? How do you like your prince's kiss?"

"I loved it."

"That much?"

Her breaths were shallow and shaky, as if she was having difficulty controlling them. And then her tongue flicked out to moisten her lips, sending fissures through Lee's restraint. Reaching up, he held her head and lowered his mouth once more, delving inside for another taste. This time he allowed his tongue to brush against hers. When she didn't object, he did it again, firmer, slower, savoring her velvety texture. Remarkably, she lifted hers in response. Blood humming in his ears, he touched it again and again, stroking, caressing. Her response grew bolder, matching stroke for stroke, caress for caress.

His restraint shattered.

His blood heated, flashed through his body and pulled tight in his groin. Pressing his mouth to hers, he stroked her harder, rougher, then drew her tongue inside his mouth to suck it, drawing every last bit of taste out of it. Then plunged in again, invading now, tasting, licking. Then he suckled her once more, drinking deeply of sweetened champagne. And the more he kissed her, the harder he grew. Wildly frustrated, he tried to fill the need by taking everything from a kiss, doing with his lips and tongue what he couldn't do with the rest of his body. His arms tightened around her until even through the blood pounding in his ears, he heard her moaning.

Or groaning. Frightened. Christ, what was he doing?

He jerked his head up. What in Christ was he doing? This was not a gentle reminder to Jess of what she was missing. It was a savage rape of a kiss.

She stared up at him, her lips a bruised red, her face flushed rose, her eyes wide in dismay. She was breathing heavily, and even through the din in his mind he could feel her trembling in his arms, which had wrapped themselves around her in a tight grip. Abruptly he let her go. She almost fell, and he had to reach out to steady her.

"Jess—" he started.

"You . . . you kiss . . . very intensely, don't you?"

He clenched his jaw and said in a rasping tone, "I'm sorry. It was unkind."

She smiled shyly, tentatively. "Unkind? Harsh, maybe. But I liked it."

He froze. "Did you?"

"Mercy, Lee, you can make a girl's toes curl."

"Jess," he said, trying to control himself as his trousers became tighter, "that was the least intelligent thing I've ever heard you utter."

She swallowed. "Why?"

He stared hard at her and shook his head. "Forget it."

"I told you I like kissing."

"It seems quite true." She continued to stare at him, her mouth open, and he couldn't for the life of him resist one more kiss. This one soft, gentle, a mere sweeping of his tongue because much more and he'd lose his mind.

"Now," he said. "Off you go. I shall see you tomorrow at the train depot."

She nodded, stepped inside and closed the door. When she was gone, he leaned his head against the wall, attempting to rein in his rampaging lust. Every cell in his body cried out for release, a release Jess swore she could not give him. Damn, damn!

He shoved away from the wall, spun on his heel and took the stairs two at a time. A woman. He needed a woman, tonight, now, or in a few seconds he'd be banging the blasted door down to beg on hands and knees for Jess to give him just five minutes use of her lovely, frigid body.


The acrid smell of coal smoke and steam filled the air as Jess and Michelle stood on the platform, turning this way and that in an attempt to find Lee's tall figure among the rapidly dwindling throng. Damn him, Jess thought frantically. A typical man! The train was due to depart in a few minutes, and by the look of things this one was actually going to leave on time. Damn the railroad, too.

"There! Oh, there he is, Jess," Michelle squeaked and waved her white-gloved hand. As usual Michelle was dressed to perfection, if not a little ostentatiously, in pink velvet. A girl never knew, Jess thought with a touch of cynical amusement, when Wealth in search of Beauty would sit next to her. Jess couldn't wait to see Lee's reaction. Her heart took an abrupt turn as she peered in the direction of Michelle's wave. Then, as she too spotted Lee, it began beating much too fast. He made his way swiftly toward them, and with each long stride she eagerly scanned his face, recalling exactly how it had looked last night—while dancing, in the carriage, before and after he'd kissed her. Goodness, such kisses . . .

In another few strides he stood in front of them, ticket in hand.

"Lee, *mon ami!* You are almost late."

Lee's eyes flickered over Michelle briefly, then fell again on Jess. They were darker than usual, lacking the sparkle of merriment she'd come to expect—and adore.

"I'm sorry, Michelle. Jess, sweetheart, I came to say good-bye."

Her heart shuddered to a stop. "Good-good-bye?"

"I can't make this train. I'll catch one tomorrow and meet you in Denver."

"What? Lee, what are you talking about?" Michelle cried.

Ignoring her, Lee continued to focus on Jess, whose heart had started up again, in hard, irregular beats. And then—while she tried to convince herself that she didn't really feel anything, not dismay or concern or fear—an unusual fragrance arose, mixing with Lee's soap and wood-smoke aroma.

"Listen, the tickets Robert bought are in the main compartment, the immigrant car. Quite uncomfortable, so I purchased these. First class, Pullman."

He held out two tickets as the smell registered in her brain. Perfume. Cheap perfume. The kind she'd smelled on Everett many, many times. Comprehension exploded inside her like shattering glass, scattering tiny shards of pain over her skin. Gasping, she stepped back.

The train's whistle blew, the conductor called "All Aboard," and Lee frowned in bewilderment. "Jess?"

"We don't want them."

Michelle stepped forward. "*Mais oui*. Of course we want them," she said taking the tickets.

Barely breathing, Jess shook her head. "I don't. You can't buy me, Lee."

"Buy you?" he growled. "What the hell does that mean?"

He'd gone to another woman. When? This morning? Last

night? Did it matter? It shouldn't matter. It shouldn't matter at all.

"I do not understand, *mon ami,* why will you not join us?"

"A game, *chérie,* on the next train," he said, flashing his eyes at Michelle a moment. "High stakes poker. Jess, are you going to answer me?"

"Ha! It is always cards!" Michelle exclaimed disgustedly.

"I meant I'm not for sale," Jess said, stepping back, away from him, away from the mixture of the past and the present, cheapened by perfume. "I'll buy my own tickets—"

"Robert bought those!"

"And my own clothes and my own meals. I don't need you."

Jaw clenching, Lee took a breath and stepped toward her. "I know that. Christ, Jess, don't you think I know that? I'm merely trying to make it a little easier for you." He held out a hand in supplication.

"You're not." She stepped backward.

He dropped his hand as his face creased in anger. "No. Goddamn it!" He shook his head. "I can't believe we're having this conversation. What the hell's come over you?"

She was shaking, holding back sobs of pain while alternately summoning up the ragged remains of her dignity. "Sanity," she said, then whirled around and all but blinded by tears she lunged for the train stairs. A few short steps and she was handing the conductor her ticket.

Behind her, Lee called out. She heard the sharp, fast clip of his boots as he gave chase. The conductor wished her a comfortable trip and handed her the ticket back. She climbed into the car as the conductor asked Lee, "Have a ticket, sir?" The last thing she heard from Lee before she lost herself in the throng of passengers, was, "No, you goddamned sonuvabitch! I don't!"

# Chapter Eleven

Why? Jess thought, leaning her head against the window, oblivious to the beauty passing by as the train climbed through the Sierra Nevadas. Why did women cry, but not men? Could they check their tears, or did they just not feel them? If that were true, she wished she were a man. Men had so many things women didn't. Money, opportunities, strong stomachs. When men hurt, they drank. She couldn't drown her sorrows. If she did, she'd drown every bucket on the train.

Oh, God!

Finally, in spite of her best efforts to control them, tears spilled down her cheeks. She turned to look out the window, bound and determined that no one see her cry. Certainly not Jon, seated next to her like a small, thin watchdog with a handlebar mustache. *Leave this woman alone. She is not interested in male attention. Oh, Jon,* she thought in despair, *don't you know men aren't interested in* me?

Certainly not Everett. Not Lee, either. Obviously she wasn't enough for either of them. She'd fallen in love for the second time in her life, and again her reckless heart had chosen a cad, a scoundrel, a philanderer.

"Jess? Are you all right?" Jon asked.

"I'm fine," she sniffled.

"You don't sound fine."

"I have a cold."

A cold that infused her entire frostbitten body. Of course Lee didn't want her! Of course he fled to the arms of another woman! How could she blame him? What did she expect?

Nothing. She expected nothing, except for him to give back the heart he'd stolen. Why, oh why, would he do such a thing? Why hadn't he just *let her be?* In spite of her best efforts, a little sob escaped her mouth.

"Jess?"

She pressed her forehead against the window and tried to hold back the mounting sobs. But she kept seeing him in her mind, his eyes, his mouth, his long fingers, tall wide body . . .

A few more sobs broke free, strung together.

"That's it. The train's pulling in for dinner. I'm finding Michelle."

Ignoring him, she ground her teeth. By the time the train stopped a few minutes later, misery had sunk so deeply into her bones, they actually ached. As the passengers rose, Jess wrapped her arms around her stomach. She imagined the sound of Lee's deep-timbered laughter combined with that of a faceless woman, effectively drowning out the din of her fellow passengers pushing and shoving to get off the train. More sobs racked her body until she finally surrendered to a flood of suffering. He'd left her, he'd left her, he'd left her . . .

"Jess? Jess, honey, what is it?" Michelle asked from behind her.

She refused to answer, for she hated Michelle as much as she hated Everett and Lee; Michelle was the kind of woman they went to when Jess's body betrayed her.

"Oh, honey," Michelle breathed, sitting next to her. She turned in her seat to take Jess into her arms, enveloping her in waves of French perfume and velvet. Hate or not, it felt good to Jess's battered heart. She sunk into her friend's embrace and yielded to a bout of self-pity.

"Ma'am," the porter interrupted them, "I need ta sweep there."

"Oh, do go away," Michelle snapped. "Can't you see we're busy?"

Steps and then silence again. Presently, Jess sat up and, with a weak, watery smile, took Michelle's proffered handkerchief. It, too, smelled of perfume, but Jess realized it lacked the staleness she'd smelled on Lee and Everett.

"There, now. Are you feeling better?"

Jess nodded a little. Her heart still hurt like hell, but at least it had stopped exploding.

"Good. Now what is this all about? It's Lee, right? Honey, he'll be along in Denver just like he said."

With a little hiccup, Jess replied, "I don't care. I don't ever care to see him again."

Michelle frowned and shook her gold curls. "I don't understand. Does this have something to do with the ball? From what you told me this morning, you had a grand time! You were so happy and excited! And now you're nothing but salt and water. Jess, it doesn't make sense, and what is more it's made your eyes all puffy."

Jess let out a shadow of a laugh. "Oh, Michelle, if that was all I cared about, I would be as cheerful as the day is long."

"Which is what I've been telling you for months. A shallow, vain heart, Jess, is so much easier to live with."

"And," Jess said, tears filling up her eyes, "I wish to Heaven that I possessed one."

"Oh, Jess, don't start crying again. You can have one! Just think shallowly!"

"Easier said than done!"

Michelle heaved a sigh, turned, reached into her purse and withdrew an etched silver flask. "Here, a little drink will help."

"What is it?"

"Sherry."

Nodding, Jess took a few gulps, while Michelle settled her

hands in her lap. "Now, Jess, I am shallow-hearted, so it will be difficult for me to understand, but I'm listening anyway."

"Oh, Michelle," she said, "it's madness. I think I've fallen in love with Lee."

Michelle's eyes widened in astonishment. "In love? But how could you? You're in love with that cad who I spit on!"

"Everett."

"The cad who I spit on! You can't love Lee!"

"Oh, but I do!"

"And the cad? You no longer love him?"

For months she had allowed Michelle to believe she still loved Everett. It made Michelle's unremitting desire to find Jess a new love easier to deal with. "He's my husband."

Which Michelle took as an affirmative for she had never heard the whole truth of Jess's marriage. Not her or anyone else, for it still hurt far too much to expose to the fleeting emotions of her fellow actors. "I think," Michelle said, cloaking herself in her motherly role, "you'd better shrink that heart, too. Two loves is one too many, honey."

"I think one love is one too many."

With a deep sigh, Michelle took the sherry back. "Now *I* need a drink." She took a few quick swallows. "I'm sorry, Jess. When I decided to throw you two together, I never thought that you'd fall in love with Lee. He's not really your type."

"My type? For the love of Pete, Michelle, he is exactly my type! Dissolute, intemperate, sensual! All my heart holds dearest!"

"Well, Lee *is* handsome. But you're thinking of the cad, too, and comparing them. I see no comparison. Everett is poor. Lee is rich."

"Good God, Michelle, do you think of nothing but money?"

"Often. I think of all the things I can buy with money."

The train whistle hooted and Jess sighed, leaning against the window. The passengers, having wolfed down a frantic fifteen-minute lunch, streamed back onto the car, frightened of being left behind. Jess reached for the sherry, which was going to her head rather quickly. "Michelle, did Lee ever take you to one of those parties?"

Michelle burst out laughing. "No! Me, at a society party? That's absurd."

"But you and he are so close—"

"Jess, I'm an actress. I don't belong at a party like that. I don't *want* to belong at a party like that. All those stuffy conservative people would made me mad."

"I'm an actress, too."

"You never had stage fever, Jess," Michelle said gently. "Acting is your job, it's not who you are."

She swallowed that, then continued. "Do you know much about him? Has he ever told you anything about his background?"

"No, why should he? Lee's past doesn't interest me."

With a shake of her head, Jess took another drink, while Michelle, eyes brightening said, "You know, Jess, I still have that ticket for your Pullman seat. It is far better than this. There's gas lighting and I expect the porter has already made up the beds. Come, it's cold in here and the sleeping arrangements are better." She frowned as she eyed two passengers bartering with a man selling boards for making beds out of the benches.

"No!" Jess snapped, suddenly angry again. "I will not take anything from him!"

"And you'll sleep with Jon instead? Or is there someone else in this compartment you'd like better?"

Jess flinched and surveyed her fellow passengers—cowboys with the range still stuck to their boots, a woman of questionable repute sipping from a flask, her eyes glazed over.

"No."

"Fine," Michelle said, grabbing her purse with one hand and Jess's wrist with another. "We'll use Lee's tickets and tell him that you slept in here, where you were cold, miserable, hungry, and were almost accosted by many horrible dirty men.

I don't know what he did to hurt you, but he'll feel guilty for sure and it serves him right for making *mon amie* cry, the cad."

They never made it to Denver. In Cheyenne, where they switched trains for the Denver and Rio Grand, Robert, for some inexplicable reason, decided that the whole troupe would take a three-day detour to the small town of Grant. At this pronouncement Michelle broke into hysterics, and it took all of Jess's patience to load her into a passenger car before Robert fired her. With gentle persuasion, Jess convinced Michelle that she could quit the troupe if she wanted, but she must wait until they arrived in Denver where she could find another job. Michelle, crying pathetically as the train lurched forward, declared that she *would* return to San Francisco. Jess didn't have the heart to point out that she didn't have a dime to her name.

Neither did Jess.

Robert swore up and down that he'd get her money to her—in Denver. The playhouse owner, apparently, had given him only half the profits and would telegraph the rest to Denver. Jess railed and threatened to no avail. Robert didn't have the money and a body couldn't squeeze blood from a stone.

Grant was small, dusty, dry, and, in Michelle's opinion, uninhabitable. The troupe took every room in one of two hotels, and a couple in the other. On the second night they performed in the saloon, where a makeshift stage was created by pushing the tables against the walls and setting the chairs up in rows. Robert gave his actors a set of three scenes from different plays, for this audience was definitely not ready for a complete rendition of *Hamlet*. The scenes he chose were of the warmer variety, and greeted with amusement, cheers, and clapping. At least, Jess reflected cheerfully, they refrained from throwing rotting vegetables.

As to why Robert decided to bring Shakespeare here of all places, rumor ran rampant among the nine actors and actresses.

Michelle stood by her claims of madness, but neither that nor any other rumor could be substantiated. Jess had her own suspicions. She thought she saw a familiar face in the audience. Although she'd been too angry in San Francisco to look closely, Jess could have sworn it was the girl from Robert's office. But, as Jess accompanied Michelle back to the hotel, she wondered what the woman would be doing here, in Grant. It seemed unlikely that Robert would follow her, for he'd never shown the least tendency to monogamy before. It wasn't, she thought ruefully, a trait that sat well in her profession. They entered the hotel and she started up the stairs, just as a voice called out.

"Jess! Michelle!"

Lee's voice. Her blood ran cold. And then as she turned to see him crossing the small lobby, heat burned her nerves like frost-numbed appendages suddenly warmed in front of a blazing fire. She clamped her jaw shut.

"Lee!" Michelle cried out. She practically tripped as she ran down the few stairs to throw herself into his arms. With an agonizingly familiar chuckle, he dropped a kiss on Michelle's forehead. "*Chérie,* you'd think I hadn't seen you in weeks instead of days."

Jess stood paralyzed, torn between the longing to feel his arms wrapping around her and the need to run as fast she could to save her poor heart from further destruction. A sandpaper-rough sob rose in her throat.

Lifting his head, Lee gave her a large, full-faced smile, dimple and all. It froze on his face when their eyes met. A second, and then Jess fled up the stairs.

"Oh Lee, you have done it again! You have made *mon amie* cry!"

"Cry?" he snapped, staring at Jess's fleeing form. "What in hell is the matter with her?"

"That is for *you* to tell *me*. What have you done to her, you . . . you . . . you bully!" she cried and hit him in the chest with her small fist.

"Me!" Lee said, looking down at Michelle. Her face was bright pink, her bosom heaving with indignation. "What did I do?"

"You know very well what you did!"

"I didn't do anything." She continued to stare hard at him, tapping one delicate foot as if that would somehow draw a confession from him. "What? What!? I swear to you that I have no idea why she's upset. I didn't *do* anything!"

"You did. Jess is not like me. She is sensible. She does not run upstairs for no reason!"

"And what the hell did you mean by 'again'? When was she crying before?"

"On the train, for hours! And she would not come be comfortable with me, *non!* She stayed in that filthy compartment with those dirty cowboys! Miserable! Cold! Hungry! And it is all your fault."

Goddamn it, how'd it become his fault? What was his fault? He hadn't done anything! By God, he would never understand women, never.

"Fine. It's my fault. Now be a good *chérie* and go up there and retrieve her so I can apologize." And that'd be one hell of an apology, apologizing for making her cry over nothing. But, he thought with a tugging at his heart, he'd rather utter inane apologies than see her hurt.

"No. She does not want to see you, this she told me. Instead, you will take me to eat the pig-slop supper and tell me what you did."

"I want to see her. I want to see her *now*."

"It is too bad. She does not want to see you."

Clenching his teeth, Lee considered pounding up the stairs and tearing the door off its hinges. But, as much as that would cure his frustration, it wasn't apt to help the situation. "Ah hell," he muttered and rubbed his neck. Perhaps she needed time to herself. For reasons unknown to man, women sometimes wound themselves up over nothing, and often, given time, they managed to unwind themselves. "All right, I'll take you to supper. Pig slop you say? Sounds appetizing. Would you mind explaining to me what in hell you're doing here in the first place? I was a stone's throw from buying a ticket to Denver when I heard someone mention a troupe traveling to Grant. What the hell is Madison thinking? I'm ready to wring his neck."

"*Oui,* the neck wringing. This I understand. Jess, too, is for the wringing of Robert's neck. I am fortunate to have friends who would do such violence for me."

Lee laughed. "All manner of violence, Michelle, especially where the infamous Robert is concerned."

Hugging her knees to her chest, Jess sat on the bed that she and Michelle were sharing. It was shoved against a wall in a generally barren room, which Michelle had declared too decrepit to house *un cher*. Lit by a single lamp, the room closed comfortingly around Jess as she laid her tired head upon her knees and flipped a page in her book. Her eyes stung from crying but the stabbing in her chest had eased enough to allow concentration on Othello and his murderous jealousy. Oh, but that Iago was a devil!

A knock echoed through the room. Jess lifted her head. "Yes?" she called out. Her heart pleaded for Lee to answer, her brain for anyone but.

"It's Jon."

Her eyes burned, her heart sank. But, her brain firmly told her heart as she rose to open the door, it ought to be grateful. The more distance between it and the man who was determined to break it, the better.

Jon held a tray in his hand, loaded down with a plate covered by a napkin. With a little flourish, he flipped the napkin off. "Voilá! Supper is served."

"Is it really?" Jess asked, surveying it warily. Some kind of meat sat on the plate, covered with a gelatinous glob, which pretended to be gravy.

Jon grinned. "Best I could do, Jess. Michelle said you refused to come eat with us."

Lifting her eyebrows, she asked, "Can you blame me?"

Grinning, he strode into the room and laid the plate on the bedside table. "It's not so bad. We're leaving tomorrow and who knows what other pleasures the road holds for us."

"Tortures more like. Thanks all the same, Jon." She closed the door, sat on the bed and pulled the table over. For a moment she stared at her plate, then took up a fork, and gingerly moved the food around. "What do you think it is?"

"Some kind of beef thing," he said, taking the only chair in the room, a rickety piece of furniture that creaked under Jon's light frame. "Or sheep thing. Michelle called it pig slop."

"Michelle is not fond of anything Western," she said, smiling as she sliced the meat.

"She liked San Francisco well enough."

"She seems to have her directions mixed up a bit."

"Sometimes," Jon said acerbically, "I think she has her countries mixed up."

Jess smiled, took a bite, chewed, and then said surprised, "You're right. It's not so bad if you forget what you're eating, which," she said as she cut more of the mystery meat, "isn't very difficult, considering I still don't know what it is."

"Yeah, I didn't think it was so bad. That Montgomery fella agreed."

Flinching, Jess nodded and continued to eat.

After a few minutes, Jon broke the silence. "It's him, isn't it, Jess? He's the reason you've been so upset these last few days."

She sucked in her breath. Mercy, but she definitely didn't want to talk about *that*. "I'm still angry about the money Robert owes me."

"Yeah, I heard about that, too."

"He says he'll pay me in Denver. He claims that the playhouse owner from San Francisco will have it waiting for him in a bank there."

"Yeah," Jon said, the chair creaking as he shifted his weight. He glanced out the window, rose to turn up the flame on the lamp, then leaned against the wall, watching Jess with a pained expression on his face.

Sighing, she shoved the meal aside. "Okay, Jon, what is it?"

Grimacing, he dragged the chair next to the bed and sat in it, leaning forward earnestly. His brow wrinkled with concern. "Listen, Jess, I thought maybe I oughtn't to tell you. It's none of my funeral, really. But the point is . . . damn it, Jess, it's just not right."

She frowned. "What's not right?"

"Last night after we settled in, I went to the saloon for a touch of whiskey." He shuddered as if the memory was bad and continued. "I stayed late. There was a—well, I stayed late and I, uh, kinda went out the back door."

"The back door?"

"Yeah. See, Miranda came looking for me through the front door."

"Miranda? Why—"

"That's not important. What *is* important is that I went by this room on the right, in the back. The door was open a bit and when I chanced to looked inside, I saw a group of men sitting around a table playing cards."

Jess bit her lip. It had to be Lee. No doubt Lee was there and he hadn't . . .

He took a deep breath. "Robert was at the table."

Jess frowned. "Robert? Gambling? Jon, we all know he gambles."

"Yeah, but, Jess, there was a lot of money on that table. I mean a *lot* of money. And after what he told you, well, where did he get that money?"

A chill ran down her spine. "How . . . how much is a lot, Jon?"

"There were hundreds of dollars on that table, I'd swear to it."

# Chapter Twelve

Jess tried to sleep after Jon left, but she tossed and turned, her anger with Robert growing with each passing minute. It didn't help that Lee kept sneaking into her mind, and that he'd left with Michelle and that Michelle hadn't returned yet. Whenever Jess thought of them together, in Lee's hotel room, no doubt in bed enjoying the pleasures her cold body refused her, flashes of jealous rage burned her already charred nerves. She spent hours reasoning with her heart that it was acting illogically, that a night's sleep would clear her mind. In the morning, fully refreshed, she could face Robert with composure.

But when the clock struck twelve, Jess finally threw back her blankets and rose to light the lamp. Michelle hadn't returned, and her stomach sloshed with the kind of queasiness she'd experienced all those long nights that she'd waited for Everett's return.

She took to pacing.

It didn't work.

Her whole body ached: her neck, her shoulders, her heart. Finally, she could bear it no longer. She faced betrayal on all sides, from Michelle, to Robert, to Lee. In truth, she'd been facing betrayal for years and damn it all she was *not* going to stand for it any longer. For once she was going to make someone else pay.

Forgoing a bustle, she quickly dressed in her blue calico gown. She dragged a brown woolen shawl around her shoulders, then marched down the stairs, across the empty lobby, and out the door. With every step she felt better. Action, that's what she needed, action.

From the saloon across the street the sound of drunken revelry punctured the night air. Lee's laugh? She wouldn't think about that. She'd think about Robert, the weasel, and she hoped to God that he had that little tramp of his in bed with him. The more she embarrassed him, the happier she'd be. Revenge, damn it all. She was getting revenge.

As she approached the hotel lobby, a light scream cut through the night air. Good God, she thought disgustedly. Screaming, too? What kind of town was this, anyhow? San Francisco had its dens of inequity, but even they closed down sometime, didn't they?

The lobby lay empty and silent as she crossed it and climbed the steps. She walked down a long corridor to Robert's room, last door on the right. She didn't bother to knock since he hadn't bothered to ask before stealing her money. With a quick turn of the knob, she opened the door and stepped inside, her mouth open to yell bloody murder at him and that little slut.

Instead, her words emerged as a tiny guttural squeak. For Robert wasn't in bed. Robert was facedown on the floor, a pool of liquid rapidly curling around his body. The flickering yellow flame of a hurricane lamp turned the blood seeping from his neck a dark, nauseating brown.

Gasping, Jess fell to her knees next to him. "Robert! Robert! Oh, say something!" She slowly turned him over and let out another strangled cry. His white shirt was almost black from a deep, slashing wound running the width of his neck. Warm, sticky blood flowed freely, gurgling a little so that at first she thought he might still be alive. Frantically, futilely, she covered his neck with her hands. But his eyes were wide and lifeless and nothing would save him. He was dead.

"Well that's it for me, *chérie,*" Lee said, and gathered his winnings. "I'm ready to turn in. You keep playing if you want, though."

Michelle, sitting at the saloon table with three others of her troupe, looked up. After a night of playing penny-ante poker, her eyes still shone, very much awake. Rising, Lee stretched, then smothered a yawn as if exhausted. Truth be told, every muscle in his body was tight, and had been since seeing Jess. Neither the hours spent pacing his room searching for a reason for her behavior, nor the two hours of poker had eased it.

"Oh, must you, *ami?*" Michelle asked.

"I must. I'll see you in the morning, Michelle, gentlemen." He repressed the urge to bow, a habit from his Bostonian up-bringing. He'd learned early in his Western career that there were few ways more likely to get a man beat up than display-ing such manners.

Everyone exchanged pleasantries except for Horatio—Jon—who eyed him warily. Lee left, shrugging his shoulders to re-lieve the tension in them as his thoughts returned to Jess. What was it about that woman that constantly tied him up in knots?

He stepped off the boardwalk and strode across the street. He patted his empty vest pocket, absentmindedly searching for the cigar he smoked earlier.

"Lee . . ."

Lee stopped at the sound of his name, whispered from somewhere behind him. Frowning, he turned, searching for the source and spotted a figure standing next to the hotel. It took a moment to recognize Jess, who stood still, first regard-ing him, then her hands and then back again. Lee looked at her hands to see what she found so fascinating. Something black and oily drizzled off them. Something, he thought with a tightening of his throat, something that resembled blood.

He was in front of her in three long strides.

"Jess? Jess, sweetheart, what is that?" he asked, wrapping his fingers around her wrists to lift her hands toward the moon's light. "Did you hurt yourself?"

"It's blood. He's . . . he's dead, Lee, and now I have his blood on my hands."

"Dead?" Lee asked bringing her hands down once more. Fear coiled in his stomach like a rattler, ready to strike. "Who's dead?"

"Robert. I went to see him. Jon told me he was gambling my money away. I went to tell him . . . to tell him . . . and then, there he was. His neck—there's blood all over the floor. Dead. I felt his pulse. It wasn't there. That means he's dead."

Good God, Lee thought, and flashed his eyes around the deserted street. Grabbing her wrist, he pulled her into the building's shadow and attempted to read her eyes in the darkness. "Where? In his room? Did you come out the front door?"

"No, the back was nearer and I wanted to get out of there. I thought I'd go for help. Get a doctor. And then, I saw you. I thought you could help. But you can't, can you? Because he's dead and once you're dead, that's it. You can't be alive anymore."

"That's true." By God, but he could use a brandy. "Listen, perhaps you'd better take me to him. Up the back staircase, if you would, instead of the front door."

"But why?"

"Sweetheart, I don't think we want anyone to see you this way. Not with blood on your hands."

"There's no one in the lobby."

"All the same," he said, mounting the stairs, Jess trailing him. "I suspect you're in shock."

"Shock? Yes. Maybe. I do feel strange, as if I'm walking on air or going mad, like Lady Macbeth. 'Out damned spot.' I think I could do her right now. It'd be a first-rate performance."

Wispy tendrils of amusement floated through fear as Lee

started up the back stairs. "Certainly. And you have the blood on your hands, so there's one less prop you'd need."

"Yes. Convenient. And thrifty. Robert would appreciate that," she said, and then a sob escaped her. "But he's dead, Lee."

Damn, she was going to bawl. He reached the landing, waited for her to climb up beside him and then replied gently, "Jess, I need you to be strong right now, all right? Take a few deep breaths. That's right. Better?"

"He's still dead."

"You won't help him by weeping."

She drew in another breath, closed her eyes and nodded. "Okay, but promise you won't leave me alone with him? I'll . . . I'll cry later."

"Good." He opened the door and waved her in as he glanced around the street again. No one. Still, he had a bad feeling about this. Prickles rose on his neck as he closed the door behind them. His hand slipped on the knob. He looked down. Blood—from Jess's hand as she was leaving.

Clenching his jaw, he looked across the hall at a partially open door. Robert's room, no doubt. Throat tight, he strode purposefully forward, pushed through the door, and came to a stiff-legged halt.

Robert's head had all but been cut clean off his body. Blood had pooled around it and gleamed a rust brown in the dim light. Dead. Very dead.

Jess followed him and he reached out for her arm. She stopped. He felt her staring up at him as his fingers tightened, while his lungs battled for breath and every nerve cried out to run.

"Lee."

Closing his eyes, he allowed one huge shudder to run down his spine. He fought off the next one and taking a deep breath, turned to Jess. "You're right. He's dead."

"Yes." She stared down at the body, flinched a little, then

raised one shaking, blood-covered hand and pointed. "I think that's the knife," she said in an oddly hollow voice.

He followed her gaze. A long, thick knife lay next to the body. The blade was indeed covered in blood, the steel hilt speckled with the sticky stuff and shining evilly in the lamplight. Carefully stepping around the body, Lee leaned over it to retrieve it. The hilt was thick and woven with dragons. Lee had bought it in San Francisco for his father.

The sound of boots at the end of the hall broke through the rasping of his own labored breathing. One, no two pair, coming fast. Bloody *hell!*

"'Murder, most foul, as in the best it is,'" Jess abruptly quoted, her voice eerily soft in the dimly lit room. "'but this most foul, strange and unnatural.' Hamlet. Act one, scene five."

The footsteps were coming too fast for mere curiosity. The owners knew Robert was dead. The door burst open and a large, heavy man strode in, yelling, "What's going on here? Someone heard a scream."

Unnaturally composed, Jess surveyed Robert's partially severed head, then shook her own. "I don't think so."

The man's tin star glinted in the lamplight. A marshal. Or a sheriff. Law and order, Western style. Another man entered, passed his eyes over the scene and stumbled out. Seconds later came the sound of vomiting. And Lee could do nothing but stare at Jess, stone still, her face frozen with horror. In a cold, slowly-moving mist of unreality, he saw her as the marshal did—bloody hands, bloodstained dress.

Eyes narrowing, the marshal called to the man outside. "George, get in here. I need help."

His gaze flashed to Lee. "You there, what's your name?"

"Leland Montgomery."

He jerked his head toward Jess. "And her?"

"Jessica Sullivan."

The marshal drew his gun and trained it on Lee. "Well,

Montgomery, you're gonna come along with me. I'm arresting you for murder."

*This can't be happening,* Lee thought, closing his eyes. But when he opened them, the marshal was still there. "The gun's unnecessary," he said in a shaky voice. "I'm a peaceful man."

"Sure. Drop the knife, then."

Lee looked down at the cold steel gripped firmly in his hand. With a shudder, he let it fall to the floor. It hit the puddle of blood and made a ghastly splashing noise. The marshal backed up and motioned Lee out of the room. "George, I got this one. You take the lady there."

"We're arrestin' a woman?" George asked in wonder.

"You stupid sonuvabitch, didja take a look at that dress? She held him down while this one did the slicing."

# Chapter Thirteen

Jess rose reluctantly through the gray fog of sleep, a soft, luxurious way to avoid the complications just on the other side of consciousness. But in Deadwood she'd learned too well about the consequences of ignoring problems. She opened her eyes.

She lay on her side, facing a poorly plastered wall with peeling white paint. The mattress beneath her, thin, lumpy, and covered with a rough sheet, smelled faintly of urine. Her dress peeked under the edges of a scratchy gray blanket.

Her dress—she'd slept in her clothes.

Dark recollection swept away the last vestiges of sleep—memories of Robert's bloody, half-decapitated body and Lee's face, hard as granite, as they were handcuffed and led from the death room to the marshal's office. To jail. With a groan she sat up, ducking her head to avoid banging it on the sagging bunk overhead.

"Morning, Jess," Lee said in a ruthlessly level voice, as warm as a Nebraska blizzard. "Or is it afternoon?"

After rubbing her gritty eyes, she looked across the tiny cell to where he stood with his shoulder propped against a wall, staring out a tiny barred window. Normally so neat, he appeared worn and tired, his clothes hopelessly wrinkled, his face shadowed with a night's stubble. Grimacing, she continued to take in the cell: four plaster walls and one strong wooden door, with a small barred window in the center. A smoking potbelly stove was shoved into one corner. In front of it sat a tray of food and, in the opposite corner, a chipped blue bowl and earthenware chamber pot. Her bladder tightened in demand.

"You're rather quiet this morning," he said in that horrible desert-dry voice. "Cat got your tongue?"

"Could it be that I'm not accustomed to jail cells?"

He turned his head toward her. His face was sharply creased along now-unused smile lines, and the emotion in his eyes, more hazel than green, was unrecognizable. "I suggest you become so." He nodded to the tray. "There's your breakfast. Or you may call it dinner, since it appears we aren't getting anything else."

Her stomach grumbled at the mention of food. Shoving aside the blanket, she started to rise, but slammed back down on a wave of dizziness when several rusty brown blotches on her gown caught her attention.

Blood. Robert's blood. Swallowing nausea she looked at her hands, which had been sticky with Robert's blood last night. Clean now. She had a mist-shrouded memory of Lee washing them for her, sitting on the bunk next to her, as silent as a corpse.

Except Robert was the corpse. Dead, six years friend and mentor, swine though he'd been in the end. For a few minutes memory clogged her thoughts, of Robert kindly offering her a job, of years of encouragement and teaching as she learned how to play her parts. Tears blurred her vision, but then her eyes found the prison bars once more. No time for grief. Last night shock had masked the desperation of her situation; today she couldn't afford that luxury.

Steeling her backbone, she crossed the room and squatted next to the breakfast tray. It held two cups, one empty, one full of coffee so cold that it left a ring around the rim. Also, two plates, one empty, the other holding a kind of gelatinous glob and a biscuit. She took the biscuit and the coffee, leaving the glob to transform itself into its next horrible form. Breakfast in hand, she returned to the bunk. She drank the coffee in deep swallows to avoid the taste, between bites of the biscuit that, although hard around the edges, was soft and flaky in the middle. When finished, she laid the cup on the stone floor and warily eyed the chamber pot. "Lee," she said hesitantly, "I need to relieve myself."

"There's a chamber pot," he said, staring out the window.

"I'd rather not use it in front of you."

"Fine, I'll bust down the door and wait for you in the marshal's office."

"Sarcasm is not appreciated."

"Neither is priggishness."

She flinched at the ice in his voice. "Can't you call the marshal?"

"He left about an hour ago and has yet to return."

She sighed in frustration. "I can wait."

"You can try."

She held silent for a few minutes, until the pain in her lower extremities became unbearable. She admitted defeat. "I can't wait."

"I'm not lookin'."

She glanced at the pot. "But you'll hear it."

He turned finally, his eyebrows lifting as laughter sparked in his eyes. "Hear it?"

"The sound—it's embarrassing."

"And what precisely would you suggest I do? Clap my hands over my ears and hum a little tune?"

"Actually, I was hoping for the 'Star Spangled Banner.'"

"A little unpatriotic, isn't it?"

"But ever so long."

He chuckled finally, the deep warmth breaking the tension in their cold cell. "Go ahead and use the pot. I'll turn around and cover my ears."

He did and she took care of her needs, then called out. "I'm done."

Laughing, he dropping his hands and turned. "I know."

Her face warmed, but she couldn't resist his laughter. "I ought to have made you sing."

"Believe me, sweetheart, you're very glad you didn't."

She chuckled, then asked tentatively, "Would you care for some privacy, too?"

"Thank you, I wrangled a visit to the outhouse while you were sleeping. I would have woken you, but I thought you'd wish for a few more hours of peace."

Sighing, she returned to the bunk and wrinkled her nose. "Not the best of accommodations are they? Why do you suppose they put us both in the same cell? Not that I don't *adore* your company," she added tartly.

He flashed a forced grin. "As I do yours. Apparently, they have only the one cell. I suspect they didn't think we'd care, given our occupations. An actress and a gambler aren't precisely known for arrow-straight respectability." With a bitter bark of humor, he added, "Hell, we're murderers. What would we care about proprieties?"

"But they can't *really* believe that. For me to kill Robert, why, Lee, it's preposterous!"

"It's not only preposterous," he answered, rubbing his neck as he took three long strides to cross the cell, then slide into a sitting position in front of her, his back against the wall. His eyes flashed back and forth to the window. "It's impossible. A woman couldn't have wielded a knife strongly enough to make that cut. They don't believe you killed him. They think I did."

*"You?"* she asked, head spinning. "But he stole from me, not you."

"Which is where our relationship comes into play. Some might conjecture that, with a certain sort of . . . persuasion, I'd kill for you."

"But we're . . . we're only friends. Besides," she argued,

shaking her head, "you're rich, Lee. Wouldn't it be easier for you to just give me the money?"

A rueful smile creased his face as he raised an eyebrow. "Are you now saying you *will* let my buy you? Amazing what a night's stay in jail does to the will!"

"Don't be ridiculous!" she snapped. "I was discussing *their* thoughts, not my own!"

His face softened. "I'm teasing, Jess. I couldn't resist the opening."

"So you've told me before. Your resistance, Lee, is questionable."

The barest flash of desire flickered across his face. "I have some."

Jess's tired heart jerked, then settled in her throat as she recalled the smell of perfume on his clothes. "Little enough."

"But enough," he said. He lifted his eyes to the window and started to rub his arms as if cold. Sighing at the senselessness of men, Jess rose to close the shutters. When she touched them though, Lee burst out in a loud guttural voice, "No!"

Startled, she turned. Panic contorted his face, his breathing came in quick, hard gulps. Frowning, she dropped her hand. One more gulp and he rasped, "I don't care for small spaces."

"I thought you were cold," she said surprised.

"Not that cold. If you are, you may have my jacket."

"I'm fine," she said, sitting on the bunk and saying with a sigh, "I'm sorry I've dragged you into this, Lee, but, really, I can't believe we'll be here much longer."

His eyes mere slits, he leaned his head back and took several steadying breaths. "No," he said in a tortured voice, "they're going to hang us just as quickly as possible."

Lee watched Jess's eyes widen, but she retained her composure, sitting ramrod stiff with her hands neatly folded in her lap. "They can't. They have no evidence."

"The knife is mine. No doubt the murderer stole it while I was playing poker last night, expecting to implicate me."

"Playing poker? Last night?" she said, eyes lighting up. "But then you have an alibi."

Those walls seemed even nearer. Taking a deep breath, Lee trained his eyes on Jess. Her coolness eased his panic. "Not for the entire night. After supper I spent a couple of hours in my room trying to figure out why in hell you were so angry with me."

Her eyes flickered as dark wrenching anguish passed over her face. Why, damn it all! What had he done to cause that?

"That doesn't matter," she said shaking her head. "If the knife was stolen while you were playing poker, then Robert was killed"—she took a breath—"while you were playing poker. Your alibi holds."

"I can't prove that the knife was stolen after I left my room, nor do we know when Robert died. As far as a jury's concerned, I may have killed him before I went to the game and left the knife there by mistake." He gave a small laugh. "Not only am I a murderer, but stupid as well."

Jess frowned and lost herself in thought. Grimacing at her unusual seriousness, Lee stared out the window and wondered when in hell the marshal intended to restock the coal bin for the stove. If they didn't get some fuel soon, they'd have to close those shutters.

"Do you remember the girl who was with Robert when we went to get my money?" Jess finally spoke. "I saw her in the audience yesterday. I hear that she lives in Grant."

Lee rubbed his chin and grimaced at the stubble. "I'd seen her in San Francisco at a gaming table with Robert and her father, a man named Temple."

"Really? Then maybe," she said slowly, "he lost to Robert, owed him a large sum of money, and skipped town because he couldn't pay it. Robert came to Grant to collect it—Jon told me he seemed to have a lot of money suddenly—and Temple decided he wanted it back. A fight ensued and he killed Robert. There! We're free!"

"Possibly, but Robert was a notoriously poor gambler. His

nickname was Payroll." She winced and he added gently, "I'm sorry, Jess, I would have told you sooner but you'd already given Robert your money."

She rubbed her eyes. "I was a fool," she said, her voice rife with self-disgust.

"You trusted a friend."

She smiled ruefully despite the pain lurking in her eyes. "Then I'm a remarkably poor judge of character. I'm not certain that's better." She took a breath. "Is it possible that Temple killed Robert because he compromised his daughter?"

"It's possible," Lee said. "I do believe Temple murdered Robert. There are just too many coincidences. But his motive is currently irrelevant to our circumstances. Temple's fairly well connected, a railroad man and in the pocket of several congressmen, influence he may use to intimidate people—the marshal, a prosecutor, even a jury."

She lifted a shaking hand to rub her temple. "And if he set us up for the murder, he'd want a quick trial and hanging before anyone was the wiser. Which is what you said earlier."

"Indeed." Lee swallowed as he recalled a hanging or two. A man's neck didn't always snap—sometimes he swung for several minutes, strangling under his own weight. Ah hell, now he was shaking, too. "To win this, we must exert our own influence. I sent a message to Michelle to telegraph my father, who also knows congressmen. In the meantime, we must hire a lawyer to convince a judge to delay our trial. They'll be loathe to hang a woman. That's in our favor, at any rate."

They heard a door slam, jerking Lee's head around. From the marshal's office came the sound of voices—the marshal's, low and gruff, and a higher, more feminine one with a thick French accent, interspersed with French. Bad French.

"Okay, okay!" the marshal shouted in exasperation. "What the hell do foreigners come to this country for, anyhow?" A couple seconds later, the marshal opened the door. "Oughtta at least learn the blamed language," the marshal grumbled as Michelle entered carrying a tray of food. "Drag me from the saloon for a couple murderers. Give 'em the food, lady, then git."

Manners exerting themselves, Lee rose.

"Oh, but why must I leave?"

"Them's the rules, no visitin' but from a lawyer."

"Oh," pouted Michelle prettily, an expression few men could resist. "You cannot think that I, *un petit* girl, would cause difficulty, eh? Not with such a big, strong man just behind that door!"

"Oh, all right. But behave, you hear?"

*"Oui, oui, naturallment!"* she said, laying the tray on the floor.

With a few more grumbles he left, and Lee, glad for her soft, shallow company, folded Michelle in his arms. "Ah, Michelle, *chérie*, it's so good to see you!"

"And you, too, *mon ami,* and not hanging from a rope!" She gave him a squeeze, then slid from his embrace to hug Jess warmly. "There. Now we are greeted. You will eat and I shall tell you my *bon* news!" she said, bouncing on the bed next to Jess.

"What good news?" Lee asked, picking up two plates from the tray and handing one to Jess. She took it and pushed around the food skeptically, as if afraid it'd bite. He couldn't blame her. It looked like even more of a mystery than their last meal. "Did you send my telegram?"

*"Oui* and with no French at all! All good English. I asked Jon first. He has very good English, *n'est pas?"*

Lee smiled and Jess laughed, a soft, tinkling sound that went up and down the scales of his heart. He loved her laugh. It reminded him of his mother's, the warmest of all his boyhood memories. "Yes, Michelle, his English is good. Now tell us the news."

"I have hired you the best lawyer in town."

"The best?" Jess asked, lifting her eyebrows. "How do you know that?"

"It was easy. He is also the only lawyer in town."

Jess chuckled, and Lee grinned. "That does limit the scope."

"Yes, but I have arranged for him to save you from this villainous plot!"

Jess bit her lip, Lee suspected, to keep herself from laughing. "I'm certain you have, Michelle," she said. "Does this lawyer have a name?"

"*Oui,* it is Monsieur Temple."

# Chapter Fourteen

Lee and Jess groaned.

"What? What is this moaning and groaning?" Michelle asked.

Disappointment settled like a block of ice in Jess's stomach. "We think Temple may have killed Robert."

"No," Michelle gasped. "No, but *Monsieur* Temple, he seems so nice!"

"I'm sure he is when he doesn't have a six inch blade in his hand."

"Oh, but why would he kill Robert? What reason?"

"It's a long story, Michelle," Lee said. "Jess, sweetheart—"

"It's gotten worse, hasn't it?" she said, with a deep sigh. "If our lawyer is the murderer, he's not going to delay our trial."

"He'll push our case through just as fast as possible."

She shuddered, trying not to picture her body swaying from a gallows.

Lee drew a deep breath. "Michelle, did you say urgent in that telegram?"

*"Mais oui!"* Michelle said, as she looked back and forth between the two.

Rubbing his neck, Lee sighed. "Damn, I could use a drink."

"Oh, but I have brandy!" Michelle withdrew a flask from her purse.

Lee leaned forward to take the flask. Michelle stared blankly into space, then rose abruptly. "I have a plan," she said and crossed the cell to the door.

"A plan?" Lee asked suspiciously. "What sort of plan?"

"First I must find *mes amies*. Marshal!" she yelled through the bars. "*Monsieur* Marshal!"

"But, Michelle, how—"

The marshal opened the door, swinging his keys. "Done, are you?"

"*Oui.*"

"Damn it," Lee swore under his breath, and then, "Marshal, if you please, before you leave, the lady and I would appreciate trips to the outhouse."

"I took you this morning," he said, as Michelle swished by.

"The chamber pot's full, but if you wish to keep emptying it . . ."

The marshal scowled, then drew his gun from his holster and waved Jess over. "Ladies first."

A half hour later, Jess, worry etching her heart, watched Lee enter their cell. The sheriff slammed the door and locked it behind him. A few seconds later the front door slammed, leaving them alone in the building. Jess sighed as Lee crossed to seat himself next to her. Looking at the bunk above them, he grimaced. "Awfully small in here, eh?"

She smiled. "Did you sleep at all last night?"

"A little," he said, retrieving Michelle's flask from the floor.

A moment of silence passed before she asked hesitantly, "Lee, do you think we'll truly hang?"

He took a swig of brandy before answering. "I don't know. People will hesitate to hang a woman, but I don't know for certain how strong Temple's influence is."

She rubbed her temples, pictured her body swinging again, and shivered. "How bad do you think it is? Hanging?"

He winced. "I've heard of worse ways to die."

"Why, thank you, sir! That is a comfort!"

With a chuckle, he wrapped his arm around her shoulder and gave her a hug. "You know, sweetheart, if I have to be stuck in this situation, I'm glad I'm with you."

Such a warm, strong arm, far more comforting than any words. So easy to lean into him and lay her head on his shoulder. She sighed. "I'm a little sleepy."

"Do you wish to lie down?"

"The sheet smells like urine."

"Ugh. Let's scoot back here against the wall then," he said, sliding his backside along the bed, pulling her with him. "You can sleep on my shoulder. How's that?"

The smell of soap and wood smoke, a touch of cigar, and traces of brandy arose from him. "It's wonderful."

"Not a trifle close?"

She glanced at him. His jaw was clenched as he looked up at the bed just two inches above his head. "Not to me," she said. "Will you be okay?"

Smiling, he kissed the top of her head and took a deep breath, stirring her hair. Another breath and he leaned back. "Grab me that pillow there and I shall be fine."

So strange, as if he took comfort from the smell of her hair—like she did from him. She leaned forward for the pillow and a minute later he had it behind his head. Her own sunk back down to his chest. She fell asleep with the sound of his heart—strong, constant—thumping in her ear.


Lee roused to the sound of scraping metal and his name being whispered loudly. "Lee! Jess! Wake up!"

The night encircled them, only the gray light streaming through the window to break the darkness. It fell upon Michelle's pale face, peaking through the door. "Michelle?" he hissed.

"Yes. Hurry! I'm breaking you out!"

"Breaking us out? How?" he asked, as Jess stirred. Then she silently pulled out of his arms and slid across the room. He

rose, shaking the sleep from his head, and followed her through
the door into the marshal's dark office. Against a wall the marshal's cot lay unmade—and empty. Suddenly abandoned?

"Oh! Shhh," Michelle hissed. "Your boots are too loud.
Walk softer, Lee!"

Frowning, he lightened his steps as they navigated the furniture. Michelle stopped next to a window, lifted a shade and
peeked out. Lee reached behind him, searching for Jess's hand.
A touch, and then he wrapped her fingers around hers, cold and
shaking. Gently squeezing it, he pulled her nearer. Doubtless
Michelle's plan was outrageous, comical, and untenable. And
yet his heart quickened and blood raced through his veins.

"Not yet," Michelle whispered. "They're looking this way. A
minute more! Oh, Miranda," she whispered against the window
"you must work harder! Wiggle those hips! Marvelous! Lee, you
first, out the door, *quietly*. Slink over to the side of the building,
run through the alley and wait in the back. Quickly now!"

With a deep breath, Lee slipped out the front door and then
stopped dead in his tracks, his attention caught by the presen-
tation diagonally across the street. The marshal and a small
crowd of men had gathered in front of the saloon to watch
three partially nude women dancing on the boardwalk. Damn!
For several seconds, Lee stared in frank appreciation.

But nude women weren't worth swinging for. He tiptoed
across the porch, leaped over the rail, and sped down the
alley. A half minute later Jess joined him, silent except for
short, fast breathing. The excitement and fear pulsing through
him sharpened his senses and strengthened his courage. Without thinking, he bent over and kissed her, fast, hard, rough.

He lifted his head at the sound of running footsteps. Mi-
chelle hissed, "Lee, later, for God's sake!" and grabbed his and
Jess's hands. She dragged them at a run through the dark.
Good God, her plan better not be a foot race.

The silhouette of a tree formed a few feet from them,

followed by horses, packed for travel. Yes, by God, yes! Horses.

Approaching the horses, Michelle apologized breathlessly, "I'm sorry, Jess, it's not a sidesaddle. You have blankets, though, and other necessities!"

"Riding astride is safer," Jess answered, then took a step forward to hug Michelle. With a sniffle in her voice, she said, "Thank you, Michelle. You are my very best *amie* and the best fairy godmother a girl could wish for."

"And you my best Cinderella!" Michelle replied, then released Jess and pushed her toward the smaller of the two horses. "Quickly now, honey, you and your prince must ride, ride like the wind!"

Jess nodded, took the reins in her hand, then grabbed the pommel to hike herself aboard. The horse danced a bit, but Jess controlled it easily. She could ride, thank God.

Michelle turned to Lee. Taking her gloved hands in his, he dropped a chaste kiss on the cheek of his former lover. "Thank you, *chérie*. That was quite a scene."

"We all helped, the whole troupe. And we are not done yet! In the morning, when the marshal learns of your escape, several people will have seen you riding north, for Cheyenne. Head south. They'll never expect that."

He flashed her a rueful grin. "And so, Michelle, you prove you have a fine brain after all."

She laughed. "When needed. Listen." She lowered her voice. "About Jess. You'll take care of her, right? Don't you hurt her, you hear me!"

He smiled, leaned over and whispered in her ear. "I love her, Michelle. I'll guard her with my life."

And with that, he leapt on his horse and turned it southwest. Michelle, quickly recovering from her shock, clapped her hands gleefully. "Oh, I knew it! *Bon chance, mon ami! Bon chance!*" she called to them as they disappeared into the night.

# Chapter Fifteen

Pulses racing, Jess followed Lee's lead, urging her horse across the prairie at a dead gallop. When they reached the road, he turned them south, reining in his horse to a mile-eating, bone-jarring lope. The cold night rushed by them; the pounding of hooves and the harsh sound of her laboring horse filled Jess's ears. Slowly, as the new moon eased across the sky, its ghostly rays gleaming on the dry prairie grasses, Jess's panic eased. Finally, Lee pulled his horse to a walk, signaling for Jess to follow suit. "Are you sure that we ought to slow down?" she asked. She took deep gulps of the dust-laden night air, sweetened by freedom.

Lee, took a breath, too. "Unless you'd prefer to kill these animals."

"I'd prefer not to hang."

"We won't," he said with conviction.

"Do you think they've noticed we're gone yet?"

"I doubt it. I daresay Michelle will fix our bunks to look like we're sleeping. And she's got a scheme to send whatever posse they gather north for the border."

"And for the train," she said, doubtfully. "Which would make more sense, wouldn't it?"

"Except that Temple's a railroad man and will telegraph

ahead with our descriptions. Nor do we have any notion of when the next train is due to leave Cheyenne. Even if we did, they could very well catch us before we reach the border. I agree with Michelle's plan. Heading south is far more intelligent." Lee twisted his neck back and forth to stretch the muscles. "Lord, Jess, it feels good to be out of that cell."

"It does," she agreed as she slowly turned over this new wrinkle in their "adventure." Not, she thought as she glanced at Lee riding tall in his saddle, such an ill-adventure, really—except for the rope that might await them at its end. She gulped and fought to control the urge to knee her horse into a fast, horse-killing gallop. "So, Lee, we're free. What now?"

He shrugged. "We stay free."

"How?"

"I'm open to suggestions."

After a few moments thought, she offered, "We might turn ourselves in."

He jerked his head around, his face harsh with astonishment. "What? You want to go *back* to jail? How does that keep us free?"

"Of course I don't! But I don't want to spend my life looking over my shoulder, either. We didn't do anything wrong. Why not find another town and explain everything to the marshal there? Not Denver," she added quickly. "Not if Temple knows congressmen, but somewhere far enough south to be beyond Denver's influence."

"All right," he took a deep breath. "I think it's lunacy, but if you insist we'll consider it. Tomorrow morning—no this morning," he corrected nodding to the sun peaking out over the plains, "we ride into the nearest town—"

"It has to be a good size to have a marshal."

"The nearest *large* town, walk up to the marshal and inform him that we're wanted for murder. I'd hazard to guess that the first thing he does is throw us in jail."

"Surely not!" she said with a tiny laugh. "You're far too large to be thrown."

"Claps us in jail, then. Better?"

"Yes, except that I disagree. You said yourself that it's impossible for us to have killed Robert. Assuming the marshal has some intelligence, he'll see that."

"He might, except for two things. First we've broken out of jail, which makes us appear guilty."

"Yes, but—"

"And your gown is stained with blood."

"Oh."

"You don't appear precisely innocent."

"Well," she said, glancing down at her bulging saddlebags. "It's more than likely that Michelle packed me some sort of clothing. She might have forgotten food," she said with a trace of mirth, "but not a gown."

"No doubt," he said with a laugh. "Probably silk, too."

"And so, I change—"

"In the middle of the plains."

"Behind some trees."

"There's so many of them," he said, waving over the flat, naked land surrounding them.

"Enough. I change and then we talk to the marshal."

Silence, and Jess glanced at him. As the sun spread its rays across the grass lands, she was better able to see his expression. Amusement touched his voice, but the muscles on his face were taut with excitement. He was enjoying this. "Even if he believed our story," Lee said, "lawmen aren't generally known for permitting suspected murderers to run free. Townsfolk frown on that."

"He wouldn't have to tell them."

"If he were honest he would, and we are looking for honesty, correct? And so it'd be a jail cell for us again."

"Not if we offered to stay in town. After all, we must gain some respect for turning ourselves in."

He frowned. "I suppose that depends somewhat on your explanation."

"Why, the truth of course!"

"Which is?"

"That Temple murdered Robert, but schemed to have us charged for it."

"He'll ask for details."

"I'll tell him that I went to see Robert about the money he owed me—"

"Which he lost gambling. There's your motive, Jess."

"But not *proof*."

"You went to him in the middle of the night."

"But I'd only just learned that Robert actually had money—"

"And were so enraged that instead of waiting until morning to confront him, you visited him, a single man, in his *hotel* room."

"You make it sound so sordid!"

"Just stating the facts."

She sighed. "Okay then, I'll explain that Robert and I were only friends. After I found him dead I went looking for you—"

"Which makes it even more sordid."

"I was frightened!"

"Or guilty."

Vexed, she growled, "I met you and we investigated."

"Instead of finding the marshal."

"I admit that was a mistake."

"A mistake then, guilty as charged now."

"Okay, okay. Maybe we ought to start the story by telling him about Temple."

"Fine, we tell him we're wanted for a murder that our lawyer committed."

She sighed. "That doesn't sound good, either."

"Just stating—"

"The facts. I know. But if we tell him everything we know about Temple, and how he owed Robert—"

"But, Jess," said Lee, his voice tight as his patience began to wane. "We don't *know* that. It's pure supposition on our part. And the second thing the marshal will do is telegraph Grant for their version of the story. Remember this mythical marshal never saw the body and doesn't know that Robert was just about decapitated. All he knows is they found me holding a bloody knife, *my* knife, your dress covered in blood, and Robert owed you money. All our supposition in the world won't alter those facts."

She sighed. "Well, at least we'd have a little of that time you said we needed."

"It'd take a day for Temple and his gang to retrieve us. They might very well shoot us on the road back to Grant, claiming we were trying to escape. It eliminates the trial altogether and whatever unease a jury would have about sentencing a woman to hang."

The thought of being shot, lying bleeding and dying in the middle of the dusty Colorado prairie, appealed to Jess less than hanging. "Okay, okay," she finally agreed. "It won't work. What's your idea?"

His eyes narrowed as he thought a moment. "I have friends who own a ranch southwest of Pueblo. They may take us in."

"Ah, the stint on the ranch. And you think they'll be predisposed to taking in a former employee and an actress, both of whom are wanted for murder?"

"The McGraws are no strangers to trouble."

"All right," Jess said, and added wearily, "You know, Lee, I'm already a deserted wife, I'm not particularly excited about adding escaped felon and murderer to my resume."

"You won't. My family will clear us of the charges soon enough."

She looked at him, trying to read his face. "Are you sure?"

He turned and gave her a comforting smile. "Absolutely. Don't worry, sweetheart. We hold the trump card. Still," he said glancing behind them, his eyes narrowing, "Temple and the marshal must pretend to chase us. Ready to run again?"

Her backside ached, but the pain was better than being hanged. "I suppose."

"Oh, Michelle!" Jess sighed in disgust, holding up Michelle's crushed red velvet gown. They'd stopped to water the horses along a river running to the right of the road. Cottonwoods lined it and Lee had suggested Jess take the opportunity to change from her bloodstained dress. "*Not* traveling clothes," she said, grimacing at the plunging neckline.

Lee stood leaning against a tree, drinking from a canteen as the horses grazed. "I rather like it."

"You would! Damn it, Lee, this is an evening gown! It'll cause comment."

"Bloodstains will cause comment *and* curiosity."

"They won't be seen if I keep my wrap on."

"And if you're required to remove it?"

She sighed. "Point taken. I'll change over there. Promise you won't look?"

Grinning broadly, he turned. "I'm the very epitome of discretion."

"Oh, yes," she said, as she hid herself as best she could among the trees. "And Michelle could be nominated for sainthood!"

"I'm certain a few men called to God when she—"

"Lee!"

"All right. I'll shut up."

She struggled with the dress, reaching behind her to fasten it shut, but she couldn't reach all the buttons. When she smoothed it into place as best she could, she noted that the top of her breasts peaked over the neckline, damn it all. Making a face, she emerged from the trees to find Lee collecting a pile of various-sized sticks. "What are you doing?" she asked, confused.

"Collecting firewood," he said, breaking a thick piece of wood over his knee. After throwing it on the pile he turned. "It's a precious commodity on—" His eyes fell on the low neckline, cutting off his sentence. When his eyes met hers, the amused sparkle was eclipsed by a warm glow. "Lovely."

"It needs a bustle," she said, reaching around to pull at the overlarge back.

Raising an eyebrow, he ran his eyes up and down her body in frank admiration. "It appears to possess all the important parts."

A blush warmed her face, as a swift, hot memory of his kiss shot through her mind. A moment later she recollected the smell of stale perfume clinging to him at the train depot. Biting her lip to contain the flash of jealousy, she decided not to ask for help with the remaining buttons, but to cover herself as best she could with her wrap. But when she reached forward to retrieve it, Lee's sudden intake warned her that that, too, was a mistake. "Chriiist," he breathed, dragging up other recollections—his voice floating to her bed from the parlor that first night when Michelle convinced him to stay against his better judgment.

Setting her teeth against the longing yanking at her heart, Jess looked up and caught his gaze fixed upon her breasts, now pressing hard against the neckline as if fighting to break free. The glow in his eyes had become a fire; raw desire etched his face. Swallowing hard, she straightened and shoved the same corresponding emotion down her throat. Desire was a dead-end road: hot kisses, cold body.

Lee took a deep breath and rubbed his neck. "Come here and I'll help fasten the gown."

"It's okay, I think."

His jaw tightened and he caught her eyes. "It's not. And we'll *both* be much happier if it's fastened."

She swallowed and clutching the bodice against her chest, strode over and turned her back to him. He carefully brushed her hair aside, and her skin burned where his fingers touched. His breath came quickly, flowing over her neck in soft tendrils of desire. Every touch of his fingers as he pulled the gown together sent warm thrills over her nerves. A moment later, he stepped back. "I think I'll finish with the wood now," he said in a rough voice.

She turned. "Do you need help?"

He took a breath. "It would go faster."

They worked silently for a few minutes. Jess finally ventured, "Lee, what are we doing this for?"

"Firewood's scarce on the plains. The more we can gather, the better tonight's campfire."

"Campfire? What campfire?"

"We're on the dodge, Jess. It'd be best to steer clear of any town large enough to have hotels and sheriffs."

"I don't care for sleeping in the open."

"I don't care for jail cells."

"But what about snakes?"

"What about 'em? They make good eatin'."

"Eating!" she exclaimed, eyes widening as she straightened. He'd bundled the sticks together and was lashing them to the back of his saddle.

"Sure. They're a delicacy roundabout these parts. Rattlers are especially tasty."

"Rattlers are poisonous."

"Only if they bite you."

"I don't believe you. You'd never eat a snake."

"Sure I would. They taste a little like escargot. In fact, I know the perfect white Burgundy to accompany rattlesnake," he said and turned. A grin spread across his face from ear to ear and his eyes twinkled. "A Chateau Michaud, seventy-five, I think." When his eyes lit upon her, staring at him openmouthed, his shoulders started shaking.

"You're pulling my leg," she said, holding back the hiccup of laughter bubbling up.

"You're right. One should never age white wines."

"And a girl oughtn't ever to expect a word of truth from you!"

He laughed outright at that. "Are you ready to ride?"

She glanced down. "The skirt of this gown's a little tight. Maybe I ought to cut it."

"Cut it?"

"Do you have a knife?"

Shrugging, Lee reached into his pocket and pulled out a jackknife. For a minute he stared at it, a frown creasing his brow. Then he tossed it to her. She opened it and cut a slit up the side of her skirt as he mounted up. His gaze followed her as she swung into her saddle and tucked her skirt as best she could around her leg. He held his tongue and then, with a pained expression tightening his face, wheeled his horse around and set it to an easy lope. Jess followed.

# Chapter Sixteen

"How is it?" Lee asked as he used a gold-plated dinner knife to spread caviar on a piece of hardtack.

Jess lifted her eyes from scowling at the canned partridge that made up her supper, Michelle's notion of traveling food. With a flutter in his belly, Lee noted the reflection of the campfire dancing in the depths of her eyes. Her cheeks were pink from cool night air and her black curls, after a day's hard riding, fell riotously around her face, regardless of her attempts to tame it. Michelle had remembered the dress, a flask of brandy, the rather interesting food and utensils, and a few basic camping essentials. Somehow she'd forgotten a brush, and now Jess looked like a woman who'd been recently, and very thoroughly, tumbled. The rush of blood to his groin testified to the fact that he had not been the lucky fellow.

She took a bite of partridge and made a face. "It's dreadful."

"Would you prefer the caviar?"

"I'd prefer snails."

He laughed. "You have to eat it at any rate. We need to keep up our strength."

"Do we? I wonder if there's a rattlesnake available." She glanced around, then shuddered. "Then again, maybe I don't want to know." Frowning, she took another bite, swallowed quickly and reached for the flask. She took a deep gulp and shook her head as the brandy washed down her throat. "So how far is this ranch? Assuming I survive this supper, that is."

"A couple days hard riding should bring us south to Colorado Springs, where we might catch a train to Pueblo. If all is well, we might spend the night in town and make it to the Bar M the following evening."

"We'd have to camp out one more night?"

He nodded.

"Not a town?"

"Not this far north. Not unless you want to risk sleeping in a jail."

She scowled down at her pheasant. "The sheriff might feed us better," she grumbled. With a fortifying breath, she forked two more bites of pheasant into her mouth, washed it down with brandy, and then shoved the empty can aside. "I finished it. Satisfied?"

Satisfied? He'd be far more satisfied if she'd take off that wrap, lay herself down on the blanket, and let him very slowly remove her breasts from the tight confines of the bodice. A picture rose in his mind of her hair spread out and his— He coughed to loosen the tightness in his throat. "There's more food if you're still hungry."

"Not hungry enough."

"All right, then. If you're cold, you can slide under the blankets there."

She leaned forward, grimacing as she lifted the blanket with one finger.

"Jess?"

"Looking for snakes."

"Ah."

Finding none, she slid under the blanket and faced him. "So, Lee, tell me how you went from ranching to gambling."

"Ah, ranching. I left home believing all the dime novels I'd read about cowboys. I was convinced it was the most exciting job on earth, so I signed on with the Bar M. And, at first, it *was* marvelous. But then I met the cows."

Jess chuckled. "You didn't meet the cows right up front then?"

"Not until the roundup. My experiences with the cows were not, shall we say, enlightening and I, uh, quit. A short time later I discovered that I have a talent for gambling. How can I explain this so I don't sound like a lunatic? When I'm playing cards it's as if I can see the other players' hands. It's a gift I inherited from my father. At any rate, you can imagine how useful that would be in poker." He leaned back and added some wood to the fire. "By and by I learned to read men's faces also, and I started winning regularly. In fact, I earned a reputation for being unbeatable, which isn't quite as advantageous as you might expect. People avoided playing with me. After that I learned to slip in a losing night here and there to keep 'em coming back."

"Ah, deception. You seem to have a talent for that, too."

He flashed his dimple. "Michelle taught me."

She laughed. "More likely you taught her."

"Possibly." He reached for the two blankets that Michelle had provided him, while mustering his courage to tackle the next obstacle in this continuing catastrophe. "Jess, sweetheart," he said as coolly as possible, "you'll have to scoot over."

Her eyebrows drew together. "Move over?"

Holding her gaze, he nodded. "I'll need a little room."

"A little room?" she asked warily.

He nodded. "It gets quite cold on the plains at night. We shall both be warmer if we combine our body heat."

Her eyes widened. "I will not!" she snapped.

Damn, he'd done it poorly, but for the life of him, he couldn't devise any better way. "It's only for the warmth, Jess."

"I'm not that cold!"

"You're shivering."

"I'm trembling with rage."

He chuckled. "You are not, you little shrew. You're cold.

Come, be logical. If you shiver all night, you won't sleep and you'll be falling out of your saddle tomorrow."

"Which means I ought to sleep with *you*?"

He shrugged. "Why not? I need the sleep, too, you know. I swear upon my honor, Jess, to hold you only for warmth. As far as propriety—honestly, sweetheart, we're in the middle of nowhere. Who's going to know?"

She set her teeth and stared at him. Her eyes calculated; he reminded himself to breathe.

"I get the side nearest to the fire," she conceded and scooted over.

"Whatever you wish," he said. He removed his jacket and folded it into a pillow. Sliding in behind her, he rested his head on his newly constructed pillow, and slipped his arm around Jess's waist. He gritted his teeth and pulled her against him, summoning up pictures of decrepit old women with missing teeth and dry, withered bodies.

It didn't work.

Jess's sweet woman's scent mixed seductively with the musky smell of horse and leather, provoking erotic images of her riding naked across the prairie. The feel of her slim waist, clothed in velvet warmed by the heat of her body, made his hand itch with the urge to stroke it, to slide his hand under her wrap to cup her half-naked breasts. When her bottom curved to mold neatly against his thighs, hot blood surged downward, bringing his staff to attention and Jess jumping out of her skin.

"Lee!" she exclaimed, trying to jerk free.

Clenching his jaw, he held tight. "Jess, it's nothing," he ground out.

"Oh no, it's not! It's a whole lot of something!"

"It's a natural reaction. Nothing to concern yourself about. I won't act upon it."

"No! We can't possibly sleep this way!"

Good God, her squirming hips rubbed against him,

transforming desire to white-hot lust. "Your moving only exacerbates the situation."

"Then let me go!"

With a groan of frustration, he released her. She jerked away so fiercely she almost ended up in the fire. Still on her knees, she whirled around to face him, hair flying, eyes flashing with anger and something else. Tiny sparks of desire. For a moment he was breathless.

"Give me my blankets!"

He swallowed and said in a husky voice, "You're taking this far too hard, Jess."

"I want my blankets."

He rammed a shaking hand through his hair. "Will you just please listen, for a moment? Please."

Her throat worked spasmodically as she searched his eyes. He held perfectly still, and presently she calmed down and nodded.

He took a deep breath. "When a man's with a woman things happen. He hasn't got any control over it, but he can control what he does about it and Jess—come now, sweetheart—you must know I'm no rapist."

She bit her lip and Lee resolutely shut down his god-forsaken imagination. "But how can you sleep? That's what this whole . . . arrangement . . . is about, isn't it?"

"It will ease, trust me. And it's better than the cold."

She took a deep breath. The anger in her eyes slipped away, leaving behind sweet compassion, never far away from her tender heart. "Are you sure you'll be able to sleep?"

"By and by."

"Okay," she said, and moved gingerly back into his arms. "Everett wouldn't have."

"I'm not Everett." Once more he pulled her against him, sucking back a groan as her soft bottom settled against his hardened staff. Clenching his jaw, he forced his hands to remain perfectly still. Lightening his voice to the best of his ability, he asked, "Are you warm enough?"

"Ye-yes. You'll tell me if it becomes . . . unbearable."

It already was. "Of course."

She fell silent. Soon her light breathing told him she was asleep, and his body slowly softened enough for him to follow suit.

# Chapter Seventeen

Lee put his hand to his forehead to shade his eyes from the sun. Standing up in his stirrups, he scanned the horizon. Here and there dust clouds floated along the road but none large enough to warn of a posse.

"I don't see anything," Jess said, standing up in her stirrups, too. "Do you?"

"No. And this hill's the highest yet. I think we're home free."

"I think so, too," she said with a lilt in her voice. Damn, but it was good to hear that, he thought as he turned. She was smiling. For the first time in over a week she appeared happy. "Does that mean—"

He shook his head. "No hotel. There's no good reason to risk getting caught."

"There's every reason. Better food—"

"No," he said, wheeling his horse around to start south again. It wasn't just the risk; it was the tormenting, titillating joy of spending a full night with Jess's curvaceous body pressed against his. Was it illogical to willingly put himself through that torture? Since when did logic rule desire? "But if you wish," he said when she caught up with him. "We might try to get something to eat at one of the ranches along the way."

"Maybe they'd offer to let us stay the night," she ventured hopefully.

Lee frowned. "After asking us a whole host of questions that we can't answer, like why we're traveling so lightly."

"Won't they ask anyhow?"

He rubbed his neck. "True. Perhaps we're better off avoiding the ranches altogether."

"Mercy, but you're stubborn! Wouldn't you sleep better in a bed. *Alone?*"

Memories of his dreams the night before heated his blood. He'd sleep more, but not better. He flashed her a smooth, easy grin. "Last night wasn't so bad."

"Oh, all right! You know, I'm beginning to think you're enjoying all of this!"

"And you aren't?"

Her eyebrows shot up, before she let out a chagrinned laugh. "Maybe a little. It *is* exciting."

"Sometimes, Jess, I think there's a bit of the scoundrel in you."

Her eyes sparkled. "It's possible. Shall we run them again?"

"If you wish."


They stopped about ten miles out of Colorado Springs to set up camp beside the Plum River. It had been a torturous day for Lee. The day before had been difficult enough with Jess frightened and nervous, biting her lip to keep from asking for comfort or rest. With the load off her shoulders, though, her grimaces had turned to smiles and laughter—and flirtation. The previous night's sleeping arrangements had led to nothing sexual, and she appeared to have concluded that Lee was unaffected by her attractions. For several long, intoxicating hours he'd been exposed to the woman Jess might have been had her heart not been stolen by a bastard of a man too stupid to realize the woman he'd deserted was worth far more than the money he'd stolen. While attempting to check his rising desire, Lee inwardly damned Dunne to hell, perdition, and every other manner of suffering that he could imagine. Doubly so when, hot under the autumn sun, she unfastened the top buttons of her wrap, revealing a tempting morsel of the treasure hidden beneath.

Torture, pure torture, and he would have cherished every last second if he could count on satisfaction in the end. By the time he swung off his horse he'd decided that she damned well owed him some measure of satisfaction, however small.

Without bothering to tie his horse—it could head for the hills for all he cared—he strode over to Jess's. Reaching up, he helped her down, slid his arms around her and pressed his mouth desperately against hers. She let out a small moan of surprise, but as soon as he delved inside, she responded passionately. She met him stroke for stroke, before sweeping his mouth with her small, velvety tongue. When she drew him inside, it was so much like the actual act itself that he forgot everything she'd ever told him and slid his hands down her back to stroke the feminine curves of her soft round bottom. The heat of her skin burned through her dress and petticoat, enflaming him. Not enough—not enough at all. He shifted and slid his leg between hers. While pulling her forward with his hands, he moved his thigh slowly back and forth to rub against her soft, sensitive parts. Taking her resulting shudder as surrender, he lifted his mouth.

Her eyes were almost black, her face flushed rose-red. His blood caught fire and roared through his body. This wasn't the reaction of a frigid woman. This was full-steam-ahead lust.

But then her eyes widened. She shifted her gaze to regard his hands on her hips, and jerked backward.

"Oh my God!"

He didn't want to let go. She took another step back, breaking free of his hands and banging into her horse. It moved slightly.

"Jess, sweetheart," he said, lowering his voice to hide its shaking. "It's all right."

"You promised to leave me alone!" she exclaimed between deep breaths.

Damn it, why had he broken off the kiss? Fool! Fool! "Jess, that reaction wasn't anything like—"

"I told you, I don't like it!" She turned away, tears in her voice as she started to unpack her horse.

"That's not what you said with that kiss!"

She dropped her saddle to the ground. "I'm not going to talk about it."

"Jess—" he said, stepping toward her.

"No!" she cried out, spinning around so fast she spooked his horse. Lee lunged and snatched up the reins before it ran. It shied a little and with a sigh he realized the horse needed gentling even more than Jess. He strode forward slowly, speaking in a low soothing voice. Carefully, he reached up and stroked its neck, speaking all the while, and the animal calmed, comforted by the sound, not knowing that Lee was repeating every swear word he'd ever learned.


The fire crackled and spit as they ate their supper in bone-chilling silence. Lee's mind churned, every thought marbled with despair. His body had long since softened but his heart ached for her smile, and his lips for her kiss. She'd wanted him, at least for a few moments, he was sure of it. But then something had gone terribly wrong.

He glanced up from his supper of mushy canned caviar. Jess was sitting in the center of the blankets, her nose wrinkled in distaste as she took small bites from her can of oysters. With a quick flick of her wrist she drowned the taste, and probably the texture, too, with more fine Napoleon brandy.

"Jess, we need to talk."

"I have nothing to say."

With a sigh of resignation, he laid down his supper. "I think

this started that last day in San Francisco, at the train depot.
Do you remember it?"

"It started the day I was born," she snapped.

"Do you remember it?" he insisted.

She lifted her head and scowled at him. "What of it?"

"At first you appeared happy to see me. Then it was like
someone had thrown a bucket of cold water over you."

"I was tired. We'd been out late the night before."

"Michelle said you wept on the train." He pictured her
caught in the middle of a loud, boisterous crowd as tears
streamed down her face. The image stabbed at his heart.

She shrugged, refusing comment.

He sighed. He'd hoped she'd back herself out of whatever
corner she'd sidled into, but apparently it was just too deep,
too dark a corner.

"There were tears in your eyes when I met up with you in
Grant. You ran from me."

She pretended intense interest in her oysters.

"I think I deserve an explanation."

She shrugged again. "There's nothing to explain."

"Don't you think I ought to be the judge of that?"

"No," she said with a mirthless laugh, "I think I ought to be
the judge of that, and just about everything else, truth be told."

"I'm not amused."

"Why, then, that must be a first for you. You're rarely serious about anything."

"Goddamn it, Jess!" he said, ramming his fingers through
his hair. "I want an answer!"

"Well, Lee," she said and leaned back on her palms. She
caught his gaze. Her face was tight, her eyes dark and hollow.
"It's good for you to want. From what I know of your past,
there's been precious little wanting in it."

Well, she sure as hell had altered that situation. "Was it
something I did? Before the ball? During? After?" Something
flickered in her eyes, and he pressed onward. "It was the kiss,

wasn't it?" She shifted her gaze to stare out into the night. And bit her lip. "You told me you liked it. You appeared happy when I left."

More silence, but he detected a tremor in her arms. He could apply but one interpretation to that clue. "Sweetheart, did you expect me to follow you inside?" He swallowed at a new, breathtaking thought of a missed opportunity. Had he left her wanting? Lord, but for a time machine to go back and do it all over again.

"Lee, where did you go after you left?" she asked abruptly. She took that godawful moment to catch his eyes. Damnation! His mind whirled, searching for an answer to extract him from this trap as swiftly as humanly possible.

"I smelled perfume on you at the train depot," she said.

He sucked in his breath. Her eyes narrowed, and he felt a fleeting desire to stab himself in the heart for his damnable male appetite.

*Lie.*

*I can't.*

Holding her gaze, he said slowly, "Jess, sweetheart, you kiss like the very devil, you know? I've no doubt that you love kissing. What you do with something as simple as a kiss could break a man."

She blinked, pain creasing her face. "Not everyone. Just you and Everett."

"Well, I don't know about Everett. But after that kiss, I was just about mad from wanting you. Lacking any hope of satisfying that desire, I confess, I sought out another woman."

Flinching, she closed her eyes as if unable to bear the sight of him. It ripped at every last nerve. "You're a remarkably lovely woman," he said gently. He took a breath. "But it's not like I haven't known some beautiful women. Michelle isn't exactly last night's canned beans." She winced. "But I've never wanted them like I want you. Do you know what I think about every time I look at you? I think about removing your clothes and stroking every last inch of your body until you're wild with desire. I think about your smell, your taste, your touch. The sound of your moans. I'm truly sorry, Jess, but kisses aren't enough to satisfy that need. I don't have your passionless nature."

She shuddered. Revulsion? Desire? *Lord, please, make it desire.*

She stared down at her nails. After a moment, she said, "Like Everett."

"Everett?"

"He wanted to . . . to . . . I don't quite know the words."

"Have relations?"

"Have relations. All the time."

"I daresay it's generally that way when people are first together."

"Maybe. Anyway, I was willing at first. It hurt, but he promised it would get better. It didn't and I became," she paused, "not so willing."

"You refused him?"

With a trembling hand, she shoved her hair behind an ear. "Lee, it was all the time! Morning, noon, night. It was exhausting and then, well, in time I started vomiting."

He jerked in alarm. "Vomiting. Good God, Jess, it was *that* bad?"

"Yes, after . . . when—" She stopped, then shook her head, as if trying to clear it of some horrid memory. Lee frowned, his mind swiftly sifting through the information. Vomiting?

*Pregnancy.*

Damn the man to hell.

She continued in a small, choking voice. "Everything was so wonderful in the beginning. We . . . we took my inheritance and went to New York to try our luck in the market. We were so young . . . I was sure Everett would hit it big, be rich and pay back Jason. And I was just as sure that, *that* part of our lives would improve."

She bit her lip and, rubbing her temples, continued. "I was

wrong. Everett lost money in the market and quickly became disillusioned with New York. Two months later we moved on to New Orleans. A new city, a new venture. New Orleans is beautiful, but very different from Illinois. I felt lost. And I was *so* tired. At any rate, Everett bought a share in a riverboat. For a few months we thought we'd made it. But Everett's friend sold the boat on the sly and skedaddled with the money. Then Everett heard about a ranching partnership being organized in Denver. We moved again . . ."

Her voice trailed off and, tension biting at his shoulders Lee prompted, "And so with the exhaustion and the . . . illness . . . you denied him."

She hesitated, then nodded. "Occasionally. And so Everett sought pleasure elsewhere. He'd come back smelling like perfume. I was . . . I was especially sick on those nights."

"Good God, Jess, he took you then?"

She swallowed. "Sometimes. I wanted to be a good wife and a good wife doesn't deny her husband his marital rights. On those occasions he was especially amorous," she said with a little catch in her breath. "I don't understand. Why would a man want to go from one woman to another one like that?"

Lee winced, remembering times he'd had two women, in the same room, in the same bed. "Some women like it that way, too."

"*Women* do? Goodness! I can't imagine wanting—although, in truth, I don't want . . ." her voice trailed off.

After a moment, he said softly, "Regardless, Jess, I'm not like Everett."

She turned her hurt eyes to him, face creased in confusion. Lord, to take that pain away; right now he'd cut off his right arm if it'd help. "What?"

"I don't want just any woman. I want you."

She jerked. For a moment the pain seemed to retreat. "The night of the ball," he added. "That woman was only for release. I didn't want her. I wanted you." Wisps of hope floated across her face. He reached out to run his knuckles over her soft skin, and his heart melted when she leaned into his hand. "Everett's an idiot. *Any* man who'd leave your bed for another woman is a blasted idiot."

Her face tightened. "Not if I wasn't 'particularly satisfying.'"

A vision of her lying naked in bed, black curls spread across a pillow, her lips swollen from kissing, crossed his mind. His blood heated. His hand shook and he dropped it. "I don't believe that." More tender hope smoothed the creases on her face. "And now, sweetheart, it's long past time for bed."

She nodded and they slipped under the covers. Although it was a warmer night than the one before, she slid up against him as if they'd slept together for years and it was perfectly natural to curl her body into his. With a grim smile—her scent warmed his nose and his body reacted—he wrapped his arm around her pulling her nearer. If she felt him leaping to life, she didn't mention it.

For a while, he let his mind sift through their conversation. Her revelations had been painful, and he had no wish to cause her more. Still, she'd left out large pieces of her life with Dunne. Curiosity got the better of him.

"Jess? Still awake?"

"Ummm."

"I was wondering, sweetheart, and you don't have to answer, it's not my business, but your illness—the baby—did you miscarry?"

Her body turned to stone in his arms. "No."

"Then you gave it up? An orphanage, perhaps?"

For a moment he thought she wouldn't answer. When she did, her voice was thin and thready, as if anything stronger would intensify the memories. "After Denver it was gold in the Black hills. Near Deadwood. I was eight months along and . . . and very tired. We lived in a tent near the mine. It was spring and the rains came. I became feverish and went into labor early." Her voice trembled. A deep breath did nothing to dispel it. "There weren't any other women to help. When the pain became unbearable Everett poured whiskey down my throat. After sixteen hours, I delivered little Janey. Oh God, Lee," she said on a strangled sob, "she was so beautiful. Big blue eyes, blond fuzz for hair. But so very small. She didn't cry, just whimpered a little."

Damn it, Lee thought, his arms tightening around her. He was the most idiotic man ever born. Why had he asked her? Why hadn't he left well enough alone? She didn't need to live through this again.

Another small sob. "She barely had the strength to nurse, and I was so sick. Everett drank and drank and then, on the third day, I woke up and he was gone. Just like that. No note, no good-bye. I don't know how—how could he? I loved him." She paused, swallowing hard. "The fever broke, but I was still so tired, so sore. My milk"—she drew in a deep, shaking breath—"my milk never came in. I tried and tried and tried, but four days later Janey took one little breath and . . . and that was it."

Jess rolled over and buried her head in his chest. She started crying, harsh racking sobs. Helpless, Lee rubbed her back crooning softly, "Jess, sweetheart, don't cry. It's all right, sweetheart, it's all right. Don't cry." But her heart seemed dead set on breaking. He gave up and rested his chin on her head. "All right, then, you go ahead and cry. Let it all out, I'm here. I'm here and I won't leave. I'm not leaving." But even as he spoke the words, his heart grew heavier, for, like Everett, faithfulness wasn't his strong suit. He loved Jess right now. But if he *did* seduce her, what then? Fading interest? Another love for his fickle heart? Like Everett, he'd probably break Jess's sweet heart, but he couldn't bear to let her go and so he promised, over and over again, that he wasn't going to leave her, more lies for his swiftly deteriorating soul.

# Chapter Eighteen

Coffee. The familiar, slightly bitter aroma wafted under Jess's nose, convincing her to open her eyes. They felt swollen and gritty, reminding her that she'd fallen asleep crying in Lee's arms. Warm, strong arms and his soft, soothing voice whispering the kind of comfort she'd so dearly needed six years earlier.

As she sat up, rubbing her back, aching from two nights sleeping on the cold, hard ground, her gaze fell upon Lee. He was sitting a short distance away in front of a small campfire. Glancing at her, he took a long stick and carefully moved a can sitting at the edge of the fire toward her. She raised an eyebrow.

"Coffee," he said.

"Coffee? In a can?"

"Michelle provided the beans, but not the pot. I realized this morning that I could boil the water in your leftover oyster can. It's hot, though. Be careful."

Amusement skittered through her stomach as she reached for it. It was hot, but not unbearably so. Avoiding touching the ragged edges with her lips, she poured some of the dark, thick brew into her mouth. After a second of letting it coat her tongue, she swallowed.

"How is it?" Lee asked.

"I don't know. Is this what coffee's supposed to taste like?"

He laughed. "Shrew. Here, hand it over." He leaned forward to take it and she snatched her hand away.

"Not on your life! Get your own oyster coffee!"

"Why should I when I can drink yours?" He stretched across her lap to try to grab the can. Laughing, she let him have it. Eyes twinkling he sat back and took a sip, then wrinkled his face in disgust. "It's terrible." He picked up the empty caviar jar sitting next to him. "Still, it's better than nothing."

He poured a little in the jar and gave her back the can. For a couple minutes they sipped the brew, an uneasy silence poisoning the cool morning air. No doubt Lee was contemplating how to remove himself from the emotional tangle he'd unwittingly plunged into the previous night. Generous as he'd been with his comfort, he was nonetheless a man dedicated to bachelorhood. A tight spot formed in Jess's heart. The least she could do this morning was let him off the hook.

"Lee," she said. When she caught his eye, she lowered her voice to keep it steady. "I wanted to thank you for last night. I . . . I appreciated the comfort." Appreciated. Past tense. Oh why, oh why did it hurt so much now?

An unusual intensity built in his eyes, even while his face went blank. After a moment he said in an even voice, "I was glad to offer it."

"Yes, well, I just wanted to . . ." She let her voice drift off, no longer certain what to say. Did he regret holding her? Questioning her? It was impossible to tell when he held his face so still, not moving a muscle. "Is that your poker face?" she asked, tilting her head slightly.

His eyebrows suddenly knitted together. "Pardon me?"

"Your face was completely expressionless. It must be your poker face."

He shook his head. "I smile when I'm playing poker."

"Because you're so happy about taking everybody's money?"

He barked a small laugh. "No, shrew. A blank face is much

harder to maintain than a smile. Any facial movement at all can give a player away."

"You smile all the time."

"Exactly."

"Then in a way, you're always gambling, aren't you?"

That self-same smile settled on his face and he leaned forward to kiss her on the cheek. "I smile for you, sweetheart." A light thrill ran over her nerves. He rose. "I'll pack while you finish your coffee. We ought to reach Colorado Springs in an hour or so. With luck we'll be in Pueblo tonight. I'll telegraph Michelle of our progress, and then if there aren't any signs of a posse, I promise you a hotel and a good dinner. Would you like to sleep in a bed tonight?"

"My-my back would appreciate it," she stuttered and then made of job of sipping her coffee, afraid any attempt at further speech would come out in squeaks.

They scarcely spoke during their short journey to Colorado Springs. Nor did the loud, jolting train ride allow much conversation. They arrived in Pueblo in the early evening, where Lee found them hotel rooms and a sizzling steak dinner. Caught between raging hunger and exhaustion, Jess almost fell asleep over it. Back in her room, without benefit of a woman's aid, Jess slept in her clothes in a backbreaking rope bed. She was awoken an hour later—or so it seemed— to knocking.

"Jess," Lee said softly through her door. "Time to rise, sweetheart. We have to start early if we're to reach the Bar M tonight."

She opened one eye to the semigloom of early morning. "Go away," she grumbled. "It's not even light out."

"Do you want to camp tonight? Those are rain clouds outside your window."

Jess opened her other eye and glared at the sky through the dirty panes. "Damn you," she growled, then stomped over to the door to let him in. "If it's going to rain," she said, running her fingers through her tangled curls, "why don't we just stay here?"

Smiling, he entered the room and handed her a brush. "I bought it last night," he explained. "We're not entirely out of danger. If for some reason Temple *does* want to catch us, we're only a telegram away from Grant."

She dragged the brush through her hair, wincing when it caught. "Okay, okay. Then give me a minute to freshen up before breakfast."

"Yeah," he said, rubbing his neck, "about breakfast . . ."

She sighed. "Okay, we'll leave now."

Several hours later, as the sun started its daily descent into the mountains in front of them, Jess decided her backside had bruises on top of bruises. It had been a long, uncomfortable day, especially after the wonderful reprieve of train riding. Lee rode silently until, summoning up her greatest acting abilities, Jess teased him with a lightness she didn't feel about his unusual reticence, to which he answered, amusement quivering underneath the sarcasm, "Well, Jess, I can't talk *all* the time, can I?"

"No?" she questioned. "But you generally seem so intent upon proving otherwise."

He chuckled slightly and then, a challenge in his voice, said, "What about you? Have you nothing to say, either?"

"I . . . I talked the other night."

A brief silence followed. "You told me about one year— one very unhappy year—of your life. Certainly there were good times before that. You once told me you wanted to go home. So, Jess, where is home?"

And so she told him about home, about growing up in small-town Illinois, about the men who left to find their fortune in Chicago, about the ones who stayed behind to farm and marry and raise children. About how those who remained were too shy, too dull-witted, to create even a spark of interest in her. About her life as the daughter of a cooper and a teacher.

"A teacher," he said. "So that's where you obtained your education."

"Only that of a schoolteacher. As much as my mother wanted me to have a back-East education, I was never much interested. Nor did my father like the idea."

"Considering your mother's profession, I should think he'd have understood the usefulness of an education."

"Father allowed mother to work because the town needed a teacher, but he would have preferred she stay home like most women." She continued to talk about his sternness, his belief in women as being morally superior to men, but far, far *inferior* intellectually, emotionally, physically. Her mother had raised her in that manner, working to instill in her a deep sense of humility and duty to home and hearth.

"And so," Lee said, when at the end of an hour and a half of talking, Jess ran out of conversation, "Everett came along and you were primed to run."

"I guess so," she said. "I never thought I cared. I'd always been the good daughter, but Everett ignited some rebellious spirit in me. So I went with him. All of which must seem remarkbly dull in comparison to the advantages of your youth."

"Money aside, my father wasn't much different than yours. Except for a few notable exceptions he follows a straight, narrow line and did all he could to ensure that we followed it also."

"Which," she said smirking, "he failed miserably with you."

Lee flashed twinkling eyes at her. "That assumes my father's surrendered. He never does. He still expects to find some redeeming quality in me."

"A hopeless task."

"He doesn't know the meaning of the word 'hopeless.'"

"He sounds frightening. And, it's *your* turn. Tell me of your home life."

Lee kneed his horse. "Later. We need to make up some time."

They rode fast until the horses were laboring, and then Jess asked again about Lee's childhood. "I expect your arrow-straight father disapproves of your gambling."

"He hates it."

"And what would he prefer you do?"

Lee stiffened. Three days in the saddle and Jess's lovely body pressed against him for two nights had successfully distracted him from contemplating his family's reaction when they received his telegrams. He'd rather not think about it at all, never mind discuss it. But after her revelations, answering her questions was only fair.

"He'd rather I return home and settle down."

"Marriage?"

"And children. I'm the oldest son, and it seems that my brother's wife is incapable of having children, never mind a son to pass on name and fortune."

"Name and fortune . . ." she said, her voice drifting off. "No doubt they have specific ideas of the kind of woman you ought to marry."

"They do."

"Like the women at the ball. A debutante."

He swallowed. "It's expected."

Not an actress, not a divorced woman. He refrained from making the comparison out loud, but he might as well have. It rode between them like a phantom.

"And will you?" she asked after a moment. "Return home and marry your Boston debutante?"

Her voice was calm, but thin. He hesitated, not wanting to cause her further distress. "It doesn't concern us, Jess."

She sucked in her breath, and he glanced her way. She looked like he'd struck her. "Of course not," she replied. "We're only friends."

He winced. "Indeed. Now, have we hurt each other enough or do you wish to continue shooting arrows?"

"I don't see what there is to be hurt about."

Except that her face resembled sculpted marble. "If you must know, I don't particularly wish to marry a debutante."

"I'd think you'd prefer not to marry at all."

"Precisely. Nor do I enjoy disappointing my family."

"I find that surprising. You're always so casual about everything, Lee, including this situation—the murder charge."

He barked a laugh. "You've not met my father when he's been thwarted. Most days I'd rather face a hangman's noose."

"Is he violent then? Mine could be on occasion."

At that Lee really laughed. "Violent? Lord no. Ward Montgomery would never even consider anything so common. No, Dad is more like a steel wall—unmovable, intractable."

"*Ward?* As in Montgomery Ward, the catalog king? Oh, Lee, you must be joking!"

Soothed to hear laughter lacing her voice, he smiled down at her. "I'm not. I see you're amused."

"Well, you must admit, with a name like that he hardly sounds threatening."

"Trust me, he can be. As for the name, you might consider how his and mine combine. My father was once a sea captain."

"Leland Ward? Oh no, *leeward!*" she exclaimed and started laughing again. "No, that's absurd. A man so frightening would never do that."

"It was my mother's idea. As was my sister's name, Star for starboard, and my brother Port. Although, his full name is Porthos, from the Three Musketeers."

"She's sounds amusing."

"She is. She was all that made growing up in society bearable for Star and me. Port, however, follows comfortably in my father's path. He lives in New York part of the year and associates with people like Ward McAllister and Mrs. Astor."

"Mrs. Astor? *The* Mrs. Astor?"

"The Queen of New York society herself."

Jess drew a breath, trying to fill suddenly tight lungs. She recalled walking past Mrs. Astor's mansion with Everett, who spoke of it in low, hushed tones. San Francisco was the social hub for the West Coast, but in comparison to Mrs. Astor— why, no one compared to Mrs. Astor.

"Star and I, well, let us say our positions in society were always more tenuous. Star's full of more fire than a bible-thumper, and she's a woman's reformist to boot." From there he related amusing tale after amusing tale of minor high jinks played at parties, balls, and social functions, of the many different ways they'd avoided lessons and, on occasion, dragged a much-chagrinned Port along with them. It seemed to Jess that there'd been few serious moments in Lee's childhood, and little had changed until he'd met her. Now he was an accused murderer on the run from the law. She was an ill influence on Lee, she thought with wry amusement. Definitely morally inferior to Lee's high-society ladies, who strictly followed the code of conduct set down for the 1880's woman. And yet, *he* believed her to be straitlaced. He wouldn't if he knew her true reaction to last night's kiss.

A tiny shiver ran down Jess's spine and she glanced at Lee, silent for over an hour now. In the fading light, she let her eyes slide over his profile. Today he was a long chalk from the dapper, debonair man she'd met in San Francisco. His boots were dull and scratched, his clothes wrinkled from three days of wear. Gloveless and cold, he'd pocketed one hand, while easily guiding his horse with the other. He wore no hat, and his dark hair was windblown, his face slightly tanned under four days of stubble. No, not dapper, certainly not a dandy. But he was handsome in a rough and tumble way, and just looking at him set her heart to tripping over itself.

He turned to look at her and flashed his dimpled smile, turning her nerves to mush. "How are you doing, sweetheart? Not much longer now."

She nodded mutely and focused on the road again.

Oh no, she was not nearly as straitlaced as he imagined her or as passionless as she'd believed. That had become perfectly obvious during that last kiss when he'd slid his hands down her back while rubbing his thigh against her soft parts. The combination of his lips, his hands, and that delicious, erotic caress had sent the world spinning, heating her blood in ways she'd never dreamed possible. Desire. No, stronger than desire. Lust—harsh, pulsing.

Until recollections of another woman's perfume had risen in her mind, chilling her. Temporarily. Seconds after she'd shoved him away, she'd been trembling again, a deep throbbing ache where his thigh had been. Remembering warmed her face. Her lips twitched for his kiss, her skin begged for the feel of his hands on her hips again, for the consummation of that promise. Every last nerve yearned to experience what she'd been missing for all these years. Desire, lust, satisfaction. And she could have it. Right here, she thought feverishly, right now. Ask, just ask.

Another quick glance. It was dark now, and she could hardly see Lee's face. Thank God. He was far less dangerous that way.

For he *was* dangerous. As much as her body craved his attention, as much as she wanted to weep with frustration over those cold, passionless years, her mother had raised her to revere chastity. To understand that, in those rare cases when a "good" woman felt any of the baser urges, she learned to resist temptation, keeping herself untouched until her wedding night. After that she assumed the duty—with neither physical nor legal recourse—of keeping her husband's desires under strict control and regulating the expulsion of energy on physical passion. Too much of such activities could damage his health.

Recollections of Lee's kisses flashed into her mind, dragging her body along on a wet, rolling wave of passion. Regulate that? Resist those? How—and, she thought with another hot flush, why?

Because, a reproving little voice in the back of her brain reminded her, she was married. Married as in a license, a ring, and vows. For six years she'd kept those vows, resolutely adhering to the lessons taught her at her mother's knee. Even if Everett was dead instead of gone, as a "good" widow she must keep men at a certain distance. As much as she wanted Lee, she firmly told the shameless voice whispering in her other ear, marriage and morality forbade her to take him.

Another shudder.

She drew a deep steadying breath.

And Lee was a gamble, a philanderer, a consummate bachelor. How could she possibly consider giving herself to such a man, one who hadn't even promised her tomorrow, never mind forever? Hadn't he told her straightaway that he wasn't particularly faithful? He'd already gone from her to another woman. No doubt if he seduced her, he'd leave her, just another medal on his chest. Could her pride take that? Could her heart? Bedded and abandoned by another man—she shut her eyes against the sudden crushing in her chest, and let out a deep wavering sigh.

"Jess," Lee said abruptly. "I'm sorry, sweetheart. It's not that much farther. We're already on the McGraws' land. See those trees to the left? They border the river that feeds the McGraws' valley. The ranch is at the end of it."

She turned to look at him. In the dark she could not see his expression, but his voice sounded compassionate. Swallowing, she drew upon her wealth of cynical humor, the only wealth she possessed. "So you've told me several times over the past two hours. I swear we've changed direction twice in that time. You wouldn't mind expounding upon your definition of 'far' would you? Just how far is not much farther?"

"Just trying to keep your spirits up," he said, a smile in his voice.

"By lying to me."

Shrugging, he said, "A mere broadening of the truth."

"If you keep broadening the truth, we'll end up in Alaska."

"'Frisco more like. Alaska's north."

"Marvelous. We could've caught a train in Cheyenne and been there days ago!"

"Now, Jess, where would the fun be in that?"

"Fun. Of course. Sleeping in the cold and eating oysters out of a can is everyone's notion of fun."

"I offered you the caviar."

"Just a fancy name for fish eggs."

"It's a delicacy."

"So are snails. I'm beginning to think you know so much about wine because you have to be damned drunk to eat all those delicacies. Do you judge a delicacy based upon its slime content?"

He laughed and pointed ahead. "Look there, Jess. See those lights? Behind the trees? That's the Bar M. And I assure you, you'll have no delicacies from the McGraws."

"My," she said, gulping as she ran her eyes over the distant lights. "There are a lot of lights, aren't there, Lee?"

"Are there? I never noticed."

He never noticed any amount of wealth, Jess decided a few minutes later when the road cut through the trees and the Bar M spread out in front of them—a barn, stables, a long low building and the ranch house. The last compared in expanse to Michael Hathaway's house, although it lacked the elegance. Made of logs, it rose two stories into the air and boasted a wide front porch with a swinging chair. Lamps hanging on either side of the door lit up the porch.

"They've added on," Lee commented as they rode into the yard. A couple of men emerged from the long low building, a bunkhouse no doubt. A tall, lanky young man in a battered Stetson spoke, "Howdy, stranger. Somethin' we can do for you?"

"We've come for Jim or Nick. Are they at home?"

The front door to the house opened and a dark-haired man of average build stepped out. "I'm Jim McGraw," he said, walking toward them. "Something I can help you with?"

"Man alive, Jim, I could think of a shipload of things you

could help me with," Lee said, swinging down from his horse. He strode forward, extending his hand. "But for the present, I'm just damned glad to see a friendly face."

"Monty? Lee Montgomery, by God, it is you!" Jim exclaimed. A grin spread across his face and he grabbed Lee's hand and gave it several hearty pumps. "What the—" His eyes flickered over Jess a moment, he paused, then said in a cooler voice, "What the dickens' brought you all the way out here? You staying in town?" he asked, turning to yell back to the house. "Nick, hey, you Nick in the house. Come out here you lazy cuss!"

Another man appeared at the door, taller and slightly wider than the first. He yelled back. "Lazy cuss my ass! Who the hell's so damned important you gotta interrupt our game? That sonuva—" He stopped when his eyes touched Jess. "Uh, Jim?"

"It's Lee Montgomery and . . . friend."

"Lee Montgomery? Lord almighty," Nick said, swiftly crossing the yard. "Won't you just look what the cat dragged in?" He gave Lee a good long handshake. "And by the looks of you, a big damned cat, too! What brings you out our way?"

"The pleasure of your company. But I'm forgetting my manners. Allow me to introduce my traveling companion," he said, and stepped back to help Jess down. Holding her elbow, he brought her forward. "Jessica Sullivan, this is Jim McGraw and his brother, Nick McGraw."

They nodded and welcomed her to the Bar M, their eyes flashing over her speculatively. Lee, resting his hand on her back—almost possessively—commented. "There's rather a chill in the air tonight, isn't there?"

At that, Jim laughed. "Asking for an invite, huh? 'Rather a chill.' Blast, Nick, I'd forgotten about all that fancy speech of his."

With a smile, Nick nodded to the man who'd first approached them. "Take the horses, there, Ned. Grab Harry, unpack 'em and bed 'em down." Turning back to Lee he said,

"Well it's mighty warm by the fire. You and your lady friend come along inside."

As they started forward, Jim said, "And I reckon you're staying the night, now that I see those bedrolls. So we'll get you warmed up and Melinda'll rustle up some chow, and then you'll tell us what this is all about. You in some kinda trouble, Monty?"

"A heap," Lee said.

# Chapter Nineteen

"There," Melinda McGraw said, sliding a tray onto a small table that she'd dragged in front of Jess and Lee, seated together on a leather sofa. The tray held a plate of thick ham sandwiches, pickled cucumbers, a mug of beer for Lee and a cup of steaming tea for Jess. "Help yourselves." With a swish of blue-flecked calico, she gracefully seated herself next to Jim, who sat across from Jess and Lee on an identical leather sofa. Melinda was a pretty woman, about five years Jess's senior with dark brown hair arranged in a simple chignon, and big brown eyes. "Are you comfortable now, Jessica? May I take your wrap?"

Jess would be damned in hell before she took off her shawl and displayed the dress—or lack of dress—underneath, no matter how hot the fire in their enormous stone fireplace. They'd been sitting in their well-lit, male-decorated parlor of the McGraws' house for nearly half an hour now, and the longer she spent with them, the more her stomach hurt. They appeared to be good, upstanding citizens, church-going folk and respectable beyond boredom. While Melinda had prepared a quick supper for Lee and her, Lee had casually mentioned Jess's stage career. The look of consternation that flashed between the two brothers, followed by Jim's plea *not* to tell Melinda, warned her of their sentiments toward the limelight.

"No, thank you. I'm still cold."

"Well, all right then," she said doubtfully. Nick, seated in a chair before the fire, leaned back to throw a piece of wood—a whole tree trunk by the looks of it—on the fire. The fire hissed, crackled, then lapped the wood greedily. Jim and Melinda's young son, Dickie, sitting in front of a forgotten chess game, moved his chair away from the fire.

"We camped in the cold for two nights, Mrs. McGraw," Lee said. "It may take some time before she warms up."

"I've had Stella make up a fire in your room, Jess," Melinda said, as Jim draped his arm around his wife's waist. "And another in the front room, next to Nick's for Mr. Montgomery. They should be warm enough by the time you retire."

Lee sat back, took a swig of beer and said, "The name's Lee, Melinda."

"Monty," Nick contradicted, moving the chess table aside to drag his chair into the circle of family and friends.

"Monty," Lee repeated in disgust. "I never understood why in blazes you made such an abomination of my name and left Winchester alone. Why not Whinny, like the horse?"

Jim laughed and took a sip of the brandy Nick had poured when they'd first entered the house. "Rick would've hit us."

"I might have hit you, too."

"You laughed," Nick said.

"You'd have gotten more laughs out of Whinny."

"We would've gotten shot," Jim said.

"Ha! I worked with Rick for six months, but never once did he prove his reputation for the fast draw. That man had the coolest temper I ever saw."

A shadow fell across Jim's face as he glanced at Nick. His dark blue eyes calm, Nick shrugged. "That was before Lilah," Jim said, swirling his drink.

"Yes," Melinda interrupted with a smile, "But I know Rick and Lilah's story. I believe we'd all like to hear Lee's."

Jess was surprised to see Jim wince, and a slightly pained expression enter Nick's eyes. Rubbing the stubble of his chin, Lee said, "Well, we're in some trouble, as you've supposed, ma'am. The truth is, you may wish us on our way when you've heard it all, and I shall not blame you in the least." Lee turned to Nick, the older of the two brothers. Even with his coarse language, he seemed the more conservative of the two. "It's law trouble, Nick. We've been accused of murder. We're innocent, I'd swear upon my mother's grave. Neither Jess nor I touched the man, but we stand accused regardless."

Jess, intently watching Nick's eyes, heard Melinda gasp. Flinching, Jess shifted her gaze toward Melinda, while quickly sifting through her mind for words to dispel her dismay and disgust.

"Your mother died?" Nick asked with rough sympathy.

"Ah, no," Lee said with a grin. "But I should swear upon it if she had."

"Murder," Melinda whispered. Oddly, she didn't look revolted. Actually, her eyes were alight with excitement. "Oh, whatever for?!"

Jess lifted her eyebrows and glanced at Jim. He'd bent his head slightly and worried the bridge of his nose between forefinger and thumb. "Oh, Monty, didja have to say it?" he muttered.

"All right, Monty," Nick said, "let's have it all."

Lee told them their story, from the time he'd arrived in Grant to the time they'd left. Jess flinched when he spoke of her lost money. With Robert dead, she'd never recover it. It was a sad reflection on her character that distressed her more than Robert's death.

When it came time to mention Jess's stage career, Melinda gasped again and turned to her with childlike wonder in her eyes. No revulsion with the bawdier aspects of the stage life here but appreciation. Stage fever! Jess's tension eased.

"And so," Lee finished, "we're here."

"You're a stage actress?" Melinda said.

Jess nodded, gulping back a laugh at the increasingly tortured expression on Jim's face.

"Oh, I have *always* wanted to be an actress. Is it very wonderful? It must feel like Heaven when the audience claps for you!"

Jess's mouth twitched. "Most of the time it's very nice. When they throw things, however, it can be a bit daunting."

"Throw things?"

"Generally rotten vegetables, although I have had a drink or two splashed on me."

"My goodness! How terribly rude!"

"Western audiences aren't known for their social polish."

"Perhaps it's the plays you choose," Melinda said, frowning. "What do you do?"

"I'm in a Shakespearean company."

"Shakespeare," Melinda breathed, her eyes sparkling. "Romeo and Juliet, maybe?"

"I played Juliet a time or two."

"I saw it when I was in school back East. It was very romantic, but ever so sad. Is acting—do you feel like you're living the part?"

Jess glanced at Jim, who was shaking his head, his face a mask of comic misery. Nick's appeared deeply amused. Jess realized that she was actually enjoying herself. As much as she disliked Lee's San Francisco friends, she liked these. But then he hadn't liked those in San Francisco, either.

"There are times when an actor or actress becomes swallowed up in the role," Jess said. "But you know, Melinda, Shakespeare isn't pure romance. Many characters die."

"Oh, but to die so romantically!"

Lee submerged a chuckle in his brandy.

"And so painfully, too!" Jess said with a small laugh. "Many of Shakespeare's characters die at sword point."

Melinda's forehead wrinkled and the sparkle in her eyes dimmed. "But Romeo and Juliet died from poison."

"Romeo did. Juliet stabbed herself. Hamlet's stepfather and

Laertes, his one-time friend, both died from a sword. And Othello stabbed himself, also."

Melinda's eyes widened. "He did? Why?"

"Why, because he'd killed his wife and couldn't bear to live without her."

Gasping, Melinda leaned forward. "Oh, why? Why ever would he do such a thing?"

"Jealousy. Later, however, he learned he'd been deceived by his friend."

Hand to her heart, Melinda turned to Jim. "Oh, Jim! We must see that play!"

"Sure, honey," he said, raking his fingers through his hair. "I'd love to watch a man kill his wife. Some days it seems like a fine notion to me."

Jess felt Lee's shoulders shaking with silent laughter, and she bit her lip to check her own.

Melinda flashed Jim a wavering smile. "But I've never given you cause for jealousy, have I?"

Jim's tension melted into a smile of love and chagrinned amusement. "No, honey, you haven't. But I promise if you did, I'd kill you in an instant. And then, by George, I'd kill myself, too."

"Would you?" she asked. For a moment her face lit up with the romance of it. But then she ran a measuring look over him and her shoulders sank. "No, you wouldn't. You're too practical. Besides, you didn't kill yourself the last time I died, did you?"

It proved more than Lee could bear and his laughter cracked the air, followed by Nick's deep chuckle. "Last time you died?" Jess asked in a shaky voice.

Jim shook his head in exasperation. "It's a long story. Melinda, honey, forgive me. I was young. I swear I'd do it today."

"But who would care for the children?"

"Nick would, wouldn't you, brother?"

Nick patted Dickie on the back. "Sure. Problem is, we don't have any swords."

"You have guns, though," Lee interjected.

"Oh, now you're just having fun with me!" Melinda said, and turned to Jess once more. "Still, I'm sure the audience appreciates your performance and that makes the sadness worth your efforts."

Jess nodded solemnly. "True. I even had one young cowboy who fell head over heels in love with my Juliet, which, uh, caused a commotion."

"Oh! Do tell!" Melinda said, bouncing in her chair.

The fire crackled, the lamps cast a cheerful yellow glow around the room, and the warmth of companionship floated around Jess like a balmy spring afternoon. She smiled, settled herself more comfortably in the sofa, and proceeded with her story slowly, for maximum effect. "Why, he was merely rambunctious at first," she said. "But when he saw me about to drink the poison it was too much for him. He jumped onto the stage, dashed the cup out of my hand, and tried to drag me off. I believe he said something like, 'No, you don't Juliet! Ain't no good can come from drinkin' that stuff.'"

"Oh dear!" Melinda said, eyes widening. "What did you do?"

"I resisted him as best I could, but he was very insistent. Then Romeo—played by Jon, do you remember him, Lee?" He nodded and his eyes gleamed down at her with amused appreciation and affection. Her heart tripped. "Romeo, was a little, uh, involved in his character and felt it incumbent upon himself to spring to Juliet's rescue. He grabbed a sword and brandished it about hollering something like 'Unhand her, you villainous cur.'"

"And did he?" Lee asked, grinning.

"Mercy, no! He drew his weapon shouting. 'My Colt beats your puny little sword you lily-livered coward. You ain't got no honor if'n yer thinkin' on forcin' this here girl to drink poison and that's a fact.' Then in words decency forbids me to repeat, he swore that Romeo was illegitimate and he'd 'for sure and for certain' rescue me from the no-account coyote."

"Were you frightened?" Melinda asked, awed.

"Did you go with him?" Lee asked, amused.

"By that time I was too angry to be frightened. But before I had a chance to do anything, Romeo decided to test the gun-against-sword theory. For future reference, the gun wins."

"So the cowboy shot Romeo?" Jim asked, shaking his head. "Man alive, I would've liked to see that play!"

"Actually, no. Romeo lunged with his sword—a stage sword, mind you, point-less. The cowboy aimed his gun. That's when *I* decided that we *didn't* need to test the theory. I'd finally freed myself and tried to force Romeo backstage. The bullet clipped me in the shoulder."

Lee jerked. "Good God, Jess you were *shot?*"

"I was. I stumbled and knocked down Romeo, and then proceeded to fall upon him, bleeding all over creation! I may have screamed, I don't know. Anyway, the cowboy dropped his gun and started crying, which gave the Friar the chance to tackle him and drag him offstage. Meanwhile, Romeo slid out from under me, hollering 'Juliet! Juliet!'—he'd forgotten my real name. At that point someone had the presence of mind to drop the curtain. The audience exploded, stomping their feet, clapping and shouting. There was only about a hundred people but it sounded like a thousand. It was," she said smiling at Melinda, "very exciting."

"Oh, my goodness!" Melinda said, clapping herself. "It sounds it!"

"But, Jess," Lee said, his brow creasing. "You'd been shot!"

She shrugged. "The audience believed it was part of the play, and it was a clean wound. Two days later we opened to standing-room-only. We tried, truly, to do the show correctly but they'd have none of it. Cat calls, boos, all that. Midway through, one of the actors dressed up as a cowboy and tried to abduct me and shoot Romeo. Again, the audience exploded. For the remainder of our time in that town we played it that way. To this day, those people believe guns existed back in the 16th century!"

Nick burst out laughing. "I never knew the limelight could be so dangerous!" he exclaimed.

"Nor did I," Lee said. "Jess, does this sort of thing happen often?"

She laughed, tossing her hair. "Goodness, no! How many gun-brandishing cowboys do you think like Romeo and Juliet? Besides, after that, Robert insisted that all guns be left at the door."

Lee nodded, appearing relieved. "That I remember."

"Well, that decides it for me then," Melinda said with a delicate shudder. "I'm now very happy I never pursued the stage."

Jim took her hand and kissed the back of it. "Me, too, honey."

"So," Melinda said, after a minute's pause. "How are we going to rescue Lee and Jess from Mr. Temple?"

Jim winced and flashed a pleading look at Lee. "Lee said his family would do that."

"But they're in Boston. What if they don't make it here in time? We need another plan, just in case."

Lee looked skeptical. "I doubt they'll come at all, Mrs. McGraw. I daresay my father will conduct his business through the telegraph, lawyers, and perhaps hire a Pinkerton."

Surprise brightening Melinda's chocolate-brown eyes, she exclaimed, "Oh, but that won't do it. Pinkertons and lawyers are no use against a lynch mob!"

"As I said, we saw no sign of a posse," he said, his eyes twinkling.

"Oh, but you don't always *see* a posse, do you, Jim?" she asked, turning to her husband.

Nick leaned forward, touched Dickie's arm as if in apology and said, "Son, you're a tad flushed. You feelin' poorly?"

Dickie's eyes registered quick, but reluctant, understanding. "I'm tuckered, is all."

Jim leaned forward. "You sure? Not coming down with a fever are you? Dang, it's late, too!" he said glancing at the mantel clock. "Quarter to nine, long past your bedtime!"

"Oh no!" Melinda said, moving from the sofa to kneel at

her son's feet. Face traced with concern, she placed a hand on Dickie's forehead. "You are warm, honey!"

No doubt, Jess thought, due to the fire blazing just behind him.

Dickie shook his mother's hand off his head. "I'm fine, Ma!" But at Nick's encouraging nod behind Melinda, he added grudgingly, "My stomach hurts a *tiny* bit."

"Then it's off to bed with you!" She grabbed his hand and rose, then pulled him through the parlor and the dining room to a door carefully hidden among the wallpaper. "I *think* I still have a little of Lilah's stomach medicine."

"Oh no!" he called, looking back at Nick, his eyes wide in distress. Nick smiled broadly and winked at him just before Melinda shut the door with an authoritative click.

Jim drew a huge sigh of relief. "You owe that boy, Nick."

"I know. I'll take him shootin' twice this week."

"Shootin'? You ever *try* that medicine?"

"Okay, I'll allow him a turn with my new Remington. How's that?"

Jim thought on it a moment, then nodded. "That'll settle it."

Lee sat back and, as if it were the most natural thing in the world, dropped his arm around Jess's shoulders. "And so, gentlemen, what did Melinda mean by another plan?"

Jim barked a laugh. "I dunno, but you can be sure it wasn't gonna be very simple—"

"Or very good," Nick added.

"But *ever* so romantic—" Jim said.

"Most likely with you, Monty, giving your life for Jess," Nick interjected.

"And," Jim said, chuckling, "you, Jess, killing yourself out of guilt, heartache, or both."

"Escape hanging by suicide then?" Lee asked, dimpling.

"Sure," Jim said, "but think of the legend you'd make!"

"A man can't be a legend and remain alive?"

"Not a good legend, anyhow," Jim said decidedly.

"I believe, Jess," Lee said, smiling down at her, "we'll avoid the redoubtable Melinda McGraw's plan for immortality, shall we?"

She laughed. "Yes, but only if you promise not to force any more delicacies on me!"

"Done! Jim, Nick, we choose to live!"

"Well, then," Jim said, "you'll have to give me a few hours alone with Melinda. Most days I can talk some sense into her but only if there's no, ah, distractions."

Jess smothered a stage yawn. "I *am* tired. If you wouldn't mind pointing me in the right direction, I think I'll find my bed."

Nick nodded approvingly. "Good idea. If you're in bed, Melinda will leave us men to talk alone. You go up these stairs here, turn left, it's the third door on the left. Second is Melinda's bathroom, which is more'n likely why she put you there. Your room has a connecting door."

"A bathroom? You have one?"

Jim nodded. "Sure. We added one a few years ago after seeing one at a friend's ranch. There's a bathtub, stove, and a pump, tho' it doesn't work so well in the summer. Water's scarce 'round here then."

A *connecting* bathroom! Oh, sweet luxury dead center in the middle of nowhere! "It sounds marvelous," Jess exclaimed, rising. "And now, I'll bid you all a good night!"

"I'll show you up," Lee said, rising, too.

For a few seconds, Jess could only stare at him. First the hand on her back, then his arm resting across her shoulders, and now this. When had Lee become so attentive?

"Honestly, Lee," she said, puzzled. "I'm capable of locating my own room." In San Francisco, at the ball?

"Doubtless you are," he answered as he crossed the room to the front door where he retrieved their saddlebags. "But you'll want your things tonight, won't you?"

Or before that? After their picnic in the mountains? "I'm also perfectly capable of carrying them myself."

"Indeed, you are," he said, throwing one set of bags on his left shoulder. "But with a big hulking thug like me at your service, why should you?" He heaved the other bag over his right shoulder with a loud, theatrical grunt.

She ran her gaze over his large—but far from hulking—form. "Oh, yes! Every woman *dreams* of being accompanied to her bedroom door by a thug, *hulking* and all!"

"Not *every* woman. Only women being chased by lynch mobs. Under those conditions it's generally considered helpful to have a thug at your service. Just ask Melinda."

She sighed dramatically, avoiding eye contact with the McGraws, for she was enjoying herself and they couldn't possibly approve of this flirtation. She followed Lee to the stairs. "And will you, o' thug of mine, leap in front of a gun to save my life?"

He nodded to the stairs. "You first, my lady," he said with a low bow. "I will most certainly throw myself in front of gunfire," he continued, following her up the stairs. "But for the sake of argument, what *kind* of gun would that be?"

"Does it matter?" she asked, reaching the landing. She strode down the hall toward the door Nick had directed her.

"Well, if it's a Colt I shouldn't think twice. A shot gun, now, might give me pause."

She opened the door and entered a pleasant room decorated in gold and tan. A wood fire danced merrily in the fireplace and a few lamps filled the room with soft yellow light. A large oak bed with a patchwork quilt called to her from the middle of the far wall. To her left, toward the front of the house was another door. The bathroom!

Lee dropped her bags on the dresser as she turned to him, smiling broadly. "No doubt, you'd consider the kind of gunfire quickly, as I could be dead in a split second."

"A mere flash in my brain, my lady, I assure you. You shall, no doubt, assure *me* that, as I lay dying in agony from being gut shot, you'll weep profusely and swear vengeance!"

"Of course! And I might even promise to bury you, too!"

He laughed. "Always a well of compassion." He glanced around the room. "Not bad, eh?"

She frowned a little. "Very handsome. Tell me, Lee, do you have any friends who *aren't* wealthy?"

His eyes twinkling, he stepped toward her. "Yes. You."

"Then I must be a constant source of enlightenment for you!"

In a heartbeat his smile softened from raw merriment to deep affection. Reaching up, he brushed her lips with his thumb. "A continual, delightful source of enlightenment, sweetheart. And now, your hulking thug shall take payment in a kiss." He touched her lips with his, lightly stroking them with his tongue. Just as she was raising her arms to pull him nearer, he lifted his head. Eyes gleaming, he stepped back.

She frowned. "That wasn't much of a kiss, My Lord Thug."

"Complaints, my lady?" Lee asked, raising an eyebrow. "I thought after last night . . ." his voice trailed off.

Mercy, what on earth was she *asking* for? Another kiss like yesterday's and her restraint would dissolve like sugar in hot coffee. Goodness, just the thought and she was melting.

Biting her lip, she shook her head. "No. No, of course not."

The hint of a smile etched the corners of his mouth and knowledge leaped in his eyes. With a hot shiver, she watched the gleam of desire warm into a glow. She crossed her arms over her chest and looked about for distraction. Her eyes fell on the bed. "It'll be odd sleeping in my own bed tonight."

"You had your own bed last night."

"A rope bed. It was more for fainting than sleeping."

He tilted his head to one side. "Are you saying you might be lonely?"

She nodded. "I suppose. Not so with you I expect."

"Very lonely," he said firmly.

This was *not* the right conversation! But with Lee in a certain mood, there was no right conversation. "But not," she said, her voice trembling, "so frustrated."

He stared in silence, his eyes hot now, yet that shimmering

affection remained, more seductive than anything he could ever say. "The frustration was worth every minute, Jess."

Her heart climbed up her throat and lodged there, beating frantically. She tried to swallow it to no avail. "I think," she said in a low voice, "you'd better leave now."

"All right. Sleep well then, but not too late! You'll have real food and real coffee for breakfast. Unless," he said with a sudden spark of mirth, "you'd rather I find that oyster tin?"

She laughed, grateful for the easing tension. "Maybe another time."

Settling his saddlebag more firmly on his shoulder, he agreed. "Whenever you desire, ma'am. I made certain to keep it for the future so that I may be at your service."

As he crossed to the door, she said, "I don't believe you! You threw it away!"

"Never," he said, flashing his dimple, "would I discard something that's touched your lips, Jess." He winked at her, then pulled the door shut.

She fell asleep counting all the items that had touched her lips that he must certainly have discarded, just to remind herself that most of what Lee said was pure, unadulterated blarney.

# Chapter Twenty

Lee almost whistled as he strode to his room. Jess was close to caving, he could feel it in his bones. It was entirely possible that if he'd pressed his suit, he'd have won her tonight. But she was bone weary and he'd yet to clean up after four days on the dodge. When he took her for the first time he wanted more than mere surrender; he wanted her wild with desire and ready to climb the walls. After all this time a few moments of passion would scarcely satisfy him. Hell no, he wanted an explosion of pleasure, wanted to hear her sing his name when he touched her, wanted his body to ache in desperation before he buried himself deep inside her—a hot shudder ran down his back. No mere surrender, but complete capitulation.

Neither exhaustion nor dirt was conducive to those conditions. Instead, he found his room, tossed his bags inside, and switched his thoughts to his two old friends. With a lightness in his step he descended the stairs, smiled broadly, and seated himself once more on the sofa. "She's settling in, I think," he said, taking a sip of his drink. "It's been rather difficult for her these last few days. She's not a native Westerner."

"No kidding," Jim said with a sarcastic smirk. "I couldn't tell!"

"So, Monty," Nick asked, "where in hell did you meet this

woman, you lucky sonuvabitch? What the devil does she want with you? She's damned near the most beautiful woman I've ever seen."

Smiling in spite of the discomfort stirring in his belly, Lee answered, "A mutual friend introduced us. That other actress we told you about, the one who helped us escape. Michelle."

"*Two* actresses?" Nick said, as Jim rose to retrieve a cigar box on the mantel. "Sounds a little seamy to me."

Narrowing his eyes, Lee rubbed at the crick developing in his neck. If Nick and Jim took a sudden dislike to Jess, it could cause trouble. "It didn't come about the way you're thinking, Nick. In truth, Michelle and I have been—friendly—for years. But Jess is a far cry from Michelle. They're friends, and that's where any resemblance ends."

Jim took a cigar for himself and handed one to Lee. Nick scowled at Jim, who shook his head and said mildly, "You quit smokin'. I promised Rick I'd look after you."

"You're havin' one."

"Never had the addiction to smokes, so it don't matter to me. But you smoke one, and before you know it, you'll be puffing away again day and night, and hacking like a lunger."

"Damn it," Nick grumbled, "stupidest promise I ever made." Still scowling, he turned back to Lee. "I dunno, Monty, that tale the lady told was a little racy."

Jim flashed amused eyes over Nick and said, "Oh, for the love of God, Nick, sometimes you're a damned prude! Melinda didn't mind it and you know when it gets down to bedrock, she could spot that kinda woman miles away." Turning to Lee, he said, eyes brightening. "Two actresses, Lee. How in hell'd you catch *two* of 'em? I could never make a mash with even one."

Lee grinned. "It helps to have charm."

"Yeah. Reckon I forgot that," Jim said sarcastically. "Okay, so she's an actress whose mind slipped when she met you. And you explained all right and tight how you ended up in this murder difficulty. But what's too many for me is why you didn't separate, maybe in Colorado Springs. And why come here? You could've 'run for the border' without our help. As an actress, she can find a job most anywhere. You came from 'Frisco, right? Why not just send her back?"

Shifting in his chair, Lee tried to maintain some humor in his voice. "I thought I should see the thing through."

"Uh huh," Nick said, and picking up on Jim's teasing voice, continued for him. "I'd bet the ranch that if she weren't so pretty you would've run for cover long before this."

Lee laughed. "Certainly. But with Jess," he let out a small whistle, "Lord I'd nail my eyelids open just to watch her sleep."

"Yeah, well," Nick said, "with a woman like that, you stay long enough and she'll hook you but good. And I'm not talkin' just a ring on the finger, man, I'm talkin' one through the nose. I thought you were a sworn bachelor, like me."

"I am."

"For now," Jim said. "I better warn you, Monty, Melinda's more 'n likely already planning your wedding."

"Hell, Jim, she's probably checking out her gown right now to see if it can be altered," Nick said laughing.

"And the *last* time she set her mind to a wedding, her brother Steve got hitched. Fact is, she'd gotten all five of 'em hitched in nine year's time. Only one who's escaped is Nick, 'cause he's smart enough not to show a partiality to any woman shy of a couple soiled doves in town."

"Amen!"

Oh, damn it to hell, he'd like to have avoided this. "Well, she'll be foiled this time, gentlemen. Jess doesn't love me."

"Hogwash!" Jim laughed. "She will when Melinda's through with her!"

"'Sides," Nick added, "a woman don't need love to want a weddin'."

"The thing of it is," Lee said, taking a deep breath. "Jess has already had one."

Jim's eyes widened. "You're *married!*"

"I'm not. Jess is."

At which point Lee had the dubious satisfaction of seeing Nick spit out his brandy and Jim play catch with his cigar, swearing when it burned him.

"Married? Have you gone loco? She's not wearing a band," Nick said when he finished coughing.

"Damn, Monty," Jim said, stabbing out the cigar in an ashtray, "we're not gonna have an irate husband bangin' down our door, are we? I'd take the posse over that any day."

Lee shook his head. They seemed concerned, but not angry enough to heave them out. Damned, though, if talking about it all didn't burn more holes in his shallow heart. "She wears her band on her right hand. As for banging down your door, we don't even know where he is."

"Don't know where he is?" Jim asked incredulous. "Don't you think you oughtta find that kinda thing out? He'd like as not sneak up on you while you're sleeping and plug you in the back."

"Never fear, gentlemen, I sleep on my back. He'll have to 'plug me' right between the eyes."

"I'm not laughing," Nick retorted. "Sonuvabitch, man, you can't go stealing other men's wives! Especially when they look like *that!*"

"I didn't steal her. He left her."

"Likely story!" Jim snapped. "Aw Christ, Nick, he's gonna get us all killed," he moaned, running a hand through his hair.

"Nevertheless, it's true. When I met Jess she was, uh, unencumbered by male companionship."

"If you aren't the stupidest sonuvabitch I ever did meet," Nick swore. "So *he* ran from *her*. You think he'll shoot you any less dead?"

Laughing, Lee said, "My mother's not a dog, nor is my father, although I confess many disagree on the latter. Regardless, Dunne left Jess six years ago. She was young still, eighteen, and I don't believe she was quite the beauty she is now."

Nick scowled. "Eighteen?"

Lee lit a match, puffed on his cigar until it caught, then blew out a smoke ring before answering. "Eighteen. And recently delivered of a child. Apparently the strain of fatherhood was too much for him and he vamoosed."

"Oh, my God," Jim breathed with a sick twist of his face. "Where's the child?"

"Dead."

Nick sucked in his breath. "How long after she had the child did he cut dirt?"

"A few days. She had a rough delivery, the baby was sickly, and they were out of money. He left, the baby died. By and by, she found work on the stage and now here she is, grieving mother, abandoned wife, and suspected murderess. Quite a life I'd say."

Nick eyed Lee grimly. "I reckon I was wrong about you getting hooked. You already are."

Lee winced at the shot to his heart. Trying to maintain a cheerful tone, he said, "You always were remarkably astute, Nick."

"Which means," Jim said, taking a gulp of brandy, "that the answer is yes. This all has a hellishly familiar ring to it, and I don't like it. I damn near got killed last time."

"Last time? What last time?"

"Rick and Jim got into a few tight squeezes after you skedaddled."

"You mean with the Frost Queen?"

"Yeah, with Lilah."

"Nick, I was thinking," Jim said, regarding his brother. "Sure we can take care of Monty and Miss Sullivan. Worse to worse, we could hide 'em in the mountains, but—"

Nick, smiling grimly, sat forward and interrupted, "But getting them out of the state might be smarter."

Jim nodded. "And Texas—"

"Is where Rick is," Nick said, turning to Lee. "He's got a mighty nice spread down there, Monty. Posse won't chase you across the border, and even if they did, there's Winchester."

Lee cocked his head slightly. "It's unlike you to run from trouble, Nick."

Grimacing, Nick said, "I'm not. We don't have Rick's reputation, is all. At the Rockin' R you'd have both the law and his gun on your side."

Lee'd only known Rick for six months before he'd left the Bar M. Still, in that short time, he'd developed a strong affinity for the man whose rough frontier humor had hidden a quick, well-educated mind. He'd never fully believed Rick's reputation, but if others did and it kept Jess safe, then who was he to argue? "All right, let's talk about it."


"And so, Jess," Lee said, "Jim and Nick believe we'll be safer at the Rockin' R."

Settled in a leather chair in the library and warmed by a crackling fire, Jess has listened with only half an ear to a not very detailed story about Rick and Lilah Winchester, friends of the McGraws' and one-time fugitives. Her mind had, instead, focused upon the pure pleasure of being at the Bar M, where, after less than a day, she felt more at ease than anywhere else in the past six years. The easy camaraderie between Melinda, Jim, and Nick enveloped her in a soft cocoon. The three children, rambunctious and outspoken, tickled her funny bone and massaged the ache in her heart for her own lost baby. Home, she thought abruptly, this was what *home* felt like, complete with Lee, seated across from her in borrowed denim pants and a gray shirt.

Except that Lee could never be home—not an unsteady gambler with a wandering eye.

But right now his eyes were watching her steadily, and all too easily, her heart created a happy home with him at the center.

"But," she protested, as much to her heart as to the other occupants of the room—Nick, Jim, and Melinda, "what use would Mr. Winchester's fast draw be? If he shot one of the posse, wouldn't that just make him a murderer, too?"

Jim, sitting behind a gleaming mahogany desk, shifted uncomfortably. Nick lounged on top of the desk, with a glass of brandy in hand and one leg swinging lightly. Melinda sat perched on the arm of Jim's chair. "Not Rick," Jim said. "He, uh, has a way of forcing self-defense."

"If," Melinda said, "they were unwise enough to try it. I think it's a marvelous idea. It's been ages since we've seen Lilah and Rick!"

With a deep sigh, Jim turned to her and set his teeth. "You weren't invited, honey."

"Nonsense. Lilah's always happy to see us. I'll bundle up the kids and we'll all go."

"There's no time. We leave tomorrow morning."

"So soon?" Jess asked. Oh, but she wanted to stay just a little longer, to pretend—

"It's for the best, Jess," Lee cut off her thoughts.

"You see, Jim," said Melinda, "even Jess would like to wait another day. I can pack us all up and the carriage will travel just as fast with the children as without them."

"We weren't taking the carriage."

"But you'll need it to carry the clothes I'm going to lend Jess."

Amusement bubbled up inside Jess. "Melinda, I really don't need *that* much."

"Oh, but you do! It will take days and days."

"Not," Jim ground out, "if we travel light."

"A carriage isn't that heavy."

"Mercy, Lee," Jess said in a low voice, "was she always this stubborn?"

"I don't know, sweetheart. Last time I was here, she was dead."

Nick, about to sip his drink, burst out laughing. "By God, Monty, why'd we let you go? You were the funniest cowhand we ever had."

Jess tilted her head in confusion. "He told me he left because he hated the cows."

"Well," Nick said, smirking, "I reckon he did, but he hated those bulls more, right, Jim?"

Grinning from ear to ear, Jim nodded. "Sure did," he said, then whispered something in Melinda's ear that brought a smile to her face.

"Bulls?" Jess asked Lee.

"Now, gentlemen," he said, flashing a warning glance between the two men. "We don't need to discuss this in front of the ladies, do we?"

"I don't know. I reckon this is something Jess oughtta know," Jim said, reaching for the bottle. "See, Jess, Monty liked to moo."

Raising an eyebrow, Jess turned to Lee. "Moo?"

"Moo," Jim answered decidedly.

His eyes twinkling, Lee heaved a sigh. "I told you, I didn't like cows. They mooed and bawled all the time. God, but they are the loudest blasted animals on earth. Kept me awake half the night! So," he said, with a shrug, "I mooed back. In self-defense."

"And he was good at it, too," Nick chimed in.

"The cows, they liked it," Jim said.

"They mooed more," Nick interjected.

"Anyhow, one night," Jim went on, "the men had a tad too much of the o-be-joyful, and started makin' bets that Monty could get those cows to come right on up to him. Maybe make brandin' easier."

"So they got a cowhide," Nick interrupted, "and tied it to Monty. Then they put him in a pen with a few cows and told him to moo."

"Problem was," Jim took up the reins, "we plumb forgot there was a bull in the pen. So Monty starts mooing, the cows moo back, and they all wake up the bull. Now that bull's feelin' frisky and those cows ain't been in heat for months. Next thing we know, the bull starts after Monty, so Monty cuts dirt. He's just about to the fence when he stumbles over a cow pie. And the bull, he sees his chance to get *real* close."

"Monty would've been fine if he just stayed put," Nick added.

"Easy for you to say," Lee growled. "You ever been raped by a cow?"

"Bull," Jim said.

"So," Nick continued, "Monty tries to escape—"

"He wasn't mooing anymore," Jim offered.

"And the bull gets, uh, irritated, and tries to hold him still with his horns."

"And they're all *laughing!*" Lee interjected.

"But not so much that Winchester couldn't get a shot off. Once the bull was down, we dragged Monty out and patched him up enough to get him to the doctor."

"And *that*," Jim concluded, "is the tale of How Monty Lost His Moo."

"Oh, dear," Melinda said, wiping tears of laughter from her eyes. "I never heard that story before."

Jim shrugged. "It was from before your time."

"When you were dead," Lee said, and Nick chuckled again.

"I don't understand this. When she was dead?"

"It's a long story, Miss Sullivan," Nick said.

"And not very interesting," Melinda said firmly. "Why don't you come with me, Jess? We'll go through my clothes and see if I've got something to lend you for your trip to Texas. And then," she continued as Jess nodded and rose to follow her, "I expect you'll want to rest before supper. You must still be exhausted after your adventures."

Nick shook his head. "Give her credit, Jim, she's the only woman alive who'd have the perfect outfit for a run to the border."

# Chapter Twenty-One

"Jess," Lee called out, after knocking on the door to her room for the second time. She had to be in there. She'd left the library a couple hours earlier and he hadn't seen her since. He'd come hoping she was still asleep, lying in bed wearing nothing but her chemise . . .

His blood quickened as he twisted the doorknob. The knife, he reminded himself. He was here for Jim's knife, which he'd lent her to slit Michelle's tight red dress, exposing one long, perfectly shaped leg. He'd been damned jealous of that knife.

He opened the door, "Jess, do you still—"

The room was empty; the bed was made. Damn it! His eyes flashed around, searching for her, and fell on the door to his left, standing slightly ajar. He heard a light splashing. The bathroom. Bloody hell, she was in the tub!

Visions of her naked bursting through his mind, he crossed the room in three long strides calling, "Jess." When he knocked the door swung open.

She lay in a large brass tub, her hair pinned up and the bubbles that skimmed the top of the water imperfectly hid what lay beneath. His breath caught in his throat as his eyes fixed upon her breasts floating just below the surface of the water, her nipples peeking dark red through the suds.

Then she gasped, "Lee," and sank deeper in the tub while covering herself with one arm. Her face turned deep red, not, Lee decided, unlike the flush of a woman on the verge of climax. "Oh my God, don't you know how to knock?" she exclaimed.

Reluctantly, he averted his eyes as his brain seethed with various schemes to get her out of that tub and into his arms—words, seduction, deception. Anything.

"I did," he said. "You didn't answer."

"Well, I'm answering now! Get out!"

"It's no big deal, Jess," he said, shrugging in an effort to appear casual, although his heart was hammering in anticipation. If he could get her out of that tub, if he managed to wrap his arms around her and kiss those lips, stroke that body, would she struggle? Or would she moan in delight? His mind flipped to their last kiss. And her response. Delight. It'd be delight. "I've seen it all before."

"Not this particular all!"

Another shrug. "I'm not looking. I'm here to remind you that supper's in an hour. And to retrieve that knife I lent you. It's not mine, actually. It's Jim's and I thought I'd better return it." He breathed deeply of the scent of perfumed soap wafting through the air, while the sound of each popping bubble fueled his excitement. Out of the corner of his eye, he saw her dark, silky eyebrows drawing together in a frown, and even that heated his blood.

"Knife? What knife? Good gracious, Lee, this is not the place for this conversation. Come back later when I'm—" She sucked in her breath. Something about the sound made him look at her, just in time to see a flash of emotion—desire. "When I'm decent," she finished.

*I want to come now,* he thought. "Later . . . the problem is . . ." The problem was later she wouldn't be so vulnerable. He didn't want her decent; he wanted her naked. Once dressed it'd be far more difficult for him to ignite that deeply buried passion of hers. "I borrowed it from Jim a few years ago and forgot to return it. If I leave, I'll forget again."

She stared hard at him and he stared right back, refusing to turn away again. The muscles in her face tightened as she took a couple deep breaths. It required every last bit of his willpower to refrain from dropping his gaze to where her breasts rose and fell in the water.

"I think it's still in my saddlebag," she answered. "On the dresser. Go and look for it, then, and close the door behind you."

He wouldn't leave now if the whole damned house was on fire and he had less than a minute to escape. "You don't really care to have me pawing through your things, do you? Why don't you get it for me? I'll turn my head."

"Are you mad? I am *not* getting out of this tub while you're in the room!"

He chuckled. "Jess, sweetheart, as I said—"

"No!"

"All right," he conceded. "I'll try." And, he decided as he crossed the room in a few shaky strides, he'd most definitely fail.

He opened the bag, found the knife immediately, then buried it at the bottom of the bag.

"It's not here," he called out.

"Of course it is. You're not looking hard enough," she yelled back.

"No, it's not."

"Try the drawers then."

Blood pounding in his ears, he opened the drawers and slammed them shut. "It's not here, Jess."

"Oh, for Heaven's sake! Then leave and *I'll* look."

"Wrap yourself in a towel and come see for yourself."

"I'll come look when I hear that door close."

"Jess, for the love of God—all right, if you're that concerned about it, I'll close my eyes and turn my head. All right?"

"No, it's not all right! Wait outside!"

"Be sensible. How would it appear to the McGraws, to have me waiting outside your door?"

Silence. Then, "Damn it, Lee, a mule is less stubborn than you."

He heard a splash as she climbed from the tub; his heart jumped. *Easy ol' boy, just a few more minutes.* He crossed his arms, leaned against the dresser, and closed his eyes tightly. The fragrance of scented soap floated ahead of her as she padded across the floor.

"You said you'd turn your face away," she said when she was next to him.

He could feel the heat of her body. "All right," he agreed, and turned in what he thought was the direction of the window.

"Although," she said as he heard her opening the bag, the faint sound of leather against leather. "You might very well be blind. Here it is, at the bottom of the bag. Did it occur to you to move things aside? Perhaps take everything out?"

"It can't be," he said. He opened his eyes, stepped toward her to inspect the bag for good measure, then turned his head to regard her. Her hair, damp from the steam of her bath, pressed so sweetly to her temples. The pins that held it up were sticking out, begging for him to remove them—slowly. He held her gaze for several seconds. Her eyes darkened and, blood racing, he leaned in for a kiss.

"Lee—" she started in a low, entreating voice.

He smothered her words with his mouth, begging entrance, begging her to surrender to the passion electrifying the air around them. When she yielded, he surged inside. She was hot, sweet, and remarkably responsive. Her tongue met his and his staff jerked in reaction, craving the same attention. Groaning, he lifted his hands to hold her head while he deepened the kiss, trying desperately to taste as much of her as possible should she refuse a more intimate touch. By God, if she did, he'd never make it through another day. The last few had stretched his patience to the limit. Another second without relief and he'd go stark raving mad.

He wasn't yet beyond sanity, however. When she emitted a tiny moan, the sound slipped through the pounding in his ears and shot into his conscience—confound it—compelling him to break off the kiss. If she asked him to leave, he would, but it'd be by way of the window, plunging straight to his death.

She stared mutely back at him, drawing several deep breaths. Breaths, he noticed as his gaze shifted south, that strained the towel tucked around her body. Fascinated, he watched as the dark crevice between them grew ever lighter until the towel broke free and fell to the floor. With a moan of tormented anguish he fixed his gaze upon her full breasts, rose-tipped and hardening in the coolness of the room.

After a moment he lifted his eyes to hers. "Don't deny me this time, Jess," he beseeched her in a desire-roughened voice. His hand crept forward to cover one beautiful breast, allowing the tip to tickle his palm. He yearned to kiss it, suckle it, hear her moan in deepening ecstasy. Holding her eyes with his, he moved his hand to tease her nipple with his thumb. Her eyes grew impossibly wider and she gasped. Not in dissent, but with approval, encouragement.

Tremors of desire rolled through Lee's body, and he leaned in to kiss her again, lifting his hands to pull the pins from her hair. It fell around his wrists like ribbons of silk. Burying his fingers in her soft tresses, he cradled her head and swept her mouth with his tongue, savoring every last drop of sweetness. She answered in kind, provoking flashes of hot pleasure. He slipped his hands down her back to cup her bare bottom—firm and delicately rounded. When she swayed against him, he carefully shifted her backward to brace her against the wall. Then, while stroking her hips, he slid his mouth away from the wonder of her lips, to kiss and nibble the sensitive skin of her neck. Whimpering, she moved her head to allow him greater access and then gripped his shoulders to pull him against her naked body. It almost undid him.

Jess's conscience had quieted to a murmur. She knew she was making a mistake. She knew she ought to ask Lee to leave. Instead, she drew him nearer. His lips sent shivers down her spine, while the movements of his hands created delicious sensations in her lower belly. Her heart felt light, her stomach fluttered. Impossible, absolutely impossible to refuse him or the desire bubbling in her veins like champagne.

As she took several breaths, the soothing scent of wood smoke rose from his hair and filled her senses, gently blowing away the last vestiges of conscience. He blazed a path down her shoulder toward her breast, nipping and licking, light pain followed by sparkling pleasure, making her skin tingle. Her breast quivered, and as he drew nearer to them, her nipples tightened in anticipation. Breathing heavily, she leaned her head against the wall and clutched his shoulders. Kiss it, dear God, she so dearly wanted him to kiss it . . .

His left hand glided upward from her hip, to her waist, to her right breast, while his mouth traveled over the swell of her left breast. Nearer, nearer, and then his thumb brushed against one sensitive nipple and his tongue flicked over the other. Her whole body jerked. She cried out in desperate pleasure.

"Again," she rasped. "Oh, God, Lee . . ."

Another flick, and another. She moved her hands to hold his head, and he let loose a soft laugh. His hot breath cooled her nipple and she whimpered in response. It was torture.

He licked her, slowly drawing his tongue around her nipple and then over it, again and again and again. Her heart beat wildly, sending her blood racing through her body, heating her skin, her face. And then his mouth closed completely around her tormented nipple, drawing her inside. Like lightning, desire flashed from her breast to the sensitive area between her thighs. As he continued suckling one nipple and stroking the other, the flashes softened into a warm, wet glow, spreading downward, from breast to belly, to a growing pool of pleasure below. Growing pleasure, and a growing need for greater stimulation.

His hand glided over her hip, across her belly, and toward that pool. She held her breath. His fingers slid through the petals they found there. Her legs buckled.

Gasping, he lifted his head and her hands dropped away. His left hand held her steady as he slid a finger inside her. She moaned, and her body tightened around him.

"Jesus, Jess," he breathed in her ear, "you're flowing like a river." He slipped back out and moved his hand to take hers. His fingers were damp from playing between her legs. She shivered. "Open your eyes, sweetheart." She did and saw that his were so dark they were almost black. They glittered as he moved her hand down over his belly to where he was straining against the rough cloth of his borrowed trousers. "I want you," he said. "Right here. Right now."

He peered hard at her, as if expecting some reply. She couldn't. She'd lost all command of the English language. All she could do was feel, and those feelings were so incredible that nothing else mattered.

And then he was helping her unbutton his pants, untie his drawers. He shoved them down and then guided her hand to his shaft. When she ran her fingertips over the length, pulsing and powerful, he sucked in his breath. Dipping his head, he rasped, "Right here, Jess, right now."

His knee slid between her legs, gently widening the breech. "Right here . . ."

He wrapped his hand around hers, shifted, and then helped her guide him toward the opening.

"Right now . . ."

And then he was inside her, large and full, burying himself to the hilt with a deep, satisfied groan. His hips shifted slightly and *she* groaned, for the movement caused him to rub against the place where desire pulsed. She held on tightly as he slid back out, whispering harshly, "Right here, sweetheart"—he drove inside—"right now."

Out, then in again, each movement pulling at that quivering bundle of nerves, accompanied by his voice repeating the refrain in her ear, over and over again. His thighs shook, her body quaked, and he started to thrust faster. She gasped as all thought, all reason, vanished, leaving behind nothing but sensation: her perfumed soap mixing with his wood-smoke scent, her hoarse breathing and the sound of his harsh whisper, the hard internal caress of him moving inside her.

Then with a loud cry he shoved even deeper, spilling inside her and tripping a nerve that caused her body to convulse in pleasure. Her legs failed her and she slumped against him. Breathing heavily, he wrapped an arm around her waist and propped himself up against the wall with his other shoulder. Trembling, they stood that way for a long while. Jess's world righted itself again, and presently Lee spoke, amusement and passion rumbling through his voice. "Well, sweetheart, I think we've solved your frigidness."

"Goodness," she whispered against his shoulder. "Goodness, yes."

He kissed her temple. "I never really believed it at any rate."

Another minute passed, and then as if she were made of fine crystal, he leaned her against the wall. The paper felt smooth and cool to her overheated skin. "Stay there just a minute," he said and backed up to seat himself on the bed.

Puzzled, Jess watched him remove his boots and socks, then kick off his trousers and drawers. "Isn't it a little late for that?" she asked, running her eyes over his narrow hips, hard flat belly and muscular legs. Her breath caught in her throat. Mercy, but he was as handsome out of his clothes as he was in them.

His eyes gleamed as he yanked at the buttons of his shirt. "Did you think we were done?"

"But . . . but what more is there?" she stuttered, eyeing his spent member, nestled in the thatch of black curls between his thighs. It was smaller now and not nearly so commanding, but, she thought with a hot shudder, capable of such marvels when erect.

His gaze ran appreciatively over her person before finding her eyes once more. "Plenty," he said and dropped his shirt.

She could barely breathe when he looked at her like that. Suddenly she was warm again and the soft area down below was twitching—and wet. His seed was leaking from her, running down her leg. She pushed a piece of hair behind her ear. "I ought to clean up," she said in a trembling voice.

"I'll do it," he said, leaning over to scoop up the towel.

Her pulse tripped. Smiling, he rose and took the step between them. He ran his thumb over her cheekbone. "You're flushed, sweetheart."

"I'm a little warm."

Holding her gaze, he moved his hand from her face, down her neck, over her shoulders, and then inward to finger the tip of her breast. Languid desire swirled through her belly. *Oh, not possible, not again.*

With the other hand he slid the damp towel between her legs, then down the inside of her thigh in a featherlight motion that turned the simple gesture into a caress. With a gasp of delight, she leaned her head against the wall and reveled in rising pleasure. *Oh yes, again.*

"I'll do it," he repeated, his eyes gleaming. "With the towel," he said, moving it down the inside of the other thigh. "And my mouth."

He dropped the towel, and slid to his knees. The words had scarcely registered when she felt his mouth on the sensitive skin of her inner thigh. She sucked in her breath and grabbed for his shoulders as hot thrills ran up her thigh to the soft area between her legs. Her legs shook and the world started to slide away. He trailed kisses up her thigh toward the juncture of her legs. Oh no, she thought. Not *there.*

Oh yes!

Oh, she couldn't breathe! She slumped against him, her legs no longer able to support her.

He let out a deep, rough laugh. "Sweetheart, this will be impossible if you close your legs."

She couldn't move, could hardly think.

"All right," he said, rising to his feet. He wrapped an arm around her waist to hold her up and glanced around the room. Through the mists of desire, she saw his eyes fix upon something a few feet away. He leaned over to retrieve the towel, then led her to the dressing table chair, where he spread the towel over the buff velvet upholstery. Carefully, he settled her in the chair, then sank to his knees once more. Oh yes, she thought wantonly. *Oh yes!*

The towel felt soft on her bare skin as he placed his hands on her hips and slid her forward to the edge of the chair. Gently he spread her legs, and then took a deep, satisfied breath. "Damn, Jess," he said on a sigh. "You smell like passion itself." His words sent shivers up and down her spine, and he bent his head to the inside of her thigh. She felt his lips, then his tongue. She closed her eyes and leaned back in the chair, surrendering to sensation. Alternately kissing and licking, he made his way along her inner thigh toward the V of her legs. She trembled with anticipation.

He reached his target. Crying out, she gripped the arms of the chair. His tongue moved leisurely though the petals until he found her opening. A quick flick, and then he delved inside for a taste. Jess cried out, her hips jerked, and she held tightly to the chair to keep still, to keep him doing what he was doing to her.

He lifted his head.

No, she thought, opening her eyes. No, he couldn't stop now. Her body was fairly pulsing with desire.

He was staring at her. His lips twitched into that deeply seductive smile. "It's better if you watch."

She couldn't possibly . . .

Holding on to the arms of the chair, he pulled himself up to kiss her, plunging inside to sweep her mouth. With each stroke of his tongue came a new taste—salty, musky, strangely intoxicating.

He drew back, still smiling. "Like it?" Holding her eyes with his, he slid his hand from the chair arm to the V of her legs. "That's what you taste like," he said, slipping a finger inside her. "Right here. Like ambrosia, sweetheart. The food of the gods."

She gasped, and her body contracted around him. Not enough. More, it wanted more. "Lee . . ." she whispered.

His smile grew, his eyes warmed with some tender emotion. "I like the sound of my name on your lips." He slid his finger back out and touched her mouth in a chaste kiss. As he explored the petals between her legs, he pressed more kisses along her neck, her shoulder, her breast. The languid pleasure in her belly spread downward, pooling between her thighs. He suckled her nipple and the pleasure grew until it was a pulsing ache. She squirmed in the chair and he lifted his head. With a small laugh, he moved back to a kneeling position. His hot breath warmed her, and then his tongue resumed that marvelous dance, sliding, gliding, leaping through her petals.

But always missing the hard bud at the center.

She whimpered and moved her hands from the chair to his head.

His tongue slid over her bud, and lightning flashed over her nerves. Her hips bucked. He moved his hands to her thighs, firmly holding them in place, and then licked her again, leisurely, thoroughly, as if enjoying her taste. Again and again and again. The ache became a frenzied need and blood roared in her ears. When her thighs started shaking, those soft wet strokes came faster and faster. Pleasure mounted, then concentrated in an ever-tightening band deep inside of her. Too much . . . too strong . . . she couldn't bear it . . .

Her climax came in an explosion, followed by rushing, writhing waves of heat, flushing her skin, and racking her body with contraction after contraction. Her voice emerged in one long, low cry. Shifting his mouth, Lee found her opening again, and his tongue flicked out to lap up her juices. More contractions. Unable to bear the emotion, she started to weep.

After a moment, Lee rose and drew her into his arms. "It's all right, Jess." He rubbed her, crooning in her ear. "It's all right. It's all right."

Presently the trembling eased and, emotion spent, she stopped weeping. The world started to right itself and she took a deep breath. But before she could take another one, he took her chin in hand, forced her head up and kissed her. He swept through her mouth, suckled her tongue, igniting passion once more. With a moan, she leaned into him and kissed him back.

His lips moved to the corner of her mouth, then to her ear, which he nipped at playfully. "So, Jess," he said in her ear, "do you like that taste?"

She sucked in her breath. "Oh God, when you say things like that, Lee, it makes me mad."

"But do you like it?" he asked. He took her hand and guided it downward, to where he was hard and throbbing again. "You can taste it right here, sweetheart. Or," he said, as he wrapped her fingers around his erection. "Or I could just carry you to bed and we'll see how I feel inside you."

Her breath caught in her throat; desire pooled between her legs. She closed her eyes, melting under the rising heat. Her hand tightened around him, and he gasped. "Crissst. All right, to the bed."

A few short strides and he yanked back the bedclothes to lay her down on the thick feather tick. "Roll on to your stomach for me, sweetheart," he said, kneeling next to her.

"My stomach?" she asked as he turned her over.

"I'm coming in from the back this time," he said. He slid his arm under her belly and pulled her up on her hands and knees.

"No," she cried out in shock. "Lee, I don't—"

"Not sodomy," he soothed, positioning himself behind her. "This way." And he slid inside. Eagerly, her body stretched to welcome him. He withdrew, then slid in again, his staff touching a part of her that he'd missed before, bringing a different kind of pleasure. "All right?" he asked.

Another slow, caressing thrust and she whispered, "Yes."

Balancing on one hand, he lifted the other to stroke her breast in time with each movement of his body. "See," he rasped in her ear in a soft, seductive whisper, "there are advantages to this. I can touch you here"—his thumb brushed her nipple—"or here." He shifted his hand to roam over the tender skin of her inner thigh. And then inward to find her pleasure point. She cried out and fought the urge to collapse. He stopped thrusting to stroke her and her body contracted, trying to reach a quick peak. Impossible with him buried inside her, and the pleasure built higher, higher—And then he stopped. Everything. Thrusting, touching, leaving her balancing on the edge of sanity.

"Say my name," he whispered in her ear.

One easy syllable. "Lee . . ." she rasped.

He sighed in her ear, a wisp of breath, bringing a quiver of pleasure. "Again, sweetheart."

"Lee . . ."

More breathing in her ear, and then his fingers started that sweet torture again. He continued to demand, "again, again, again," until she was gasping his name over and over, as her body tried to find a peak. When he started moving inside her, his words changed to flattery, to tender encouragement. The combination of his fingers and his staff working together, his voice in her ear, the fragrance of her soap mixing with the musky scent of love, and his taste on her tongue sent her senses reeling. His name became an endless, breathless plea for release. Her body shook, her arms started to lose their strength and then he drove deep inside her one more time. Climax came in a heart-pounding explosion, followed by a deep guttural shout from Lee. From somewhere far off, she heard herself scream his name, high, loud, and full of love.

* * *

Lee thrust one more time, his mind numb to everything but the sheer pleasure of having Jess soft and wet around him. She came first, in a huge, hugging contraction that ripped his own climax from him in a burst of spine-tingling pleasure. As her cry—his name—rang in his ears, he pumped deep inside her. When he removed his hand from her petals, her arms gave way and she collapsed on her stomach. He held himself steady a moment longer, then fell next to her, sucking in deep, harsh gulps of air. Wrapping his arms around her, he pulled her against him. "God, Jess. Jesus."

No answer, but no tears, either, only heavy breathing. His own throat was dry, as if his climax has sucked every last drop of liquid out of him. Closing his eyes, he breathed in her lovely fragrance and an extraordinary sense of peace settled over him, as light as down. For once his restless mind was silent, his wandering heart at rest. Quiet, for the first time in thirty years . . .

Time passed—seconds? minutes?—and his body returned to normal. For her, too, apparently, for when he opened his eyes, hers were riveted upon his face. She reached up to trace his cheekbone, his lips, with her fingertips. "I'm sorry," she said softly.

What the hell? "Sorry?"

"You wanted me to, umm, take a taste—" she said, blushing.

"No, Jess, listen I would never want—"

"And I would have, except that I couldn't get the words out."

A shudder of anticipation shook his body. He flashed her a chagrinned smile. "Perhaps I should have waited for your reply."

She smiled back, a remarkably shy smile considering that she lay naked in his arms, filled to the brim with his seed. "I'm not sure I could have given you one."

Brushing her forehead with his lips, he said, "Next time then."

"Next time?"

"Sweetheart, I don't think this body's going to work again for a few hours. You've completely drained it."

"Oh." She was quiet a moment, then said timidly, "Lee, you make me feel so reckless."

"Funny," he said tenderly, "you make me feel protective."

"That's nice," she said with a soft smile, and snuggled deeper in his arms. "I think we missed supper."

"And cards or whatever other kind of entertainment the Mc-Graws had planned for us," he said, pulling a blanket over her.

"Mmmm," she said. "That makes me sleepy."

"I'm not surprised." He nuzzled her ear, then flicked his tongue over the lobe.

She shivered. "You're making me excited again."

"I can't help it."

"Yes, well, that was my point, now, wasn't it?"

He laughed. "Shrew. All right then, shall I leave you to sleep?"

"I wish you didn't have to leave at all," she said wistfully. "Won't you stay just a little longer?"

"All right, until you're asleep," he said. She closed her eyes, and in a few short minutes the sound of her easy breathing told him she was sleeping. Carefully, he slipped from the bed and tucked the covers around her. After blowing out the lantern, he dropped a kiss on her temple and whispered softly, "I love you, Jess."

# Chapter Twenty-Two

Lee descended the stairs, his gaze flickering over the empty dining room to his right. He reached the bottom stair and turned left, toward the company assembled in the parlor. "It appears that I missed supper," he said, striding forward. "I apologize."

Melinda sat in an armchair before the fire, scowling fiercely at a sampler in her hand. Jim was leaning against the fireplace mantel, frowning down at her, and Nick sat a full sofa's length away, reading the newspaper. As Lee settled on the empty sofa, Melinda lifted her head. Her dark brown eyes, generally filled with warmth, flashed anger at him. "It looks that way, doesn't it?" she snapped.

Lee looked at Jim. Grimacing, Jim shrugged, and Lee focused on Melinda once more. "I am sorry, ma'am. I'll make up for it, I promise."

"And Miss Sullivan? Will she make up for it, too?" Melinda asked.

For some reason, she was enraged. To soothe her, Lee employed his best woman tamer, his dimple. "I'm certain she'll express her sincerest apologies in the morning."

"Of course." Melinda stabbed a needle into her embroidery, and Lee had an uneasy feeling that it was serving as a surrogate for him. "The children were *very* disappointed. You promised Dickie a game of chess."

The dimple wasn't working. Charm then. "I'll play with him in Texas for certain. And may I add, Melinda, that your gown is lovely on you. You have excellent taste."

"Sure," she said. She rose, tossed her embroidery into her basket and closed the lid with a fearsome snap. "I'll have you know that I am not at all impressed by your flattery!" She spun on her heel, then stomped across the room and through the dining room door, slamming it so loudly that Lee jumped.

Puzzled, he stared after her a moment, then turned to the two remaining McGraws. "She's a trifle angry, eh?"

Jim frowned. "You missed supper."

"And what does she do if you miss her birthday? Take an ax to your head?"

The frown slid away and he shook his head. "Right now she'd more 'n likely take it to a different part of your body."

"Ah," Lee said, nodding in dawning comprehension. "So it was the *reason* we missed supper. Well hell, Jim, you have three kids! I suspect you 'missed supper' a few times yourselves."

Nick chuckled and laid down his paper. "I've eaten many a supper alone."

"Sure, but I doubt we were ever so *loud* about it!"

Lee's eyebrows shot up. "I see. You heard us then?"

Nick grinned. "The vowel at the end of your name can be stretched for a mighty long time."

"Ah," he said, smiling ruefully. "Still, Jim, you were newlyweds once."

"We were. We didn't have any children, tho'."

"Children?"

"Yeah. They heard you, too. At first they thought Jess was hurting you."

Amusement bubbled up Lee's throat at the scene forming in his brain. "Of course," he said, restraining his mirth, "you explained that wasn't the case—"

"And then, a little later, Jess yelled your name," Jim continued. "But cut it off short-like. They thought you'd killed her."

Nick's shoulders started shaking.

"Oh my God," Lee said, controlling a tremor of laughter. "Jim, really—"

"So they reckoned they'd better check up on you. Dickie grabbed his rifle and was halfway up the stairs before I caught him."

"And," Nick added, "you're damned lucky he did, 'cuz that kid's a good shot and his aim's just about groin level."

Lee tried desperately to summon up remorse. "Jim, honestly—"

"But that wasn't so hard, because by that time *she* was yelling, so we knew she wasn't dead."

Nick was holding his stomach now, and Lee was losing his fight with remorse. "If I can do *any*thing—"

"Samantha thought she might be pleading for her life. Melinda tried to tell her that Jess didn't *sound* like she was in pain—"

"*Any*thing—"

"But Sam thought she sounded as if she was, uh, begging for mercy and it kept getting louder, and louder, 'Lee! Lee! Lee!' until it turned into one long scream. Melinda's face turned so red, I thought she was going to burst into flames. The kids were out of their chairs, I had hold of Dickie by the collar, Nick had Sam by the pigtail and then *you* yelled. It sounded like 'Yowie!' to me, but Matty swore it was 'Jess, don't kill me.'"

"Which," Nick interjected, "is when Melinda went for her dinner knife."

"I reckon if I didn't get hold of her hand, she would've come up the stairs and cut the voice box right out of your throat. Next time, Monty, d'ya think you could stuff a bandana in it or somethin'?"

"Whatever you want, Jim. I'm very sorry, believe me. I swear I'll apologize to Melinda tomorrow."

"It's okay," Jim said, with a slight grin. "She'll get over it."

"Yeah," Nick said, rising. "And now, gentlemen, I'm saying good night, too."

Jim glanced at the clock. "Early for bed, isn't it, Nick? Nick?" he called, as Nick headed for the front door. "Where you off to?"

Nick grabbed his hat and gun belt. "Town. After Lee's display, I'm of a mind to see if I can't make a little noise myself. I'll see you in the morning." He nodded and left.

"Well, Jim?" Lee asked. "What shall we play? Cards or chess?"

Jim shook his head. "Neither. I'm going to find Melinda and, uh, give her your apologies. See ya in the mornin', Lee."

Lee glanced at the mantel clock. Eight P.M. With a sigh he took a deck of cards from the mantelpiece, "Looks like solitaire then."


Jess awoke early, an unusual feeling of contentment threading through her heart and relaxing her muscles. The touch of cool linen sheets against her naked skin reminded her of where that contentment had come from, and she smiled. Who would ever have thought that lying with a man could feel so incredibly wonderful? Oh hundreds of women no doubt, but never cold-blooded Jess. And yet now, after all those years of believing she had less passion than an animal, she'd discovered in one night that she was, in fact, *normal*. Well not Dr. Acton normal, but not frigid, either. With a blush she recollected the more intimate details of the night. Had she really done all that? Said all those things? Had he? A hot shudder tripped over her nerves. Oh yes, he had, and she'd responded wantonly, wildly. And she wanted to do it again. Again and again and again. She suddenly understood why Everett had been consumed by desire even when it left *her* cold.

Of course, with Everett she'd been in the family way.

Suddenly horrified, she sat up in bed, gasped at the cold air, and swiftly pulled the blanket around her body. She'd not thought of that! Oh, but life could not be so cruel! For eighteen long years she'd been a good girl. For the last six, in spite of the temptations constantly paraded in front of her, she'd continued to be a good girl. Surely she'd not be punished for a few moments of pleasure.

Her stomach growled. Regular hunger or the needs of a woman carrying a baby?

*Ridiculous!* she castigated herself, throwing back the blankets. That kind of hunger took months. It was merely the fearful imaginings of her guilty mind for having lain with Lee. Although, really, they'd done precious little lying. Another delicious shiver ran over her nerves, warming her body in the most remarkable way. As she rose to wash and dress, her mind floated over recollections of the evening. A chaste woman, a moral woman, would not dwell on such wanton behavior, but after all the years of believing herself abnormal, she couldn't help it. By the time she descended the stairs twenty minutes later, she was close to forgetting the consequences.

Everyone was already gathered around the breakfast table. When her eyes caught Lee's, she forgot everything, save the glow in his eyes: a heady combination of affection and desire. For a moment, she could scarcely breathe.

"Miss Jess! You're okay!"

Jess jumped a little and braced herself just in time to prevent being toppled over by Matty McGraw, who threw herself at Jess's waist. Puzzled, Jess stroked her blond hair.

Melinda groaned.

Jim, with the slightest hiccup of a laugh in his voice, said, "Matty, I told you she was."

From outside came the sound of a horse approaching, fast.

"Matty hush!" Sam hissed.

"Of course I am, honey," Jess said. "Why would you think differently?"

Lee, eyes still sparkling, appeared slightly embarrassed. "I think, sweetheart, you'd rather not have that answer right now."

Boot falls on the porch and just as she was about to ask why not, the door burst open. Nick, a piece of paper in hand, his face sharp with concern, strode to the table. "You have to leave. Now." He slapped the paper down in front of Lee.

Lee glanced at it; his eyes widened. "Damn it to hell!"

Jim rose. "What is it?"

Lee's head jerked up. "It's a wanted poster. Jess, there's a bounty on our heads."

"Oh no!" Melinda exclaimed, lurching out of her chair. "Are they on their way, Nick?"

Removing his hat, he ran his hand through his hair. "Not yet. The posters just went up this morning, but if there's posters, you can be sure there's a posse."

"The men are already packing the horses," Jim said.

"I saw 'em. I told 'em to move a mite faster and lighter."

Swiftly, Jim crossed to the coatrack as Nick said, "Lee, Jess, no time for breakfast. If these posters are in town now, they'll be farther south by the end of the day. Cross-country, Jim. No stopping in Pueblo or Trinidad, right? Better steer clear of towns."

"No breakfast?" Jess asked, terror and hunger fighting for control of her stomach. She didn't want to hang; she dearly wanted to eat. No breakfast, and no beds, either. Oh no, she didn't want to camp *again!*

Melinda grabbed her hand and pulled her to the door. She took her Ulster from the coatrack and a set of fur-lined gloves from the pockets. "These will keep you warmer than your gloves, Jess. Oh, Jim, I wish you didn't have to leave so quickly. I scarcely have time to say good-bye!"

He leaned over and kissed her. "It won't be long. In a couple days you pack up the kids and get one of your brothers to escort you on down, right?"

"You're coming, too?" Jess asked.

Melinda gave Jim a large, teary-eyed smile. "Jim agreed last night."

Lee shrugged into Nick's slicker. "I'll return it as soon as possible, Nick."

"Bring yourself with it," he said, opening the door. "I'll telegraph Rick, let him know you're coming."

"Good. And my father. I'd be obliged to you if you would inform him of the state of affairs. If you get me a pencil and paper, I'll give you his address."

"Sure thing," Nick answered.

A few minutes later they were mounted up and racing across the valley toward the Colorado prairie—again.

# Chapter Twenty-Three

"I know it doesn't look like much from the outside," Jim said, as the Rockin' R rose out of the Texas prairie. "The original house was built to protect the owners from Indian attack. It's better inside."

Goodness, it was a fortress, not a home, Jess thought with a dismayed gulp. A huge, square adobe structure, which grew more intimidating with each passing minute. It stood two stories high with mere slits for windows and an entrance guarded by two massive wooden doors more suitable for a castle than a ranch house. Not even the leisurely winding river in the distance could soften the appearance.

"If I were an Indian," Jess said, "and I saw that, I'd head for the hills."

"It's really great on the inside," Jim reassured her. "There's a courtyard."

Twenty minutes later, as the sun started sinking, a couple men exited the matching outbuildings and jogged toward them to take their horses. Jess, trying to control her shaky nerves, dismounted as the fortress doors flew open. A tall blond-haired man in denim and blue cotton walked out, his arm around a smallish woman with raven black hair and a sharp, blank face. Rick Winchester, no doubt, and his wife, Lilah.

"Jim! Just got your telegram yesterday. They're having trouble with the wires. You're a day early. Made good time, did you?" Rick said; a large welcoming grin spread across his handsome, slightly creviced face. Two dimples joined smiling crystal blue eyes.

"Been shot at by bounty hunters before, Rick. I thought to avoid it this time," Jim said, moving forward to give Rick a quick back-slapping hug. "Lilah, Melinda sends her love and warns that she'll be joining us in a few days, children in tow."

Lilah's eyes flashed over Jess and Lee before she gave Jim a small smile and allowed him to hug her. "Nicky will be glad to hear that."

"Not," Jim said laughing, "if Sam has anything to say about it. Rick, you remember Monty, right?"

"Remember him, Christ, Jim, I'm counting on him!" Rick said, reaching out his hand to capture Lee's in what looked like a bone-crushing handshake. "Tell me, boy, how's your moo? I could use a man capable of honeyfugglin' a cow or two."

Lee laughed. "I haven't mooed in years, Rick, and I've been too old to be called boy for fifteen."

"Yeah, but it makes me feel young."

"Ah, and a man your age would appreciate that, eh?"

Rick stared a moment, then laughed. "Touché, Monty. Here, you remember Lilah don't you?"

"We had only a few days together, but the memory is, uh, indelible. Mrs. Winchester," he said, a devilish light in his eyes as he took Mrs. Winchester's hand and kissed it. "*Au chante,* madam."

Rick eyes narrowed and his smile tightened, "Well, she sure as hell is enchanting, Montgomery, but if you ever kiss my wife again, I'll take those lips clean off your face."

Everyone froze. Jim winced and Lilah's body stiffened as she turned her head to watch her husband. Jim said Rick had a way of forcing self-defense. Jess could well believe it. The man just about radiated danger.

Only Lee maintained the former levity as he raised eyebrows. "Jealous, Rick? And how many married women have *you* kissed?"

Rick's eyes narrowed slightly. "Only one in the past nine years."

"Ah, then I suppose I'm a few up on you," he said, and Jess flinched.

For a moment Rick stared at him. Then he let out a low laugh and took Lee into a slap-on-the-back bear hug. "Man alive, have I missed you. How come you've never visited before?"

"Well, sir, there were all those women . . ." he said, hugging Rick back.

"An exaggeration, no doubt," Rick said, stepping back. "And is this the lady I've heard so much about? Miss Sullivan?" he asked, and taking her hand, brushed his lips across her knuckles.

"Is that retaliation, Winchester?" Lee asked, scowling although his eyes sparkled. "Do it again, and I'll take you clean *out.*"

"My gun's a mite faster than yours. I'd beat you to the draw every time, boy."

"Ah, but I should beat you to heaven."

"And St. Peter would kick you right back downstairs," Rick retorted. He jerked his head toward the door as his men took away their horses. "Come on in out of the cold. We'll get you settled in and then talk about your difficulties over dinner."

"Sounds good," Lee said, taking Jess's elbow lightly. Biting her lip, she followed Rick, Lilah, and Jim through the doors into a foyer and stopped dead in her tracks.

"My goodness," she gasped.

From the outside a fortress, from the inside a palace. The foyer was small, but the line of windows at the other end opened upon a rectangular courtyard. At the front stood a fountain, at the back a rose garden. A couple of trees along with plants in various containers decorated the stone walkways, and here and there wrought-iron benches offered several views. Long windows and doors of various rooms flanked it along the first floor, and above, along the second story was a veranda with wrought-iron fencing, creating a sort of outdoor corridor.

Jim strode forward to peer through the glass. "Finished the second story, huh?"

"A few months back," Rick said, shutting the front doors. "Like it?"

"Melinda will be thrilled."

"Apparently the cattle business has been good," Lee said, amused surprise in his voice. Jess glanced at him. He was smiling, far less stunned than she. But then he was accustomed to such splendor.

Rick grinned. "Yeah, that and the fact that Lilah has a talent for investing in the stock market. Ah, here's Consuelo to show you to your rooms . . ."

After rinsing her hair, Jess sank deeper into the hot water. Luxury, pure luxury! Like the McGraws, the Winchesters had a bathroom—*two* actually, one upstairs also. This one, part of the Winchesters' original bedroom suite, connected to her bedroom and Lee's. She closed her eyes and listened to the fire crackling merrily to her right. Dinner wasn't for almost an hour and she was going to soak.

The door opened.

Her eyelids flew up. The door to Lee's room. Crossing his arms over his chest, he propped a shoulder against the doorjamb as if he meant to sprout roots and grow there. His hot, appreciative eyes followed the lines of her person, perfectly visible under the clear water. She ought to grab a towel and cover herself, but the wanton released four days earlier at the Bar M reveled in the slow, sensual caress of his gaze. "Jess," he greeted her in a husky voice.

Oh no, this was not good. For the entire length of their journey, Lee had acted like a perfect gentleman, without even the tiniest sexual innuendo either in or out of Jim's presence. If not for the constant desire gleaming in his eye and the way his gaze occasionally rested too long on certain body parts, she'd have thought their night together had no more substance than a dream. Maybe, she'd reasoned, he'd decided not to pursue her any further. It both distressed and comforted her, for the prospect of pregnancy shadowed her thoughts.

But now, the languid smile spreading across Lee's face proved otherwise.

"Don't you ever knock?" she snapped, hoping to deter him with a shrewish temper.

He raised his eyebrows. "I'd hazard to guess that if I had, you'd have sent me away. And I don't particularly wish to go away."

An ill-advised attempt—Lee had always liked her shrew.

"Lee," she said, closing her eyes against the seduction of his voice. She tried to collect her strength and courage, then looked at him again. "We can't do this."

His brow wrinkled. "What can't we do?"

How was it, she wondered as her heart jerked into an uncomfortable patter, that a man with four days stubble on his face could still be handsome? His kiss would scratch. It ought to repel her; it attracted her. "This. I-I think you'd better leave."

His eyes narrowed slightly. "All right, but dinner's in three quarter's of an hour and I hoped to have a chance to bathe beforehand," he said, running his eyes swiftly over her person before settling on her face again. "And I thought we'd done *this* extremely well."

A shudder ran down her spine. Mercy, but she surely should not be discussing this naked, in a tub! "My point wasn't the . . . the quality, but—"

"I believe," he cut her off, "that the *quality* was your objection from the start. Your entire reason behind every rejection, Jess, was your inability to enjoy such a relationship. Didn't we prove that incorrect?"

"Yes, but—"

"Then I don't understand the objection."

"Well, if you'd stop interrupting, I'd explain!" she snapped, tension coursing through her veins. A baby. She pictured Janey's pale face and her throat closed up. A baby and she alone and destitute, unable to earn enough to care for it. Not even Lee's loving was worth that.

"All right," he said, watching her carefully. "Fire away."

She took a deep breath. "We must think on the consequences of our actions."

"Consequences," he said slowly, his eyebrows drawing together. "If you're speaking of diseases, Jess, I assure you, I have none. My grandfather died of syphilis, which has made me exceptionally cautious. And you have been without male companionship for years, unless . . . damn, Dunne didn't—"

"No!" she exclaimed. "That was the one thing Everett always took great care in."

"So," he said, smiling, "that settles it. And as much as I should love to watch you bathe, we're running out of time—"

"There are consequences beyond disease."

He frowned, bewildered. Then understanding dawned in his eyes and he straightened, dropping his arms. "A child. I hadn't considered that. Still, you can't know so quickly, can you?"

"No, but if we continue this way it's likely to happen."

His eyes narrowed as he contemplated it. After a moment he glanced at the clock. "Fair enough. It certainly warrants discussion, but I now have only thirty minutes to bathe and you have yet to dress. After dinner, perhaps?"

"O-okay. We could meet in the library."

"No, this requires the utmost privacy. My room or yours shall do."

A bedroom. "I don't think that's the proper place for this discussion."

Lee's eyes slid over her. As her traitorous body warmed, thoughts of Janey slid away. "This is a much worse place. You're not exactly dressed for the occasion."

"All right," she said, for if he kept looking at her that way, it would be her undoing. "Your room then." Which would mean she needn't eject him after the conversation.

"Splendid. Now, if you don't mind? The tub?"

Although the food tasted remarkably good after four days of riding and the company was entertaining, dinner seemed interminably long. Jess had been placed directly across the table from Lee who, washed and shaved, could not have looked more handsome. His hair shone blue-black in the light gleaming from the silver chandelier. His borrowed clothes fit well—too well. Before being seated, she noted that Lee's black denim jeans hugged him far tighter than a set of dress trousers. Worse still, his forest-colored shirt patterned with thin black stripes, turned his eyes an arresting shade of green, setting her heart tumbling every time he looked in her direction.

Which happened far too often for her frazzled nerves.

As the night wore on, his gaze grew progressively warmer and more appreciative. It disconcerted her. The gown Lilah had lent her was very pretty, soft blue velvet, trimmed in black lace and pink rosettes, with a low, but far from eye-catching neckline. Still, his eyes strayed there over and over again creating a sort of rising hysteria in her chest. He'd agreed, at least nominally, to suspend "relations" between them until they discussed it further. Under those circumstances, oughtn't he avoid looking at her altogether? She ought to have, she decided passing him a dish of butter, insisted they carry on their discussion this evening in the library or the study or any other room in the house.

His gaze caught hers as he took the butter from her, his fingers brushing over hers in a swift caress. "Thank you," he said, and the gleam in his eyes implied that his gratitude was for far more than the butter. She quickly dropped her trembling hand back in her lap, coloring up when Rick's eyebrows raised at the interchange. Seconds later he turned to Jim and made some innocuous comment.

Lee had nominally agreed to cease relations. Nominally was the key word. With a flip of her stomach, she realized he'd never truly agreed to anything—and when he looked at her like that all consequences appeared trivial in comparison to the warm, languid desire creeping over her.


Marriage. The word reverberated through Lee's mind for the first half of dinner, driving him to distraction. He could find no other solution should Jess become pregnant. Over the last ten years, he'd studiously employed the sort of protection that allowed him to enjoy the company of many different women without any of the consequences. Ten years of complete freedom, all the play, without any of the pay. But he'd played with the wrong woman this time and it could very well mean marriage.

That word again, and once more he waited for an invisible noose to tighten around his neck. Once again, nothing. He tried out fidelity. No different. A lifetime with Jess, never to lie with another woman. Would it be so terrible? When he regarded her across the table, her eyes shining a brilliant blue and that damned tight dress, he couldn't remember any other woman. All he could remember was the silken feel of the skin hiding under the soft, velvet bodice.

He'd scarcely thought of another woman since he'd met her.

He took a deep swallow of Cabernet and snapped out a comment to something Rick said, provoking a roar of laughter.

He had no French safes with him and no way of obtaining any in the near future. Bedding down with Jess tonight would be a pure gamble, and losing meant losing access to all women, for—damn his honor!—he didn't believe in the sometimes-fashionable concept of love outside of marriage.

Marriage and children. Ties far stronger than the thin threads of his family, stretched across the country. Children meant responsibility, something he'd never been particularly adept at. Truthfully, children had never interested him much.

And yet he'd thoroughly enjoyed playing chess with Dickie. And he'd watched the way Jess had played with and talked to Jim's children. Within minutes of meeting her, they'd adored her. She'd make a capital mother; she'd make a capital wife, both in and out of bed.

Jess leaned forward to grasp the pepper mill and pass it to Lilah. The movement offered Lee a spectacular view down the scooped bodice of that gown and the curves that filled it. Memory of kissing those curves, of Jess's hot, wet reaction, flashed through his mind, and desire flooded his body, making it difficult to breathe.

Fidelity, he reminded his racing heart. One woman for life.

But what other woman could suit him better than Jess? He'd expected that lying with her would lessen the intensity of his feelings for her, but instead they had doubled—tripled. Impossibly, he wanted her more than ever. Damned if she wasn't worth the gamble . . .

Noting the butter next to Jess's plate, he smiled across the table at her and asked, "Will you pass me the butter, sweetheart?"

By dessert, Jess could bear no more of the ever-increasing tension. The flush that rose when she'd passed Lee the butter— such a simple act!—now warmed her face permanently. With luck everyone would accept it as a sign of illness. Lord knew she felt feverish! When the maid started to slide a piece of pie in front of her, she shook her head. "No, thank you. If you don't mind, Lilah, Rick, I have a horrible headache. I think I'll skip dessert and retire."

Lee's eyes gleamed. "All the traveling, no doubt," he said. "Do you require an escort?"

Damn him! Bad enough to make her blush with those appreciative looks, must he add to her embarrassment with speech? "It's only across the courtyard. It's unlikely I'd lose my way."

"I never said so. If the headache has made you dizzy, however, it's a distance. You could fall and hurt yourself."

The bland expression on his face belied the mirth in his eyes. "I'm not so frail," she snapped.

"Indeed," he said in a voice marbled with laughter. "You're a veritable Amazon, six foot five at the least. I apologize, Jess, I'd forgotten."

A tiny laugh escaped her throat. Oh why was it always so difficult to stay angry with him? "You are incorrigible! It's unfair of you to make me laugh when I have every right to be furious with you!"

"Do you feel better?" he asked, eyes sparkling.

"No, I don't! My head hurts *more,*" she lied. She turned to her hosts. "Lilah, Rick. Thank you very much for your hospitality. Good night!" she said, and slipped out of the room.

Lee leaned back in his chair, sipping his wine as he watched the swing of her hips through the glass doors. After a moment he turned to the other guests. "Anyone for cards after dinner? A little whist, perhaps?"

Rick laughed. "Christ, but you're a devil, Monty. You're not playing cards. That lady's waiting for you!"

Lilah stirred uncomfortably in her chair. "Rick, really," she said, a trace of censure in her voice.

"Waiting for me?" Lee asked innocently. "She has the headache."

"Maybe, Lee," Jim said, frowning at Rick, "you'd like to check on her before we play cards."

"Sure," Rick said with a laugh. "And you could take the rest of that wine there, too. I've heard it cures the headache real well."

"Rick!" Lilah exclaimed.

"Perhaps he's right, Lilah," Lee said, standing. Just the thought of Jess waiting for him set his blood to boiling. "I ought to see if she, uh, needs anything." He tried to hold an even face in front of Rick's smirk. "Good night, Lilah, gentlemen."

After they were gone, Rick sat back in his chair and let out a whistle. "Man alive, did you see how those two were looking at each other?"

Jim grinned. "Could we miss it? You should've seen 'em on the trip out here. Made you two look like pikers."

A picture flashed in front of Lilah of those days nine years earlier—trapped in a hotel room, and Rick's out-of-control temper carving out pieces of her heart. She flinched.

Rick's mind-reading gaze flashed over her, then to Jim again. "Reckon the circumstances were different."

"Yeah, reckon so, " Jim said, his face wringed with sympathy. "I'm turning in, too." He stepped toward her. Warm brown eyes smiling affectionately, he dropped a kiss on top of her head, sending little rays of sunshine into Lilah's stomach. "It's great to see you looking so well, honey. Reckon this lug of yours is treating you as he ought to?"

"As I have for nine years, Sir Galahad," Rick snarled, drawing a laugh from Lilah.

"You'd better. You have a lot to make up for!" Jim said and exited, leaving Lilah encompassed in a warm glow.

"So about Monty and Jess, darlin'," Rick said, his eyes gleaming with mischief, "I'm thinking we ought to see about arranging a visit with a preacher for them while they're here."

Lilah shook her head. "I think you ought to let them alone."

His deep laugh turned the ice in her veins to warm honey. "But Lilah, darlin', where's the fun in that?"

"It's not fun, it's manipulation."

"It's fun." He took her hand in his and gently rubbed the back with his thumb. "Come, love, promise you'll talk to Jess for me. I'll make it worth your while."

"Damn you, Rick, you'd make it 'worth my while' anyway. All right," she snapped as her treacherous body reacted to his touch, "I'll do it, but I'm not promising anything. I'm not good at woman talk."

Grinning, he pulled at her hand, drawing her into his lap. "You're good at everything that matters to me, darlin'."

* * *

Jess was sitting on her bed rubbing her temples and trying to compose her quaking nerves when the door connecting to Lee's room crashed open. She had barely a chance to acknowledge his entrance before he crossed the room and dragged her from the bed to crush her mouth under his. He parted her lips and delved inside, touching, tasting, heating her blood and sending her heart flying. Seconds later he took possession of her tongue, sucking on it as if to drink every last taste, creating a wet tickle down below. She moaned in response, pressing her body against his, shuddering when the evidence of his excitement pressed back.

By the time the kiss ended, she was shaking, her knees barely holding her upright. "By God, Jess," he rasped in her ear, "I thought dinner was never going to end. Where are the damned hooks to this gown? Oh, the hell with it. I'll take it off later."

"Lee," she gasped, as his mouth moved down to kiss her neck and still lower. "I thought—ohhhh!" she sighed when his tongue slid down the crevice between her breasts. Hot, wet thrills shot through her and she could scarcely breathe. A moment later he pushed her back on the bed and reached under her skirt to find the ties to her drawers.

Excitement flashing like lightning in his eyes, he said huskily, "Women wear entirely too many layers of underclothes." He reached under the linen to touch her, making her cry out. His eyes closed as if in a kind of tortured ecstasy as his fingers moved gently through her folds. "You feel so good." Finding the pearl at the center, he stroked, creating a hot, aching need. "Lord almighty," he whispered. "I can't wait." He withdrew his hand. She groaned in disappointment. Trembling, desperate for his touch, she watched as he made short work of his clothes, then completely naked, flipped up her skirt to rid her of her drawers, too. He shifted her into the middle of the bed, straddled her and kissed her again, long, hard, as he parted her legs. He whispered in her ear. "Hold on tight, this is going to be fast and hard." With those less than loverlike words he slid inside, gently the first time and then with the next thrust drove deeply, rubbing hard against the sensitive places his hands had just stroked. When she cried out he pasted his mouth to hers, sweeping inside with gentle caresses as he drove into her, fast, furious, creating a kind of pained-pleasure, a building need for more—harder still, faster still, until release came in an intense burst of pleasure, rocking her down to the very core of her being. A few seconds later he shoved even deeper inside and filled her, causing another little explosion. She gasped as he let out a growl of satisfaction and collapsed beside her.

"Damn," he gasped between deep breaths. "Damn that felt good."

She was shaking, her private places were tender and bruised, and her face cold from the slowly draining flush. Her heart slammed hard against her ribcage and her nerves sparkled with the remnants of her climax. "Good," she said as she tried to catch her breath, "good is ice cream on hot summer nights. I don't think I'd call that good."

"No?" Lee asked, rolling on his side to lean on an elbow. "I'm sorry, sweetheart, was I too rough? Did I hurt you?"

"Hurt," she said, licking her lips. "Yes, but I . . . I didn't mind."

He let out a small, humorless laugh and slid his hand along her bare thigh. "That's not precisely a resounding recommendation, is it?"

She smiled, and ran her fingertips over his lips. Rough, male lips, capable of so much pleasure and so much laughter. "And who would you have me recommend you to?"

He smiled back, the amusement in his eyes dim. "As a brute and a monster? No one I can think of."

"You really are distressed!"

"This may surprise you, Jess, but I don't enjoy hurting women, you least of all."

Why did "least of all" make her heart flip? Silly, silly heart. Blushing, she said, "You're no brute, Lee. I just never thought a gentleman like you would be so rough. It was exciting."

A glimmer of a smile. "Exciting. Pleasurable, too, perhaps?"

"Yes."

The smile grew and his eyes twinkled. "Very pleasurable?"

"Y-yes."

His dimple emerged and his eyes glittered. "More so than when I do this?" he asked, sliding his hand higher on her thigh.

"Yes," she said, sucking in her breath. She grabbed his hand. "But we were supposed to *talk* after dinner, remember?"

He shrugged, gently trying to work free of her grip. "But this is so much more enjoyable."

"And less productive. Lee, I'm serious. We can't go on like this."

He sighed. "All right." He sat up, fluffed a pillow behind his head and leaned against the etched mahogany headboard. "I gave it a deal of consideration during dinner."

She lifted an eyebrow. "Your thoughts seemed focused on other things."

He grinned. "You were something of a distraction. Here's the situation. When we left Grant, we had only the clothes on our backs and the few items Michelle packed. She certainly didn't provide for this situation, thus I lack the usual methods to prevent conception. Furthermore, with the price on our head and the general illegality of such items, I don't anticipate being able to purchase them in the near future." He turned on his side. He held her eyes with his, his expression unusually sincere. "It could be weeks, sweetheart. Weeks with you in the bedroom next to mine. We could attempt abstinence, but frankly, I don't imagine it working. It was difficult enough before and now—" His face twisted briefly with an odd kind of torment. He rubbed his neck. "In any event, you may already be with child. So my plan's simple. If you should become pregnant, then I'll marry you."

# Chapter Twenty-Four

Jess jerked, her eyes opening impossibly wide. "Marriage!" she gasped.

"Marriage," Lee repeated, his heart racing. From fear? Or anticipation? He didn't know. He couldn't seem to get a grasp on his emotions these days. "It's the generally accepted remedy."

"But," she sputtered, "you don't wish to marry me. You've sworn never to marry at all."

He had, but perversely as soon as she assured him he didn't want to marry, there was nothing he wanted more. "I wish far less to abandon my child."

"No," she said, shaking her head. "This is madness. Marriage is not a solution."

"Have you a better one?"

"Yes. You leave straightaway and we avoid each other like the plague."

"I meant one that would work."

"It could work!"

"Not if you're already with child."

She took several breaths. A thought flashed though her eyes. "I'm already married."

"True. We'll need to locate Dunne and sue for divorce." Her eyes brightened with unshed tears, stabbing deep into his chest. She couldn't possibly care for him after all he'd done, could she?

Not after everything Lee had done, too.

"Regardless of your feelings for him, Jess, I won't allow my child to bear another man's name."

Her forehead creased; her eyes narrowed. "That's right," she said slowly. "My child wouldn't be a bastard, would it?"

He didn't like the calculating look in her eyes. "No. But if you wish for my support, you'll marry me."

"I might—" she started stubbornly.

"Jess," he interrupted, "nothing you do could possibly equal the advantages I could give our child. You know that." When she appeared ready to balk, he mustered his courage and added gently, "A penniless life may have contributed to Janey's death. How could you possible deny this child?"

With a hiccup of a pain, she said, "You're not playing fair."

"I only want what's best for my child." He raised a hand to caress her cheek, hoping to link her heart to his with a touch. "And for my wife."

"You shouldn't touch me like that!" she said with a shiver. "It's how we ended up in this mess!"

"You have the smoothest skin," he said, and leaned forward to kiss her, slowly, persuasively. She smelled musky-sweet after her bath. Like lilies-of-the-valley. That was her scent, the smell of cool mossy woods on a hot summer day. And her hair, when he buried his fingers in it, felt like rivers of satin. He imagined it falling around her naked shoulders, brushing his chest as she mounted him— Blood coursed downward and he broke off the kiss. Leaning back, he took several deep breaths. They didn't calm him. His body was leaping to life.

Jess regarded him almost dreamily, her eyes were wide and dark with the beginning of languid desire. Her face was flushed a lovely rose red and her hand had loosened on his, allowing him to slide it farther up her thigh. "That decides it, doesn't it?" he said.

She sighed softly. "If you insist upon kissing me, it does."

"I can't resist," he said.

"Well," she said, biting her lip in that damnably seductive way, "it might not happen in the end anyhow. Sometimes a baby doesn't take."

Which, he thought as he moved his hand between the juncture of her thighs to spread her lips, was a singularly unpleasant thought. Then she whimpered and all thought evaporated.


Jess glanced around the Winchesters' empty parlor. Lilah had yet to arrive from tutoring her son and Jess breathed a sigh of relief. At breakfast she had requested a few moments of Jess's time to "chat," a sort of entertaining necessity. But Jess had no notion what they'd talk about. Her hostess, regardless of all references to the contrary, appeared to be a staid and conservative housewife. What had she, as actress on the dodge, in common with Lilah?

Jess crossed the room to the armchair closest to the bank of windows that bordered the courtyard. Like every other room in the house, the parlor was luxurious and large. Its chairs, sofas, and tables were placed around the room to section it off into several separate sitting areas. And, like every other room, the appointments were understated and tasteful. Decorated in shades of green and rose, the parlor had enough gilt and marble to proclaim wealth, but not so much as to dazzle the eyes. The heavy rose curtains had been pulled back to let in the low November sun, which warmed Jess's aching shoulders as she seated herself.

Lilah entered and crossed the room with such silence and grace, she might have been a wisp of air. In her years of travel, Jess had met many women. None of them had ever made her feel large and clumsy like Lilah did.

"It is good of you to join me," Lilah said stiffly as she sat across from her.

"It's my pleasure," Jess replied.

And that was it. They had nothing left to say. Silence filled the huge room, and Jess glanced around, anxiously searching for a topic of conversation.

"Are you comfortable?" Lilah asked after a moment.

Jess focused on her. Lilah's hands were clasped tightly in her lap. Her frosty eyes were leveled on Jess. "I meant your room," Lilah added. "Is there anything I might get you?"

"No, thank you. Everything has been wonderful."

Lilah nodded, paused a moment as the clock on the mantel-piece ticked away sixty long seconds of unease. "And the clothes? You're a little taller than me, but they do seem to fit well."

"Oh," Jess said, running her hand over her white muslin gown. "They're beautiful. Thank you, they fit just fine."

Another uncomfortable silence filled the room again. Lilah drew in a deep breath, and a flash of vulnerability crossed her blank face. "Forgive me, I'm not very good at small talk."

Jess bit her lip. "No, I must beg *your* forgiveness for intruding upon your lovely home. Please understand, it wasn't my idea. If you wish, I'll try to convince Lee to find another place."

Lilah shook her head. "You misunderstand me. I'm not asking you to leave. And Rick wouldn't allow it even if Lee wanted to."

"Your husband is rather, uh, forceful isn't he?"

Sudden mirth twinkled in Lilah's eyes. "You have no idea."

Jess smiled and relaxed a bit. "I'm not used to seeing Lee overruled. He likes to control situations."

"All men like to control situations, especially when they're feeling vulnerable."

"Why, then, they must feel vulnerable all the time!"

"I believe that was my point."

Jess laughed. The corner of Lilah's mouth twitched as she rose. "Would you care for a drink?" she asked, crossing the room to a table in the corner.

"A glass of water would be nice."

"Were they very rough on your trip?" Lilah asked as she

poured a small amount of amber-colored liquid into one glass.
She poured water from a pitcher into a second glass and crossed
the room to hand it to Jess. "Are you sure you wouldn't care
for something stronger?"

"Uh—" She looked at Lilah's glass, then lifted her head to
gaze into Lilah's eyes. Amusement had vanquished the coldness,
and Jess realized with a shock that her eyes were quite beautiful.
Emerald green and thickly fringed. "What are you having?"

"Whiskey."

"Whiskey!" Jess sputtered in shock. It was only eleven-thirty!

"There's sherry if you prefer. Or would you care for tea?"

Jess shook her head. "You're a very unusual woman, Lilah."

"So I've been told."

Jess hesitated. Drinking alcohol, never mind at eleven-thirty,
was contrary to everything her mother had taught her. But
Mother was dead, and Jess had tried so very long to be a good
girl. All for naught. The harder she tried, the more mistakes she
made. Since meeting Lee, she seemed to make them hourly.

She handed Lilah her glass back. "I'll take the sherry, please."

Lilah's mouth twitched. "So they *were* bad."

"Awful."

"I assumed so based upon your arrival," Lilah said, crossing the room to pour Jess a glass of sherry. "The trip usually
takes four or five days." She handed Jess the glass and made
herself comfortable again.

"Jim wouldn't slow down, not for love or money."

"Really? Jim's generally a little cooler."

"Not with us, he wasn't. Every morning it was 'daylight's
burning.' Honestly, Lilah, isn't daylight *always* burning? Or
are there days when the sun actually *doesn't* rise?" Lilah let
out a tiny, burbling laugh, and Jess grinned. "Mercy, but he
was always so cheerful about it, too!"

"That's Jim," Lilah said with a rueful shake of her head. "And
Lee?"

"Oh, he'd groan, but then drag himself up and start packing

before I even unglued my eyelids. I swear one morning he took my blanket off me and had it packed before I was awake. At times, I actually prayed the posse would catch us. At least then I'd get a cup of coffee."

Lilah's eyes sparkled. "Not even coffee?"

"I drank my own spit."

"Did you ask for coffee?"

"Every night, before bed. And every morning after 'rise and shine.' They ignored me entirely."

"Ah, that was the problem. If you'd asked to be dragged from your bed and tossed on your horse, they'd have made the coffee."

Laughing, Jess said, "And forced it down my throat at the first sign of a complaint!"

"Because men like to control situations."

"Because they were doubtless feeling vulnerable about having only *one* woman to abuse!"

Lilah stiffened. "Abuse?"

"If dragging a woman from her bed at the crack of dawn doesn't constitute abuse, then I don't know what does!"

Raw pain flashed through Lilah's eyes. "No, I don't imagine you do." She paused a moment, then asked abruptly, "Do you love him, then?"

Jess started. "Pardon me?" Mercy, but this woman had a disconcerting way of tossing out personal questions!

"I was asking if you love Lee," she repeated.

Jess stared. Should she lie and lead the conversation back to easy, polite chatting? What easy polite chatting? Lilah wasn't good at small talk. An understatement. "I'm attracted to him," she answered slowly.

Lilah shrugged. "Attraction and love are not always the same thing."

With Lee, she thought, her heart tightening painfully, it was the same thing. Oh yes, she loved Lee, loved him more with each passing day, a heartbreaking love with no happy ending. He'd never displayed any sign that his heart was engaged and she was not free to accept it, anyhow. And his proposal? Why, that was mere desperation.

"Does it matter? I'm married, after all," she said, more to herself than to Lilah.

Lilah's hand froze on her glass. Shock drained the emotion from her face. "You're married?"

Jess winced. She was an adulteress. Would a once-upon-a-time fugitive find that disturbing enough to throw Jess from her house? "He left me six years ago. I don't where he is."

For a moment longer, Lilah stared. Then she stood abruptly, crossed to the door and leaned into the courtyard. A quiver of apprehension shot through Jess. She'd gotten them kicked out! Then Lilah called out, "Maria, would you bring us coffee, *por favor? Gracias.*"

Jess lifted her eyebrows as Lilah sat back down. "I thought we were drinking liquor."

"I'd prefer to keep my mind clear for your story. Tell me about your husband."

Jess swallowed. "You're not angry then, about my . . . relationship . . . with Lee?"

Lilah slowly shook her head. "I'm the last one to judge you."

Jess would have preferred to keep her business to herself, but Lilah's eyes were cool, compelling. With a deep sigh, she started, "I was eighteen. . . ."

Whistling cheerfully, Lee crossed the courtyard and entered Rick's study. Jim sat lounging in a chair, an expression of consternation on his face, as Rick frowned at a lone piece of paper on his desk. Although it was a bright balmy afternoon, in the tan and mahogany coolness of Rick's study the atmosphere was decidedly somber.

"You sent for me?" Lee asked as he slumped in a chair near Jim.

Rick lifted his head to regard Lee, his eyes calculating. "Where's Jess?"

Lee frowned. "Taking a nap, I believe. The trip wore her out some."

"Good," Rick answered, shoving the piece of paper across the desk toward Lee. "Jackson went into town this morning and picked up a telegram from Nick. It's a couple days late. Still having trouble with the wires, I reckon. Anyhow, it seems like everything's been cleared up in Colorado."

Confused at Rick's unusually grave air, Lee crossed the room to take the telegram.

"Also says that Melinda and the kids are on their way," Rick continued, "as are your father, sister, and brother."

*Father?* Lee thought. His eyes widened as he read the paper.

*Monty's situation resolved. Melinda on her way, bringing M's father, brother, sister. Reply, Jim's arrival.*

Lee sucked in his breath and leaned against one of Rick's leather arm chairs. "My father?" he repeated aloud, his mind whirling with all the implications. Dad's reaction to Jess and worse, Jess's reaction to his family. "What the devil's he doing in Colorado?"

Rick grinned and shook his head. "Reckon he came out West to see you. Lilah's having rooms readied and has sent for Consuelo's nieces to help."

Lee ran his fingers through his hair. "It doesn't say when they'll be arriving."

"Melinda said she'd leave a couple days behind us," Jim said. "Add another day to load up your family and five for them to travel by carriage. I expect they'll be arriving Monday."

Monday—two days to prepare Jess. "Damn, Rick, I never expected to put you to so much trouble. Listen," he said, "if you could hold these cards to your chest, I'd be obliged. I'll tell Jess myself when I've had time to figure out how."

"Okay," Rick said with a puzzled shrug. "You have bigger

problems than those, anyhow. It's about Everett Dunne. Lilah tells me he's Jess's husband."

"He is. What about him?"

"When Jackson was in town he heard that Dunne had been there, making inquires about Jess. Stayed a couple days, then cut dirt."

"Bloody hell," Lee whispered, and shifted to sink deeply into the leather chair behind him. Fresh shock waves slammed into him. Dunne—here. Coincidence, or had he finally come to claim Jess? Damn, had Lee's revenge scheme actually *worked?* "What sort of inquiries?"

"Reckon he saw the wanted posters of you and Jess. He'd heard you'd headed this way and was asking if anyone knew where Jess was staying. He asked about you, too. Wanted to know if you were from Boston."

Boston? Hadn't Jess mentioned that Dunne was from New Hampshire? If so, he'd no doubt heard the Montgomery name. Was he sizing up the competition? Dunne would come up lacking in most categories. Except, perhaps, for love.

Lee's stomach took a godawful lurch. She couldn't love him. He had asked her once, but she'd not fully answered him. It hadn't mattered at the time, but now it seemed to be the most important thing in the world.

He rubbed his neck as tension yanked at his muscles. It would be mad for her to love him after everything he'd done. Illogical. But what had logic to do with a woman's heart?

He lifted his head to see Rick and Jim regarding him. Jim's expression was soft with pity. Rick's eyes, however, were cold. "From what Lilah says he's a no-account bastard," Rick said. "I'd be happy to get rid of him for you."

"Damn, Rick," Jim growled, "you can't just go shootin' everyone you don't like!"

"Why not?" Rick asked, with a glint in his eyes and a hard smile on his face.

Lee shook his head. "Thank you, Rick, but it's not necessary. I'll handle it. Just give me a day or two to talk to Jess first."

Rick sighed and his shoulders drooped. "Ah, hell, if that's the way you want it, okay. But I still say shootin's the answer."

Lee folded the paper and shoved it in his pocket. By and by, he and Jess must deal with Dunne. But first he was going to make damned certain she loved him, not Dunne. "Maybe next time."

# Chapter Twenty-Five

Perched on the edge of the fountain, Jess ran her hand through the water, enjoying the silky coolness of it flowing through her fingers. The tinkling, trickling sound filled the courtyard, and a breeze delicately laced with the smell of roses wafted by. Jess breathed deeply of the scent as her mind wandered over the last three nights spent with Lee. Magic, pleasure-filled nights putting to rest once and for all Dr. Acton's fable of her frigidness. Three nights followed by three marvelous days, enjoying the luxury of the Rockin' R, rejoicing in the warmth and laughter of Lee's company. With few exceptions he'd spent every minute with her, his eyes filling with regret and disappointment when, for purposes of civility, he occasionally left her to join Rick and Jim, as he had this morning for a tour of the ranch. He'd left her with a kiss and a promise to return as quickly as humanly possible. He could not return fast enough for her, she thought, sighing dreamily as her mind filled with recollections of his dimpled smile, his deep laughter, his hard naked chest as he slid inside her . . .

It was wrong. It was adultery.

She shoved the thought back into her conscience, and slammed the door and locked it. Plenty of time later for regrets.

An entire lifetime to beg forgiveness. Unless she became pregnant, sued Everett for divorce, and married Lee.

"Ah, there you are, sweetheart."

Her heart jerked at the sound of his voice. She turned to watch him cross the courtyard. He was dressed in borrowed jeans and a green wool shirt, deepening the glow of gentle affection in his eyes. Or was it love? Oh no, impossible, she told her racing heart. Scoundrels didn't fall in love . . .

He reached her and leaned forward to drop a kiss on her forehead. "Miss me?" he asked.

"From the moment you said good-bye," she replied, her voice hoarse with restraint.

His face softened and he lifted a hand to touch her face, brushing his thumb against her cheekbone. "I started missing you as soon as I agreed to join Rick and Jim," he said, tenderly. He took a deep breath and flashed an embarrassed grin. "Which sounds idiotic, I know. But it's true nonetheless." He leaned in to kiss her.

Jess's heart hammered both from his admission and the feel of his mouth on hers. Primed by three erotic nights, her body responded with a rush of heat, reviving the wanton in her. Better, she assured herself, to kiss him back than to blurt out her true feelings and destroy everything. Lee liked loose, no-tie relationships.

He groaned and deepened the kiss. His hand slid down to stroke her breast, sending flashes of heat across her ragged nerves. The heat became a fever. She wanted more, much more. She reached behind him to grasp his buttocks and pull him between her legs.

Gasping, Lee shifted his mouth to her ear. "Jess, sweetheart you can't—" He stopped, breathing heavily as she felt him grow hard and hot against the soft, pulsing juncture of her thighs. "Damn it, Jess, I can't seem to get enough of you. You're like an addiction."

"Then it's one we share," she whispered, sighing when he

slipped his hand between her legs. While nibbling her earlobe, he caressed her, the heat of his hand burning through layers of cotton. Jess closed her eyes in tormented ecstasy. Blood pounded in her ears, her face warmed and her thighs shook as she neared climax.

"Lee? Is that you? Oh my!"

Lee's movements stopped abruptly. He lifted his head, leaving her ear suddenly cold. Slowly, Jess opened her eyes, trying to make sense of it as he slid his hand to her thigh and turned his head in the direction of the voice. Voice? Oh dear God, had someone spoken?

"Star?" Lee said.

Star? Jess thought. What star? It was daytime.

"And this is your actress I presume?" a woman said, merriment marbling the disdain in her voice. "She *is* rather pretty, isn't she?"

"Bloody hell—"

"Lee, there you are!" a male voice spoke. The flush on Jess's face turned to embarrassed humiliation as her eyes found the owner of the voice, a tall, slender man dressed to the nines. He came to a staggering halt several feet away, behind an equally tall, finely dressed woman. The man's eyes flashed over them and disgust creased his face as he spat out, "Good God, man, have you no discretion at all?"

"He never has before, Port," the woman answered, lifting an eyebrow over light brown eyes, almost amber in color. The laughter living in them reminded her of Lee.

*Star.* Good gracious, it was Lee's *sister.*

"Why would you expect it now?" Star finished.

"When in hell did you arrive?" Lee asked, his voice a rough mixture of anger and embarrassment.

"Just now. Father—" Port started, but was interrupted by another man, walking along the pathway. Rick accompanied him, his expression displaying strong amusement. This man carried a cane and wore his severely cut clothes as if born to them.

He had Lee's build and harshly sculpted face, but the careworn creases and gray stripping in his hair testified to his age—and his connection. Mercy, it could not be . . .

"Leland," the man interrupted Port. "I see we've finally found you, son." His gaze flickered over Jess, devoid of any warmth. "And Miss Sullivan."

It was the stuff of nightmares, Lee thought, for his father, the epitome of discretion, to find his son in such a position, with a rock-hard erection and Jess a few caresses shy of climax.

"Sir," he said, swallowing hard. "I hadn't expected you until tomorrow."

"Apparently not," his father said dryly. Lee winced. At his driest Ward Montgomery was also at his angriest. "Perhaps you'll be so kind as to introduce us to your lady friend."

"Oh *yes,*" Star answered, her voice warm with mirth, "please do, Lee. I've been dying to meet her ever since we first heard about the murder."

Over the course of his boyhood, Lee had threatened Star with murder many times. Someday, by God, he was damned well going to do it! "Forgive me, Sis," he said with dark sweetness, "I've been backward in my manners. " He pivoted, pulling free from Jess's thighs, and stood beside her. Her face had gone from the red flush of desire to ghost-white. He couldn't blame her. His father's scowl could scare the hell out of Satan.

Lee reached for her hand. It was cold and trembling, damn his family. Linking his arm in hers, he brought her forward. "Jessica Sullivan," he said, "please allow me to introduce my sister, Star, my brother, Port, and my father, Ward Montgomery."

His father's bow could only just be called that, and Port's was hardly any better. In spite of the laughter in her eyes, Star beamed at Jess and held out her hand. Tentatively, Jess placed hers in Star's meticulously gloved one. Star covered Jess's hand with the other one, saying in a singsong voice, "It is a great pleasure to meet you, Miss Sullivan. I've heard many interesting things about you, I'll have you know!"

"And I you," Jess said.

"Has Lee told you about us then? Why, isn't that intriguing!" Star exclaimed. Her voice rippled with laughter. She lifted an eyebrow. "I'd not thought he'd care so much . . . about us."

Definitely murder. Lee opened his mouth to fire a retort, when Rick interjected. "Excellent. Now that the introductions are over, why don't we adjourn to the parlor? Lilah's busy settling Melinda and the children, but I expect dinner will still be in half an hour."

Ward Montgomery passed one last disgusted look over Lee, before nodding to Rick. "Thank you, sir. You're quite generous. If you'd be so obliging, however, I'd like to change before dinner."

"Oh, as would Port and I!" Star agreed brightly. "Perhaps you, too, Lee?" she asked, her eyes running over his rumpled shirt. The devil take Star, murder was too good for her.

"I would. Shall we continue our reunion over dinner?" Lee answered through gritted teeth.

"Sure," Rick answered. "Lilah's had rooms prepared for you, if you'll follow me."


"Your family! Your *family,*" Jess exploded, throwing open the door to Lee's room. As soon as she returned to her room, she'd marched right through the bathroom and into his. Her blood was boiling with humiliation and fury, and she couldn't contain either a second longer. "When in the name of all that's holy were you going to tell me about them?"

Flinching, Lee sat on his bed. "I only heard yesterday that they were coming. I thought they wouldn't be here until tomorrow or I'd have told you sooner."

"You knew they were coming and still you . . . you . . . good God, Lee, the position they found us in!" she exclaimed, blanching as she took several short, quick breaths in an attempt to fill her tight chest. "How *could* you do that to me?"

With a poker-blank face he answered, "I merely kissed you. You initiated the rest."

Port's appalled expression rose in Jess's mind, followed by Mr. Montgomery's disgust. Jess sank into a chair, rubbing her aching temples. "It doesn't matter. The result's the same. Oh God, how can I possibly face them?"

"Jess, honestly, sweetheart, it's not as bad as all that. They're only people."

People who viewed her as the dregs of society. *And this is your actress I presume?* Jess knew the Bostonian reputation of conservatism, but had never seen it in practice. And she was supposed to dine with them? "I can't meet them again," she rasped. "Tell them I'm tired or sick or dead, I don't care. I'm not going to dinner."

"And what about breakfast? Or lunch? You'll have to face them at some point."

Fresh waves of horror washed over her. They wouldn't be staying for a day or two, but for much more. Oh, she couldn't bear it! But if they'd come this far— "If your father's here, then we've been cleared, haven't we?"

Lee peered at her a moment, before nodding slowly. "Nick said so in the telegram."

"And you didn't *tell* me?" she asked, aghast.

"I didn't think you cared anymore."

"How could I not care? It means we're free, *I'm* free!" she said, relief flooding her taut nerves. "I may leave at any time."

His eyes narrowed and his face tightened. "You can," he answered slowly. "I can't."

The words fell with a thud between them. An aching silence filled the room. Lee ventured in a low, pained voice, "They've traveled three thousand miles to see me, Jess."

She swallowed, but the lump in her throat refused to budge.

"They hate me," she said in a strangled voice. "Do you understand what you're asking? They *hate* me!"

"You won't change their feelings by hiding in your room."

"I can avoid them entirely by leaving. Except," she said with a gulp as reality took another painful turn, "I don't have any money."

"Then stay," he answered. She could only stare back, trapped by the tenderness in his eyes, trapped by her financial situation. Absolutely trapped. Tears welled in her eyes as she searched her mind for a way to escape the Rockin' R, and her foolish, foolish heart.

Lee crossed the room to squat down in front of her. Taking her hands, he stared into her eyes, sincerity quashing the usual merriment in his voice. "Just for a week or so, and then we'll leave together. I'll take you to Denver and you may meet up with your troupe. We'll spend Thanksgiving with them, and discuss what to do next."

And what exactly did *that* mean? It didn't matter for it was pure lunacy, the whole situation hopelessly muddled! Another flash of Mr. Montgomery's face crossed Jess's vision. "Lee, they *hate* me—"

"They don't even know you. When they do, they'll love you. Just the week, sweetheart," he pleaded, dropping one of her hands to brush her tears away.

The desperation in his eyes turned Jess's heart to mush. And where would she go without any money? "Oh, all right! But no more than a week!"

His face broke into a dimpled smile and he rose, pulling her against him. "Splendid. It shall all turn out capitally, Jess. I promise."

She'd never faced a more hostile audience, Jess thought, peering under her lids at Ward Montgomery. He sat across the dinner table from her, with Rick to his right and Melinda on his left and

Port next to Melinda. Lee sat three seats down from Jess, unable to protect her from his father's scowl or the disgusted looks Port periodically shot at her. Lee's family had gathered up Lee's and her trunks in Grant, and dressed in his dark green suit, Lee had appeared as dapper as ever. Jess, on the other hand, in her faded and much-mended blue calico, felt dull and dreary.

As Consuelo served oysters and soup, Mr. Montgomery studied her. Judging from his expression, she came up wanting. He shifted his gaze to his son. "If you'll forgive my candor, Leland, I must say you appear remarkably uninterested in how your situation has turned out."

"I suspect you'll tell me in your own good time, sir," Lee answered in a tight voice, "although I'm not overly concerned. You've never encountered a 'situation' you couldn't master."

Mr. Montgomery inclined his head briefly in appreciation. "Very prettily said, son."

"Yes, Lee," Star commented, laughter sparkling in her voice, "you can't know what a comfort it is to know that you've not lost *all* your manners, circumstances speaking to the contrary this afternoon."

Jess sucked in her breath. Next to her, Jim whispered, "Easy, Jess."

"I daresay you're not fully acquainted with the circumstances," Lee snapped.

"Oh, I apprehend them well enough. Boston or Texas, Lee, I'm not blind."

"Well," Rick interjected, "I for one am interested in the outcome. If you would, sir?"

Jess glanced in his direction. Rick's manner was calm and pleasant, almost urbane. His Western bluffness was gone; his diction, even his southern drawl, altered to sound educated. It unnerved Jess.

Lee took a deep breath. "I *would* like to hear why Temple assembled a posse. From what we deduced, capturing us could hardly have been in his best interest."

"That is because you discounted his daughter," Mr. Montgomery said, as the main course was served, "who was engaged to Senator Keene's son. Temple had invested heavily in railroad equipment, believing that through the marriage he would receive some lucrative beef shipping contracts to the Indian reservations in Dakota territory."

"To Dakota territory? I suspect they have enough beef up there to feed the Indians."

"I never said his plan was good. Regardless, all appeared to be running smoothly when the Temples went to San Francisco. There Mr. Temple won quite a large sum of money from Robert Madison at the gaming tables," Mr. Montgomery said, as they started to eat dinner. He continued between bites. "Madison, however, didn't have the money, and decided that the best way to settle the debt was to seduce Miss Temple and use that as leverage. A despicable business, and yet it would have worked had Madison stopped there. However, he continued to gamble until he was just shy of bankruptcy. It was then he came upon his next scheme."

As Mr. Montgomery chewed his food, Lee provided, "To continue the blackmail."

Mr. Montgomery nodded. "He sent Temple a telegram requesting more money or he would tell Senator Keene 'the truth.' He was traveling to Grant with witnesses to prove it. "

"Jess and me," Lee said with a groan. "We found them together in Madison's office. Temple learned that from his daughter and decided to eliminate both the witnesses and blackmail by murdering Madison and pinning the blame on us. A couple hangings and he'd be free."

"Not knowing, of course," Port added haughtily, "the Montgomery name."

"And how did you learn all this?" Lee asked.

"Miss Sullivan's troupe," Star answered. "They'd already done most of the detective work. Very *interesting* people, Lee.

Especially Miss Dubois who had no compunction about explaining the more *intimate* details—"

"Shut up, Star," Lee growled.

Mr. Montgomery flashed a deeply disapproving scowl at Star and continued. "As Star said, the troupe found Miss Temple—"

Star leaned toward Jess and asked, "Why do you suppose men always shut women up when they express their views?"

"Envy," Lilah interjected softly, "for they're so incapable of expressing their own."

Rick laughed, and Mr. Montgomery continued without a hiccup in his speech. "Who was staying with her aunt in Denver. Miss Temple, it appears, was very much in love with Madison and carries his child. She's furious with her father. When we explained—shall we call them the financial benefits?—of telling the truth, she agreed to testify against him. I discussed it with Senator Keene, the charges were dropped, and the wanted posters ripped up. Which, Leland, leaves you free to roam the West again at will." The sharpness in his voice made the statement a harsh reflection on Lee's life, as did his gaze, falling cold, black, and damning on Jess once more.

"Why, thank you, sir," Lee shot back. "It is good to be free. Now perhaps you'll explain why in blazes *you* came when you could have hired a Pinkerton agent just as well."

A scowl darkened Mr. Montgomery's face. "I'm here because that telegram you sent was the only communication we've had from you in four months."

As Jess winced, Star waved her hand to dismiss all. "Splendid. Lee is a vagabond once more. Now let's move on to something far more interesting like that *divine* Nicholas McGraw."

Jess's head pounded as Port groaned, "Good God, not the cowboy again! She would talk of nothing else, Lee, for the entire journey here."

"Nick!" Lee exploded, eyes widening in shocked anger. "No! Star, you'll dig your claws into that man over my dead body!"

"Oh yes! They'd make the most wonderful couple!" Melinda exclaimed, bouncing.

A week of this—Jess could not bear a week! "I think," she said, standing up in the middle of all, "that if you don't mind, I'll retire. I'm not feeling well."

Lee turned to her, face creased in concern. "Do you require—"

"No, I can manage. Thank you, Lilah, for another marvelous dinner." She turned and fled to her room, where she immediately locked the doors—both of them.

# Chapter Twenty-Six

"Dad," Lee said, entering Rick's study to find his father sitting comfortably before a small fire. "Rick said you wished a private moment with me."

"Why, yes," he said, laying his book on a table. "I wished to relate your mother's regards."

"Only regards, Dad?" Lee said with a smile as he sat in a chair across from his father.

Ward Montgomery's brown eyes peered at Lee from under the heavy bone of his brow. "No. She also requests that, your situation now settled, you turn your attentions eastward for the holiday season."

Lee rubbed his neck. "I'm not certain I shall be available this year."

"Indeed. Would you be obliging as to explain why you wish to disappoint your mother in this matter? She makes few requests of you." When Lee hesitated, he added, "It's this woman, correct?"

Lee shifted uneasily, then leaned forward to throw a log on the smoldering fire. No need, for the room was warm enough, especially with Dad's "I will brook no opposition" tone of voice.

"I should like to assist Jess out of some difficulties."

"And what difficulties would those be now that the murder

charges are no longer in effect?" his father asked, his tone changing from roughness to a damnably silky tone.

"For one thing, she's currently without funds or employment."

"I see," his father answered. "There is, I believe, an opera house in Denver. You may move her there, see her settled in another role, and possibly still be home in time for Thanksgiving dinner."

Turning, he glowered at his father. "Perhaps I wish to spend the holidays with Jess."

"Surely, son, your mother deserves your company more than this actress of yours."

"If she wishes my company so much, you need only invite Jess also."

His father's back stiffened and his face darkened. "I will not. If you must bring the girl, you may find her an inn. I dislike it but shall concede if you abide by your mother's request."

"If I find Jess an inn, sir, I shall stay there as well."

"You shall stay in your own home! In Marblehead, where your mother will do her best, as always, to provide you suitable entertainment." His father took a breath, settled his temper, and continued. "If you choose, you may visit the girl from time to time."

The implication of Jess as his mistress tightened Lee's shoulders. "Those being the conditions, I must decline."

"Good God, man, she is an *actress!* You shall not insult your mother by foisting such a female upon her!"

"Jess," Lee said through clenched teeth, "is not an insult, and I refuse to abandon her for you or any other man, woman, or child."

"I'm not asking you to do that," his father said, calming. "You are a man of honor and the woman is in need. I expect you to assist her. All we ask is a month of your time. Should you require female companionship during that time, Boston is but twenty—"

"Goddamn you, Dad! God*damn* you and your snobbery! I want Jess and if you want me, sir, you must take *her!*"

"Take her—what in the name—" Ward cut himself off abruptly, eyes widening, "Good God, you're in love with her!" Lee clenched his jaw and said nothing. His father stared, stunned, then shook his head. "It's impossible, son. She's an actress, and Irish, too."

"Her vocation is irrelevant."

"She's a member of a traveling troupe. She cannot even claim attachment to serious artists like Booth or Neilsen. I expect she does burlesque," he added disgustedly.

"She's a Shakespearean actress and a damned fine one at that! I've done some traveling, sir, and I assure you, the Bostonian view of the Irish is mistaken. Only a few are of the ilk proving their bad reputation."

His father, concern creasing his harsh face, ran his hand through his hair. "Leland, you are obviously smitten beyond logic. You must know she's entirely unsuitable. She'll never be accepted in polite circles."

"That," Lee said with a laugh, "is a benefit."

"By God, this is no laughing matter! You are set to break your mother's heart!"

"I never pretended to care for society, Dad," he said gently. "Mom knows that."

"Entirely understandable in youth, but as a married man, you must see the advantages—"

"I'm not discussing marriage."

Ward frowned. "But you love the girl. Enough it seems to cause your mother considerable discomfort, which you have always found distasteful."

"I love Jess enough to cause the whole world considerable discomfort. And I'll do my damnedest to keep her."

"I never expected less. Unless you're attempting to inform me of a need for funds," he said with a small cough. "I can rec—"

"I don't want your money, for Christ's sake. I have my own! Have I asked for so much as a dime the last ten years, Dad?"

"No, and it's a blasted shame! Your trust fund, Leland, has more than tripled in value, and still you persist in earning your bread by gambling, the most dishonest of all professions—"

"You lecture me on gambling? You taught me!"

"I played for entertainment, never to feed or clothe myself."

"I play for entertainment also. The benefits are secondary."

"It's abominable."

"It is independence," he said slowly, remembering similar words from Jess. *I will not take your money, Lee. I can take care of myself.* With a sharp pang he realized they were more similar than he'd first considered. Both seeking adventure, both determined to be self-sufficient, and, Lord, both missing their respective homes. If he could take her, he'd go in a minute. But without Jess . . .

His father continued. "We drift from the subject. I request, again, that you come home for a month, perhaps several. Your actress may await your return in Denver."

"Jess," Lee replied, his muscles taut as bowstrings, "will accompany me or I won't come at all."

"You cannot love her if you refuse to marry her!"

Lee played with the stopper on the bottle. "I do not refuse her. She refuses me."

Silence. Total painful silence, except for the smallest of movements across the room. His father declared flatly, "I don't believe that. She has no reason to refuse you."

"She doesn't love me."

"She's scarcely in the position to demand love in marriage. You have wealth, prestige, and countenance, more than enough to recommend you."

Lee took a large swallow of his drink, and said softly, "I believe she loves her husband."

"Husband? She's married? Good God, son, what are you about here? Are there children?"

"The one child they had died shortly after birth."

"And her husband. Where is he?"

Lee hesitated. "I'm not precisely certain."

"Then how do you know if the story she tells is true?"

"Oh, for God's sake," Lee spat, rising to lean against the mantelpiece. "I know better than to fall in love with a liar."

"I should think you'd know better than to involve yourself with a married woman!" his father shouted, anger boiling over once again. "You shall heed my advice, sir, and *not* drag your family into such a scandal!"

"Scandal! Who are you to talk of scandal after your marriage to my mother?"

"You mother was nobly born!"

"She was disgraced, disinherited, and disowned!"

"Her lineage was impeccable. This actress of yours," he shouted, waving a hand toward the courtyard, "has no lineage whatsoever!"

"Lineage! What is she a horse? For the love of God, Father, this is America!"

"She is *married!*" Father roared.


Jess tried to rub the pain from her eyes, but it was useless. Her head ached with unshed tears as the sounds of Lee's voice and his father's reverberated through the courtyard. She could not make out everything they said, but she'd spent enough time standing outside the study window to understand the gist of it.

Foolish, dim-witted girl, why was she so shocked? She'd known for weeks about Lee's background, the sort of family he came from, had seen the disgust in their eyes. She'd known from the moment she'd stepped over the threshold of the Hathaways' home in San Francisco that no permanent bond could ever form between them, regardless of feelings. They were from such different worlds! And love, she told herself with a horrible cracking in her chest, love could not build bridges that large.

But, she thought as angry tears formed in her eyes, Lee was a gambler! How much better was that? A philanderer.

For a man, gambling was common, and philandering part of his nature, both lapses in judgment, forgiven by society. But a woman's fall from grace, that lasted a lifetime.

For a few moments her stubborn streak surfaced. Lee loved her. He'd stood eye to eye with his father, defending her against every slander Mr. Montgomery had hurled. He was, after all, not a boy, but thirty years old and master of his own life. He'd do as he chose and he chose *her*. He'd even sounded as if he—as if he wanted to *marry* her. A wonderful, little explosion of excitement blew through her stomach. Maybe she wasn't just a passing fancy, but real love.

Except that he was a rake—and she was married—and Mr. Montgomery loved his son.

And it seemed that Lee was some sort of descendant of English nobility. Mercy, but it truly was impossible. She couldn't stay, she couldn't leave; she could see no way out of this that didn't include tearing her heart from her chest and stomping on it until it was mush.

"Jess? May I join you?"

She lifted her tired, aching head to see Lilah standing above her. Usually she found the woman's cold eyes daunting. But the emotion rampaging through her heart made Lilah's coolness feel like a breath of clean mountain air on a blazing hot summer day. With a lump in her throat she nodded.

Lilah seated herself and said, "I heard the argument."

"It rages on," Jess answered, nodding to where raised voices drifted through the courtyard.

"They've yet to dispense all their anger."

"If they continue in this strain, they'll end up dispensing a shotgun."

"From the little I know about Lee and Ward, they will part in anger but forgive in time."

"Forgive faster if the cause of the argument is removed."

Lilah stared across the yard a moment before saying, "Lee loves you very much."

She took a deep agonizing breath. "He loves his family."

"It seems he'd choose you."

"Have I the right to force that choice?"

"Are you forcing him?"

She closed her eyes and tried to swallow the lump in her throat. "My situation does."

Lilah was silent a minute. "Perhaps it wouldn't be so difficult if you were to examine that situation."

Jess opened her eyes. "What is there to examine? It is what it is."

Lilah took a deep breath, "No doubt Lee and Rick and all the rest will curse me for this but . . ." She paused. Jess frowned in confusion as Lilah drew a breath and finished. "Your husband was recently in town inquiring after you."

Stunned, Jess couldn't move for a moment. Then, her heart shaking, her hands trembling, she asked in a low voice. "Everett? In town?"

"A ranch hand informed us two days ago. He disappeared before we could find him."

"Disappeared? But why?"

"I don't know. After learning about your difficulties with the law, he may have decided to protect you by lying low. Or he may have heard of your relationship with Lee and thought to leave well enough alone. Or perhaps he needed to leave for some reason but means to return. The point is, he's in the area if you wish to see him."

"I-I'm not certain I do, not after all he did," she answered even as her heart, aching from losing Lee, took a leap of hope. A way out, maybe . . .

"He treated you very poorly, I understand. But memory is a

tricky thing, Jess. Time puts a certain patina on our memories, youth exacerbates it." Lilah's eyes narrowed. "Confronting your husband will tell you if what you remember is real or illusion."

"And if it goes badly?"

"Then you'll know for certain. It's impossible, Jess, to live fully without accepting your past. I know that well."

Jess looked down at her hands. She could still see Everett's brown eyes, warm with love as he stroked her hair. Was that the illusion? Or was her disgust in the marital bed and his betrayal illusion? Could betrayal be illusion? He had deserted her in the most desperate of conditions, leaving her penniless with a sick and dying infant. For a moment her vision blurred and the ashes of rage almost choked her. She took a breath, then resolutely she swallowed the anger. Everett was her husband and she was still bound to him, legally, morally, spiritually. Did that make her bound to try to forgive him? They'd both been so young back then, maybe too young for the responsibilities of marriage and a baby. But six years had changed her from the wide-eyed, dreamy girl she had been then, maybe it had changed him too. Could six years turn a boy into a man, could if offer the recipe to change young, impetuous love into something stronger, deeper, aged gracefully like fine wine?

Lee's voice suddenly clear, echoed through the courtyard. "I will do as I please!"

His father returned in a tone thick with fury, "You shall do as I say, or you shall do all without your family!"

Without his family. Abruptly her own father's voice trumpeted in her mind, "Marry Dunne and you'll be no daughter of mine!" Horrible, gut-wrenching pain tore at her belly and she clutched at it. Guilt followed hard on that, along with sorrow and black grief. She missed him, wished with all her heart she could have but a few minutes to hold his gnarled hand as he lay dying, to comfort him, to beg forgiveness.

Maybe there was no way for her to get through this without stomping on her own heart—or Lee's for that matter. But she could prevent him from even greater harm. Lee would never live through the agony of losing his family. Not if she had any say in it.

"You know nothing about her!"

"I have known her kind! A vaudeville actress who shows no compunction about consorting with a gambler!"

"Goddamn you, she refused every advance—"

"Until she learned of your connections no doubt! How could you be so stupid, son! It is the oldest trick in the book!"

"I must leave," Jess said, tears pooling in her eyes. "I cannot allow this!"

"I know," Lilah said, reaching into her pocket. She withdrew a roll of bills—twenties—and pressed them into her palm. "This will ease your departure."

Jess stared at the money. "I can't take your money."

Lilah placed her hand on Jess's and gently closed her fingers around the bills. Noticing that Lilah's trembled, Jess looked up at her. Unshed tears sparkled in Lilah's eyes. "I know what it is to feel trapped," she said in a low, husky voice. "Worse to be tied to a man by money, hardest still to love that man. It is hellish." A small, quivering breath and she said with the slightest of smiles, "Take the money and find Dunne. Then you'll have your answer."

"Lilah, I can't—"

"Do it for me."

"Damn you, Father!" Lee shouted and then the door slammed. Jess and Lilah froze, until they heard Lee's footsteps moving swiftly away from them.

Jess tried to breathe through frantic heartbeats. "Okay, then, but I *will* pay you back, I promise."

"I never doubted it."

* * *

Lee paced in his room for half an hour before his temper calmed. In the end he conceded that his father was a snob and an ass, and he couldn't change that. But the argument had solidified the decision he'd been struggling with for days. Far from fading after lying with Jess, his feelings for her had strengthened tenfold. A hundredfold. Beyond measure. Love was too small a word for what he felt, and the idea of spending another day without her in it, never mind the rest of his life, tore the very breath from him. Even if she still loved Dunne, her response to him must register some sentiments toward himself. It was far past time to declare his love and beg for her hand in marriage.

Heart pounding, he left his room and was about to knock on her door when he saw her in the rose garden. She sat on a bench, holding her head between her hands as if it hurt. Damn. She'd heard the argument.

She lifted her head as he approached. Her eyes seemed slightly red, her expression pained. "Did you hear us then?" he asked.

She narrowed her eyes a little and then looked down at her hands. "Some of it."

He sat next to her, his thigh rubbing against hers. She moved her leg. Not a good sign, he thought with a thud in his chest. "I'm sorry, sweetheart. For the worst parts of it, at any rate, but not for what I said about you."

She remained silent. Lee reached over and snapped a pink rose off a bush. While turning it in his hand, he summoned all of his courage. "It's time to confess the truth, Jess. I've fallen in love with you." *Confess.* Stupid fool! It sounded like he was guilty of something.

He glanced over at her. A light pink flush stained her skin. She sat regarding her hands, her eyes, those windows to the soul, turned away. An interminable minute crept by. "No answer? I must tell you, sweetheart, I had hoped for a warmer reception."

She turned to him, her eyes mere slits, effectively hiding her feelings. "What would you have me say?"

He flashed her his dimple. "That you love me, too, madly, passionately. That you'd gladly spend the rest of your life in bed with me, forsaking everything including food and water."

"My goodness!" she said with a faint chuckle. "What would I say for an encore?"

Amusement. A good sign. He reached for her hand and held it tenderly, while giving her his best smile. "You wouldn't say anything. You'd do it."

She smiled a little. "I do like food, Lee."

"All right. I shall allow you food *occasionally*."

"Everett and I tried staying in bed. It worked badly."

Damn the man! "I thought *we* managed it fairly well."

With a sad smile, she removed her hand from his. A huge, ocean-sized ache started deep in his chest and rose up his throat. "You do, Lee."

"Do you love me at all, Jess?"

"What use would it be?" she asked.

He leaned back, squinting against the sun. "Love isn't useful. Love just is."

She studied her nails, pushing at one of the cuticles. "Lilah told me Everett is in town. I would have expected to hear it from you."

Damn! Why in hell would Lilah do that? He rubbed his neck, and watched an ant making its way over a rock, not a care in the world. "I was waiting for the right moment. You realize, I expect, that knowing his location allows you to sue for divorce."

"But I love him."

Lee's heart slowed to a halt. "I should think you'd wish him to the devil."

"We had many happy times together."

"You had much suffering!"

She lifted her head to look at him. Her eyes were glassy, but her expression cool, immobile. Even with all his gambling experience, he couldn't read the emotions of an accomplished actress. "I mismanaged my wifely duties. I was young, inexperienced. After this last week, I may manage them better."

White-hot fire flashed down his spine and then spread through his body, scorching everything in its path. "I think you'd better clarify that."

"You understand perfectly well."

"That you would go from my bed to his," Lee growled, making fists of his hands.

She jerked in reaction. Swiftly, though, she regained her composure. "You're not generally so crude."

"You're not generally so cruel."

She bit her lip. "'Cruel only to be kind'" she quoted in a low voice. "Far kinder to burn the bridge now than to spend years believing we could cross it."

He could scarcely breathe. Images of life without Jess, nightmares of her lying with another man, ripped through his mind. "And what if you're carrying my child?"

Her eyes narrowed. "My monthly came today."

Another shot, this one to the gut. He hadn't realized how much he'd wanted that child. "And if it doesn't work out with Everett?" he asked, grasping at straws.

She turned away again. He wanted to grab her chin and yank her face around to face him. But the thought of her reaction to such violence calmed him.

"Then I'll resume my career."

"I'll take you," he said roughly.

Again she faced him. Her eyebrows lifted. "You will?"

"I will."

"Even after I've gone back to Everett?"

He ground his teeth. "Even after."

Her eyes narrowed as she tilted her head. "How long after? Days? Weeks? Months?"

More hellish images. "Any amount of time."

"And what if I decided to have several affairs to make him jealous? Would you take me then, too?"

After killing every last one of them. "Yes."

"And you and I could enjoy each other's company in between, and you could call me Michelle."

"Goddamn it, Jess!" He crushed the rose in his hands. The thorns dug into his flesh. He barely felt it as rage yanked at his muscles. "Why are you saying this?"

"To burn the bridge," she said, her voice cracking. A tear escaped her narrowed eyes and she dashed it away.

"You're crying," he whispered, his anger dissolving in the face of her distress.

"It's difficult to say good-bye."

"Then don't. There's no reason we can't remain friends, is there?"

"I can't," she said, a hitch in her voice. "Married women do not remain friendly with ex-lovers. It tends to strain the marriage."

"But if Everett refuses—"

"I am not," she started. Her voice abruptly strengthened as she sat back. "I am not the woman I was before. And I *will* make this work. I want to be married, Lee." She swallowed. "I want children. I want a home. I'm sick of adventure."

"But that's what I'm offering, Jess," he said, spreading his palms in supplication. "The ring, the wedding, babies, the whole shebang."

"I'm already married."

"That can be rectified!" he growled.

"No. It wouldn't *work,* Lee. You and I are too different! But Everett and I are not. We're both from small towns. We speak the same language—"

"You and I are more alike than it first appears."

"I wear wool and you wear silk! We are as dissimilar as mica and gold!"

"A difference in financial circumstances doesn't constitute incompatibility!"

"Oh!" she exclaimed jerking to a stand, dropping her fists

to her sides as anger flashed through her eyes. "If you aren't the most mule-headed man . . . Aren't you listening? I don't *want* you, Lee! Need I say it again? *I don't want you!*"

Any nerve not already scorched burned to a crisp. He pleaded in a low, harsh voice. "I don't believe that. Not after these last days—"

She was shaking now, eyes unnaturally bright in her pale face. "Physical compatibility, nothing more."

"It's a helluva lot more than Everett gave you!"

She sucked in her breath. "It's over, Lee. There's a stage-coach headed to Abilene tomorrow at eleven A.M. That was Everett's last known direction. I'll bid you farewell now. I know how early hours disagree with you."

"At least give me a day!"

"I don't wish to miss Everett." She turned on her heel and headed up the path to her room.

"A night then. Jess. Jess!"


Jess closed the door, then slumping against it, knees weak, closed her eyes and covered her ears to block out Lee's voice calling her back. Oh God, why did doing the right thing always hurt *so* much?

Because she'd done the wrong thing to begin with. It wasn't doing the right thing that hurt, it was correcting the wrong.

Breathing deeply, she fought back tears. Every fiber of her being wanted to throw herself on the bed and cry until her body could produce no more tears. But she couldn't. Tears produced red eyes and swollen lids, the telltale signs of her shattering heart. Lee would notice, and use it to keep her by his side. His knowing would destroy them both.

She stayed there for a long time, visions of Lee flashing through her mind as her stomach rolled. She lurched toward the chamber set and vomited into the basin. Afterward, she sank to the floor, pulling down a towel to wipe her mouth. For a time she stared blankly at the wall, shoving aside all thought of Lee until her brain was empty. Slowly the unshed tears receded, leaving behind a throbbing headache.

She rose and opened her trunk to pack her few items. By and by, she'd have to cry it out. But not today. Maybe tomorrow night when she was miles away, in a hotel room with no one as witness.

When she was done, she pushed aside the curtain to peer out the window. No sign of Lee. With a sigh, she opened the door and stepped out. After a minute of searching she found Maria. She managed quickly to convey her wishes—supper in her room tonight, for she suffered from a painful monthly, and a bottle of sherry to ease the pain. Twenty minutes later she had both. Locking both doors, she poured herself a glass of wine and then raised it. "To you, Ev. May you prove to be worth at least some small portion of all this suffering."

# Chapter Twenty-Seven

Apparently, Jess thought, eyeing the only other passenger in the stagecoach as it pulled out of town, no one wanted to go to Abilene. He sat slumped in the corner, a poncho covering the upper portions of his body, a large sombrero-type hat pulled low over his face. He seemed to want to sleep. Jess settled herself diagonally from him and moved the curtain to peek around it. She watched as the Winchesters' buckboard with Lee sitting tall in the back faded from view. Every nerve ached as she leaned back and closed her eyes, fighting back tears. Tonight, she promised herself. Tonight she would cry.

They'd been traveling for half an hour when the man stirred. She looked at him briefly, then opened the curtain to watch the passing scenery. She had no desire for conversation.

He pushed his sombrero up on his head. She risked another glance. His brown eyes gleamed at her, his lips forming a broad, friendly smile, accented by blond sideburns.

"Everett!" she cried out, her stomach jerking.

"Hello, Jess. Fancy meeting you here."

"Oh my goodness, Everett!" she said, leaning forward, the heaviness in her shoulders lightening. "I can't believe this! What are you doing here? In this coach? Ev, darling, I was coming for you. I'd heard you'd been making inquiries . . ."

Her voice trailed off for he said nothing, made no move at all. Slowly her eyes shifted downward to see his hand peaking out from under the poncho. A gun. Pointed at her.

"Ev?"

"Like my gun, Jess?" he asked almost proudly.

She smiled tentatively. "I suppose. Must you point it at me?"

"I do. See, I need money."

Had he gone mad? "Well, I don't have much money but what I have is yours. You don't need the gun. For heaven's sake, Ev, didn't you hear me? I was coming for you."

Licking his lips, he leaned forward, his eyes glittering. "You have money? Did that Montgomery fella give it to you? How much?"

"Three hundred dollars."

His face fell and he leaned back. "Three hundred's not enough."

"Damn it, you're in trouble," she said, disgusted. Why had she thought Everett was the answer to her problems? It was all coming back to her, and none of it was good. "How much?"

*He's your husband,* her conscience reminded her.

"Four thousand."

*You're legally—*

"Oh, Good God, Ev, how *could* you?"

*—and morally—*

He grimaced. "Gambling. I've been losing."

*—and spiritually—*

"You always lost."

*—bound to him.*

"Well, this fella's not the kind you forget to pay, you know?"

Her shoulders sank. Out of the frying pan and into the fire. It hadn't been such a hot pan and this fire, Lord, she'd been down this road before. "All right, put the gun away. I'll help you."

"You can't. Unless you could convince Montgomery to give you the money?"

"Not a dime. We're . . . we're not together anymore." She frowned. "How did you know I was going to be on this coach?"

"I've been planning this for days. Then I saw you buy the ticket and, well, you dropped right in to my lap. See, Jess, this isn't a stick up. This here's a kidnapping."

Everett pushed the door open and motioned Jess inside a small, dark sod room. Its ceiling was barely high enough for their heads. Glancing up, she rubbed her arms and wondered if there were snakes in that ceiling. Strangely, the soddy had windows and wallpaper, along with a big four-poster bed, a dresser, night table, and chamber set. So if she actually had to touch a snake, she could wash up afterward. Hallelujah, she was saved.

"It's ugly," she said.

"Yeah, but the stage station owner won't talk; he needs the money. He used to rent it out to passengers before the train came through. Don't bother yelling for help; he's mostly deaf."

"Lovely," she said, as Everett closed the door and dropped her trunk just inside. It fell with a clunk, for the floor was made of wood, which made not a word of sense. Why have a wood floor and sod roof?

Oh, none of this made sense and try as she had to make Everett understand that Lee believed she'd gone to Everett on her own, he'd refused to listen. Finally, too disgusted with the situation to quarrel anymore, she'd agreed with him. Lee would surely pay five thousand dollars for the return of Everett's long-lost wife. Why not? He had more money than Midas.

"Okay, now, I'm going to have to tie you up, here," he said, grabbing a rope from the dresser, while keeping the gun trained on her.

"I'm not going to try to escape. Why should I? For the love of Pete, Ev, I was coming for you!"

"Get settled comfortable-like there on the bed. It'll be better than the chair. I'll tie you to the post."

She rolled her eyes and with a flounce, sat on the bed, and dropped her purse on the ground next to her. Everett strode purposefully toward her. Almost gingerly he placed the gun on the beside table. "I'm putting my gun down, but I can grab it if I want, okay?" He knelt down next to her, pulled her arms behind her and then lashed her to the post.

"Everett, this is absolutely unnecessary!"

"I'm sorry. It's gotta be done." He finished and she felt his hands fumbling with the buttons of her sleeves. A moment later he rolled back the sleeve of her right arm. "Okay, this is gonna hurt a little," he said, rising to fish through his trouser's pocket. Her eyes widened in alarm when he pulled out a knife.

"What in hell do you think you're doing?"

"Just a little cut," he said, leaning over.

Horrified, Jess jerked on her bonds as she watched the knife come down slowly to slice the flesh of her lower right arm. "Ow! You goddamned bastard, what are you doing?"

"Lord, but your language's taken a dive. Where's you bag? Oh, there it is," he said, reaching down.

"What do you expect after six years in the theatre! Everett, I'm *bleeding!*"

"'Course you are. That was the point! Little pun there," he said, digging through her bag. "Aha! Here's your handkerchief. Plain white. You don't treat yourself much, do you?"

"Are you going to bandage me? Shouldn't you use your own handkerchief, since you're the one who cut me?"

"Lord no!" He bent over and gently wiped up the blood. He stared down at it and shook his head. "I don't know if that's enough."

"Enough for what?"

"To convince Montgomery that you're in danger. I figure the more worried he is about you, the more likely he'll be to fork over the gilt."

"You could have damned well bled yourself!"

Everett looked slightly chagrinned, and a little accusatory. "You know how much I hate pain, Jess."

"And I like it?"

"You take it better."

Trying to summon up patience, she closed her eyes and took a deep breath. "The blood's running down my arm."

"Hey, that's great!" he said, and sopped up more blood. "Here, take a look. That looks like you're plenty hurt, huh?"

She glanced at the handkerchief, then glared at him. "I could slap you right now!"

"Ha! You did often enough when we were together!"

"Well," she snarled, "I wouldn't have if you'd kept your hands off other women!"

"Other women?" he repeated. He slid off the bed, then took a piece of paper and pencil off the dresser. Dragging a chair over to the night table, he shrugged dismissively. "I never understood why that upset you. I always came back to you."

"Because I loved you, you bastard!"

Pencil poised, he lifted his head and smiled at her with those soft brown eyes. For a split second she was transported back in time, to when they'd first married and she'd still loved him. "I love you, too, Jess."

She stared, marveling at the gentle affection in his eyes. He did love her. But it made no sense at all! She shook her head. "Have you never heard of faithfulness? Did you miss that part in the vows, Ev?"

Frowning, he looked down at the paper and started writing. "See, Jess, that's where you're wrong. We weren't married."

"Weren't married? What the devil are you talking about?"

He lifted his head. "You better stop hollering. I need to concentrate on writing this ransom note."

"Not until you give me an answer!"

With a sigh he reached into his pocket again, causing Jess a moment's compunction. Oh no, he wouldn't use the knife again.

A handkerchief. And a bandana. "I didn't want to do this," he said, "but you aren't leaving me a choice."

"Do what—" she started. As soon as she opened her mouth, he stuffed his handkerchief in it, smothering her words. Furious, she tried to spit it out, but before she could, he covered her mouth with the bandana. While she twisted her head this way and that to escape, he tied the bandana securely in place. Oh God, she'd kill him when he freed her. What did he mean they weren't married?! Of course they were married.

Ignoring her, he sat back down to compose his note. And Jess, exhausted, leaned against the wall behind her. She closed her eyes, and tried to stop the whirling emotions tugging at her sanity.

# Chapter Twenty-Eight

Lee stared into the library fire. *Hamlet* lay on the table next to him. Idiotic idea, searching for Jess in a book. He clenched his teeth against the wave of heartache. How long did past loves haunt rakes? Months? Years? Lord, but he'd loved being a scoundrel!

The door opened and Lee lifted his head. His father's eyes fell on him and after a quiet click of the door, he strode across the room, purpose in every step. Wincing, Lee leaned back in the chair and closed his eyes. "I have nothing to say to you, Father."

His father took the chair opposite Lee, saying gently, "I have much to say to you, son."

"What, did you miss something in your last lecture? Or have you come to gloat?"

"I came to apologize."

Lee opened his eyes at that. "Apologize? I didn't know you made mistakes, sir."

"About once every ten years, it seems. Would you be so kind as to pour me a glass of brandy? Thank you." Lee obeyed and handed his father a glass. After taking a sip, he sighed appreciatively. "Excellent. I shouldn't have believed such civilization in the West." He took another sip. "It's come to my attention that Miss Sullivan has left."

"She has."

"Did she hear our argument?"

"Dad," he said on a sigh, "they heard it in El Paso."

"Her reason for leaving, I expect." Lee nodded and his father contemplated the fire a moment before continuing. "When you left home eleven years ago, I believed you were behaving like a spoiled child, determined to have your way at the cost of your family and your future. These last days have compelled me to revisit that belief." Another sip of brandy, as Lee turned in his chair to watch his face. "The very people you despised in Boston and New York were always the least trustworthy and most pretentious. The Winchesters and McGraws, however, possess strength, loyalty, and kindness. I like them. Quite possibly you are a better man now, son, than if you had stayed."

"And," Lee said with a small laugh, "society is much better off also!"

His father smiled slightly. "Perhaps. These friends of yours seem to have a great deal of respect for Miss Sullivan. Or is it Mrs.?"

"Sullivan is her stage name. Her married name is Dunne," he replied and took a long, fortifying gulp of brandy.

"Regardless, I mistook the situation, and the woman. I am not generally so poor a judge of character." His father took a deep breath. "Miss Sullivan is extraordinarily beautiful." He paused again, then continued peering at Lee with his intense, hard gaze. "You've always been close to your mother. You are alike in so many ways—the restless spirit, sense of humor, and dislike of society."

Lee smiled. "And yet she pursues the social life."

"For the family's sake. She'd wish them all to the devil if she could."

"Which," Lee said with a small chuckle, "she often did in the confines of our family."

"It is her only relief. Yet, you are my son, too, Lee. Montgomery blood runs through your veins, blood that has run very hot for generations. Not only in temper but in the sensual arts as well."

Lee frowned. "Yes, you've told us about Grandfather—"

"Not just your grandfather. But my grandfather as well chased women, and his father before that. And it follows through the less direct lines also. Rob behaves decently, but his brother in Worcester, my aunts in New York—" He shook his head. "It's not something we're proud of. Suffice it to say that I fully understand your nature. Combine that with all else, and it seemed to me when I met Miss Sullivan that her beauty had swept you away. That you had mistaken lust for love."

"Dad—" Lee started, shaking his head.

His father raised his hand to stop Lee's words. "I was wrong. She left to spare you pain and embarrassment. More important, I know you, son. You've always, even when young, displayed a strong sense of integrity and honor. For all your waywardness, you judge character well."

Lee sipped his drink to hold down the pain in his throat. "She's a jewel."

Ward sighed. "I ought not to have interfered."

"It makes no difference."

"What I don't understand is why you let her go."

"Could it be due to her marriage?"

"You may file for divorce. It's difficult but obtainable with the right amount of money and the proper connections. I understand the Dakota territory has a fairly easy divorce law. And your lady's husband has certainly given her ample grounds."

"And the scandal?"

His father grimaced. "Unfortunate, perhaps socially insurmountable in Boston and New York, but as you pointed out earlier, you may find that beneficial."

Lee envisioned his family attempting to defend Lee to their friends. "Not to Port or the rest of you."

"Port!" Ward barked a laugh. "Lee, Port *makes* society. Besides, Jess may yet have a champion in McAllister. She made quite an impression upon his brother in San Francisco. You, I must point out, behaved abominably."

Lee winced. "You heard about that, did you?"

His father's lips twitched. "Did you think we wouldn't? I don't know what demon possessed you to expose the poor girl to that set, but McAllister liked her tremendously. 'As charming as she is lovely,' he said. Of course he knew nothing of her background."

With a deep, shuddering sigh, Lee took another long swallow. "It doesn't matter at any rate. Jess loves Dunne."

"I think she loves you also."

"Not enough."

With an impatient intake of breath, Ward said, "If I loved the woman, son, nothing short of mortal wounds would keep me from her side."

Lee laughed a little. "No, sir. As I recall Mom stabbed you."

Ward's eyes gleamed. "It was but a slight wounding. It scarcely deterred me."

"Nor did anything else, as I recall. By 'any means, be they fair or foul,' correct? It's a miracle that she forgave you my birth."

"It was," his father said truly smiling now, "my greatest triumph. You proved quite useful, son."

He bowed his head. "I have always endeavored to please, sir."

"You rarely endeavor to please. But my pleasure and your obedience is not at issue. I made a mistake with Miss Sullivan. I hope to prevent you from making a worse one."

Lee shook his head. "It was different with Mom. She loved you. Jess does not."

"Are you certain?"

He sighed. "I'm your son, Dad, not your servant. Regardless of your dictates, I offered to obtain a divorce for her so that she could marry me. She declined. Strongly. She swears she loves Dunne."

"No doubt to turn you away."

"She's indicated that she did from the moment I met her. I chose to disbelieve it."

"Still, son," Ward said, taking a sip of brandy, "you have much more to offer than this Dunne. In all probability he is still penniless. And to abandon his wife under such circumstances, you must concede that he can never make her a decent, never mind good, husband. If you pursued her—"

"Jess cares nothing about the money, except to say she won't be bought. She truly believes in this marriage, Dad, it's what she *wants*. She loves him, for God's sake! And, loving her as I do, I can't stand in the way of her happiness."

"Not married!" Jess spat when Everett removed the bandana. After finishing his note, he'd dropped a chaste—despicable!—kiss on her head and told her he'd be back. She'd spent hours trying to remember if Ev had always been so stubbornly stupid, and wondering what he meant by "not married." It had to have been hours, for she couldn't see the sun shining through the cracked windows. It was still daylight, but the sun was starting to set.

"Still on about that?" he asked. "I've brought you dinner."

He'd laid the plate on her table, complete with utensils and a napkin. The smell of the food caused her dry mouth to salivate—beefsteak, potatoes, and a can of sarsaparilla, one of Everett's other loves.

"I'm not hungry!" she snarled. She was starving. And furious.

"You? Not hungry? You were always hungry when we were together."

"I was carrying your *child!*"

He had the good grace to wince. "I'm sorry about that Jess. I . . . I reckon Janey died?"

Tears sprang to her eyes and she turned away, setting her

teeth. It was a moment before she could speak. "Three days after you left."

He sighed, and pulled the chair up to the table. "I thought so. Jess, about that . . . you understand . . . I couldn't stay. I couldn't bear to watch."

Anger and pain battled in her heart as she jerked her head around. "You couldn't bear anything."

He shrugged. "You were always stronger than me. I think that's why I love you so much. Here, lean forward and I'll untie your hands so you can eat."

It was the second time he claimed to love her. Now that she thought on it, love had never been Everett's problem. He loved easily—just not very deeply.

Lee claimed to love her also. As shallowly? No. Mercy no, not if he'd been willing to buck his father's wishes and risk losing his family for her.

"You're not eating."

She eyed the knife, considering how to use it as a weapon and escape from Ev's latest mad scheme, sure to fail, as always, and submerge her in suffering. She'd been wrong, she thought with a sinking in her chest. Everett wasn't her answer. He never had been. "My hands are numb."

"I'll cut your food," he said helpfully.

She swung her legs around the edge of the bed and pulled the table toward her.

"You still haven't explained—oh hell!" she spat, as an unpleasant reminder wafted under her nose. She slammed the fork down. "You were off with a woman weren't you? I can smell the perfume! Damn it, don't you ever *stop?*"

"I'm better than I was," he defended sulkily.

"You could scarcely be worse," she spat back. She took a swig of sarsaparilla, and then started eating. "What did you mean about not being married?"

Off the hook for his whoring, he flashed her his impish grin. "We weren't."

"I was at the ceremony."

"I paid a man ten dollars to conduct it. He did a nice job, didn't he?"

"Ev, I have the marriage certificate in my trunk!"

He shrugged. "Another ten dollars."

She shook her head and took another bite. Never married. Not for all the last six years during which she'd followed the ten commandments to the letter, no adultery, no coveting, except for Lee— Oh God, she wasn't *married!*

A warm shiver fluttered through her heart.

*She wasn't married!*

Swallowing, she lifted her eyes to him. "Are you certain?"

"Sure I'm certain. I paid the man. You aren't angry?"

*Not bound legally, morally . . .*

"Absolutely, positively certain?"

Frowning he said, "Jess, I'm certain. I did want to marry you, but, see, I'm already married."

She dropped her fork.

*Already married?*

The world spun. She took several gasping breaths. Then her *marriage* had been adultery . . . but she hadn't known! Did that count? It shouldn't if she didn't enjoy it. Oh God, what did it matter, for she'd lain with Lee when she thought she was still married to Everett. Wasn't it still a sin if she intended to commit adultery?

She'd stolen another woman's husband! What could she possibly do to make amends now? "'Though all that I do,'" she quoted in a cracking voice, "'is nothing worth, since that my penitence comes after all, imploring pardon.'"

Ev frowned. "Is that an insult?"

She focused on him again, catching his eyes. Bland, guileless eyes. A child in a man's body. "It's Shakespeare. Henry the Fifth begging forgiveness from God."

"You haven't done anything that needs forgiveness. That's what I'm trying to tell you."

She stared at him a moment and then shook her head. It wasn't worth explaining. He couldn't understand. Hands shaking with emotional fatigue, she continued eating.

After a minute, he ventured, "This Montgomery fella, Jess. You like him?"

"It seems so," she answered between bites.

"But you were coming for me."

"I was."

"Listen, then, I have a plan," he said, leaning forward enthusiastically.

Her chest tightened with dreadful recollection of past plans. She slowly lifted her eyes. "A plan?"

"You think he'll pay the money right?"

She nodded.

"But you want me more."

Frowning, she gave her head a little shake to see if it would help his words make sense. It didn't. "I don't understand."

"Well, Montgomery will have some rich friends. You stay with him a little, then take up with another of his friends. I'll stay nearby and keep low, and you can come to me anytime you want. Then, when you think the new fellow's ready, we do it again. You know, the kidnapping, the ransom. We'd be rich in no time."

Oh no, oh no, he couldn't be serious. "You want me to take another rich lover. And you capture me and hold me for ransom again? That's what you're saying."

"Yes."

"And, in between kidnappings, I sneak off to be with you when no one's looking?"

He grinned. "It'd make it more exciting!"

A whore, he wanted her to be a whore. For him. Her breath came in short shallow spurts. A score of conflicting emotions collided into each other, then formed into a black ball of rage. "Are you aware of the fact that I have a fork in my hand?" she asked in a low voice.

"A fork?"

"And I am going to damned well stab you with it, you *bastard!*" She jerked to a stand and brought the fork down on his hand. Only he was too quick for her; he jumped away, knocking his chair over. The fork hit the table, sending jolts of pain through her arm. As Everett backed toward the dresser, she yanked the fork from the wood and then gave chase. His fingers curled around the gun handle just as she lifted the fork to stab him in the arm. He whirled away and pointed the pistol at her. It shook in his hand.

"Hold it right there, Jess!" he said, his face creased in fear.

"You *fool!*" she hissed. "You don't have the guts to shoot me!"

"I will if you come any nearer with that fork!"

Her mind filled with a fog of rage, she stepped forward, holding her fork in front of her, determined to shove it deep into his black heart. He stood steady, his eyes narrowing. He cocked the gun. For a moment she stared at it, and then suddenly the absurdity of the situation struck her.

No! Oh no, she wouldn't laugh! She was damned well going to stab him!

But she couldn't help it. Hysterical laughter shuddered through her, and she dropped the fork. She turned and sank into the bed. Between peals of laughter she gulped air. Oh, to actually threaten a man with a fork, when he was holding a fully loaded six-shooter. And *he* to look frightened! She couldn't wait to tell Lee; she could almost hear his deep, masculine laughter.

Except that she left him.

The vision shattered. The next peal of laughter came out as a sob. Tears ran down her cheeks. Fool, she was the fool, not Everett.

Everett's answer to her hysteria was to carefully lay the gun on the table, and then tie her up again. At length, her sobs subsided and she fell asleep. Some time later, when the moon was high in the sky, she awoke to the bed squeaking as Everett lay next to her. Then, just as she was falling back asleep, his hand slid up her waist to caress her breast. The smell of cheap perfume stung her nose. Mercy, she was going to vomit.

Lee's smile flashed through her mind, followed by recollections of his touch. Damn Everett to hell!

She waited until the other hand joined the first. Then, with lightning swiftness, she bent her head to bite his wrist. Hard. Very hard. She tasted blood, the bastard.

He recoiled, squealing like the pig he was.

He didn't try it again.

# Chapter Twenty-Nine

Lee stared at the chess pieces, marvelous constructions of black and white marble, and could not decide on a move to save his life. The Winchesters' parlor was lit brightly against the night, and a fire crackled in the grate. His family and his friends were scattered in small groups around the room, talking and laughing as if nothing was wrong, as if the world had not turned sideways on its axis, as if Lee was not sporting a huge gaping hole in the center of his chest. The companionship around him ought to ease his pain, but it only made him lonelier.

"You might consider," Star suggested across from him, "moving your bishop."

Star—flirt, women's rights activist, and blown-in-the-glass genius at chess. They'd been playing this particular game for nearly an hour and he'd made several stupendously bad moves. She'd ignored them.

He glanced up. Her amber eyes, generally bright with suppressed mirth, watched him compassionately. He swiftly shifted his gaze back to the board, even more miserable, for only true suffering could touch Star's merry heart.

"I'm considering my king," he said.

"Why, yes, that *is* the purpose of the game. I'm merely

pointing out that your bishop may be helpful in protecting your ever-suffering king."

"I know how to play the game, Star," he answered through gritted teeth.

He waited for the sharp rebuke. It didn't come. Instead, she answered in a gentle voice, "I always thought you did."

The double meaning stabbed, and he sucked in his breath. Then the door opened and a maid stepped in. Lee watched her bring a piece of paper to Rick. He took the letter, read it and shook his head. "Well, if that don't beat all! Thank you, Consuelo."

Lilah, sitting next to Melinda, who was talking intently about the children, turned to him. "I don't enjoy suspense, Rick."

"Not generally, darlin', I know," he said affectionately. "But this is Monty's business." He held the note out to Lee.

Frowning at the gleam in Rick's eyes, Lee crossed the room and took the paper from him. It was heavily blotched with ink, but the letters themselves were clear and painstakingly formed.

> *Dear Mr. Montgomery,*
> *I got Jess. She is fine.*
> *So am I.*
> *This letter is to inform you that I am holding Jess captive. If you want to see her again, bring $5,000 to the place marked on the map.*
> *Sincerely yours,*
> *Everett Dunne*
> *P.S. Tomorrow. At noon.*
> *P.P.S. To the spot marked X. On the map. The black X. Not the X that's crossed out, but the black X.*
> *P.P.P.S. I'm changing it to a O. Tomorrow at noon at the place marked O. Not the X but the O.*
> *P.P.P.P.S. My pen broke. Bring the money to the place marked C. Not the O, but the C. Not the X neither. The C.*

"What is it, Lee?" Star asked.

His mouth twisting into disbelief, Lee regarded Rick. "It's got to be a joke."

Rick's eyes sparkled. "I dunno. He said he was sincere. Right there where it says 'sincerely yours.' Here's the map." Rick handed him a second piece of paper.

It was a mass of lines and squiggles and eraser marks, with half an O in the middle of the page.

"A map? Why would someone send you a map, Lee?" Port asked.

Lee looked at Rick. "Are these places real? It looks like a child drew it."

"I have a general idea of the area. I bet Lilah can pinpoint it."

"Pinpoint what?" Lilah asked, as Lee distractedly sank into a chair next to Rick. So Jess had found Dunne. Or he'd found her. And she was fine. And so was Dunne.

Lee ruthlessly swallowed a chuckle. It wasn't a laughing matter.

She couldn't possibly love Dunne after this.

"Son, what is it?" his father asked.

"A ransom note."

Melinda sat up, her eyes wide in shock. "A *ransom* note? For who?"

Jim jumped up. "The children—"

"Settle down, Jim, it's not the kids," Rick said. "It's Jess."

"But," Melinda sputtered, "who would kidnap Jess? Oh, not that angry cowboy, is it?"

Lee bit the inside of his cheek. This was serious. Jess could be in trouble. Especially if he couldn't figure out where the X was. Or the O. Or the C. "It's Dunne."

"That's absurd," Port said, shaking his head as the room erupted into excited conversation.

"Oh no," Star exclaimed, bursting into laughter, "he *must* be joking!"

If Dunne intended to ransom Jess, didn't that imply that

she wanted to leave Dunne? A man couldn't ransom a woman who wanted to stay, could he?

"Or he's plumb loco," Jim said. "A man can't hold his wife for ransom. Who'd pay?"

"Apparently," Rick said chuckling, "he thinks Lee would."

Lee could picture Jess's outrage when she learned of the scheme. Which, had Dunne a brain in his head, he'd keep to himself.

If Dunne had had a brain in his head, he'd never have left Jess in the first place.

"Why of course Lee will pay it," Melinda said warmly. "He wouldn't leave Jess to Mr. Dunne's dastardly plotting!"

Rick's chuckle turned into full-throated laughter. Star and Jim joined him, while Port exclaimed, "He shall not!"

"How much, Leland?" his father asked, a voice of calm in a sea of laughter and indignation.

"Five thousand." He'd have paid ten times as much and still consider it a bargain. "And yes, Melinda, I'll pay it," he said, raising his eyes to Rick's. "That is if you'll loan me the money, Rick. I'm short—"

"Not a problem," Rick interrupted, staring at something in his hands.

"That's unnecessary, sir," his father said. "I shall cover the expense. It's the least I can do."

"Father, no," Port sputtered. "You can't mean to bow to blackmail. It's inconceivable!"

Lee's lips twitched. "I believe, Dad, that the least thing you could do was to save us from the hangman's noose."

His father smiled. "Why, then, this is the second least thing I can do."

"I shall pay you back."

"If you insist."

"I do. Rick what's that?" Lee asked, watching him turn over a piece of white cloth.

"A handkerchief. It came with the letter. I think there's blood on it."

*"Blood?"* Lee exclaimed.

"Now don't fret, boy. I reckon Dunne's just trying to scare you. Most likely Jess scratched him and he wiped it with her handkerchief."

*"Quite* likely," Star said, laughing. "Oh, Lee, I *do* like her! She would make a capital sister-in-law."

Sitting back once more, Lee grinned. "She would, wouldn't she?"

"I'm not certain she's safe," Lilah interjected.

"Of course she is," Port said. "A man dim-witted enough to ransom his own wife is of no danger to anyone."

Rick peered at Lilah, and laying his glass on the table next to him, leaned forward. "Okay, out with it, love."

Dismissing Port, Lilah focused on Lee. Ice cold eyes, chilling his insides. "What do you know about Dunne? Was he ever unkind?"

Lee frowned. "He left her penniless with a dying infant. I'd say that was unkind."

Irritation ran across Lilah's face. "You misunderstand me."

"You might try explaining it better," Rick said gently.

She shifted her focus to her husband. "Rick, she's been kidnapped."

"We're aware of that."

Lilah closed her eyes as pain settled on her face. Emotion transformed it. Suddenly the Frost Queen was gone, replaced by a very beautiful woman. A woman who regarded Rick with a mixture of hurt and deep, deep love. Envy plucked at Lee's heart.

"You must understand she's completely in his power," she said.

Damnation, Lee thought, his heart jerking to a halt. She meant *sexually.* His stomach turned over at the thought of Jess being seduced by that snake.

Rick answered gently, "She's in love with him, Lilah."

*No, she's not! Not anymore!*

Lilah swallowed. "That might make it worse."

"Would it? I'd think it'd be easier. Even pleasurable."

Incredibly, tears formed in Lilah's eyes. A melting glacier. "No, Rick. It would not."

Rick drew a deep breath, and reached for Lilah's hand. "I never meant you harm."

She flinched. "I know that now. But *then* . . ."

Another breath, and he lifted an arm. "Come here."

She rose and Rick pulled her into his lap, where the Frost Queen curled into his arms, contrary to all convention and every thought Lee had ever had about the woman. "I'm sorry, love," Rick crooned softly. "I'm sorry."

Lee set his teeth and stared down at his glass, unable to bear the bittersweet scene in front of him. Their love filled the room, pressing against the bloody wound in the center of his heart. For years he'd avoided marriage and its complications like the plague. Now, watching Rick and Lilah, those years yawned dark and empty behind him, lost, wasted years. He wanted Jess. He wanted her with him just that way.

Rick lifted his head and focused his eyes on Lee. "She's right, Monty. Jess may be in a deal of trouble. She may love Dunne, but I doubt he feels the same way."

Lee frowned. "And?"

"And a woman can still be raped by her lover."

Lee's muscles jerked in shock.

Rick continued on, his face hardening. "As he's her husband, it's perfectly legal. He can do whatever the hell he wants with her."

Rape . . . Jess pinned spread-eagled to the ground as a faceless man rammed into her. Screams of pain, of humiliation—tears running down her face.

"I'll kill him!" he snarled.

Through a black fog, Lee saw Rick grin—cold, brutal. "Now you're speaking my language, boy."

And with that, the glass in Lee's hand shattered.

* * *

Jess shivered under the hot Texas sun, her entire focus on the steel barrel pressing into the small of her back. A pistol, with Everett's finger on the trigger. He'd never intentionally hurt her, but he wasn't particularly proficient with firearms.

"You'd better stop shaking, Jess. You're making me shaky, too."

Oh God, she didn't want to die! "Ev, darling, it's not too late. You can still walk away."

"There's a carriage coming."

She jerked her head around to see a shiny black coach entering the valley. Lee had come! For love? Or, she thought with a sick thump of her heart, for honor? Five thousand dollars was a drop in the bucket to Lee, and honor was everything to his family.

What honor was there in saving his mistress?

It didn't matter. Everett had a gun and his hand was shaking. "Ev, you've got—"

"Too late, Jess. Show's on." He pushed the barrel deeper into her back. "Down the hill now."

Someone could get hurt. Lee, she thought with a catch in her throat, could get killed.

As they reached the bottom of the hill, the carriage came to a halt. "Nothing brave, Jess," Ev whispered in her ear. "I'll kill him, you understand?"

"Everett, this is madness," she hissed. "You don't want to kill anyone. Give me the gun and I'll hold him off long enough for you to get away."

"I need the money."

Lee, wearing a long black frock coat, white silk shirt, and trousers exited the carriage. His head was bare; his black hair gleamed in the sun. She wanted so much to throw herself into his arms that her body actually ached.

"I'll get the money for you somehow. Ev, please," she whispered desperately.

Too late. A black leather valise in hand, Lee strode toward them. His eyes were fixed upon her, his face as hard as granite.

"That's far enough," Ev said, when Lee was about fifteen feet away. "Drop the case and back off."

Lee halted, his eyes moving hungrily over Jess's face, sending tiny thrills across her nerves. Love—oh that had to be love. "Are you all right, sweetheart? Did he hurt you?"

"You saw the bloody handkerchief!" Everett threatened.

Lee's hand jerked on the valise. His face creased with anger, and fear shot through Jess. She had to keep him calm. "I'm fine," she said, rolling her eyes for good measure.

"For now," Ev said. "Now you open that case and count out the money so I can see it."

"You want me to count five thousand dollars out in the middle of the Texas prairie?" Lee snapped in disbelief.

"Ev, for the love of God!" she hissed so that only Ev could hear her. "Do you really think he'd come all the way out here with an empty sack?"

"Do it!" Ev said, and the gun dug deeper in her back.

Lee eyed him warily. "What assurance do I have that you'll release her?"

"You have my word."

Lee barked a laugh. "The word of a man who'd abandon his wife and baby in a mining camp? How good is that?"

"God, Jess," Everett whispered. "You *told* him?"

"He wanted to know how I ended up on stage," she said out of the corner of her mouth.

"But it sounds so bad."

"It was bad!"

Lee scowled. "Release her first."

"That's not part of the plan."

"It's part of *my* plan."

"Lord, Jess," Everett whispered in her ear, "he's a stubborn cuss."

"You have no idea."

"Jess stays with me," Everett said in a normal tone.

"All right, then let her step away from you. Keep the gun on her if you wish; trust me, I won't take any chances with her life."

He shook his head. "She's my shield."

Lee stared a moment and then slowly placed the case on the ground. Kneeling down, he opened it and with slow precision withdrew each packet of bills. "Five hundred, one thousand, fifteen hundred, two thousand . . ." When he was done, he lifted his head. "Satisfied?"

"Put it back in the case," Everett said. Frowning, Lee complied. Afterward, still on his knees, he raised an eyebrow at Everett. "Good," Ev said. "Now back away."

"Release Jess."

"No. Bring another five tomorrow and then maybe I'll let her go."

Lee's shaky composure melted. "Tomorrow! You said today!" he roared.

"Ev!" Jess hissed. Oh God, he was going to get them all killed!

"You found that money mighty fast. Seems to me you must have more. Bring another five tomorrow and you can have her."

"You sonuvabitch," Lee said through gritted teeth. "I want her *now!*"

"Jess," Everett said, breathing excitedly, "unfasten your cuff. Show him that cut."

"Are you mad? Better to kick a wounded bear!"

"Show him!" he said, digging the gun into her back. Her heart jerked and she obeyed.

Everett raised her arm to show Lee the injury. "Bring more money tomorrow or there'll be more of this."

Lee's eyes flashed green fire. His hand moved inside the

case, and with a sudden stomach-turning certainty, Jess realized he had a gun in there.

Chaos erupted.

She whipped around to shove Everett out of the way. From up on the hill, a rifle went off. Blood burst from Everett's sleeve. Everett lifted his gun, and fired. Lee fell. Another shot. A bee flew by, stinging Jess's upper arm. One more shot, Ev fell into a heap, and Jess finally dove for cover.

# Chapter Thirty

For a moment everything was eerily silent. Her arm stinging, Jess lay perfectly still and waited for someone to scream, for the hysteria that followed sudden death and foretold of lives changed forever.

Everett moaned, and someone atop the hill yelled, "Hey down there! Is Jess okay?"

Lee jumped up and crossed the small distance between them. He fell on his knees next to her. "Jess, my God—"

Lee was alive. Perfectly alive.

"I'm all right," she said, and placed her palms under her chest to push herself up. The bee sting stabbed and her arm buckled. Bewildered, she glanced at her arm.

Blood. Not a bee sting, but blood.

"That bastard!" Jess swore. "That bastard shot me!"

Lee helped her into a sitting position, then moved aside the torn fabric. "It doesn't seem too bad. The bullet passed through."

"He *shot* me!" she said through gritted teeth. She'd warned him, damn it, she'd *warned* him someone would get hurt, but he hadn't listened, and now her arm was on fire. "Where's that gun?" she snarled, lunging for Lee's valise.

Lee, his arm encircling her waist, stopped her. From her left Rick and Jim came jogging down the hill, toting rifles.

"Don't move, Jess," Lee said gently. "You'll only make it bleed more."

"Then get the gun for me, so I can shoot the bastard."

"Jess, no!" he said, amusement marbling the concern in his voice.

"Damn it, I ought to have brought my fork!"

"Your fork?"

"To stab him."

"Oh right. Of course."

"You okay, Jess?" Rick asked. Jim knelt on one knee next to Ev. "How's the husband?"

"He's not my husband anymore," she growled.

"Well, hell, I thought I missed him," Rick replied. He removed his Stetson and ran his hand through his hair.

"He's alive," Jim said. "Shot in the shoulder is all."

Lilah dropped a haversack on the ground and knelt down next to Jess.

"Ah, Christ, really?" Rick asked. His tone was one of disgust, but his voice had lightened.

Lilah glanced at Lee as she pulled a pair of scissors from the haversack. "It's only a graze. She'll be fine." She unfastened Jess's cuff, then cut the sleeve up to her shoulder.

Lee nodded. He said to Jess in a low voice, "Did he hurt you, sweetheart? In any other ways?"

"Other than *shooting* me?" she snapped. Her mind was awhirl. People were appearing from nowhere, and she was shot, and Ev wanted to make her his whore.

Lee's eyebrows drew together. "Yes."

Puzzled, she stared, until his meaning sank in. More fury burned her chest, but this was followed by grim satisfaction. She flashed a triumphant smile. "He tried, but I bit him."

"Bit him?" Lee asked, raising his eyebrows.

"Yes, until he bled."

Mirth lit Lee's face, wiping away the anxiety. "Was that before or after you stabbed him with the fork?"

"I never did stab him. He ran too fast, the bastard."

Lee's eyes sparkled. "Then you chased him with the fork first?"

"I did. But he pointed his gun and I had to drop it."

"Ah, yes, well, a gun does beat a fork. But perk up, sweetheart. All is not lost! The course of true love rarely runs smoothly."

"Smoothly! Smoothly! Are you *mad?* That rat," she started, pointing furiously at Everett, "that bastard—" Lee's lips twitched. She wanted to choke someone, but the amusement in his eyes was infectious. "Oh my goodness, Lee," she said on a sob of a laugh, "can you believe he kidnapped me!"

"To his regret, apparently."

"He brought me to a sod house—with a wood floor."

Lee laughed. "A wood floor? You'd thin—"

"That they'd use it for the roof! I couldn't believe it! And I kept looking for snakes."

"Hungry, sweetheart?"

She emitted a tiny laugh, but her amusement faded as the whole horrid incident came back to her. Tears formed in her eyes. "I could have used some of that white Burgundy!"

"Oh, Jess," Lee said tenderly. He pulled her closer, and nuzzled her neck. A shiver ran down her spine. "I missed you like hell."

She let her head drop against his chest. He felt so good, so right. "It was only a day."

"It felt longer."

"A lot longer when you're expecting snakes!"

The sound of his deep chuckle sent bittersweet hope rushing through her chest. With another tiny sob she started crying. He tried to wrap his other arm around her too, but accidentally jogged her shoulder. She cried out. Swearing, he shifted his body, then pulled her against him, laying her head on his shoulder. Lilah, too, shifted, to placidly continue inspecting her wound.

"It's all right, sweetheart," Lee whispered in her ear. "It's over now."

Such a kind voice, such compassion, twisting her heart. "He went out," she whispered between gulps of air, "and came back smelling like perfume."

"Lord, Jess, I'm sorry," he said in that soft-sweet tone. "But I have you now, and this time I'm not letting you go."

"No?"

"Never," he said, harshly. "Not even if you beg. I-I can't."

"Good," she said, "for I don't want to leave."

"Promise?" he said, reaching down to lift her chin. She stared into his eyes through a mist of tears.

"I promise."

"Jess," he said on a sigh. He smiled tenderly. "A kiss then, to seal it."

His lips were so soft, so familiar. She closed her eyes, and when he demanded entry she yielded with a sigh, reveling in his taste as he swept through her mouth. And she was going to give this up? Oh, she must have been mad—absolutely mad.

Someone was coughing. Loudly. Persistently.

"Lee!"

The method behind her madness. Ward Montgomery.

Lee lifted his head. He flashed her one of his breath-stealing smiles, then shifted his gaze to his father. She took a steadying breath and also faced Mr. Montgomery.

"Time for that later," Ward said, scowling. "Mrs. Winchester needs to tend your lady's wounds."

*Your lady*. Not your actress. The words touched Jess's tattered heart. Fragile hope set her body to shaking. But Ward Montgomery despised her, thought her a conniving, money-hungry hussy. He'd all but sworn to do everything in his power to separate her from Lee.

Compassion abruptly warmed Ward's dark eyes. He bent over to hand her a silver flask. "Brandy, my dear. It will ease the pain."

Blinking back tears, Jess took it and noticed for the first time that they'd been joined by Star. And Melinda, who clasped her hands to her chest. "Oh, that's so romantic!" she sighed.

Jim, who was sitting cross-legged on the ground a short distance away, shook his head in amusement. "You think so? Want me to get Dunne to shoot you, too?"

"Jim!" Melinda said sharply.

Lilah withdrew a small brown bottle from her haversack. "Dunne didn't shoot her."

Everyone turned to stare at her. She opened the bottle and looked at Jess. "Take Lee's hand in your right hand and squeeze hard. This is going to hurt."

"What?" Lee asked. "No. Lilah—"

Before he could get the words out, Lilah poured some of the liquid over the wound. It burned, and the smell of alcohol shot up Jess's nose. She yelped. "Mercy, Lilah!" she cried out as the burning spread down her arm.

"Alcohol's the best thing to prevent infection. That's enough though. I'll bandage it now. The pain will ease in a minute."

"It hurt less when he shot me."

"It would hurt more if it became septic," she said practically, and started winding bandages around her arm.

Jess took a couple breaths, and the pain started to dissipate. Jim tilted his head in confusion. "Why do think Dunne didn't shoot her, Lilah?"

Lilah answered as she wound bandages around Jess's arm. "If you look closely, you'll see a hole in the valise. And there next to Star is a rock with a small chunk taken out of it," she said, indicating the area with a nod of her head. "The bullet shot through the valise, ricocheted off the rock and grazed Jess."

Star, standing next to her father, shook her head. "How can you know that?"

"For one thing, Jim and Rick are too good to miss Dunne by that much. And the valise's hole lines up with the rock."

Chagrin spreading over Lee's face. "Are you saying I shot her?"

Finished, Lilah leaned back to survey her work. She turned her eyes to Lee. "The gun went off when you were trying to pull it out, didn't it?"

Lee winced and looked down at Jess. "Sorry, sweetheart."

She sighed and smiled at him. Her arm didn't hurt so much, Mr. Montgomery didn't hate her entirely, and Lee had come for her. All was right with the world. "It's okay. I still love you."

Lee's heart flipped. For a moment he wondered if he'd heard right. Her eyebrows drew together, puzzled by his expression, as if she hadn't said anything special, anything tremendously important. "Say that again."

"It's okay—"

"The other."

"I love you." The words shot through him, piercing his heart with a deep, stabbing pang. *Jess loved him.* The pang transformed to a kind of golden heat, spreading through his chest, through his whole damned body, silky soft. Lifting a quivering hand, he reached up to touch her face, tracing her delicate cheekbone and her beautiful, magical lips, capable of making him mad with desire, of tickling his funny bone with words, of touching his heart with laughter. Lord, he wanted her, wanted to kiss every last inch of her, show her by touch the pleasure she gave him just by *being.*

"That deserves another kiss," he said huskily, leaning forward. By God, she felt good. He loved the champagne taste of her, bittersweet and intoxicating. He could never drink enough.

"Good God, he's at it again!" his father growled. "Winchester, is that man ready for transport yet?"

Jess leaned into the kiss. Then her shoulders shook and she broke away to move her lips over his ear. "You're going to give your father apoplexy," she whispered.

"Jess," he whispered back, chuckling, "all I want to do is tear off your clothes and kiss you all over. What's so bad about that?"

"Transport," Rick called back. "Where?"

He felt a tremor run through her body. Desire threaded through her soft laughter. "You'll kill him."

Lee grinned, then, one arm still around her waist, he leaned back to focus his attention on Rick. Everyone else had their eyes riveted on him also. Rick had his boot on Dunne's shoulder, an expression on his face like a cat toying with a mouse.

"To jail, of course, to await trial," his father replied.

"Yeah, I'm thinkin' widowhood would be a mite quicker for Jess than divorce."

Out of the corner of his eye, Lee saw Star's eyes widen in shock. A second later, Jess spoke up. "But that's impossible. I told you earlier. We're not married."

All eyes turned to Jess. Lee's brain seemed to freeze. "What do you mean? You married him six years ago."

"So I believed, but last night Everett informed me that he'd paid a man to pretend to marry us and draw up a fake license," she snarled, and added under her breath, "the bastard."

Ward peered at Jess, his face dark and unreadable. "For how many years?"

"Are you thinking of common-law marriage? It doesn't matter. Everett was married when we met. Apparently," she continued, bitterness tracing her words, "he abandoned her also, and his son."

"Abandoned *another* woman, you son of a bitch!" Rick growled and shoved his foot hard against Dunne's shoulder. The man shouted in pain and Lee, with a twisting in his stomach, realized that Rick had his foot on Dunne's hurt shoulder. "Was she pregnant, too? Answer me, damn it!" he yelled. More pressure with his boot, more yelling, this time from Dunne. "No! No! You're hurting me!"

"Damned st—"

"Rick! Stop that!"

Lee turned to look at Lilah. She sat on the ground next to Jim, whose hand rested reassuringly on her shoulder. Her eyes locked with Rick's, and the group held their collective breaths.

Slowly the rage on Rick's face faded into disgust. He glanced at Dunne again, then fixed his gaze on his father. Something flickered in Rick's eyes before he said, "I think I oughtta kill him, anyhow. As this is the United States, I say we vote. You first, sir."

Lee turned to his father. As he watched his father consider, Lilah whispered in an agonized voice, "Lord, Jim, I thought he was over this."

"He never will be completely, honey," Jim whispered back gently.

A moment later, his father, eyes holding Rick's in his keen gaze, said, "If you believe this is proper punishment, I shall not stand against you."

Star gasped and his father, his face immobile, grasped her wrist like a warning.

A slow smile spread across Rick's face. His eyes shifted to Star. "Miss Montgomery?"

"No!"

Rick gave her a polite nod and, his expression murderous, addressed Dunne. "An aye from the gentleman, and a nay from our pretty Bostonian lady. One to one, you bastard. You're lucky you have women present." He focused his gaze on Melinda. "What do you say?"

She looked at Jim. Some thought passed between them. "Shoot him."

Rick grinned. "I always did love you, darlin'. Seems, Dunne, that your actions have upset the mothers among us. Monty?"

Lee watched him narrowly. For all Jim's warnings, in his heart, Lee had always believed Rick to be fair and just. This man, though, was not the one he'd known nine years earlier. With a stone settling in his stomach, he grudgingly agreed. "I won't testify against you."

Rick chuckled. "We'll call that an aye from a man who refuses to commit himself to murder. Three to one, Dunne.

Looks like we might be having ourselves a little shootin'
party. I'd advise counting every breath from here on in."

His eyes shifted to Jess. The laugh went out of them when they
rested on her, and Lee could feel her tense. "Miss Sullivan?"

"No! This is preposterous! You can—"

He nodded and cut her off. "A nay from our beautiful Irish
actress. And one of the women, Dunne, who you've wronged.
You're damned lucky to have found such a forgiving woman.
So it's three to two. You just might live, yet. Jim?"

Jim, leaning back negligently on his palms, shrugged.
"Can't see that he's serving any useful purpose. Kill him."

Rick smiled again, big, broad. "Four to two. Better prepare
to meet your maker, Dunne."

Dunne started to groan, a small continual plea—"No, oh
God no, you can't, no—"

Regarding him with tears in her eyes, Jess grabbed Lee's
sleeve. "Lee, you must stop—"

Holding her firmly, he whispered in her ear, "Hold your
horses, Jess. Something's up."

Rick turned to Lilah. "In the interest of true democracy, we
all vote. Lilah, love?"

Ice coated her voice. "Would you like help?"

Rick let out a cold, cutting laugh. "Last vote, aye, from my
lovely wife, who," Rick said, turning now to Dunne, he
cocked his rifle, "is not so forgiving. Five to two. You lose."
Rick aimed and a shot split the air, its reverberations rolling
across the silent prairie.

Jess lurched forward, crying out. Star covered her eyes and
buried her face in her father's jacket. Muscles taut, Lee could
only stare. He hadn't believed Rick would do it . . .

Dunne moved. Rick's voice, harsh with suppressed anger,
rasped out, "Scared Dunne? Thought that was it, didn't you?
Thought you'd cashed in your chips. But I just shot that bug
there. But now, I'm gonna kill another bug. A big, slimy,
woman-abusing *bug*."

Rick cocked his gun. Lee tensed. Jess sat still as stone in his arms.

Another shot.

Dunne screamed.

"You sonuvabitch, did it *hurt?*" Rick snarled, bending over. And something inside Lee suddenly clicked, then leaped in rage as he recalled Jess crying in his arms, her heart breaking for her lost little girl. The veneer of civilization dropped from his soul, replaced with dark, brutal satisfaction. "Did it hurt real, real bad? Well, that'll give you some notion of how your wives felt bearing the children *you* abandoned, you worthless piece of shit!"

He cocked his gun again. Jess sucked in her breath.

Another shot.

Another cry.

"Chicken-livered bastard, I didn't even nick you that time. Bet you're plenty scared, though, aren't you?" He cocked his gun. "Maybe now you've got an idea of how frightening it is to be a woman on her own. Abandoned, not a dime to her name, without family or friends. Alone, damn you, in the goddamned wilderness. *Do you, now? Do you?*" he shouted, digging the barrel into Dunne's throat. "Talk to me, you sonuvabitch!"

"Rick!" Lilah hissed. Her voice was harsh and low. Rick froze. "That's enough." She rose and walked toward him.

Slowly he turned to her, a sort of furious agony creasing his face. "Yeah?"

"You've tortured him enough."

Grimacing, Rick shifted his rifle. "I still think I oughta kill him."

"No, you don't," she said gently, reaching her hand out.

He took it in his and smiled down at her. The anger on his face melted. "I reckon not." He gave Everett a kick in the ribs. "Sit up you sonuvabitch and take those boots off."

Eyes wide, Everett obeyed. His other shoulder bled a bit, but not as much as his first gunshot wound. Apparently Rick's shot had only caused a superficial wound. Jess sighed in relief.

When Everett finished, Rick nudged him with the rifle. "All right, start walking. That way," he said, pointing away from town. "The stage station's only five miles away."

"But my feet!" Everett cried out. "There are scorpions and spiders—"

"Close associates of yours, from what I've observed. You get to that station, take the earliest stage out of the county. If I ever hear of you kidnapping or 'marrying' another woman, I'll find you. And if I ever see you again, I *will* kill you. Understand?"

"But—"

Rick cocked his gun. "*Understand,* Dunne?"

Eyes wide, Ev nodded and with hands up, started walking backward. "I'm going! I'm going!"

"Not fast enough. You'd better damned well *run* before I start shootin' at your heels."

Ev, one last glance at Jess, turned and ran. Within a minute he was climbing the next hill.

Rick turned to Lilah. He smiled, then leaned over to whisper something. She laughed a little and replied in the same tone.

Jess watched for a moment. "Well, sweetheart," Lee spoke next to her. "I think that's the last you've seen of Everett."

She laughed a little breathlessly. "I expect so."

He smiled. "Are you all right?"

Jess searched her heart. It felt lighter, brighter. Six years of bitterness had finally lifted. It wasn't entirely gone, but was greatly diminished. She nodded. "You know, I think I am."

He kissed her forehead. "Good." He turned his attention to Jim, who was rising with Melinda's assistance. "Jim, I owe you an apology. You were right about Rick."

"Hey, that wasn't so bad," Jim said with a shrug. "Dunne's still alive."

Star, pale and leaning on her father's arm, asked, "Are all cowboys like that?"

Jim smiled kindly. "No, ma'am. That's just Rick."

Her shoulders relaxed. "Oh, good."

Lee scowled at her and started to open his mouth when Rick joined them, Lilah's hand clasped in his. "Well, ladies, gentlemen, what do you say we continue this discussion back at the ranch? I think we might," he said, grinning mischievously at Lilah, "have some planning to do, just like I ordered."

Lilah shook her head in disgust. "I think you ought to stay out of other people's affairs."

"No, ma,'am," he drawled. "No fun in that at all."

# Chapter Thirty-One

"And so," Ward Montgomery said as Rick handed him a glass of wine. He sat straight as an arrow in an armchair in front of the fireplace. "It appears, as our host has implied, that we're to plan a wedding. Star, you shall, I assume, assist us?"

The parlor filled with silence as Jess, cuddled on a sofa in Lee's arms, frowned. A wedding? "Pardon me?"

Mr. Montgomery's black eyebrows lifted. "Could it be that you didn't know, my dear?"

Remembering that horrible argument ringing through the courtyard, she shuddered. He had surely softened toward her, but after that argument—oh no, this was some kind of perverted trap. And yet, to refuse Lee's offer in front of everyone would humiliate him. He would never ask again. Goodness, but he hadn't asked to begin with . . .

And then everyone chimed in.

"Oh, yes, Jess, you must marry him now that he's saved your life," Melinda gushed, leaning forward in her chair.

"If you don't marry him, Jess," Star said merrily, seated on a sofa next to Port, "he'll be unbearable, and then Mother will feel it necessary to lift his spirits by throwing a truly fatiguing amount of parties. I'm certain she's planning them as we speak."

"You must, Miss Sullivan," Port said languidly. "It's a tradition in our family to marry those that we stab—or shoot."

Amusement threaded through Jess's panic. "Stab?" she asked.

Mr. Montgomery locked eyes with her. She was shocked to find them warmly apologetic. "It happened many years ago. However, I never wished it to become traditional," he said with a slight smile. "Nor did I ever wish to pass along the tradition of Montgomery stubbornness. I hope you'll forgive a father blinded by his loyalty for his son."

"That's an apology, Jess," Star interjected. "We're traditionally poor at those also."

"Come now, Jess," Jim cajoled, perched on the arm of Melinda's chair. "You've got Ward's blessing. Now you have to marry Monty!"

"If you don't," Rick said, from his position in a chair across from Mr. Montgomery, "he'll doubtless try to shoot himself, but being such a poor aim, miss and hit one of us. Marry him, ma'am, and save a life."

"Do what you want, Jess. No one should pressure you into marriage." The last came from Lilah, sitting on a small chair next to Rick. Her comment effectively silenced the group, and drew a scowl from Rick. Lilah merely shrugged at him.

Lee, after flashing Lilah a frown, addressed the room. "My father's apology not withstanding, I believe ladies and gentlemen, I'm capable of making my own proposals."

"Last time she said no," Port pointed out.

Rick grinned. "In all fairness, Port, last time she was married."

Chuckling, Lee looked down at Jess. "Well, Jess? They have us against a wall, sweetheart. I suspect they'll imprison us if we disagree, except for Lilah who seems determined to keep me in a permanent state of limbo."

"With so many voices, I'm not sure who I'd be marrying."

"It appears you'll wed them all! Still," he said, his eyes glowing, "you'd be my wife."

She sighed. "Well, I suppose it'd be rude to disappoint so many people . . ."

"Excellent," Rick said, and clinked glasses with Lilah, who smiled. "Congratulations everyone, we've done it! Darlin' this deserves some champagne, don't you think?"

Lilah rose and slipped silently across the room, as Ward leaned back and smiled broadly. A dimple—goodness, Lee's dimple!—emerged. "Welcome to the family, my dear. Leland, I shall telegraph your mother tomorrow and inform her to expect one more for the holidays."

Star played with her earring and thought out loud. "A Christmas wedding then—yes, I believe we can carry it off, Port. Knowing Mother, she's already making arrangements."

"Christmas?" Jess said, confused. "Arrangements? Lee, what are they talking about?"

"Apparently we've been invited back East for the holidays, at which time they intend to marry us off with so much pomp and circumstance that you'll no doubt leave me at the altar."

"No," she said, firmly, "that won't do. I'm not getting married in Boston."

Ward lifted his head to stare at her. Port and Star fell silent, and Lee, humor twinkling in his eyes, said, "I think you've stunned them, Jess."

"I'd like our wedding to be in Denver."

*"Denver!"* Star exclaimed

"Impossible!" Ward objected.

"Oh yes!" Melinda agreed.

"My dear girl, Lee won't even consider it!" Port insisted.

"Denver, Jess? Why?" Lee asked.

Jess, confused by the myriad voices, reminded herself with a gurgle of merriment about having been kidnapped, shot, and betrayed all in the space of twenty-four hours. She decided to ignore them all. It was, after all, *her* wedding. "My troupe is there, along with Michelle. She might travel to Boston or New

York, but you know she'd never be easy among all your family's friends, Lee."

"Michelle! Not that blond Frenchwoman! We met her, Lee, and if she's French, then I'm an Italian viscount," Port said disgustedly.

Lee grinned. "Denver it is." Port opened his mouth to object. "Later, Port, you may plan a reception back East. That ought to satisfy the majority of our friends."

"And," Jess said, flashing a smile through the room as two maids with trays of glasses and several bottles of champagne entered the room, "in Denver the rest of your chorus may join us. I believe it's customary for those who do the proposing to attend the wedding."

"An excellent solution," Ward said. "I shall telegraph your mother tomorrow, Lee, that she's to join us in Denver. No doubt she already has her bags packed."

Lee, eyes twinkling, said, "I thought she was busy planning parties to lift my spirits and making arrangements for my wedding."

"No doubt she's doing all three. She's a versatile woman, your mother."

Jess whispered to Lee, "She sounds formidable, Lee."

"You'll love her. She's just like you."

"Only richer?"

"Sprinkled in diamonds. You might experience a moment's blindness, but I assure you it passes."

"That is of great comfort."

He chuckled in her ear. "I knew it would be, sweetheart."

Port frowned in concentration. "It might be the answer. We'll of course invite a few of our closer friends to make the journey. And we have some in San Francisco who might have missed it otherwise. In fact, I believe that's how we shall present it. I regret, however, that I shan't be able to attend." He paused to clear his throat. "Meredith is in a delicate condition and I've been away too long as it is."

Lee's muscles froze, and then a huge grin spread across his face. "Port! Congratulations, brother! When do we expect the happy event?"

"February," he answered with a light blush.

"Yes, ironic, isn't it, Lee?" Star said with a laugh as congratulations bounced around the room. "Now that you've decided to do your duty by the Montgomery name, it's no longer necessary."

He gave Jess a squeeze. "I am marrying Jess out of pleasure, not duty."

"Port," Jess interjected, "I still must insist we invite Michelle. And my troupe. And you shall not make them ill at ease. If not for them we'd be dead now."

"Certainly. My good man," Port added in alarm as he watched Rick take a bottle of champagne and shake it, "what *are* you doing?"

"Shaking it."

"You'll ruin the champagne."

"I'm popping the cork," he said, loosening the tie.

"It's the worst thing you can do to champagne, and that, from the looks of it, is a very fine vintage."

Rick carefully aimed the bottle toward the courtyard and edged the cork forward. "I like the sound it makes."

"You, sir, are a heathen."

"Yessir, I am," Rick said, and the cork flew, champagne spilled over the floor.

Star laughed delightedly. "Oh dear, I *do* like cowboys!"

"Good God, Star, it sounds like a gun exploding!"

"And that," Rick said, reaching over to hand a bottle to Port, "is exactly why I like it. Here, you may open the rest. Anyone for ruined champagne?" As he started pouring glasses, he continued. "Now here's what I'm thinking. It's almost Thanksgiving. A week from tomorrow, correct, Lilah? Good. Why don't you all join us for the holiday? If Mrs. Montgomery is packed and ready to go, she could be here in four or five days."

Jess, having thought her heart filled to overflowing,

quickly pictured everyone sitting around the long, food-laden table, laughter flowing like the champagne from Rick's bottle. It'd been years since she'd had a family holiday.

"Lee, there's one thing. My brother, I'd like to invite him to our wedding."

"Your brother. Of course." He frowned and lifted his head. "I believe, also, that a husband assumes his wife's debts upon marriage, isn't that so, Dad?"

"I don't know the laws in Texas."

"It's the law," Rick said. "For a fact. In Texas and Colorado."

"And so, upon our marriage, Jess, I shall pay Jason back all that you owe him."

"Lee, he's lying! He doesn't know that!"

Rick's voice was alive with merriment. "You doubt me, madam?"

"You, sir, are full of blarney!" She turned back to Lee. "I forbid it! That was my mistake, not yours."

Laughter sparkled in his eyes. "Did you think I shouldn't make you pay for it? I warn you, sweetheart, I haven't a generous bone in my body. I shall, for at least a year, deny you all the delicacies you crave—escargot, oysters, caviar. No, don't beg me, Jess! I refuse!"

Jess chuckled, but shook her head. "Lee, it's not right."

Leaning over, he kissed her forehead. "It's a wedding present, along with tickets for your brother, aunt, uncle, and anyone else you have in mind. Perhaps Jason will give you away?"

She sighed. "You're very stubborn."

"Oh," Melinda said suddenly, bouncing, her eyes bright with excitement. "I have an idea! After Thanksgiving, we'll have Christmas at our house! We have room, don't we, Jim?"

He smiled down at his wife. "We'll make the room, Melinda, but there's still the matter of their wedding."

"Oh, we can plan it from the Bar M, can't we?"

"Won't Jess need to see dressmakers? Talk to a preacher? A church?"

Melinda's shoulders sank and Jess's heart went out to her. She opened her mouth to apologize when Star spoke up. "Melinda, how well do you know Denver? I confess, I've no notion of the best dressmakers there."

"Both Lilah and I know it pretty well. Lilah, where do you think we ought to send her?"

"Oh no, my dear!" Star said. "I'm requesting, on behalf of my mother and me, that you assist us in the arrangements."

Melinda's eyes brightened. "Certainly we'll help, won't we Lilah! We'll leave—"

"After," Lilah said prosaically, "Thanksgiving."

"And then, after the wedding, Christmas at our house!"

"Uh, the honeymoon?" Lee asked.

"Honeymoon?" Rick asked, laughing. "Haven't you had it already? What better honeymoon than two nights on the Colorado prairie?"

"You're proposing to have the wedding between Thanksgiving and Christmas?" Port snapped. "Impossible!"

"It's a splendid idea!" Star said. "We shall have the wedding as near to Christmas as possible, and you and Jess may leave for your honeymoon after the New Year."

Lee sighed. "I suggest we elope, Jess, else they'll plan our honeymoon."

Ward sighed also. "All right. It's settled. I shall telegraph your mother to join us here instead. You young people change your minds so fast my head spins."

Star leaned back, smiling like a Cheshire cat. "Yes, and we shall definitely employ Melinda and Lilah's assistance for the wedding. And of course you, Mr. Winchester, and you, Mr. McGraw, will want to join us in Denver. And perhaps your brother? What was his name again? Nicholas I believe."

Lee's head popped up and his eyes narrowed. "Star—"

"And Christmas at the Bar M. Yes, I believe that suits me quite well."

"Star," he warned, "I told you, Dad may turn a blind eye but I won't allow—"

Her eyes narrowing cattishly, Star smiled. "It's already arranged, Brother."

"Oh good God," Port spat. "She's talking about that cowboy again, isn't she, Lee?"

"Oh," Melinda said, bouncing excitedly. "Another romance!"

"And now," Star said, lifting her glass, "a toast! To my new sister, Jess, and my old brother, Lee. May you have a long and fulfilling life together. And," she said as everyone agreed, "to cowboys!"